Praise for novels by Heidi Chiavaroli

The Tea Chest

"Captivating from the first page. I couldn't read this novel fast enough, and yet the beautiful writing compelled me to slow down and experience every line. Dual tales of courage, love, and freedom proved even more poignant for being woven together as one. Steeped in timeless truths and served with skill, *The Tea Chest* is sure to be savored by all who read it."

JOCELYN GREEN, CHRISTY AWARD–WINNING AUTHOR OF *BETWEEN TWO SHORES*

"*The Tea Chest* brings two women, separated by centuries, face-to-face with the same question: What is the price of liberty? A master at writing dual timelines, Chiavaroli takes us beyond the historical connection between these two women and wraps them together with a shared spirit."

ALLISON PITTMAN, CRITICALLY ACCLAIMED AUTHOR OF *THE SEAMSTRESS*

"Seamlessly blending both the colonial and contemporary, Heidi Chiavaroli rivets readers with this compelling timeslip novel. *The Tea Chest* opens, unleashing an array of fascinating characters and complex circumstances that will have you turning pages as fast as your fingers fly till the end. I could not put this novel down."

LAURA FRANTZ, CHRISTY AWARD–WINNING AUTHOR OF *THE LACEMAKER*

"Chiavaroli proves herself a master at the intersection of history and present-day in her new novel, *The Tea Chest*. A gripping tale of the Boston Tea Party and the choices we all must make for truth, the power of forgiveness, and the freedom that comes when we realize to Whom we truly belong. Swoon-worthy romance, heartbreak, and intrigue combine for a thrilling story that will keep me thinking for a long time to come. Bravo!"

AMY K. SORRELLS, AUTHOR OF *BEFORE I SAW YOU*

"*The Tea Chest* is the rare time-slip novel that gripped me equally in both present and historical settings. Chiavaroli is once again home in the era of her evident passion and its echo into our tumultuous present. Brilliantly researched and executed with passion, *The Tea Chest* is timeless and empowering. Long may Heidi Chiavaroli reign over thoughtful, effortlessly paralleled fiction that digs deep into the heart of America's early liberty and the resonance of faith and conviction she offers as its poignant legacy."

RACHEL MCMILLAN, AUTHOR OF *MURDER IN THE CITY OF LIBERTY*

"Freedom is an innate need in the heart of humanity, and in Heidi Chiavaroli's latest novel, she takes her readers on a journey to the darkest moments and the brightest victories in the quest for freedom. *The Tea Chest* is not only a story of America's birth as a nation, but also one that reflects the clamoring in humanity's heart to soar unfettered by the weight of chains that bind."

JAIME JO WRIGHT, CHRISTY AWARD–WINNING AUTHOR OF *THE HOUSE ON FOSTER HILL* AND *THE CURSE OF MISTY WAYFAIR*

"*The Tea Chest* is an enthralling story of beauty birthed from sorrow, hope amid ashes, and healing through pain. Chiavaroli has masterfully weaved a timeless tale that kept me turning pages far into the night . . . and reminded me of the gentle truth that identity and worth are found in the eyes of Jesus."

TARA JOHNSON, AUTHOR OF *WHERE DANDELIONS BLOOM* AND *ENGRAVED ON THE HEART*

The Hidden Side

"*The Hidden Side* is a beautiful tale that captures the timeless struggles of the human heart."

JULIE CANTRELL, *NEW YORK TIMES* AND *USA TODAY* BESTSELLING AUTHOR OF *PERENNIALS*

"Heidi Chiavaroli has written another poignant novel that slips between a heart-wrenching present-day story and a tragic one set during the Revolutionary War. I couldn't put this book down!"

MELANIE DOBSON, AWARD-WINNING AUTHOR OF *CATCHING THE WIND* AND *MEMORIES OF GLASS*

"*The Hidden Side* is a brilliant portrayal of our country's worst modern-day nightmare and the struggles of its traumatic birth. A stunning novel, not to be missed."

CATHY GOHLKE, CHRISTY AWARD–WINNING AUTHOR OF *UNTIL WE FIND HOME* AND *THE MEDALLION*

"This page-turner will appeal to readers looking for fiction that explores Christian values and belief under tragic circumstances."

BOOKLIST

"Filled with fascinating historical details, Chiavaroli connects two women through an artifact of the past. This heartrending tale will engage aficionados of the American Revolution and historical fiction."

LIBRARY JOURNAL

"Both halves of *The Hidden Side* are singularly compelling, with more of a fine threading between stories than an obvious connection. There is also the shared message that even during times of spiritual darkness, with prayer and hope, forgiveness and new beginnings are always possible."

FOREWORD MAGAZINE

"Chiavaroli's latest timeslip novel does not disappoint. Both storylines are fully developed with strong character development and they are seamlessly woven together."

ROMANTIC TIMES, TOP PICK

Freedom's Ring

"From the Boston Massacre and the American Revolution to the Boston Marathon bombing, history proves the triumph of grace. . . . Evocative, rich with symbolism, honest in its portrayal of human errors, *Freedom's Ring* explores what happens when individuals reach the limit of their own ability and allow God to step in."

FOREWORD MAGAZINE

"First novelist Chiavaroli's historical tapestry will provide a satisfying read for fans of Kristy Cambron and Lisa Wingate."

LIBRARY JOURNAL

"Joy, anguish, fear, and romance are seamlessly incorporated with authentic history, skillfully imagined fiction and the beautiful reminder that good can—and does—come out of darkness."

ROMANTIC TIMES

"A powerful journey into past and present. This masterful love story of God and country both haunts and heals long after the last page."

JULIE LESSMAN, AWARD-WINNING AUTHOR OF THE HEART OF SAN FRANCISCO SERIES

"Beautifully written, a riveting debut novel."

CATHY GOHLKE, CHRISTY AWARD–WINNING AUTHOR OF *UNTIL WE FIND HOME* AND *THE MEDALLION*

"An intriguing tale of two women separated by time connected through their search for a strength they desperately need."

MELISSA JAGEARS, AUTHOR OF *A HEART MOST CERTAIN*

"From courage in the face of tragedy to the healing power of forgiveness, this book will leave you with a wonderful message of faith, hope, and second chances."

SUSAN ANNE MASON, AWARD-WINNING AUTHOR OF THE COURAGE TO DREAM SERIES

The Tea Chest

The

TEA CHEST

HEIDI CHIAVAROLI

Tyndale House Publishers, Inc.
Carol Stream, Illinois

Visit Tyndale online at www.tyndale.com.

Visit Heidi Chiavaroli at www.heidichiavaroli.com.

TYNDALE and Tyndale's quill logo are registered trademarks of Tyndale House Publishers, Inc.

The Tea Chest

Designed by Ron Kaufmann

Edited by Caleb Sjogren

Published in association with the literary agency of Natasha Kern Literary Agency, Inc., P.O. Box 1069, White Salmon, WA 98672.

Scripture quotations in the historical chapters are taken from the *Holy Bible*, King James Version.

The Tea Chest is a work of fiction. Where real people, events, establishments, organizations, or locales appear, they are used fictitiously. All other elements of the novel are drawn from the author's imagination.

For information about special discounts for bulk purchases, please contact Tyndale House Publishers at csresponse@tyndale.com or call 1-800-323-9400.

Library of Congress Cataloging-in-Publication Data
Names: Chiavaroli, Heidi, author.
Title: The tea chest / Heidi Chiavaroli.
Description: Carol Stream, Illinois : Tyndale House Publishers, Inc., [2019]
Identifiers: LCCN 2019014802| ISBN 9781496434777 (hc) | ISBN 9781496434784 (sc)
Subjects: | GSAFD: Christian fiction.
Classification: LCC PS3603.H542 T43 2020 | DDC 813/.6—dc23 LC record available at https://lccn.loc.gov/2019014802

Printed in the United States of America

26	25	24	23	22	21	20
7	6	5	4	3	2	1

To Noah,

Your creative spirit never ceases to amaze me.

While Noah Adams and the Golden Tomahawk *might not have made the cut for the title of this book, it's still all yours.*

I love you so much!

ACKNOWLEDGMENTS

WITH EACH BOOK I release, my appreciation for those behind the scenes of each title only grows.

Thank you to my agent, Natasha Kern, and my editor, Jan Stob, for coming alongside me in the brainstorming process. I am blessed to have both of you beautiful ladies, whom I respect immensely, in my corner.

Caleb Sjogren, I'm so grateful that readers don't ever have to read a novel without it first being sifted with your sharp eye and compassionate heart. If they could know how consistently you think of them and put them first, they would be writing you the fan notes instead of me. Thank you for all you do.

I am so thankful to the Tyndale team for allowing me the privilege to partner with them in getting stories out to readers. Thank you to Karen Watson, Elizabeth Jackson, Kristen Schumacher, Andrea Garcia, and to all the many behind-the-scenes people at this precious publishing home.

Thank you to my cousin, Stacy Leeds, for giving me a glimpse into what it's like to be a woman in the military. I admire and respect you so much and am proud to call you my cousin.

A huge thank-you to my critique partner, Sandra Ardoin, and my #1 fan, Donna Anuszczyk (aka Mom).

Thank you to the Boston Tea Party Ships and Museum for making that long-ago December night come to life. Thank you to the staff at Medford Historical Society—Jerry Hershkowitz, Ann Marie Gallagher, Mike Bradford, and Kat Ruth-Coleman—for answering my many questions about Revolutionary Medford.

To the many readers, bloggers, and reviewers who have read my books or stopped to give a word of encouragement or to write a review, thank you. You make it all worthwhile.

Thank you to my sons, James and Noah, for continuing to think it's pretty cool that your mom's an author. Thank you to my husband and love, Daniel, for letting me vent when I'm overwhelmed, for celebrating in the times of victory, and for continually believing that I am called to do this writing thing.

Lastly, thank you to my God and Savior for not only giving me strength when I am weak, but for renewing my joy and hope.

I know of no way of judging the future but by the past.

PATRICK HENRY

Hayley

The bell was beautiful.

Brass, harboring a thousand hidden stories, it reminded me of the Liberty Bell in Independence Hall—of the one time, pre–military life, that I'd left my Massachusetts hometown, the only man who'd ever earned my respect beside me.

Somehow, my uncle Joe knew. He knew I'd needed to get away from it all. From the silvery peels of losing scratch tickets and broken rum bottles on the scratched wood of our coffee table, hope transferred to dirty needles, caps off, lying beside them.

My mother, Lena, passed out on the couch, the logo of her Happy Helpers Housekeeping uniform just visible beneath the shiny drool along her chin.

I'd needed to get away from the screaming late at night.

The knife I kept beside my bed in case one of her boyfriends came in . . . again.

The wondering if I'd ever have enough guts to use the knife if it meant protecting myself.

After that trip to Philadelphia, after seeing that cracked, ancient, glorious bell, after listening to the classified stories disguised in fictional form that my uncle Joe used to instill hope, after exploring the exciting beginnings of our country, after knowing he believed in me . . . well, I didn't wonder anymore.

The first time I pulled the knife on Lena's boyfriend, he'd slipped into my room, his cheap cologne filling the thick summer air. His steps came heavy as I pretended to sleep, my hand curled around the knife, waiting for the heat of his hand to graze my bare thigh and inch upward. From experience, I knew what would come next. But instead of succumbing to it, instead of praying that it would all just end quickly, this time, Uncle Joe's stories came to mind. His words.

"Your worth is not in where you come from, Hayley. Your worth is what you already have inside of you—what God put there from the very beginning—the will to live, the will to fight. No one can take that away from you. You have a say in how your life goes."

All that beautiful bell symbolized—freedom and pride and country and everything outside of that stuffy room with this man who kept my mother chained to her addictions— swelled over me. In one swift motion I twirled from my stomach, the knife tight in my grasp, the small lesson my uncle had given me on the best place to kick a man well-rehearsed and executed.

As I stood over the crumpled form, knife unused, I felt a sense of power. And as he backed his skinny, shot-up backside out of my room, promising not to bother me again, I realized something. Something wonderful.

I *was* strong.

And to me, being strong meant one thing: I *wasn't* weak. I wasn't like my mother.

Now, I glanced at the bell situated prominently in the Naval Special Warfare Center. When I'd come to the facility a week earlier, I'd ignored the bell, put it at a distance from myself. While I'd already made history in becoming the first woman to enlist in Basic Underwater Demolition/SEAL training, responding to the defense secretary's announcement that all combat positions—no exceptions—would be open to women, I was determined to let that history play out. Now, having passed the intense physical screenings, the country's eyes were on me, or rather the gender I stood for, as my name hadn't been released to the press.

And I'd been determined not to let them down. Determined not to let my uncle Joe down. Not to let . . .

But I wouldn't think of Ethan now. Or of Emma, or the tea chest and the newspaper article Ethan had sent me a few days earlier. They would only serve to ruin my concentration, to ruin everything I'd worked so hard for, to ruin who I knew myself to be.

The wearing down that I had prepared myself for had begun three days earlier. With each derogative comment from one of the men, with each bloodied wound and aching muscle piled upon my sleep-deprived brain an inch away from hypothermia, with each wave pounding us in IBS training and rock portage, I felt it.

And today, for the first time, I imagined walking up to the bell outside the main office, as thirty-two of my classmates had already done, of releasing the melancholy sound from that old symbol of freedom and laying down my lonely green helmet alongside the rest. Of being done.

Quitting. Maybe even going back home.

My wet pants rubbed sand and sea salt into the open wounds on the insides of my thighs as I did squats with my team. My arm muscles burned as I tried to hold my own in balancing the log above my head, the "Up, down" directions of our instructor hazy in my mind.

I'd read somewhere that if the thought of DOR (Drop on Request) so much as enters your head during training, then you're not Navy SEAL material.

With that thought, I forced my gaze off the bell, looked instead to the back of my friend Carpenter's head, his own arms shaking with effort.

The lieutenant paced beside us, stopped alongside me as we stood from our squat. "Ensign Ashworth, that bell's looking pretty good, isn't it? A warm bed, maybe a doughnut and some coffee. Oh, that's right—tea for you, isn't it, Ashworth? A cup of tea's looking mighty fine right about now, isn't it?"

Seriously, this guy didn't miss a thing. Not my bell fantasizing, or my tea sneaking in the chow hall. I forced my arms stronger, wished I'd left the tea at home. I'd given up more to prove I was one of the guys.

It was just tea, after all.

"No, chief!"

"Then why are you embarrassing your team, me, and my instructor staff with your sandbagging attitude? Your weakness can jeopardize your entire team. Go make a sugar cookie, Ashworth. You have three minutes to hit the surf, get some sand, and decide you want to help your team. Move, move, move!"

My arms fell numb at my sides, even as the men on either side of me groaned at the heavier weight now transferred to them. "Yes, chief!"

I ran toward the beach, stumbling only once, my arms burning with relief. Sand crusted every inch of my skin— from my chafing toes to the backs of my gritty eyelids. When I hit the cold shock of the Pacific, the salt burned the wounds along my body. I ignored it. That's what I needed to do— focus past the temporary pain. I forced my throbbing legs forward.

My commander was right. These men—they were my family now. I needed to be strong for their sake. I couldn't let them down.

As soon as I'd sunk every inch of my depleted body in the water, I trudged to shore, my now-sopping uniform clinging to my skin, and rolled thoroughly along the beach until I was coated with sand. I ran back to where my team held their log.

Before I took my position, Lieutenant O'Donnell got in my face. "There ain't no room on this team for sandbagging. You hear me, Ensign Ashworth? This is a school for warriors, understand?" His warm breath met my face with each shouted word. "I don't care where you come from—I don't care where any of you come from. What I do care about is your commitment. Your attitude. If you don't have it, then get out right now."

"Yes, chief!"

"And that goes for each one of you. Decide where you stand now, before Hell Week—are you on the quitting team, or will you give everything you have for this team . . . and your country?"

He left my side and I got back under the log with my team, held my own.

And kept my gaze far from that bell.

☩

I bit into my ham sandwich with all the etiquette of a lion, chewed fast so I had enough time to eat the rest of my meal. I swigged down an ibuprofen with my water. During the first few days at the training center, some of the guys had introduced themselves, were civil, encouraging even. Others gave catcalls or the occasional crude sexual remark. There wasn't much I hadn't learned to tune out over the years. And like it or not, we were bound to one another. In the depths of training, we would need to depend on one another. Prove our loyalty. Prove our strength. When life and death were at stake—when our Tridents were at stake—a small thing like gender didn't matter.

At least that's what I kept telling myself.

Carpenter sat beside me, dark hair shorn, with the type of physique only earned by doing two hundred push-ups—one hundred on each arm—every night. There was something genuine about him. Like he didn't care about the other guys and their catcalls when he was talking to me, like he wasn't interested in getting in my pants.

Here at the training center, there wasn't any room for such things, even if one were to allow for sexual encounters, which I did not. If I was to make it through BUD/S, I needed to be one of the guys. To dish out the crude comments as fast as they came. Sure, sometimes it felt like an act. Then again, I'd acted so much in my life it was hard to tell where the real me ended and the fake one began.

After a minute of eating, the scent of our unwashed bodies now a familiar accompaniment to our food, Carpenter nodded in my direction. "Makes the confidence chamber look like a walk in the park, huh?"

If I hadn't been so exhausted, I would have managed a smile at the reference to basic Navy training, the exercise where all trainees huddled in a small room with their class and donned gas masks. After a tear-gas tablet was released, we'd been ordered to take off our masks, throw them in a trash can, then recite our name, rank, serial number, and date of birth. Hard, but yes, so much easier than this.

"You're doing good, Ashworth. Most of the guys didn't think you'd make it this long."

I hid the pleasure I felt at his words—like gold to me in this moment. Some hadn't rung the bell—they'd been kicked out because they didn't swim well enough or run fast enough. I'd passed it all, though at times just barely. Part ashamed, I wondered if the instructors thought to let me slide because they might be accused of kicking out their first female recruit. "You too, Carpenter. Ready for next week?"

"Hooyah." He responded with a confidence I didn't quite feel.

Next week—Hell Week. Five and a half days of torture. Cold, wet operational training done on less than four hours of sleep. Trainees had been known to fall asleep in their food. Well more than half of my comrades would end up ringing the bell, giving it those firm three tugs that would echo through the compound, signaling failure. The rest would go on, more than likely, to get their Tridents. I'd vowed to be counted among them, but truth be told, I was scared.

As I lay in my bunk that night, wishing for some hot water to soak a tea bag in—hot water to soak my entire body in instead of the cold blast of the decontamination unit that passed for showers—I berated myself. I *could* do this. Sure, physical strength mattered, but determination—mental strength—mattered more. Those who wanted it the most would get it. If I could make certain my mind didn't give up, then my body would follow.

I flipped over, every muscle feeling the pain of the last two weeks of training. My breath echoed hollow in the musty bunk room, as I was separated from the rest of the men at night only. Somehow that seemed counterintuitive to the entire "Never leave a man behind" mantra.

I thought of Ethan, my conscience niggling, hurting. I forced the vision of his face aside, knew it would only distract me from the task at hand.

I thought of Uncle Joe instead. He was part of the SEAL Team Afghanistan raid that had taken down bin Laden. He'd encouraged me, believed in me, and trusted me to do this honorable thing. Trusted me to make history, to not be among the two-thirds of my comrades who would ring that bell.

I thought of my high school years, every academic and extracurricular decision leading me to this goal—to be the best at military life.

I closed my eyes, imagined the gold Trident pinned and shining upon my uniform, representing the elite family I was being welcomed into. I'd been sifted, proven strong. Though I told myself it didn't matter, I imagined the press release from the Navy.

WOMAN MAKES HISTORY IN BECOMING FIRST FEMALE MEMBER OF ELITE NAVY SEALS

I imagined the pride on Uncle Joe's face, the look of respect I would receive from enlisted comrades and officers.

Yes, five and a half days of hell would be worth it.

Again, I forced thoughts of Ethan from my mind as I mentally recited the SEAL code, long ago memorized, exchanging the pronouns and nouns to fit my gender.

In times of war or uncertainty there is a special
breed of warrior ready to answer our nation's call. A
common woman with uncommon desire to succeed.
Forged by adversity, she stands alongside
America's finest special operations forces to serve her
country, the American people, and protect their way
of life.
I am that woman.

Knowing at any moment I could be awakened to go for a run or a swim or to polish the bunk floor or have my stuff tossed about and then told to clean it back up, I still refused to let myself fall asleep until I'd recited the entire code, the last line foremost in my mind.

I will not fail.

✠

FOUR DAYS LATER
HELL WEEK

The stench of so many men wore on my stomach. This—sitting in a stuffy, near-ninety-degree room among my fellow trainees—would likely be the most pleasant experience of the next five days. I looked at the clock on the wall. 2200. None of us could fall asleep, all of us too busy fully anticipating what was to come to allow our minds rest enough for a nap.

I jumped from my seat at the loud shout from outside the room. A man in black kicked open the door and entered, a machine gun going off at his hip.

I dropped to the floor alongside Carpenter, prostrate, legs crossed, ears covered with the palms of my hands as we'd been trained to do. More gunfire. The sound of it stripped me bare.

More men. More guns. And while I knew they were our instructors, it felt so very . . . real. Like maybe the compound had been taken over. I swiped the thought from my mind, quick. This was one of the ways we'd be tested. Doubt. Doubt toward our instructors, doubt toward one another, doubt toward ourselves.

The sharp scent of cordite smoked the room, and I pressed my face further into the crook of my arm. Yelling again, then a familiar voice: "Welcome to hell, gentlemen."

Then came shouts for us to leave the room. In a daze, I moved with the rest of the trainees toward the door and out to the grinder, the blacktop square in the middle of the compound.

Gunfire. Whistles. Artillery simulators.

A blast of cold wetness slammed into my middle, burning at the same time that it knocked me to the asphalt. I struggled to my feet, sputtering, but another high-pressure hose knocked me down again.

I lost my sense of direction. All I wanted was to get away from the freeze of the spraying hoses, run for the ocean. If the instructors gave us directions, I could handle that. But we were just being pummeled, hitting the grinder in our defensive positions, rubbing water from our eyes and trying to breathe in air and stay with our fellow classmates amid the goading and shouting of the men behind the hoses.

I began to shiver, the cloth of my uniform slick against my skin.

We'd been in Hell Week all of half an hour.

More whistles came, then orders to grind out a set of twenty push-ups, then fifty sit-ups. Orders to crawl onto the beach. Sand flew in my face from the movements of the trainee in front of me. Briefly I wondered where Carpenter was. My elbows burned.

We were ordered into the water for flutter kicks.

Swearing from our instructors. "The bell's right up the hill for any of you who want it. Come on, you maggots. You got more in you than that. Give it your all or ring the bell!"

Into the sand, then back into the water. Over and over

again. A guy who'd been one of the toughest talkers in the bunch headed for the main office and the bell. Others called at him, begging him not to give up.

He kept walking.

Six others followed him within the next fifteen minutes.

The sound of the bell rang through the compound, three solid chimes for each trainee.

The whistles finally called us out of the water. We grabbed boats, wrangled them to the ocean, where we paddled for hundreds of yards and back. My arms burned with tingling pain. We got out, carried the boat, ran with it, crawled with it. The wet sand ground itself into my bloodied elbows and knees.

More calisthenics, then back into the water. I'd never been so cold in my life. My body shook and I became certain I would never be warm again, certain I was on the verge of hypothermia. I looked at the ambulance up the beach, waiting for its need.

In the chow hall, I could scarce shovel in my eggs. No one spoke, just ate. Either that or stared in a trance at their food. Shivering, I felt in a dream. An apparition appeared before me—Lena, sticking a needle into her arm, a look of shame on her face.

I swatted at her but really just wanted to fall forward into the flawed warmth of her needle-marked arms. There had been a few precious times when those arms had comforted. When they hadn't been a source of bitterness or stress. Yet even now, with exhaustion upon me, something deep inside rebelled at the thought of seeking my mother for assurance and security. Embers of anger glowed within me and I fanned them to life, for I knew it was here—in my wrath—that I'd find strength to continue.

The whistles blew again and I looked longingly at my still-full plate, knowing if I reached for a last bite, I would be punished.

The instructors led us to the steel pier, where they ordered us to jump in and tread water. I forced my moving limbs to keep my head above water.

I could do this.

Mental strength, that's what I needed. It would keep my muscles going when nothing else could.

I would not fail.

Back onto land for more calisthenics, then into the sand and water. The morning dawned murky with large drops of rain spitting on us.

Daylight came and went. Another meal, more cold pool exercises including a drown-proofing practice where our hands and feet were bound before we were thrown into the water, and then night again.

I longed for sleep. I longed for rest. The past six weeks—Ethan, Emma, the tea chest—it all seemed like a dream. And in my sleep-deprived mind I wondered if it had been.

It was dark when I passed out in the middle of crawling onto the beach. The cold rush of the sea woke me, bits of sand in my mouth and nose. Disoriented, I tried to push myself up from the sand, to follow my team toward the O course.

I knew what waited there. A place of cruel force, the obstacle course was used by veteran SEALs to prepare for deployment—rope climbs, walls, vaults, sixty-foot cargo net, barbed wire, rope bridges. Hell.

This time, when Ethan's face appeared in my mind along-side an image of the tea chest, I lay in the sand, knowing I would need to get up and continue on, knowing I would not—could not—ring that bell. Yet I couldn't find the strength to shove the memories away. If I were honest with myself, maybe I didn't want to.

CHAPTER ONE

Hayley

SIX WEEKS EARLIER

REVERE BEACH, OUTSIDE BOSTON

I stripped my socks from my sweaty feet and tucked them in my sneakers. I plunged my toes into the sand of Revere Beach, America's historic first public beach. I inhaled the salty sea air, felt my mind wandering to California.

Only a few more weeks and I'd be at the prestigious training base, putting action to my dreams. BUD/S training was no joke, but I was prepared. I would make it happen.

There was only one thing I needed to do before I could clear myself for takeoff.

Too bad the thought of seeing Lena made my stomach tie itself in knots.

I sighed, leaned back against the sand, just beginning to warm from the cool night air. The sun rose early at the beach, and already it began its climb upward. I closed my eyes, listened to the lull of the shore. A seagull's call came from above. The muted sounds of lifeguards chatting a stand over, then two women talking as they passed—something about hot flashes and sweaty sheets—competed with that of the waves crashing on the shore.

Maybe coming to Massachusetts hadn't been a good idea after all.

Surely I could accomplish training without my past hanging over me. I could become the first woman SEAL by simply looking forward, by focusing on the goal instead of what lay behind. And I could do it all without laying eyes on my mother, without facing the weak little girl I used to be.

But while I owed Lena no amount of loyalty, perhaps I did owe that scared little girl some.

I suppressed the temptation to book a flight out of Boston. I'd come all the way here for something. And the woman I wanted to be—the strong woman who would soon possess one of the most honorable positions in the military—would not back down.

I sat up, my abs still sore from the sit-ups I'd done that morning. I squinted against the sun, to where a child of about five years jumped over a small wave not far from the shore.

I'd run away before. It was time to make amends. Or at least put the past to rest. If I couldn't tackle these mental and emotional demons, how could I expect myself to tackle the biggest challenge of my life?

"Does he need help?" An older woman in a sun hat clutched the hand of a big-bellied man and pointed farther out from where I'd just seen the child playing.

Only the child was no longer there.

I stood, immediately on alert, searching the waves. From behind came the deep yell of a man. "Braden!"

I ran toward the water, seeing flailing arms much farther out than I had just been searching, and I knew the undertow had taken him.

I sprang into action, my high school summer job as a lifeguard all coming back to me. I stripped off my khakis, swimsuit underneath, seeing the girls on the lifeguard stand scrambling down out of the corner of my eye. They had the rescue buoys, but I could likely swim faster—could get to the boy in what might be lifesaving seconds.

I ran past the couple and made for the bobbing head with steady strokes. Determination and a foreign desperateness pulled me forward. This was one mission I could not fail.

The cold pull of the undertow slowed me, but I forced my burning muscles on.

Closer. Closer still.

The boy went under again and didn't come back up. Terror seized my chest as I forced my kicks strong, then dove down and opened my eyes against the burning salt of the sea.

Nothing.

I came up for air, dove again, promising myself I wouldn't surface without the child.

I swam deeper and hit bottom. In the murky distance, I

spotted a shadow and swam for it. My lungs pinched, on fire within my chest. I released a small amount of air, measuring, knowing once my lungs emptied, I wouldn't have more than fifteen seconds.

The figure floated farther away. I emptied the last of my breath, grasped at the hazy form. My fingers grazed a clump of hair. Lunging for it, I fisted it tight at the same time that I pushed off the sandy bottom.

We both came to the surface, but I was the only one gasping for air. From behind, I slid both of my arms beneath his, locked them firmly, made certain his mouth and nose were above water, and used all my core body and leg strength to kick toward shore.

"Here." One of the lifeguards was behind me with her rescue buoy, offering to take him. I gave the boy over, swimming alongside the guard, making sure she kept the child's mouth from the water.

After what seemed an eternity, I felt bottom again. We carried the boy to the beach, the father beside us, his clothes soaked.

"An ambulance is on its way," another guard said.

My breath came hard as we laid the boy down. Was he alive? The guard dropped to her knees but hesitated. I pushed her out of the way, alongside the child's father. "I'm trained," I said, tilting his mouth and chin back, his skin not quite a normal color. I crouched close to listen.

No breath met my ears.

I placed my hands in the middle of his chest. Hard and fast, I used my body weight to deliver multiple compressions. A woman behind me started praying aloud, and the sound of her words beseeching a mighty God nearly undid me. I pushed my emotions away—would they forever be my downfall?

I tilted his head again, lowered my mouth to his own small one, sealed my lips over his, and breathed two long breaths.

More compressions before finally he choked and spluttered, seawater spewing into my face. I swiped at it. Someone offered their towel and I took it. After several more chokes and gasps, the boy started breathing.

I sat back on my heels, relief soothing my tight insides as color returned to the child's face.

"Thank God," the man beside me said, scooping the boy up in a hug.

I placed a hand on his arm, pushing him away slightly. "Give him some room for a few minutes, okay?"

"I don't know how to—" The man looked up at me, his words cut short as his gaze met mine.

No, it couldn't be. Not him. Surely I would have recognized his voice when he'd shouted his son's name. Surely I would have recognized his form as he was in the water with the child. No matter the urgency of the moment. I would have known.

He straightened, looked to the boy again, who seemed to be breathing clearly. He opened his mouth, slow. "You."

I looked away, ashamed. It didn't matter that I'd just saved his son's life. It didn't matter that years had passed since I'd last seen him. My guilt felt fresh now, his shock piled upon recognition making me realize that while I had been able to ignore what I'd done to him years ago, he hadn't possessed the same gift.

Perhaps my mother wasn't the only one I needed to make amends with.

I forced a small smile, but only one corner of my mouth lifted, and it felt fake. So very fake.

"Yeah . . . me."

CHAPTER TWO

Emma

*It does not require a majority to prevail, but rather an irate, tireless
minority keen to set brush fires in people's minds.*

SAMUEL ADAMS

BOSTON

NOVEMBER 1773

'Twas only tea.

I stared into the steaming cup of bohea before me. The
smoky, exotic scent rose to my nostrils from the glittering
display of glass, silver, and ceramic upon Mother's mahogany
tea table.

Peculiar how one was to surmise so much from one's tea
table. More peculiar, perhaps, how the contents in one's cup
were capable of tearing apart a town—nay, an entire kingdom.

"They are beginning to fear for their lives. The Sons of
Violence are mad with rage, demanding the consignees refuse
the tea on the ships." Margaret, my oldest sister, straightened
her shoulders, the green damask of her dress straining against

her bosom, grown larger with the child she carried. "Imagine, they tout the meaning of freedom and yet our merchants are not allowed to receive their goods!"

"Hush now, Margaret. We mustn't involve ourselves in politics. It's unbecoming for a lady." Mother placed a lump of sugar in her cup. "Your father is quite capable of handling enough politics for the lot of us."

As a customs official and one of the most strong-willed men I knew, Father certainly did handle his fair share of politics. How capably he did so, however, seemed to be in question—at least among the town.

I sipped my tea. "Not speaking of the matter won't make it vanish, Mother. We all feel the pressure—the hatred from the town. Why must we keep it bottled up?"

Mother tsked. "I fear you've spent too much time at the Fultons', Emma. It's but a select few who have a problem with the tea—the town does not wish ill on us."

To hear her say such proved how little she left the house, save for a few afternoons of social calls at the governor's house.

"I suppose they did not wish ill on the Clarkes, either." I spoke the words softly, knew the mob that had made an appearance at the Clarkes' warehouse should not be mentioned, yet felt the tug of rebellion in my own heart over Mother's preference for trite discourse.

Mother put her cup down. It clattered in its delicate saucer. "The governor has asked Colonel Hancock to keep his cadets ready for additional disturbances. And your young swain is due to arrive any day. Surely that's reason enough to keep your thoughts from politics."

All rebellion leached from my heart at the mention of Samuel.

Samuel Clarke. Half of the "sons" in Richard Clarke & Sons—one of the largest tea importers in Boston—Samuel would arrive from London just in time to claim the tea contract granted him by the East India Company . . . and my hand in matrimony.

Samuel and I had met once, three years before, when I was but sixteen. Though I tried to convince myself there was something . . . worthy in the handsome man I was to wed, my mind captured his rum-soaked breath and cocky manner more than anything deserving of matrimony. That I compared him to Noah Winslow helped none.

Margaret let her hand flutter at her chest. "A spring wedding! It will be lovely, won't it, Mother?"

"The Clarkes have mentioned their willingness to contribute to the celebration." She smiled, a smug expression on her face. "It shall be grand."

Grand indeed. "'Twould be a pity if they're counting on their East India tea profits for it."

Mother allowed her hand to fall on the table. "Emma Grace, that is quite enough! I've half a mind to forbid you to continue your work at the Fultons'. Enough—"

"And what is this, Mother?" Father's hard voice sounded behind me. "I've enough fuss out on the streets. I needn't bear it beneath my own roof."

Fuss, aye. Though I had not heard the story firsthand, I heard enough of the gossip around town on my trips to the Fultons' to know that something happened to Father during his recent trip to Falmouth. The papers reported a customs agent in Falmouth who had seized a ship without reasonable cause and been given a genteel coat of tar and feathers by a mob of riled sailors. I could imagine not only Father's humiliation, but his words—which he never seemed to filter—that led to the incident.

I wondered what Uncle Daniel would have said about it all. Uncle Daniel, whom I often visited upon Copp's Hill, the inscription of his gravestone with the skull and crossbones long memorized: *A true son of Liberty, a Friend to the Publick, an Enemy to oppression, and one of the foremost in opposing the Revenue Acts on America.*

Though Uncle Daniel and Father had never agreed on politics, I had always been Uncle Daniel's favorite. He paid me more mind than Father ever did, bringing me hair combs and teacups and silk kerchiefs from his travels to faraway lands. I could still remember his laughing eyes when he gifted me with such a present, showering me in adoration, making me feel as if I truly belonged.

I did miss him.

Mother's voice broke into my musings. "'Tis your youngest, John. I fear she may need to be wed and off to England sooner than we'd planned. Or at least away from the South End."

I opened my mouth to protest but closed it swiftly at the stare Father pinned upon me. Here, in this room, he was my father, and yet it seemed he never released himself fully to the love and care of his family, either in the giving or in the receiving. A former sea captain and army officer turned customs informer, his renowned fiery temper didn't end at his own threshold. I knew not to cross him—had borne the brunt of his hands enough when I was small to know how long the sting lasted.

Nay, I would keep quiet. I would not speak my mind.

I would not state that my employment in the South End was the most blessed thing to come into my life in a long while. I would not state that I detested how our family name was synonymous with "taxes" and "East India Company" and "King George" and everything that the Liberty Boys—and it seemed the whole of Boston—ridiculed. I would not state how I felt more at home among the Fultons than I ever had in my own home, how, in the deepest spaces and corners of my heart, I wished I belonged in their humble and modest home in the South End instead of our grand one in the North.

Even as I acknowledged this thought as my own, even as I avoided Father's gaze, I silently admitted that it wasn't only Sarah and the Fulton family that caught my fancy, but a certain printer's apprentice who often found himself in their company.

Father sat in the empty Queen Anne chair and crossed his legs, waiting for our slave girl Chloe to pour him his tea and place a lump of sugar within. "Nay, we shan't move the wedding up further. And we shan't demand Emma part with her employment."

I released a breath into the cloth of my napkin. "Thank you, Father."

"Yet as long as you are there, Emma, you shall make yourself useful to me."

Margaret leaned into the table.

The tiny hairs along the back of my neck tingled. "How

so, Father?" The three words came out at odds and angles from each other, my voice all sorts of highs and lows.

"Those Sons of Pestilence think they're quite wise, summoning the consignees to their silly Liberty Tree, demanding they refuse the tea, tarring and feathering those who represent the crown, sending mobs to the Clarke warehouse." He slammed his hand down on the table, causing the tea to slosh in our cups and the silverware to clatter. "Enough! If my own daughter is to be in the employ of those who endorse such upheaval, then she will be my eyes and ears where I cannot be."

"Father, you can't possibly mean for me to engage in such dishonorable—"

"Are we not already dealing with dishonor in these rebels? It may be the only language they speak."

"Mayhap I could speak with the Fultons. Tell them—"

"Stop your whining this instant. It repulses me. We are Malcolms, doing the duty of our king and country. You should be glad to help. And if you are not . . . you will no longer make your trips to the South End, and I will speak to Mr. Clarke about moving your wedding."

"Malcolms, doing the duty of our king and country." I wondered what Uncle Daniel would have said about that.

My breath came fast, my corset quite suddenly too restrictive. Inky spots danced before my eyes. The Fultons were my friends. How could I betray them? *Spy* upon them? And yet, my family—my country perhaps—had need of me. Why then did I feel no obligation to assist either?

As Mother and Margaret awaited my response, I cowered beneath Father's stare. I could not imagine my life without the Fultons. I could not imagine a life in London, married to Samuel.

And yet it all seemed inevitable. Deferring the inevitable was my only choice.

I swallowed down my doubts with a sip of tea. I hadn't a choice, truly I hadn't. I would have to be strong, though in this case I wasn't sure I could be proud of such strength.

"Yes, Father. I will do as you ask."

CHAPTER THREE

Emma

We'll lay hold of card and wheel,
And join our hands to turn and reel;
We'll turn the tea all in the sea,
And all to keep our liberty.
SUSANNAH CLARKE

THE WARMTH OF THE FIRE in the stove heated my back in the Fulton keeping room, where I sat in a sturdy wooden chair, finishing the last of the mending on a pair of eight-year-old John's breeches.

The scent of stew—a simple meat and vegetable dish—simmered on the hearth. I looked at the door, wondered at Sarah's unusual tardiness. 'Twould be dark by the time I made my way home. Mother would not be pleased.

I folded the breeches and savored the peace of the slumbering children. Ann, Mary, and Lydia were little sprites who could run me ragged. Not that I minded their neediness. One smile, smeared with strawberry preserves, was enough to make the constant minding all worthwhile.

The door squeaked open and Sarah entered, doffing her

cloak and knit hat. "Forgive me, Emma. There was another gathering at the Tree upon my way home. I fear I was swept up in it."

I smiled to think of the small, pretty lady before me at a gathering down the street, looking on amid the crowd of Sons. Something akin to admiration, but not unlike jealousy, stirred within my belly. To be more like Sarah. To be bold and state my opinions heedless of repercussion, of disapproval. To care for my family with such fierce love and loyalty. To not hesitate at stopping beneath an old elm to listen to a group of rebels talk tea and taxes.

And yet I did not covet the time she spent at her mother's tavern serving flip, day in and day out, trying to supplement John's meager income at the distillery, having to spend so many hours from her children.

If I were to marry Samuel, I would not have to worry over such things. I could live a life of leisure in England, surround myself with wee ones to tend to, to give my heart to.

Truly, there could be worse fates.

"And what did they speak of this night?" I asked. Not until the words were out, swaying beneath the dried herbs hanging in the rafters, did I think of Father's demand for information. I should not have asked, for I could not tell that which I did not know.

Sarah hung her cloak and smoothed her dark hair. "There's to be a meeting at Faneuil Hall on Friday."

Friday. Pope's Day. A day long known in Boston for rebellion and revelry, disorder and dissidence. Boys ringing bells and threatening to break windows, effigies of the devil alongside the pope paraded on cobblestone streets by men wearing costumes and banging drums, all ending in a great bout of fisticuffs between the North and South Ends. "I shan't be able to come Friday. Father won't allow us from the house."

Sarah's gaze caught mine, and in that brief space of time, the air grew heavy. She came to me, clasped my hands in her own slightly weathered ones. "Dear, forgive me. I feel you are part of our family, having helped us since Ann was a wee one. I often forget how we—our families—are on different sides of this dispute." She closed her eyes, grasped my hands tighter. "I want you to know that you are loved by us, Emma. You are like a daughter to me, one of my dearest confidantes. Not for any political display, for I know you keep quiet about such things as a proper lady should—as I fail to do over and over again—but for your love and care of our small ones. I only want to make that . . . clear. And if you shouldst ever feel it not be in your best interest to serve us, then though it would break my heart, I would understand."

I blinked fast, demanding my eyes stay dry. "You are like family to me also. I could never imagine leaving the girls." Five-year-old Ann, who would be carrying her hornbook to dame school before long. Little Lydia not quite in leading strings. And Mary. Dear, sweet three-year-old Mary, who captured my heart with her raspy giggles and intense love, best shown in clinging hugs.

Yet soon there would be no more giggles or hugs, talks with Sarah, or strawberry-preserve smiles. Soon we would be an ocean apart.

Sarah dropped my hands and turned to stoke the fire in the stove, her voice soft. "I can barely stand the thought of you marrying him, Emma. You needn't, you know."

Was I so apparent?

"I am not like you, Mrs. Fulton—"

"Sarah. You must call me Sarah, as I've begged you time and again."

"Feels improper. I—"

Sarah shut the stove door with enough force to make me jump. "Hang proper, is what I say! Is it proper for your parents to force you to wed a man you met but once? Is it proper—?"

"Sarah, please. Attempt to see my view of things." I tamped down my doubts, spoke truth as I was seldom allowed to do in my own house. "I can't imagine standing up to Father. He would disown me outright."

Her head dipped a bit. "I don't mean to press you outside of comfort. I care, is all. I don't want to see you make a choice that will haunt you the rest of your years."

"It is not a choice." Bitterness laced my words, as tart as the imported lemons we had the luxury of squeezing over our cod in the summers.

"And see? This is why I urge you to take a stand. There are some matters we should have a say in." Quite suddenly her gaze grew far-off, and I knew she no longer thought only of my future, but of the ships, burgeoning with tea, that were to arrive within days. She blinked, and then she was with me again, her stare fastened upon me, her hand squeezing my arm. "We would help you in any way possible. You are brave. You are strong. And one day, I hope to see you prove it— not to me, but to yourself." Her hand released me. "I have something for you." She turned and opened the cupboard, grabbed her cup from the top shelf. 'Twas one she didn't use daily, rather only to mark special occasions—if the children were sleeping and she could catch a moment's rest, or if she wished to commemorate a certain day.

When she held it out to me, I shook my head.

"Take it, Emma. I want you to have it."

Tentative fingers grasped the teacup, a simple accompaniment that Mother would never deem fine enough for her tea table, as it held no handles and was horribly out of fashion. A blue Oriental pattern adorned each of its creamed sides, and a tiny chip marred the edge of its base. I ran my finger over the imperfection. "I don't understand why you wish me to have it. Was it not a wedding gift from your mother? Should you not save it for one of your girls?"

"We have other things to pass on. I was thinking of you today . . . of your predicament. And I thought of this cup."

I tilted my head.

"This cup has survived much. It wears its journeys in the scratches and dents upon its glaze. Yet it's been strong enough to endure, and so I value it all the more. Take it, wherever your journeys bring you. But when you look at it, remember you have chosen your journey. One way or another, you have had a say. Either by standing aside and yielding or by standing up and fighting." She placed her hands over mine.

I stared at the pottery, certain that only Sarah could summon forth such a bold metaphor from a piece that held one's beverage. Even so, I knew what the cup meant to her. At the same time, I knew what she longed for me to do. Even with that knowledge, I thought to push the cup back into her hands, tell her I couldn't do as she would in my situation.

I was not brave. Or strong. Or autonomous.

I was nothing like Sarah. And while I hated the thought that I was a weak individual, being weak was at least safe. I needed only to stay within certain guidelines, and I would fall beneath the protection of what was expected. I would fall beneath the protection of Father.

"You are like a daughter to me, Emma. No matter our different worlds, you can create a new future for yourself. A new family, even."

What she offered in the simple gift overwhelmed me. I didn't have the heart to spurn it. "Thank you, Sarah." I met her gaze. "This means more to me than you know."

"Emmy!" Little Mary toddled out of the back room and reached her arms up to me. I slid the teacup into my pocket, scooped her into my arms, and pressed a kiss to her feather-light blonde hair, catching the scent of woodsmoke and lye, likely from her freshly laundered pillow slip.

"Yes, I'm still here. About to leave, though, little one. I will see you tomorrow?"

She favored me with a toothy smile and a nod.

The door burst open and in tumbled Sarah's husband, John, along with their two eldest children and—

Noah Winslow's gaze landed on me, his eyes dancing.

I tried to keep a blush from rising to my face, which I feared made it all the worse.

"John." Sarah planted a kiss on her husband's cheek and I turned away, embarrassed. I'd never seen Father and Mother so much as hold hands. "I was late coming home from the tavern and now 'tis dark. Might you walk Emma home?"

Though I did not wish to be a bother, thoughts of walking the town's streets in dusky light alone—with the mischievous

Sons of Liberty about, perhaps all too ready to mock an agent's daughter—frightened me to no end. And yet, though I could only suspect, I thought Mr. Fulton himself might be among the Sons. And he, with his tall, lanky frame and kind eyes, was not fearsome in the least.

"Allow me, Mrs. Fulton." Noah stepped forward.

I shook my head, half-appalled, half-thrilled that I should spend time alone with the young man who occupied my dreams. But without a chaperone? Would Sarah allow it?

But she only smiled, seemed amused at my wordless response. "That would be splendid. And when you are through, come right back here for Emma's stew."

I placed a kiss on Mary's soft cheek and donned my cloak and hat, the wool warm from the heat of the Fultons' stove. Noah opened the door and allowed me to pass through.

Once he closed it behind us, the dark near swallowed us up save for candlelight speckling the many nearby houses and lanterns held aloft by a traveler or two. The scent of the Fulton kitchen fire combined with Noah's distinct ink-and-paper smell to relax me. Winter's chill masked the more unpleasant scents of the gutter and horse manure.

As a true gentleman, Noah guided me down the slightly longer but more populated route along Essex Street. Though by daylight the town seemed a thicket of steeples and masts, only the Liberty Tree could be seen at this time of night. Eerie and naked in the dark folds of similar elms lining Hanover Square, her leafless limbs stretched outward and upward, reaching for . . . what? What was it that those who gathered beneath her branches wanted so badly?

My gaze traveled to the staff rising above the tallest branches. A Liberty Flag flew there.

Freedom.

"A penny for your thoughts." Noah kept up with my brisk pace as we rounded Newbury Street, the tree behind us.

I looked at him, thankful for the shroud of night to hide my ever-flushing face, despite the frigid weather. His breath came out in puffs of visible vapor. Somehow my noticing seemed an intimate gesture, and I looked back to the dim cobbles at my feet.

"I suppose I'm pondering . . . politics."

He chuckled. "Politics, is it? I'd think with your father's station you'd be up to your ears in politics."

"Aye. Sarah is enthralled with the Liberty Boys. With that confounded tree. I am trying to make sense of it—make sense of the need to risk so much for what seems so little."

A true son of Liberty.

Father said Uncle Daniel hadn't been a defender of freedom so much as a defender of his ships' profits. Was that true?

"So liberty is of little matter to you?"

"I suppose I'm not entirely convinced we're in chains to begin with." The line was one adapted from my father. Yet even as I released the words to the night, I wondered at how true they were to my own opinions. Was I no better than an exotic parrot, mimicking Father's words?

An Enemy to oppression.

Were we in chains? Nay. The slaves from Africa were in chains. I didn't see the Liberty Boys making a fuss about that kind of oppression.

We walked onward, past Province House with its weather vane depicting an Indian holding a bow, and then Old South, silence eating up our precious time together. In the distance, the clip-clop of a horse's hooves punctuated our quiet until I could no longer leave the unbearable stillness between us. "Noah . . . I know 'tis a personal question, but I've come to respect you—respect your opinion, even if we shan't agree . . ."

"That means a great deal to me, Emma. Thank you. I respect yours also. 'Tis what friends do, aye?"

Friends. Aye. We were friends.

We approached the center of town, passed the pump and Town House and Long Wharf to our right, stretching out to the frigid winter sea, where naked masts of ships bobbed heavy in the water amid countinghouses. In the morning, one would hear the bargaining at stalls, but now all lay quiet. The Clarke warehouse—and likely the lot of what was to be my wedding funds—sat at the base of the wharf, quiet and unassuming, yet in my mind full of reproach. It was the hub of vigorous Boston trade—tobacco, rum, sugar, molasses, African souls.

"And what be your question, dear Emma?"

Dear Emma . . .

Certainly the candlelight from the windows of the Royal Exchange tavern would give away my nervousness. I was bold. Too bold. Mayhap, 'twas in this boldness that I could be more like Sarah. I felt the heaviness of her cup against my thigh and tried to draw strength from it.

"I was wondering—and mind you needn't answer if you don't wish—but I was curious if . . ."

Noah put a hand on my arm, stopped walking. A gust of cold sea air washed between us, carrying with it the scent of salt. "You needn't be bashful. I am honored to be privy to your thoughts."

His voice ran smooth over my insides, churning them as rich as fresh cream. The invitation seemed so much more. Could it be my feelings for this man were reciprocated? And yet, if that were true, I was a dupe for pulling at the depths of his mind. For letting him draw near.

I belonged to Samuel Clarke.

Still, I could not leave him hanging there, the strong profile of his face full of shadows and earnestness beneath his tricorne hat. I gathered a breath, released it all in my next sentence. "Do you make merry with the Liberty Boys?"

I saw the lights of the Green Dragon tavern alive to the left of us, knew Boston's Freemasons and the Liberty Boys gathered abovestairs, and I wondered if Noah ever joined them.

Something like disappointment flashed, quick as a musket shot, across his features. He took to walking again, and I followed, feeling the immediate need to speak, yet fearing an apology might only make matters more strained between us.

"Why do you ask?"

"I was curious, is all."

Upon the bridge of Mill Creek that marked the North End, he stopped walking. My home was a block away. "What I mean is, do you ask for yourself or for your father?"

He expected no more from me than my father did, then. He expected me to bring information to my kin. It hurt that

38

he would think so little of me, but could I pretend that I had not agreed to Father's request for information?

"Is he gathering a list of names? Is that it?"

"Nay. I mean, I do not have knowledge of it if he is. Noah, I wouldn't—please believe me when I say I would never betray you." I looked down into the black waters of Mill Creek, the full truth of my words securing something within me. A surety that my loyalty to both him and the Fultons was true and real, no matter what Father threatened. "I am attempting to sort it all out. What it is the Sons fight for. Why Sarah is so certain it is true and right."

He quieted, scuffed his boot along a jagged wooden board of the bridge. "You said you don't believe the colonies are in chains, aye?"

I swallowed, the words I'd parroted now thrown back into my face. "Aye." No doubt he heard the hesitation in my voice.

"I suppose 'tis a matter of what chains we speak. Nay, the colonies may not be in prison. But we are not free to rule ourselves either, you see? Magna Carta states we are Englishmen, yet we have no say. The king stifles our voices, and that, to me, is a very bitter kind of chain. One I work to rectify at my press."

I looked toward my home, where the peak of the grand house could just be seen. Where Father and Mother attempted to suppress my own voice, my own thoughts. Where I was told they did not matter. Aye, I understood the different kinds of chains Noah referred to more than I first realized.

"There are some matters we should have a say in."

Sarah's words rattled in my mind, creating a clear picture where before there had been only muddle.

Noah gripped the railing of the bridge, his face suddenly fierce. "I don't make merry with the Liberty Boys often, though I think I should like to. And I am called to. I tell you this in trust because you are my friend and I care for you, and I long to earn your trust."

I inched my hand from the warmth of my cloak, placed it on his arm. I'd never touched him before, and the action caused a dizzying sensation to course through me.

He cared for me.

Right then, I longed to be worthy of this man. This man who was nothing but riffraff in my father's eyes, yet who to me was tenscore worthier than Samuel Clarke. "You have my trust, Noah. And now it is time I earn yours."

I was rewarded with a grin as wide as Mill Pond. He rustled within his cloak and pulled a book from his pocket.

"A gift for you. We printed them last week. I purchased one from Henry Knox's bookshop. I heard you expressing interest to Sarah one afternoon."

I took the book, warm from where it had rested beside his broad chest in the folds of his cloak.

A True History of the Captivity and Restoration of Mrs. Mary Rowlandson. The story of Mrs. Rowlandson's kidnapping by the Narragansett natives during King Philip's War.

"Noah . . . thank you. I shall treasure it forever." Two precious gifts in one night. The last gift I'd received of such value had been from Uncle Daniel. I put my hand on Noah's arm again, and this time he stared at me with an intensity that had me questioning everything I'd ever believed.

I *could* make a life with this man, in the back of a printing shop if necessary, if he would but ask. I *could* allow Father to disown me, accept that I would never see Mother or Margaret again. I *could* take up the cause of freedom. I could explore what life was—who I was—without Mother and Father dictating it all for me.

Yet Noah had not asked me to do any of those things, and in the next space of breath, reality came crashing upon me with all its expectations.

Loyalty. Father and Mother demanded my loyalty. And in many ways, was not loyalty more honorable than liberty? I was bound to my parents—truly, who would I be without them?

I slipped the book within the pocket of my cloak, knew I would need to hide it from Mother's prying eyes, as my parents discouraged my reading anything save the Bible.

We walked the remaining block to my home, where I turned and thanked Noah, my previous question longing for release. Once again, I ignored my intuition and my need to remain quiet and steadfast as a proper lady should; instead I opened my mouth.

Mayhap Sarah had influenced me after all.

"Noah, tell me which is more honorable—loyalty or liberty?"

Beneath the warm glow of Father's expansive house, his eyes twinkled. "I suppose that should depend on the worth of who or what one is loyal to, aye?"

"If men were to constantly judge the worthiness of that to which they should be loyal—God or king or mother or father—would not the whole of society collapse?"

"A fair question, and one we should discuss at length sometime—mayhap when we are not in the middle of the street."

"You dodge my question."

He stepped forward, closer to me than he'd been all night. I had the horrid sensation I should step back, run away, and the more horrid realization that I longed to press closer.

His breath came upon my forehead, warm against the night. "I think I am merely in awe of your beautiful mind, Miss Emma. And I should further like to explore it. Will you—?"

The front door of the house opened, spilling light upon us. We stepped apart. "Emma?" 'Twas Father. "In the house this instant. You are late. I've half a mind to take you over my knee." His tall, solid figure shadowed the threshold.

I rushed up the stairs without bidding Noah farewell, my father's words the epitome of embarrassment.

Noah's voice came from behind. "Forgive me, sir. 'Tis my fault. I led Miss Emma the long way home to stay along well-traveled roads."

Father descended two stairs. "How dare you presume to speak to a gentleman such as myself? Stay away from my daughter. She is not suited for a tramp. And if you dare test my demands, know that Governor Hutchinson has promised to pay me a bounty of twenty shillings for every Yankee I kill."

I stood at the threshold, my hand along the imported wallpaper Mother had labored over choosing. I shook my head, not comprehending Father's ill words toward the man I cared for.

Noah mumbled a "Yes, sir." He turned, head down, went back the way we had come.

Father stomped up the stairs, rage on his features, and I braced myself for whatever physical punishment he deemed fit for my crime.

And still, my question lingered.

Which was more honorable?

Loyalty . . . or liberty?

CHAPTER FOUR

Emma

*I am more and more convinced that man is a dangerous creature
and that power, whether vested in many or few, is ever grasping
and, like the grave, cries, "Give, give!"*
ABIGAIL ADAMS

"Ah, Miss Emma. You are lovelier than I remember." Samuel
Clarke's words slid from his tongue, smooth as the silk rib-
bon holding the queue at the base of his neck.

I smiled, thanked him as expected, wondered how Father
could think us a well-made match.

Then again, Father likely took no consideration of our
personalities when deciding my future. No, mine was a
match made with only monetary gain in mind.

The Clarkes' maid offered up a plate of chestnut frit-
ters. As I raised my hand to receive one, for no other reason
than to have something to do, the remembrance of Father's
painful grasp after Noah's parting the other night came to
the forefront of my mind. His words, like hot bacon grease,
sizzled in my memory, along with the fire of his grip.

"It will be your doing if that boy finds himself on the wrong end of my musket."

I understood, didn't doubt that he would carry out his threat. If I cared for Noah, then I would stay away from him. Mayhap I had best stay away from the South End altogether. I needn't put my friends in peril.

Beside me, in a white broadcloth coat complete with silver basket buttons to match his knee bands, Samuel scooped up a mug of hot buttered rum, the ruffles at his hands perfectly positioned so as not to interfere with his reaching. "Your father tells me you spend your time minding the Fulton children. Such humdrum for the likes of yourself."

"I don't mind. In fact—"

"Now, now, once we wed, you needn't worry about such nonsense." He moved closer and I caught a whiff of sickeningly sweet cigar smoke. "I see a time soon when we will have our own brood romping around. And I will see to it you have all the help you need in caring for them so that you can concentrate on . . . other duties."

I expelled a breath—a nervous, mortified laugh coming along with it.

I cared not a pig's tooth how much money Samuel Clarke possessed nor how my parents wished for our nuptials. How could I bear to be with him every day . . . every night? To live beside him, to share intimacies with him, to be his wife?

Sarah had attested that by my own decisions, I might change the course of my life. Something that sounded so simple but was in fact the most complicated feat I could imagine. Because to find my voice meant to speak against my parents—to speak against my world.

Sarah, Noah . . . they bade me stand up for what was true and right, for my future, and yet they hadn't instructed me how to go about summoning the boldness to do so.

Mother fluttered toward us in her blue velvet trimmed with ermine, a glass of Madeira in hand. "Isn't it simply grand to have Samuel home again, Emma?" She rested her fingers on the broadcloth of Samuel's arm. "She's been just dabbling around the house, simpering over your departure. A complete pity, truly."

"Mother!"

She turned doleful eyes in my direction while Samuel leered at me with a grin that churned my stomach.

He must have mistaken my outburst for embarrassment, not chastisement toward the woman who birthed me, for he chuckled, a cocky, amused expression on his face. "Has she now?"

I searched for my voice. But alas, again, it could not be found. And what would the recourse be if I were to outright deny Mother's words?

I had chosen to remain loyal, but Noah's words pressed on my mind. Loyal to what? Loyal to whom? This woman who told untruths about me to secure her own future—did she command the price of my loyalty?

A bitter taste gathered in the back of my mouth. "Forgive me, I fear I may be ill." I left the room, bypassed Father and the elder Mr. Clarke laughing heartily over some matter, and slipped outside.

The cool sea air swept over me, settled my stomach. I breathed it in. I felt my life was fast barreling in a direction I did not wish to go. And yet 'twas the way of things. Did that mean I should accept them?

From the direction of the Town House came the sound of conch shells being blown, of whistling and stamping and shouting.

Odd . . .

The door to the Clarke home flew open. Mother appeared, eyebrows raised. "Truly, you'll catch your death out here without your cloak. Come back inside at once, dear." She stilled, the sound of the horns growing closer, raucous catcalls now mounting upon them.

"Do you hear that?" I whispered.

Mother's face pinched. She grasped my arm, pulled me inside. "Come." She walked to Father, waited patiently beside him until he directed his attention to her. Meanwhile, the sounds outside grew louder.

"Father," I interrupted.

A look of annoyance flashed across his face before he recovered, likely for Mr. Clarke's sake.

"John," Mother started, "I fear a mob is brewing."

Father and Mr. Clarke summoned Samuel and the other men present, then ordered the women to the upper chambers.

I fled toward the stairs, along with the wives and daughters in attendance. From below, the sound of the door bolt came, its echo chasing us up the stairs. The rowdiness outside rose to a deafening pitch.

"What do they want?" Mrs. Clarke sobbed into her handkerchief as she led us to an empty guest chamber.

"They're demanding your family resign their position as consignors for the tea. They want your husband and sons to refuse the tea upon its arrival," I said. How did she not know the circumstances her husband found himself in?

The clamor grew louder and more frantic. Surely they didn't mean to harm anyone. I wondered if John Fulton were among the group, but I found it difficult to believe Sarah's husband would contribute to such a fracas.

I slid toward the window, curiosity overcoming me.

"Emma, get away from there!" Mother's voice rose on edge, but 'twas so filled with terror it appeared uncontrolled, giving me the courage to ignore it.

Outside, a crowd had gathered with tin lanterns and pine-knot torches, shaking fists.

"Listen to the Body or suffer the consequences!"

"This is our town. We won't be daunted by the likes of you!"

"Huzzah!"

Additional "Huzzahs!" met our ears.

From another window upstairs, on the far side of the house, Samuel shouted down to the crowd. "You rascals, be gone or I'll blow your brains out!"

"He can't mean it," I whispered. Though I understood the fear which would make him say such words. And Father . . . he must be near insane with rage to be locked up in the Clarke home, at the mercy of a mob . . . for once, not in control.

Was a bloody fracas to start this very night, in this very home?

The crowd called back hisses and shouts at Samuel.

The fire of a pistol shattered the frozen night air.

The women behind me screamed, the gun's explosion

echoing down School Street and all the way to the harbor. Though the mob grew silent, they certainly wouldn't take kindly to the shot. I sank back from the window, fearful to look down and see an injured person.

"Dear Father in heaven." Catherine Clarke whispered a quiet prayer, the scent of gunpowder finding its way to us.

Banging started then. Catsticks on the black iron hitches in front of the Clarke home. Then the shatter of glass and the sound of wood splitting. I crept closer to the window to see men throwing stones and brickbats at the first-floor windows of the house.

I clamped my hand over my mouth, wondered what was to become of us. Would they burn the house to the ground? Drag Father and the Clarkes away to be tarred and feathered? They seemed to grow mad, insensible. What might they do to the women in the house?

For once, I wished I were a man. Each day I hated this helpless feeling more and more. In Father's circles—in most of the world—women were to remain quiet and keep their noses out of politics. Yet here, now, we were in the thick of it, and without one opinion or claim to call our own.

From down the street I glimpsed the bob of torches. As they neared, my heart beat out a thrumming as fast as the cycle of a spinning wheel.

Noah. And John.

They did not know of my presence. Would I see them contribute to this tumult? I'd respected them, thought them beyond such measures, but truly, how well did I know either one? I'd heard that men often acted differently when outside the home, some of the less honorable visiting local brothels.

I'd heard rumors of Samuel doing so, had wondered how I could reconcile marriage to such a faithless man.

But Noah and John? Join the fomented rabble below? To fight for a cause was one matter. But with such unruliness?

A voice rose above the crowd. John's. "Men, stop this madness." I exhaled my relief, pressed my forehead against the cold pane of the window.

A few of the men elbowed one another, quieted, nodded toward John. "Let us not indulge in violence, but act in honor at all times. Surely an agreement can be reached."

A man from the crowd waved a catstick. "I've an agreement for ya. We shall disperse if the Clarkes choose to stop aligning themselves against their country and promise to appear at our town meeting scheduled tomorrow aft. Either that, or agree to reship the tea this minute."

The crowd stomped their feet, yelled hearty assent.

Samuel laughed loudly, still from the second-story window. "Fie! We shall not acknowledge illegal and underhanded meetings beneath *trees*! Especially not those with men of low rank, who choose to ruin honest men's personal property and throw our women in distress."

The crowd grew fierce at Samuel's words. I near cursed him in my head for stirring them up again when John had attempted to dispel their vigor.

A shrill whistle pierced the night air, and Noah climbed atop the Clarkes' carriage step. "Men of Boston! I beg of you, listen to reason! Is this the way to come to a solution? Out on a winter's night, yelling at one another, terrorizing the ladies in the house?" My heart blossomed tenfold for him in that moment. I knew his beliefs, but here he stood for what was moral and right. Though unaware of my presence, he defended the ladies within. He defended Father, who had belittled and embarrassed and cursed him just days earlier. "Let us not forget ourselves in this dispute. Let us not be accused of using violence to obtain that which is honorable and right. Let us not reduce ourselves to indecorum. Instead, let us conduct ourselves with poise and grace as we demand our God-given rights as people who should have a voice within our government!"

Some cheered his words, shouting, "Huzzah," stomping their feet as a sort of applause. Yet some in the crowd turned away, mumbling, likely not impressed with Noah's speech and the impasse it brought on the entire gathering.

Nevertheless, the crowd did disperse. Father and the Clarke men came from the house to clean the shattered glass left on the walkway. Noah and John stooped to help, and when I realized they would stay and aid the Clarkes, I pushed through Mother and Mrs. Clarke to descend the stairs.

I would not be welcome outside with the men, but I made busy cleaning the glass inside the parlor, staring intently until Noah straightened from his work and caught my gaze. His mouth parted in surprise, and hiding myself partly behind the drapes, I raised my hand in greeting and gratitude.

He dipped his head, the tug of a half smile upon his face as he stared at me. I hadn't seen him since the night he escorted me home. I suspected he avoided the Fultons, not wishing to garner more trouble for me by way of my father.

Yet, to see him now . . . something bold and new burst within my heart.

What Noah took part in, what he thought worthy to fight

for, who he was—titled gentleman or not—was noble. The thought made me feel at home, secure. Quite of a sudden, I longed to be a part of it.

"You there!"

Noah snapped to attention at Samuel's words.

"Do you dare ogle my intended through my father's broken windows? Off with you, now, you hear? We needn't any more aid from the likes of you."

I despised Samuel's haughty tone, the very voice of the man I was to wed.

And as Noah dipped his head again to me and then to Samuel beneath Father's glare, I knew without a doubt whose side I longed to be on.

Nay, it might not be moral for the mobs to attack the Clarke house, but neither was it moral for those of a certain station to snub their noses at others as if they were plebeians, riffraff, and blackguards. Especially the likes of Noah, who had curtailed the fury of the mob with his timely words and peaceful presence.

For the first time, I saw clearly why Sarah, John, Noah, and the Liberty Boys fought so adamantly for that which was not yet theirs.

They *were* in a sort of prison. One where the gaolers told them they mattered less than their fellow humans. One where they were denied a voice.

One where they and their families were forced to endure circumstances they didn't have a decision in, forced to bow to the whims of the so-called gentlemen of the town. Men like Samuel. Men like my father.

Watching Noah's torch bob away in the inky night, I

vowed not to stand on fence posts any longer. I vowed to do what I could for the decent folk of the town—unlike me perhaps, but worthy people nonetheless. I would follow Noah's example and stand as a light for that which was noble and right.

Samuel entered the house again, disgust on his face at the broken glass near my slippers. "Your father tells me that ruffian takes an interest in you. We've decided it best you no longer visit the South End, Emma. Now that I am home, there is no need, and you have a wedding to plan and a trip across the sea to prepare yourself for. Is that clear?"

I pressed my lips together, breathed through my nose, the fierceness of a fairy-tale dragon longing to break free. Yet I must plan my steps with care and wisdom. Succumbing to feisty feelings would not do, not if I were to truly take charge of the design formulating in my mind.

"Emma. Is that clear?"

I raised my chin to Samuel, for the first time thankful that I would not be his wife in the end.

"Aye, Samuel. You are indeed very clear."

If I could grasp this newfound courage, refuse to release it to weakness, refuse to doubt whether or not I owed my parents my loyalty, then mayhap I would find my voice after all.

CHAPTER FIVE

Emma

This tea now coming to us [is]
more to be dreaded than plague or pestilence.
SAMUEL ADAMS

DECEMBER 14, 1773

I held the forbidden newspaper to the light of the candle flame beside my bed and pressed my feet nearer to the warming pan beneath my covers. While Father preferred the *Chronicle* with its funding from the customs office and its English cartoonist's replications featuring the colonials as inferior Indians, I had been voraciously reading both the *Chronicle* and the *Gazette*, trying to come to a decision of my own regarding politics.

In the *Gazette*, I read a letter from Philadelphia, posted earlier in the month. "Our Tea Consignees have all resign'd, and you need not fear; the Tea will not be landed here or at New-York. All that we fear is that you will shrink at Boston."

I put the paper on my lap, leaned back against the head-board. The Sons were not only being pressed by those within the town; they were being pressed by Philadelphia and New York.

Three ships bobbed heavy with tea at Griffin's Wharf. The Sons of Liberty had swayed most of the town to their side, and now the time for the tea to be unloaded and the taxes paid by the people of Boston loomed before us, just days away. The soldiers at Fort William had loaded their muskets and charged their cannons to prevent the *Dartmouth* or any other ship from leaving the harbor, and it seemed the town was at a standstill, holding its collective breath, waiting to see the fate of the tea.

As for me, Father had sent the Fultons a letter after the riot at the Clarke house, stating I would no longer be aiding them in the care of their children. I no doubt disappointed Sarah, and as each day passed, I waited for a letter from her, assuring me this was not the case.

But no letter came. Yet that didn't mean one had not been sent. In our household, Father controlled the post as well.

I slid from my feather mattress, crept to the window, where a sliver of moon lit the night sky. A breath trembled up my lungs. For days—and nights—I'd been attempting to summon up the courage to do what I'd vowed I must the night the mob came to the Clarke house. And night upon night, I looked out my window onto the cold streets below, Mill Creek just beyond, and allowed fear to swallow up my courage.

Who was I without my parents? Who was I to think I could live apart from them? Such thoughts were highly irregular. What if I could not find a place with the Fultons? Father would never forgive such a betrayal. No doubt he would lock me away, humiliate me, and then marry me off to Samuel.

And yet still, the time drew nearer when the entire town might explode. Father already spoke of sending us away from "all these rebels." If I didn't act soon, it might be too late. Would I never again see little Mary, nor Sarah and the rest of the children again? Would I never see Noah?

Yet if I took action, if I carried out my plan, what of Mother and Margaret? And Father . . . Though we were at odds and I had never, sadly, felt a genuine love from him, he *was* still my father. To imagine cutting myself off from them forever seemed as absurd as cutting off one of my hands.

I thought of the book Noah had given me. I had devoured it. In it I saw how uncertain all of life is, how the Lord continues to show mercy through trials, and how He longs to free us from spiritual—and perhaps many times, physical—bondage.

I thought of how I had become much a prisoner in my own home, held captive not by a native tribe, but by Father. And this being only temporary, until I was to be chained to another gaoler—a husband.

I thought of Uncle Daniel and his legacy. *A true son of Liberty . . . an Enemy to oppression.*

There would be no rescuer. This was the time to act with boldness and courage, to find my voice, to grasp and lunge for the future I would have for myself.

Suppressing every last harrowing doubt, I stripped the bolster pillow free of its slip and shoved in underpinnings, two dresses, a comb Mother had given me when I was but ten, a few personal items, and finally, Sarah's cup and the book Noah had gifted me a fortnight earlier.

Energy rushed to my limbs and I fought off a dizzying

sensation as I acted upon my thoughts. I donned my most inconspicuous traveling dress with front-lacing stays and sat upon my bed, the embers from the chamber hearth growing dim, the slip of my pillow filled and in my lap. A note to my family lay upon the chest of drawers in my room, the latest copy of the *Boston Gazette* boldly beside it. I clutched my possessions tight to me, strained my ears for the sound of Chloe cleaning downstairs.

As the night wore on, as I became certain that all were in deep slumber, I thought to act quickly before I could scare myself with more doubts. I donned my warmest cloak and grasped my bag with clammy fingers. In my other hand, I held a candle. As I passed Mother and Father's chambers, my heart reached a pace so frantic I thought it would surely wake my parents from a sound sleep. And how would I explain my dress, my pillow slip with only my most cherished possessions? I imagined Father's stern stare and what would come if I were to be found out.

Despite the coolness of the hall, a trickle of sweat ran down the middle of my chest, wetting my stays. When I reached the stairs, I had a terrible urge to run, to never, ever look back again. Yet I held myself at a slow gait, stopped at the creak of one step, a rushing sound loud in my ears.

The feeling passed as no one stirred from their dreams. I continued with wobbly steps until I reached the entrance. I looked back toward the stairs, remembering the greenery Mother sometimes wrapped around the railings in cold winter months. Once, I'd caught Father singing a merry tune as he came down the stairs, thinking himself alone in the house. I imagined them waking, finding me gone, finding my note. Would Father search for me and, if I were discovered, demand I obey him? Or would he wipe his hands of me altogether? Would Mother mourn her younger daughter, or would she mourn her chance at a connection to the profitable Clarke family more?

The fact that I truly didn't have an answer to that last question, no matter how intently I searched my heart, prodded me to unbolt the door with shaking fingers, open it just wide enough to slip into the dark, cold folds of the night air, and shut it quietly behind me.

I inhaled a quivering breath and stared at the closed door, its wood splintered and worn from the weather. I had doubts, but nothing—nothing—was worth going back up those stairs and putting myself at risk of being caught. I scurried toward Mill Creek bridge, the flame of my candle out with the first breeze. The scent of smoky beeswax lingered for only a moment.

When I reached Mill Creek, I glanced back up Middle Street. No one followed, and as I glimpsed my house—my parents' home—through the tight confines of other dwellings, I felt an unexpected sorrow. Not so much over leaving perhaps, but a sorrow for what I wished we'd been.

And what now we would never have a chance to be.

✠

I'd never been out so late, and without an escort. The streets were empty of chimney sweeps and apprentices, of oystermen and ladies and gentlemen in their fine frippery. All lay quiet. I kept my head down, my steps quick. When I passed the dim lights of the Royal Exchange tavern, a drunken man with a tricorne hat and a cane stepped forward.

"What's a nice lass like you doing out so late?" His words slurred, and I walked faster. "Come back, wench!"

I broke into a run until I passed Old South and was certain he no longer followed. My breathing returned to normal and I walked the rest of the way without incident, save for a small stumble on a protruding cobble.

The wind sent a gust up from the sea, and when I saw the Fulton house, with the glow of candles bright among other dark houses, I near sobbed with relief.

I rapped on the door, was surprised how long it took for John to open it.

When he did, I fell into his arms, not missing the musket at his side.

He turned. "'Tis Emma!"

Within moments I was being pulled into the house, Sarah's arms around me, her warm hands covering my own chilled ones, her gaze raking over me and my full pillow slip. "Emma, what in tarnation . . . ?"

"I—I . . ."

What if they turned me away? Sarah had said she would help me in any way, that I was like a daughter to her, but now that the time to prove the words presented itself, would she live up to them? Was I asking too much? I hadn't spoken with her in days. And only now did I realize the peril I posed to her and John . . . the children. My father was many things, but a man of reason was not one of them. Surely he wouldn't harm the Fultons or attempt to persecute them. And yet I couldn't quite convince myself of that fact, which weighed heavy on my conscience.

Father's words to Noah about the governor compensating him for the corpse of a Son echoed in my mind.

The backs of my eyelids burned. I shook my head, spoke against a quivering bottom lip. "I was frightened. I thought I was being brave, but mayhap I am only foolish."

Sarah led me to the keeping room table, where I put my things down, turned, sat, and jumped at the sight of Noah in a corner chair, shadows from the dancing hearth playing across his face.

I put a hand to my chest.

"Forgive me, Emma. I didn't mean to startle you."

I shook my head. "'Twouldn't take much to startle me as of now." We shared a smile, and I suddenly felt much less lonely than I had for the last fortnight.

Sarah brought a cup of chocolate and placed it before me. I drank it, the hot liquid warming my insides, serving to calm.

"Now tell us what happened, dear."

Sarah sat beside John, the three pairs of eyes trained on me. "I—I wish to be part of your cause."

Silence.

John and Sarah exchanged uneasy glances before Sarah took my hand in both her own.

"While I can't say I'm not thrilled to hear this, you must realize, with your father being who he is—there is no turning back when it comes to this matter." She released my hand. "And while I applaud your decision to break away from an undesired future . . . I do not wish for your politics to be the excuse you use."

I felt my face flaming, doubted my motives all over again.

For the briefest of moments, I considered slipping home this very night, entering our unlocked house, and creeping back up the stairs to my chambers, where Father and Mother would be none the wiser by morning.

But was that what I wanted?

No. No, 'twas not. And I *had* thought this through.

I straightened. "You yourself have explained to me your politics, Sarah. A right to have a voice, a say in the future of our country, in the future of each of us." I pressed my lips together, chanced a glance at Noah in the corner, silent but studying me with those big brown eyes. "I don't have such a freedom. I'm destined to be wed to a dishonorable man, to leave the colonies and everything I've ever known, all because my parents demand it. I see how Father and my intended speak, what they believe, their ideals and how they act them out." I brought my gaze back to Noah. He sat, mouth parted, as if hanging on my every word. I'd never had a man, especially one whom I loved, pay me such mind. It caused a pleasant dizziness to swirl over me, making my insides light all the way down to my toes. "And then I see the honor of others— not all the Sons, I realize, but some . . . you all in this room. I want nothing more than to be a part of it."

Sarah beamed beside me, squeezed my hand.

"'Twill not be easy for you, or for any of us, if you make such a break," John said.

I looked at the corner of the book Noah had given me, sticking out from my pillow slip. My eyes landed on the round edge beside it, what I knew to be Sarah's cup. "Aye, your safety is the one thing that makes me consider going back home this very night before Father knows I ever left."

Sarah tightened her grip on my hand. "John, we do not fight for what is just by being safe. Surely we can agree on that."

He nodded. "Aye."

"I realize I am an imposition. Mayhap I could see if your mother needs help at the tavern. I could obtain room and board there."

"Nay." Noah, who had been unusually quiet, finally spoke. "I will have you board in the back of the printing shop before you live at a tavern."

My face heated.

"Noah's right, Emma. The tavern . . . 'tis not a place for a young woman. I have some years behind me, some wisdom to deal with the men while I work. But we need your help here as ever before. You'll stay with us, won't she, John? And when we make our move to Medford, we can consider our next course."

My heart grew within my chest. I thought of little Mary, her joy at finding me at her home when she awoke. Sarah. John. The children. They would be my family.

John nodded once, firmly. "For tonight, aye. But her father will no doubt come for her. Without a husband to vouch for her, I am uncertain what can be done or how I can stand in his way."

"She's a woman, not a mule to be sold to the highest bidder. Is that not enough grounds to stand by her?" Sarah said.

John rubbed the back of his neck. "I don't know. I just don't know. This is a peculiar situation."

I hadn't realized the depths and consequences of my decision. I had wanted a voice in my future, to prove myself strong, and yet here I was, once again in the hands of others.

Sarah patted my arm. "Why don't we simply see what comes of it, hmm? Get some rest tonight and we'll revisit the situation in the morning."

I nodded, the chocolate settling in my stomach like a ball of hot wax.

"We must finish our previous discussion, now, shall we?" A pleasant smile settled on Sarah's face as if all were well.

But I felt John's heavy gaze on me.

I rose, thinking he must not want me privy to whatever they discussed. "I will sneak up and lie with the girls. Thank you all, so very much."

"Emma. Sit down." Sarah pointed back to my chair, turned to her husband. "I will respect your decision on this matter, John, but has not the girl done enough to prove herself?"

John looked to Noah, who nodded.

"Very well."

Sarah turned to me, seeming satisfied. "We were talking about the plans for the tea."

I sat. "Only three more days until it will be landed."

"It must not be taken off the ship," John stated.

Noah inched his chair closer to us. "Emma, that tea will not come ashore. Boston will not pay the tax on it."

"What do you plan to do?" I whispered.

"If all other avenues of compromise fail, we must ready ourselves for more drastic measures."

Silence all around. Quite suddenly I feared what I had brought upon my head.

Noah spoke again. "If a compromise is not reached, we are prepared to dump the tea."

"Dump it?" I repeated the words so they might seep in.

"'Tis the only way." Sarah's eyes shone bright, reflecting the candles in their tarnished holders. "Though some have suggested hauling the ships to the Common and burning them, we believe there is a wiser and more peaceable solution."

I looked at Noah. Peaceable? "You can't mean . . . At best you will all be sent to prison . . . at worst, charged with treason."

Noah pressed his lips together. "If we are caught. 'Tis what we discussed. There will be a good many of us, and under the cloak of darkness. 'Twill be impossible to arrest us all, and we are taking an oath of secrecy. We are determined to be peaceful, taking only the tea."

"Peaceful while destroying private property?" Inwardly, I applauded their bravery, their audacity. Yet I also saw how much could go awry.

"We have no other choice," John said. "The consignees are unwilling to compromise. New York and Philadelphia press us. Baneful weed it is, and all for a threepence tax."

"There was a meeting today at Old South," Sarah said. "Some came from as far as twenty miles!"

"What transpired?"

"Francis Rotch, owner of two of the ships, requested clearance from the port's collector. The Body will meet again in two days' time to hear his answer. If it is unfavorable, as it is like to be, we will enact our plan." John sounded so sure, so firm.

"A disguise is necessary, John." Sarah seemed to plead with her husband.

"There is talk of such, but I rather despise the idea of skulking behind a mask."

"Then if not to protect yourself, do it to protect the Body."

My gaze landed on the hard corner of my pillow slip again, where Mary Rowlandson's narrative lay. I thought of the stories Father used to tell of the Mohawks during the Seven Years' War. How many took the side of the British, how they were compelled to fight against even their brothers in Canada. How they treasured their freedom with a fierce sort of reverence.

I thought of the weather vane atop Province House, of the *Chronicle* cartoons depicting the colonies as a petulant Indian.

I opened my mouth, wondered if my idea was foolish, yet swallowed down my doubts. "Mohawks," I said.

Sarah tilted her head. "Pardon?"

"Mother obtained a European guide to dressing for masquerade balls not long ago. I remember a picture of a Mohawk. I think it may be a . . . fitting disguise."

I waited for their responses, the only sound the crackling flames in the hearth.

John slapped his hand on his thigh, breaking the silence. "Very fitting indeed!"

Noah laughed. "Beyond fitting—flawless, I might say!"

Sarah beamed at me, and just like that, I was not only considering their side, I was an accomplice to it.

CHAPTER SIX

Emma

The profound secrecy in which they have held their names, and the total
abstinence of plunder, are proofs of the character of the men.

JOHN ADAMS

DECEMBER 16, 1773

Father did not come for me.

The fact stung as much as it brought relief.

Yet I was not free of fear. For I lived every hour quaking inside, anticipating that Father might overtake my plan to leave my family, to live a life of my own choosing.

And still, a part of me wished for him to show up at the Fultons' door—for surely he knew my whereabouts. Part of me longed for him to come, hold his arms out to me, tell me he loved me despite my politics or despite whom I wished to marry. While I determined they did not deserve my loyalty, I still longed to be wanted by the family I'd been born into. To be missed. Could we not sort out our differences?

I was a fool, perhaps, to even think it. With Father, there

never was such a thing as sorting out differences. There was only his opinion, and little else.

Instead I took comfort in the thought that if Uncle Daniel watched from eternity, he at least might approve of my actions.

A cold rain poured upon the town. John and Noah had made their way to Old South at ten o'clock that morning to await the decision of the customhouse. Hours ran precious; the deadline for the tea to be unloaded drew nigh. 'Twas quite likely that a stroke after twelve would bring customs officers and the king's soldiers to the three ships at Griffin's Wharf to unload the tea. The duties would be paid, supporting the salaries of those the Body despised—men who spoke for the king and for whom our liberties were affronted—men like Governor Hutchinson. Men like my father.

Sarah and I busied ourselves about the keeping room, anticipating the men's return, the little ones underfoot.

Mary climbed onto the chair beside me where I sat at the table. She leaned in close to the flame of the oil lamp before me, the light playing off her soft cheeks and rosebud mouth.

"Not too close, little one," I warned.

"What, Emmy?" She pointed to where I held a copper pan over the sooty flame.

I turned it so she could see the lampblack gathering beneath the pan. The smoke from the process made me cough, but today was not a day to be conducting such business outside.

"Are we making pictures today?" Ann asked.

Sarah turned from where she gathered soot at the hearth. "Not today, dears. We need all the lampblack for Papa tonight." We exchanged nervous glances, and I wondered if our plan would truly work. Would the Mohawk disguises render John and Noah and the others who planned to dump the tea unrecognizable?

And yet we held out hope that an agreement could be made. Each of us wished it to happen, however unlikely it seemed.

The door burst open and I jumped, pushed the lamp aside as if I could hide the heavy smoke within the room.

Sarah went to her husband as Noah closed the door behind him. "Has the meeting adjourned so soon?"

The men doffed their wet hats and capes, hung them on a rack by the hearth. Droplets fell from them like fat tears upon the wood floor. "Harrison denied Rotch's clearance back to London."

"That be it, then?" Sarah put her hands on her hips, looked at Mary perched on the chair, her tiny legs tucked beneath her pinafore.

"There is one more hope. One man whose authority can override Harrison's decision."

Sarah nearly snorted. "Governor Hutchinson is not like to do that."

"Still, we will exhaust every avenue before we turn to disobedience."

"The governor is in Milton," I said, knowing these facts from Mother. With the increase in violence, many of the consignees had fled to Fort William. The governor had fled to his country home.

John nodded. "Rotch is making the journey. We will convene at Old South at three to await him."

Cold rain ran on the panes of the window, and I thought what a muddy mess it would be for Mr. Rotch to make the seven-mile journey to Milton and back, likely all for naught.

I resumed the making of my lampblack. No doubt it would get its use tonight.

✠

John and Noah did not return to Old South at the designated time, though they met a messenger—an apprentice from the distillery where John worked keeping ledgers—every hour or so, who reported that Mr. Rotch still had not returned.

As dusk settled early on the dreary town, John finally stood. "It's time." His deep voice spoke of a finality, a sadness, and I realized how torn he was over this decision.

Noah had told me earlier that on Queen Street, at the *Boston Gazette*'s Long Room, Benjamin Edes's son kept a punch bowl filled for the Mohawks. The punch was said to give the men strength, physically and perhaps mentally, to carry out the deed that must be accomplished before the stroke of twelve.

John and Noah chose to remain at home. While some men hid from their families what they would do that night, I admired John and Sarah's openness and unity with one another. I longed for it, even, for Father and Mother had never once united in a worthy cause, unless of course one were to deem marrying their daughter off to a rogue such as Samuel Clarke worthy.

Yet even as the thoughts scrambled my mind, they set off a pinch of . . . something. Not quite regret, but more akin to grief. For I might not have grieved my relationship with my parents, but I did grieve what we had never had—what I saw in the Fulton family now. And although I was a part of this new home, I stopped just short of being a part of their family. I felt, deep down, that I would always be on the outside looking in, that something—mayhap only my blood—prevented me from fully belonging to this new world. And for that, I grieved.

As Sarah applied lampblack to her husband's face, using burnt cork and soot to supplement where we fell short of lampblack, I stood above Noah doing the same. The echoes of the children's feet creaked along the ceiling above us, as they were given strict orders to remain upstairs.

My fingers shook as I smoothed the sooty paste over the right side of Noah's face and worked my way around to his brow, my fingers along his skin, the intimacy of the moment not lost on me.

"These disguises are superb, Emma. All who participate this night have adopted them."

I ran the pads of blackened fingers along his forehead, brushing a stray lock of hair away from his brow as I did so. "I pray I do not come to regret them."

He scooped my fingers from his face, held them still in his warm grip. "I trust you won't. Don't you see? We are doing this as amiably as we can, following orders not to touch any property except the tea." He took a piece of paper from the pocket of his cloak nearby, held it out. "See? We are to commit no violence or mayhem. If we must do this thing, we vow to do it peacefully." The paper held many different signatures, all in different hands in a round-robin, spiraling from a printed oath at the center.

He folded the paper and replaced it within his cloak. I felt better with it out of sight, and although I admired his words, his courage, still I wondered . . . "Have you no qualms, then? I admit, I search my heart before God night after night—I feel I will never be certain. Though I do feel certain it is right that I am here, in this moment."

He ran his thumb lightly over the inside of my wrist, just against my pulse. A desire both foreign and forceful burgeoned within me. This was love, then. This wonder of life, this all-consuming feeling of flight. One that would have me disregard every other notion and cause and plight under the sun if it meant being with this man.

"I suppose, if I am to be honest, I would admit doubts in the quietest corners of my heart. Yet they are quickly silenced when I think of our freedoms and how they may be lost if we continue on this path."

Sarah's laugh came from behind. "You are shaping up to be a fine-looking Mohawk, my husband."

I slid my hands from Noah's, twisted so I could see John. Sure enough, half his face was blackened, his hair slicked back with oil.

I dipped my fingers into the lampblack, continued my work on Noah's face, my own reddening at his gaze, which seemed intent upon my mouth. I turned my attention to the task, tried not to think too much on the familiarity of it. "I am glad I'm a part of this, Noah Winslow. And if standing for freedom means I have a say in my own future . . . then I will no longer dwell on my qualms, either."

He grinned, a dent in his cheek created beneath my fingers. "Though it may make me a weak man, I think I should care for you despite your politics, Emma. But I am gladdened to have you on the side of freedom."

I continued spreading the black substance along his whiskered chin, the manly stubble foreign and appealing all at once. He swallowed and his Adam's apple bobbed beneath the smooth skin of his neck.

"Emma, I know this may be neither the time nor the place, but I want you to know that John is not the only one who will vouch for you." His voice was low enough to conceal his words from Sarah and John, and my heart threatened to gallop away at their sincerity, their implications. "Me . . . what I mean is, I wish to vouch for you. I—I wish to protect you . . . to love you forever even, if I may be so bold."

I exhaled a shaky breath, my soul taking flight. "I—I don't know what to say." Or perhaps I did. I wished to shout from the top of the Fulton roof that I loved him also, that I had never been happier to hear words from one's mouth. That in this instant nothing else mattered—not Father's disowning me or that I didn't have a true home or family to call my own or taking part in the most dangerous thing I'd ever done this very night: committing treason.

"You needn't say anything. My timing could not be worse. I much prefer the press, where I labor over my words for hours. Here, I cannot tame them near as well."

I shook my head fiercely, the lampblack now forgotten. I could not let him think himself foolish, could not let him regret those bonny words. "I feel the same," I said, my voice hoarse with emotion.

His eyes lit up from within the blackness of his face. "Truly?"

"Aye, though I've nothing now that I've left my family. No dowry, no meaning to my name—"

"I would love that you take mine. As for a dowry, I feel I would be the richest man in all of Boston if you were to be my wife." He reached his hand out where it brushed my dress, and my heart drummed beneath my corset. Was I not just lamenting that I had no family? And now the Lord had provided me a husband—the man of my heart. Not a family I'd been born into, nor a family that took pity on me, but a new one, begun from a love that had naught to do with financial gain or power or pity, but something greater.

Noah's fingers found mine, and he brought my hand to his lips, pressing his mouth to the pale veins on the back of my hand. When he drew away, a smudge of black from his face stained my hand.

I laughed, nodding, fought a swell of tears.

"Is that a yes?"

I nodded again, and Noah stood, picked me up and swung me around, planted a kiss on my brow.

I looked at John and Sarah, not without a little embarrassment. John nudged his wife. "It looks like they are having a wee bit more fun with their costume than we are, dear."

Sarah smiled, her eyes dancing between the two of us. "Well, you couldn't have picked a poorer night for the two of you to realize what John and I have known for some time."

Noah and I exchanged a glance, and I shook my head, leaving his arms, and picked up the lampblack again. "She's right. We can speak of our future later. The business at hand is more important."

Noah dropped his arms, but not before leaning toward

my ear. "Nothing is more important than our future together, Emma. But what I do this night is for a better future. For us and for the generations after us."

Pleasant heat climbed my neck. To think of being Noah's wife . . . to think of bearing his children, of having a family. One filled with love and warmth—not the cold, lifeless one that masked itself in control, like the one I had known all my life.

I worked quickly to finish Noah's disguise, adding some red ocher to his face and catching his gaze all too often, sharing one too many smiles for such an otherwise-grave night.

After his hair was slicked back and both John's and Noah's clothing was wrapped in an assortment of shawls and blankets, Sarah and I admired our handiwork.

"I would not know you if I passed you on the street," Sarah said.

I agreed. If the children came down, they would be scared witless.

John grabbed his hatchet by the door. "We will wait for the signal outside Old South. Certainly Rotch will arrive soon."

"We will speak later tonight, aye?" Noah looked at me from where he stood, merriment in his blackened features.

And then they were gone.

Sarah and I cleaned up the lampblack along with any traces that we'd been disguising Mohawks. Then she brushed her hands on her apron. "I think I shall go for a stroll and have the older children watch the little ones. Do you care to join me?"

I suppressed a nervous laugh, even as my stomach jumped

at the thought of witnessing what the men were about to do. 'Twas dark out. Cold. We were without escorts. But the thrill of seeing what was about to take place stirred up something akin to courage in my chest.

"I think 'tis a splendid idea."

The look of surprise on Sarah's face, followed by approval, would be worth my fear that someone would recognize me this night.

CHAPTER SEVEN

Hayley

I SHIFTED FROM one foot to the other, concentrated on the weight distributing itself alongside my size-six foot. The twenty-six bones in the human foot withstand a lot, and yet most of us don't give them the credit they're due. We don't focus on building the muscles around them, as with our arms; we just kind of take them for granted—that they will always be there to support us, to hold us up.

Quite the opposite of how I felt about my mother.

Now, on the cracked stoop of Lena's house, staring at a wide rip in the screen of the storm door, I wondered what I would find within. I hadn't spoken to my mother in six entire years, and for a fleeting moment I fought guilt over the texts and voice mails she'd left that I'd outright ignored. All the birthday messages, asking that I at least text her an address to send a gift. Now, I needed something from her—likely the only thing I would ever need—and here I was, on her doorstep.

I pictured her opening the door, her eyes hollowed and bloodshot, her Happy Helpers uniform wrinkled and twisted, the buttons that were supposed to be down the middle off to the side. Did she still spend most of her paycheck on scratch tickets and heroin? Did she ever win anything on the tickets? Had she ever been infected by a dirty needle?

I waited another moment, second-guessing my decision to come, feeling more than a little dizzy at the thought of actually seeing Lena. I knocked again, harder this time, swore under my breath, the hard word almost foreign to my ears of late. Why did I care? I looked at the ripped screen, felt a childlike urge to tear a bigger hole in it.

The sound of a window sliding within its casing came to my right. A shock of gray hair appeared from a first-floor window of the apartment house beside Lena's. "Miss Hayley, that you?"

I couldn't stop the grin that broke upon my face. "Mrs. Ray, how are you?" I leaned over the forsythia bush beneath the window to lift my hand to her own weathered one. Mrs. Ray was cookies and *The Price Is Right*, Lean Cuisines and soap operas—in short, the brightest part of my childhood.

"Oh, you know, can't complain. Well, I could, but it wouldn't do any good. Look at you, all grown up. Your mom will sure be happy to see you." She released my hand.

I shrugged off her words or at least tried to. It wasn't until then that I acknowledged the unspoken fear I'd held—the fear that Lena might not be here—like, here on this earth. The fear that she had OD'd, that Uncle Joe had been contacted but had been unable to respond or communicate the news to me while on a mission.

And while I stayed away from Lena, I didn't truly believe it was a forever thing. I hadn't realized how much I depended on her to be there—if for no other reason than knowing we could reconcile one day. If I wanted to. On my terms.

It would be just like Lena to up and die on me, to wreck my in-the-future plans of possible reconciliation.

But according to our lifelong neighbor, my mother was alive.

"I probably should have called first. She must be at work."

"Or Barbados."

"What?"

"She and that fiancé of hers are on vacation. Barbados."

Barbados. Fiancé. *You have got to be kidding me.* All I could imagine was Lena and one of her sketchy boyfriends lying on a white-sand beach, congratulating themselves on some illegal drug deal they'd been involved in. How else did addicts wind up in Barbados?

I rubbed my forehead. "Do you know when she's expected back?"

"Thursday. I've been getting her mail."

Three more days.

So much for getting this task out of the way quick.

I chatted with the elderly woman a few more minutes, vaguely filling her in on my time in the Navy. She was just as vague when I asked about Mom's fiancé, waving a hand through the air. "Best to leave it to her to fill you in on all the details. You can come in and watch my stories with me if you want to."

"Thank you, but I better get going." After we said goodbye, I walked to my rental car, drove away beneath Mrs. Ray's watchful eye, frustration welling up inside me.

Why did I even care about making amends with Lena? I'd tried. Like always, she wasn't available—either physically or mentally. As I eased onto the highway back toward Revere, memories overtook me. The softball finals Lena had promised to make—how I'd hit a home run and searched the stands for her proud face. How she'd been, as always, absent. How many parent-teacher conferences had she missed, how many birthdays had she forgotten? By the time she made it to my high school graduation, it was too late; I'd given up on her, scorning the opportunity to have our picture taken together.

She'd started building the wall a long time ago. All I did was make sure it stayed in place.

The dashes on the highway blurred, shaming me. I blinked, hard. I thought of Lena in Barbados. I thought of Ethan pulling the small body of his just-rescued son into his arms. I wondered who he'd deemed worthy enough to wed, to have a child with, to fall in love with—not long after we'd parted ways from the looks of it, too. No doubt they had gone home from the hospital, the three of them, a family filled with gratitude.

A family.

Why, over and over again, did I think reconnecting with Lena would help me find fulfillment? I'd accepted long ago that the military was my family. That they were better at keeping their word and commitments than Lena had ever been. That they had taught me more of loyalty and faithfulness than eighteen years with a devotedly drug-addicted mother ever had.

Why, then, had I returned to Massachusetts? Coming back here was a risk. I'd thought it had been worth it, but suddenly I wondered if I hadn't been terribly, terribly wrong.

✠

I propped my feet up on the patio table beside my iced tea and the books I'd bought at Trident Booksellers that afternoon—*A History of Boston in 50 Artifacts*, an Images of America book that chronicled a walking tour of Boston, and a book titled *Revolutionary Sites of Greater Boston*. I'd distracted myself with the trip, contemplating between bookshelves whether to fly out early to California, settle in, and focus on completing my training before BUD/S.

From some nearby grill, the scent of hamburgers found me. A breathtaking backdrop of oranges and reds streaked the sky, reflecting off the waters of Revere Beach, just across the street from the apartment rental I'd decided to splurge on that week. The salty air swept across the beach, where surfers were but black dots on the water, and made its way up to the deck, chasing away the humidity.

Somewhere between classical literature and Revolutionary history, I'd rejected the idea of leaving Massachusetts. I'd come here for a reason, and whether or not I felt like abandoning ship, failure was not an option. I'd planned two weeks on the East Coast. A couple more days of waiting to see

Lena—no matter how much I dreaded it—wouldn't be the end of me. I *would* face BUD/S with no regrets. I would not fail. To think I'd let Barbados get in the way of my plans suddenly shamed me. How could I expect to be strong enough to complete BUD/S if I was ready to run at the first sign of discouragement?

I stood from the table, feeling the need to release pent-up energy. In ten minutes, I was running on the beach just across the street. My sneakers made marks on the wet sand along the shore, and I ran the length of the beach as it emptied itself of people for the night.

When I reached the rocks at the end, I turned and sprinted hard for three minutes before slowing back to a jog. The sea air fed my soul, as it always did, and the muck of the day cleared.

The sun hovered just above the horizon and I slowed to a walk, the scratchy call of a seagull competing with the whistle of the wind.

"Hayley!"

My name didn't register at first, or rather it sounded as if the seagull called it. But then it came again, clearer and sharper, from behind. I twisted, felt the salty air sticking to my sweaty skin, the breeze pushing damp strands of hair from my face.

I recognized his form, unmistakable even after all this time. My mind raced back six summers earlier. The beach. A boy. Endless days of realizing I was falling in love. And then choosing to believe it a lie and abandoning both the love and the boy in the cruelest of ways.

Something tight lurched within my chest as I thought

of Ethan and his son on the same beach where we'd grown our young love. There was no room for regrets. Not now. I'd made my choice. I'd walked away from it all, and given the chance, I'd do it again. Even now I considered turning and running away from the man who approached me.

Ethan jogged lightly toward me, and I took the opportunity to catch both my breath and my rollicking heartbeat. I *would* make the same choices again. I would. The Navy . . . serving my country . . . making history . . . it was all worth more than a man who would have only made me weak.

He came closer until he stood before me. Quite suddenly I felt small as I stared my past in the face—shaven, a shock of hair falling in front of his eyes, a pair of running shorts and a white tank, Under Armour sneakers on his feet. My stomach trembled. He'd filled out in all the right places. No longer a scrawny teenager, everything about the man before me, right down to the small cleft in his chin, made my insides frantic. Out of control. The opposite of what I trained myself to be. The opposite of everything I took comfort in.

And Ethan himself . . . he was so very clearly *not* military— polished, more preppy than warrior. Civilian to the core. I could picture him at the bow of a pristine sailboat rather than on the hard, unforgiving deck of a Navy destroyer. In short, he had always been too . . . something. Not soft—nice, maybe? Too proper. Too good for me, really.

He cleared his throat, shoved his hands in his pockets. "Hey. I . . . I was hoping to catch you here."

"Yeah?" I was ashamed to admit, even to myself, that I had hoped to see him again before I left Massachusetts. That, while I knew it would be painful, a part of me wanted to revisit this piece of my past.

"Yeah. You—you look great, Hayley."

I often wondered if my toned physique intimidated or even turned men off. But I was proud of my body. I worked hard at what I did—at being strong. If my body showed that . . . well, that *was* me.

Why then did I have to doubt his words?

A bit delayed, I decided a "Thanks" was better than no response at all. "You look good too." I gestured toward the shore. "You want to walk?"

He fell into step beside me. "I wanted to thank you for yesterday. For what you did for Braden. I—I looked at my phone for a second. Seriously, it was a second. If anything had happened to him, I'm not sure I could have ever forgiven myself. I'm not sure I even can now."

"It was definitely a freak thing. I've never known the undertow to be that strong here. I'm glad he's okay. He got checked out?"

Ethan nodded. "He's all good. But only because of you. Really, thank you."

I shrugged off his gratitude, cleared my throat.

A half-moon hung opposite the rapidly setting sun. The squawking of two bickering gulls competed with the gentle sound of the waves on the shore.

"So what brings you back home, Hay?"

Hay. The old nickname tugged at the tight, untuned strings of my rusty heart. Made me remember the first time Ethan kissed me on Lena's front porch, the sound of mosquitoes hitting the porch light above us, the anticipation of Ethan's lips almost as sweet as the kiss itself.

That moment, bathed in innocence, would never be relived. I'd taken it for granted and hadn't realized it. Now I had no right to be thinking on it, to be walking with this man in the romantic twilight when he had a family at home.

"Just a little leave, is all."

"And the Navy. Is it everything you dreamed?"

Silence stretched before us as the question leached the life from the summer air. Was that bitterness I heard? Yes, what I'd done after high school wouldn't ever be considered the classiest way to end a relationship, but really, it *had* been six years. And clearly he'd moved on.

I felt a headache mounting at my temples. "Navy's great. I'll be heading to California soon. For SEAL training."

"SEAL training? You serious?" His bare elbow brushed mine and I moved away.

"I am."

"I—I didn't realize there were women Navy SEALs."

"There aren't. Yet."

"Ahh, gotcha. Well, if anyone can do it, it'd be you."

I searched his tone for sarcasm but found none.

"That means a lot." I looked down at our feet, caught his bare tanned leg out of the corner of my eye. "So how about you? I'm not one for social media, so I haven't kept tabs on anyone."

"I finished school, messed around a little. I own an antique shop now."

I wondered if his "messing around" was how Braden had

come about. "An antique shop? I wouldn't have guessed that in a million years."

"Yeah . . . well . . . how's your mom?"

I shrugged. "I haven't talked to her since I joined up."

He whistled, long and low. "Yikes."

Something like hot ash smoldered in my chest at the judgment in his tone. "I went to see her today," I ground out. "She's in Barbados, apparently with her most recent exploit."

He made a familiar sound—part understanding, part acknowledgment.

"What?" I stopped walking.

He laughed. "Nothing."

"That sound—that sound means you want to say something but probably shouldn't." I'd forgotten about the small characteristic until now. How many other nuances of him had I not held close?

"I was just thinking that the military hasn't served to heal any old wounds, I guess."

I wanted to be mad, but staring into his face—slightly older, slightly more weathered than I remembered but at least five times more appealing—I couldn't summon up anger. Instead, I stuck my tongue out at him. "I should get back to my apartment. Nice seeing you, Ethan."

He chased after me. "I didn't come here to pry into your life or make calls on it, Hayley. I'm sorry. I came to thank you for what you did yesterday."

"You're welcome." I stopped walking, tried out a smile. My heart beat faster when he returned it, his white teeth reflecting the light of a window across the way, the same slight dimple I remembered from high school creasing his cheek like the curve of a quarter moon.

"I've missed you," he said. The soft words came saturated with past regrets, and I tried to erect a buffer around my heart so they would not be granted entrance. He had a family. A child. Nothing good could come from this vulnerability, for either me or him.

I'd come here for closure. With Lena. That was it.

Ethan Gagnon wasn't on the list.

And after six years, one thing hadn't changed:

Anything that rooted me to this place, I couldn't afford to love. Because, quite simply, in opening my heart back up to Massachusetts, I was only opening it back up to hurt.

CHAPTER EIGHT

Hayley

THE VIBRATION of my phone woke me from a dream I hadn't wanted to leave. I was standing proud in my Navy whites, a Trident held out to me by one of my BUD/S commanders. I'd been just about to take it when . . .

I put my forearm over my head, the sun bright behind the shades. I groaned, swung my legs off the bed, and sat, swiping the drapes of the bedroom open. Outside, bright morning sun soaked Revere Beach. I thought of Ethan's appearance on that same stretch of sand the night before. He'd walked me back to my apartment, offered me a tour of his antique shop after I mentioned my book purchase.

And before I closed the door on his presence, he'd given me a hug. The friend kind. I hated to admit it, but it was kind of nice, the faint scent of day-old cologne pulling me back years earlier to other nights. Nights where something magical interlaced with the naiveté of young love, where we'd vowed to be so much more than friends.

And while I knew he'd meant nothing by it, something about his arms around me made me think that maybe he wasn't attached to anyone after all. Ethan was loyal, almost to a fault. Probably why it had been so hard for me to be faithless all those years ago. If he were married or had a girlfriend, I couldn't imagine him allowing himself to walk me home in the dark, to admit that he missed me, to give me a hug that lasted just a second too long. Yet that didn't explain Braden or whatever history lay behind the child.

I hadn't asked. It wasn't that I was afraid, exactly. Just that it seemed better not to know.

My phone vibrated again and I scooped it up.

When Ethan had asked for my phone number last night, I hadn't truly expected a text. Not this soon, anyway.

Want to come by the shop tonight? I can show you around. I have something I think you might like. Anytime after five.

He gave me an address that was just down the street, across from the beach.

I didn't reply until noon, after I'd completed an eight-mile run, a long swim, and a series of core training exercises in which I recited the SEAL code to myself no less than a dozen times, each recitation ending with those four determined, beautiful words: *I will not fail.*

When I'd completed my regimen, I could think of absolutely no excuses why I couldn't go. And truth be told, I wanted to see Ethan again.

I thought of that hug last night, the danger of spending

time with a guy I knew riled me up, a guy I had so much history with.

And what about the kid? What was the story behind him? I imagined a possible other child, a wife or girlfriend, a diaper bag by the door, Ethan spooning mushed-up baby food into an infant's mouth.

Ethan with kids. Unthinkable. These were questions that should have gotten answered before I agreed to spend more time with him, but I couldn't very well shoot them off in a text now.

I will be there, I wrote back.

I spent the afternoon listening to motivational speeches by SEALs. By the time I finished, I felt strong enough to spend some time with an old boyfriend, strong enough to go see Lena, strong enough to stare all of my past in the face and come out victorious. I would get the mission done. I would do what I'd come to do.

I dried my hair, donned some capris, a periwinkle-blue T-shirt, and flip-flops. I brushed on some mascara and lip gloss, grabbed a zip-up gray sweatshirt, the bold lettering of *NAVY* printed across the front.

Once outside the apartment building, the sea stretched before me. Its steady endlessness and strength soothed like nothing else.

I headed toward the address in Ethan's text, arriving in just ten minutes.

I don't know what I expected, but it wasn't an old two-story farmhouse with a lopsided porch filled with rocking chairs, a sign that said simply, *Revere Antiques*.

I couldn't help but feel a pinch of disappointment. I

convinced myself it was for Ethan's sake. I mean, he was a good guy. Intelligent, handsome, a heart of gold. Back in high school, he'd wanted to be an archaeologist. I remembered sitting with him on an abandoned lifeguard chair at the beach, gazing at the stars, his arm around me. He spoke of traveling to far-off places, discovering ancient civilizations, piecing together puzzles of the past. I spoke of traveling with the Navy. Back then, for one summer anyway, we didn't bother to think about how our different desires would inevitably separate us.

Now, looking at the shop, I wondered how he'd ended up here. Had he gotten a girl pregnant after I'd left, felt obligated to stay close to home? Had he fallen in love and accepted this place as his own? This place that seemed so . . . beneath him?

The sign read Closed, but after climbing the well-worn steps to the porch, I opened the door to a merry jingle of bells.

"Hello?"

"Hey!" Ethan, dressed in a Red Sox T-shirt and khaki shorts, came from a back room, carrying what might have been an old war helmet. He put it on a counter where a laptop sat. "Glad you could make it."

I put my hands in the pockets of my sweatshirt. "Sure." I looked around. Now that I was inside, I could almost make out a strange kind of order to the place. Wooden furniture seemed prevalent—and not all of it looked antique. Some of it looked refurbished or perhaps brand-new but with an antique finish.

Vintage lamps, a colonial sofa, pottery, advertising posters, and knickknacks galore. My eyes landed on a set of small stairs with intricate scrolling woodwork and wheels, likely once used for a library.

I wondered where the stairs came from, who had used them in the past. I suppose I could see the draw of being around so much old stuff. But all the time? As a career?

"You have quite the place here."

He looked around the room as if trying to see it through my eyes, something akin to pride in his gaze. "It's my home away from home, especially during tourist season."

"I never pictured you an antique kind of guy."

He shrugged. "I always loved old things. You have to remember that much about me."

"I do. I mean, I remember you wanting to travel, right? Dig up artifacts. I don't remember you wanting to sell them."

He opened a glass cabinet beside the counter, placed the helmet with care amid an array of military paraphernalia—flasks, buttons, swords, photos. "Life happens, I guess. Sometimes our dreams take a different form. I've tried to accept the form mine have taken."

There were a thousand different circumstances in his life that could have caused him to make such a statement. I tried not to ponder each too much. Instead, I looked at my unpolished toes, my thoughts flying to my own circumstances, my own dreams. I'd been so certain they would happen. For the first time, I thought of the possibility of failure. Would I be able to move on, to not allow defeat to eat me alive, as Ethan said?

"Want a tour?" Ethan's words broke through my thoughts, his grin lifting the mood, his obvious desire that I share in this . . . thing with him both intoxicating and endearing all at once.

"Yeah, definitely."

He led me to another room in the back. For areas with so much *stuff*, they really were bright and airy. The wide plank of the hardwood floors, the large windows on either end of the shop, the faint smell of pine—it all gave off a merry feeling instead of the stale, musty feeling of the few antique shops I'd been in before. And clearly he was proud of it.

Old instruments and pictures having to do with music graced one corner. Another section featured everything gardening—rusty watering cans, pottery and vases, birdhouses, worn books about flowers. I let my gaze roam over the room, each section organized but full. Suitcases and signs, wooden benches and wardrobes, irons and food scales, and an entire section devoted to tea—cups, saucers, kettles, even an ancient-looking wooden chest.

"Wow . . . how did you find all of this? And more importantly, who dusts it all?"

He laughed. "I have some help during the day. I find the stuff; Ida handles the upkeep of it. A lot of it was here when I took it over from Allison's parents, but I find a lot online, at yard sales, or other shops. Most of the furniture I've redone or built myself."

I ran my hand over a bureau with a curved face, stained a deep rustic mahogany. "Beautiful," I whispered, thinking of Allison, knowing instinctively she was important to him, that likely she was Braden's mother.

"Thanks. That means a lot to me."

I looked up to see him smiling at me, and though we were

ten feet apart at least, I felt that forbidden crackle—part passion, part tension—that seemed forever between us.

Allison. Braden.

Who was I kidding? There was no passion between us. It was all in my head, and it shouldn't even be there.

He gestured to the staircase. "There's more."

I followed him to the second level, where smaller objects—easy enough to carry down the short flight—were on display, including several table-and-chair sets for children, crates and soda bottles, figurines and decorative letters one could make words from, old windowpanes, and countless books.

When he led me back down the stairs, he cleared his throat. "So I'm not sure if you're going to write this off as lame, but ever since you . . . helped out Braden the other day, I wanted to say thank you somehow."

He was so blasted cute—his uncertainty, the way he kicked the side of his foot against the leg of a nearby table, then looked up at me with those familiar eyes, the color of an ocean on a cloudy day.

"It wasn't anything, Ethan. I was there, I have the training—what'd you want me to do, let your son drown?"

He stared at me, a smile pulling at the corner of his mouth.

"What?" I asked.

"You never were good at accepting thank-yous and compliments. And Braden's not my son."

"Oh. I thought—"

"He's Ida's grandson. The lady who dusts all this stuff. Ida was cleaning and asked me to take him for a walk. Last time she does that, I bet."

I tried to breathe around the tightness in my chest. Ethan didn't have a son.

The thought set something free within me, and I tried to capture it before it could blossom into a feeling I would regret, tried to rein in the musings that if Ethan didn't have a child, perhaps he didn't have a *someone*.

"So the accepting compliments thing. Keep working on that," he said.

I laughed and rolled my eyes.

He stepped closer, and when I realized how much I wanted him near, some gut reaction tried to get me to back away. "Remember when I used to tell you how beautiful you were? You always brushed off that compliment too."

The words sent my heart pounding like I'd just run a 10k. He smelled like that same hours-old cologne, mixed with some pine-scented furniture polish. I stopped myself from leaning into him, knew how easily I could be in his arms, where I used to find myself. I could allow things to go further than they should, all for the sake of old times. But I knew what would happen—I would leave Ethan again. And pulling him close only to run away was one mistake I was not willing to make a second time.

His gaze lingered. Almost as if he were studying me, trying to see my thoughts. Why was he doing this? Why did he bring us to this place? And he was totally right. Not about me being beautiful, but about me not taking compliments well. *Beautiful* . . . it just wasn't a word I thought to describe myself. Sure, I wasn't hideous to look at, but most of the time I didn't put too much effort into my looks. Lena had been beautiful at one time. That's what made her feeble. The guys came, and then our lives flew out of control.

Beauty was dangerous. Beauty made you fragile. Pathetic.

I'd choose muscle over beauty any day.

I swallowed, pulled away from him. "Tell me about Allison."

He straightened, rubbed the back of his neck, and turned to walk toward an old wardrobe. I thought of *The Lion, the Witch, and the Wardrobe* then. How I'd read it as a six-year-old, how I'd hidden in Lena's closet, pressing myself to the very back of it, where her winter coat hung, the scent of cigarettes heavy in the fabric. I'd close my eyes, try to reach past the wall, expect the cold snowflakes of Narnia, but always . . . nothing.

By age eight, I'd stopped believing in magical worlds where a perfect, mystical lion king reigned. I stayed out of her closet and instead started wishing I could stay away from Lena as well. Here, waiting for Ethan's answer, I had the childish urge to fold myself within the depths of the wardrobe. Maybe this was a magical cupboard—one that could whisk me back to a different reality, one where I was with my crew on the *Bainbridge*.

"Allison was my wife."

Ouch. I hadn't expected the words to hurt so much.

"She died . . . a boating accident, just a couple months after our wedding."

I opened my mouth, looked longingly at the wardrobe, then back at my flip-flops. "I'm so sorry."

"Thanks." He sighed. "It's been three years. Not that I'm

saying it still doesn't hurt, but things were definitely . . . complicated between us."

I wanted to ask what he meant but pressed my lips together instead as I did the math. He'd gotten married three years after I left. How long had they dated? Surely more than a year.

I ground my teeth at my callousness. His wife had died and all I could think about was how long it had taken for him to get over me.

He cleared his throat. "Anyway, back to my thanking you. If you don't think it's too lame, I wanted to offer you anything here as a thank-you gift. After you told me about your book purchases yesterday, I thought that maybe I'm not the only one who still has an attachment to old things."

I smiled. "So not lame."

He broke into a grin that caused my heart to trip over itself.

I started perusing the antiques along the wall. "So anything, huh?"

"Anything. Though I guess you'd want to be able to take it on your ship, huh? If you're going back, that is, with being a SEAL and all."

I tried to ignore the pride I felt at him imagining me a SEAL. It would happen. I could practically taste it. And yet there was something in his voice that sounded a whole awful lot like . . . regret? Or maybe sarcasm? I chose to ignore it, instead continuing my survey, trying to pretend his comment didn't bother me.

I gravitated toward the section of tea paraphernalia. A cup and saucer would likely be the most practical thing to take on the ship—or even to training—with me. I scanned the many options, paused over a royal-blue tea-for-one set with an Oriental picture on it. Beside it lay bamboo tea scoops, tea infusers, and books on tea, all perfect for the tight confines of my travels.

My flip-flop bumped into something and I backed up a step, squatted to see what it was. A beautiful but very old chest with a flower on it. Something foreign yet beautiful stirred within my spirit, and I reached for the object, unable to escape its beckon.

"The bottom of a chest. Likely for tea if we go by the Oriental design."

I pulled it out. The base seemed reinforced with extra wood for stability. Definitely sturdy, despite the many splinters in the ancient wood. "Where'd you find it?"

"An estate sale in Medford, just last week actually."

The chest drew me somehow, though I wasn't sure what characteristic. Certainly not its town of origin—our hometown. Perhaps the sturdiness of the thing, still strong after so much obvious wear and tear. I liked its solidness, its testament to bearing weight and trials and still finding usefulness.

Wow, I might be more into this antique stuff than I originally thought.

"I'll take it."

"Kind of big for your suitcase, isn't it?"

I hefted it off the ground. "I'll ship it wherever I need to. I like it. There's something about it . . . Besides, it's a sturdy place to store the books I bought yesterday and should fit under any bunk."

"Okay. I can bring it by for you tomorrow."

"No need. I can carry it home."

"Really? That's kind of unnecessary, isn't it?"

While the chest would be awkward, it was nothing compared to lifting logs and inflatable boats, which would be the norm for me in just a few weeks. Besides, if I took the chest, along with Ethan's thank-you, we would be finished. There would be no reason for us to see one another again. That's what I wanted, wasn't it?

Ethan shrugged and held the door of his shop open.

The sun cast a hazy glow over the evening, the tantalizing scent of salty sea infusing the air.

"If you want to wait a minute, I'll lock up and take you home."

"That's okay. I enjoy the walk."

I surprised myself with my need to flee. I wanted to believe myself a fight girl, not a flight girl, so what was this overwhelming urge to leave with this chest tucked under my arm?

And yet part of me wished to stay, the sun's end-of-day rays stretching before us, this man who drew so many complicated feelings from me filling the space of my time.

He tapped the side of his foot lightly against the stairs of the porch. "I'm glad I found you on the beach last night. I have to admit, though, for a minute I thought you were going to run away from me."

I let out a nervous laugh, wanted to deny that I would do such a thing.

But I had before, so really it wasn't so absurd.

He stared at me with such intensity I couldn't tear myself from his gaze, even as it made me uncomfortable. I shifted the chest in my arms. The rough wood scraped against my skin. "What do you want from me?" I whispered.

"Would an apology kill you?"

My defenses went up. I'd never been good at admitting failure. That's why I made sure not to fail as often as I could. Still, he was right. How I had gone about leaving was, simply put, wrong.

I inhaled a deep breath. "You're right. I'm sorry for how I left."

"But not about leaving."

"Ethan, that's water under the bridge. I didn't ask for any of this." I gestured to him, the shop, the tea chest. "I didn't ask to run into you again or—or anything. Look, I am sorry I hurt your feelings. I—I wish I could have done things differently, but you knew my life . . . you knew Lena. I had no choice."

Although he nodded, he didn't seem convinced.

I thought of my mother, of how in many ways I sought from her what Ethan sought from me. Not a second chance, but a sign of remorse, regret . . . realization that she could have made better choices. That, just maybe, I mattered to her after all.

If I wanted these things so badly, then why was it so hard for me to grant them to the man before me?

I stared at the chest in my hands. Old and worn, out of place with me—someone who didn't lug hefty things around, either emotionally or physically.

I wondered if the estate sale had been near Lena's house, if I had passed its place of provenance multiple times on one of my runs as a teenager.

Could I make the tea chest worth something? This broken, empty thing that symbolized the old. Perhaps in between my training and while waiting for Lena to return from her vacation, I could work on restoring it to something beautiful. Something useful and worthy.

Now, with Ethan standing before me, our past still very much between us, and with thoughts of Lena heavy on my mind, I wondered if it was possible for someone's soul—for my soul—to be made into something new as well.

CHAPTER NINE

Hayley

I BIT MY TONGUE to keep a curse from slipping out of my mouth as I balanced the chest in one hand, searching my pocket for the apartment key card.

Frustration welled within my chest at the rather frozen good-bye Ethan and I had given one another. I didn't know why. There was no more business between us. He'd given me the gift, said his thank-you, I'd given a halfhearted apology, we hadn't made plans to see one another again.

End of story.

So why did that thought sadden me? I hated this foreign feeling of depending on another's presence to fulfill something inside me. It's why I'd run away to join the Navy in the first place. I could depend on myself and my crew, our desire to serve our country and excel at our jobs, to remain loyal to one another. What Ethan's presence stirred within me now,

I couldn't make peace with. Because in a way that surprised me, I longed for it . . . even as it stank of neediness and regret and failure. For as loyal as I thought myself to my country and my team—even to the point of self-sacrifice—being with Ethan reminded me of how, deep down, I was still only after what was best for me.

I opened the door of my apartment, a dull throb beginning in my head. The last of the sun's rays shone into the tidy apartment, and I placed the chest on the edge of the small kitchen island, then slid onto the couch, keeping the lights out.

With the still darkness, the pain in my temples settled, leaving my head warm.

The sound of something crashing to the floor, of splintering wood, startled me off the couch.

The chest.

I groaned as I switched on the kitchen lights.

The thing truly was sturdy. I picked up the box, examined it for damage, found nothing until I turned it over.

A thin sliver of wood jutted up into the air. Certainly nothing some wood glue couldn't fix.

With care, I inserted the slice in its rightful place, but not before noticing something beneath the board. Something yellowed. It made a quiet crinkling sound when I pressed the wood back in. Like brittle paper. Some sort of padding for the bottom of the chest?

I flipped the box upward again, examined the inside. Nothing. Just wood.

Leaving the table, I went back to the couch to grab my phone, slid it to the flashlight setting, and shone it within the box. At the very corners were tiny holes, something like screws stuck into the edges. I flipped the chest back over, saw identical screws on the outside. I walked to the narrow utility closet by the door, where I'd seen a small tool kit earlier in the week.

After some searching, I found the tiniest flathead possible. From the bottom of the chest, I got to work. It took a while before I made the slightest progress, but my time working on the mechanics of a ship had taught me patience.

Almost an hour later, I had all the rusty screws out from the bottom of the chest. Grabbing a butter knife and a spatula from the kitchen, I slid them beneath the wood and pressed up gently. It didn't give easily. Perhaps I should hire a professional. The last thing I wanted was to wreck Ethan's parting gift or ruin whatever lay within. More than likely the paper was nothing—maybe a part of the box, some sort of padding that had disintegrated over time. There was no need to waste someone else's time and my money when a little patience and perseverance could accomplish what I sought.

The wood didn't come off in one piece, as I'd hoped, but in strips. Hopefully I could rebuild the bottom. The pine clung to the yellowed paper beneath, no doubt the result of time and humidity.

When I'd finally removed the wood, a folded, frail paper came away, the side that had been against the very bottom of the chest still attached to a strip of pine. Rather than yank at it and risk ruining the paper, I carefully unfolded the sheet with the wood still attached. I winced at the crinkling sound, bits of parchment falling off with each movement, its tired creases yawning in protest from a nap too long.

A circle was drawn in the center of the page. In the middle an ancient script read, *Oath of Secrecy*. Some faded words ran beneath. Stemming out from the circle were names—so many they seemed to form the rays of a sun.

I skimmed it, picked up random names among the eighty or so listed.

Henry Bass, George Hewes, John Fulton, Josiah Snelling, Ebenezer Stevens, Jeremiah Williams, Noah Winslow, Thomas Young.

They certainly *felt* old, but what did this peculiar type of round-robin mean? And why had someone secreted it away at the bottom of this chest? And what sort of secret oath had they taken?

I thought to run a Google search on some of the names, see if I could find anything, or what they had in common. But the thought of discovering something meaningful by myself niggled. In a bad way.

I ran a finger over the names, my choice wavering before me.

I had come here for Lena. That was it. But as always, my mother was absent. As always, I was on my own. And while I would need to wait for her return, I didn't have to be bored out of my mind while doing so. It was only natural that I look for a distraction in the weeks before the biggest challenge of my life—whether I found it in Ethan or the chest he'd gifted me, or now in this oath that had fallen into my hands.

I looked at my phone, wondered what Ethan was doing, how he would react to a call from me. I thought of Lena, wondered if she'd been able to travel without her drugs.

I sighed, picked up my phone, and dialed, feeling very much that I was plunging into a deep pool that I might very well come to regret.

CHAPTER TEN

Emma

Let every man do what is right in his own eyes.

JOHN HANCOCK

THE RAIN HAD CEASED by the time Sarah and I left the Fulton house, leaving us with the faint scent of water mixed with dirt and the slight tang of salt from the sea. A sliver of a moon and our lantern were enough to light our way.

As Sarah shut the door, having her daughter bolt it behind her, the loud echo of bloodcurdling war whoops came to us from the direction of Old South. They soon mixed with guttural noises and whistles reminiscent of boatswains.

Sarah grasped for one of my hands. "It appears Governor Hutchinson did not approve Rotch's request, after all."

I returned the squeeze of her fingers, drawing strength from them. I felt bonded with her in this moment, where it seemed so much depended on the events of the next few hours. With that strength came a simmering anger in the pit of my belly. I fought to quell it as I returned my hand to my muff.

They were all stubborn men, the lot of them. Men like my father, like Samuel, like the other agents and consignees. Dare I think it—like the king. The Sons were not asking for much—only a voice. A right to have a say in the duties impressed upon us, for every man and merchant to have a fair chance at providing for their families without Parliament sticking their noses in every aspect of our commerce, right down to telling us from whom we must buy our tea.

The Body had done all in their power—now 'twas time to put the tea in the hands of the Mohawks.

I quickened my steps alongside Sarah's, weaving our way to Belcher's Lane, the harbor shimmering cold to our right. As we neared Griffin's Wharf, I made out the shadows of a crowd alongside the docks. No doubt they had followed the shouts from Old South, curious as to what would be done. Yet other than a few quiet voices, all was eerily silent.

When we reached Griffin's Wharf, we pushed through the crowd, jostled and crushed by the many spectators, including a large man in a tricorne hat who smelled of rum and had little regard for sharing the tight space with others.

No longer beside me, Sarah had avoided the large man, but I pressed forward, the wharf as light as day by means of the lamps carried by both crowd and Mohawks. Aboard the *Dartmouth*, Mohawks stood fierce in their disguises, an occasional grunt traveling over the water to where the crowd looked on in silence.

With their clubs and cutlasses, the men used hoisting tackle and ropes to lift the chests to the deck. Seeing them, I found it hard to imagine Noah in their midst though I had aided him in his disguise myself. They worked quietly, methodically, as a cooperative group, and I wondered if the disguises gave them courage—if the costumes helped not only in hiding their identities but in aiding them to do what they deemed necessary.

Beneath the disguises lay craftsmen and artisans, fishermen and seafarers. Had he been alive, I could imagine Uncle Daniel among them. They each held a job, and watching them hoist the tea from where it lay buried in the hold, my heart stirred with pride.

When the sound of splintering wood filled the air, the crowd tittered with excitement, something akin to merriment wafting over the boats and the wharf. A man in the crowd who stood taller than the rest pointed toward Castle William, to the Royal Navy anchored in the harbor. Certainly they could see what transpired, and yet we were not disturbed— not as the tops and bindings were knocked off the chests, not as the canvas-covered chests were smashed, not as fresh, beautiful, fragrant tea leaves were scattered overboard, the chests dumped in after them.

"This be the largest cup of tea the fishes will ever feast upon," one man said with a snicker.

As the Mohawks continued their work, the tea leaves piled up in the shallows, spilling over the gunwales. A few lads broke up the clumps with long poles. Others waded into the flats, stomping the leaves into the mud and swirling the tea around, urging it toward the harbor. The bittersweet scent encompassed the docks.

A sudden commotion came from the direction of the *Beaver*, and several took up the cry of "East Indian!"

Though hard to see, I could just make out one man being stripped of his clothes and coated with mud.

"He pocketed the tea," came the report, swelling from the *Beaver*. "They'd tar and feather him, but they'd rather not draw more attention than necessary."

I felt a tug at my cloak and twisted to see Sarah, beckoning for me. I squeezed my way back through the crowd until we were along Belcher's Lane again, leaving the mass and the Mohawks in body, but not at all in thought.

"We must heat some water to help them when they return." Sarah seemed quiet, pensive. I wondered if she doubted the wisdom of John's involvement now that she had seen the task firsthand.

"It is going well," I ventured.

"Aye."

"There will be consequences."

"Aye. Not for them as individuals, if the men honor their oath, but for us as a town—perhaps us as a colony. There will be no turning back after this night."

Her words foretold something I knew deep in my being, for they spoke to me on a personal level as well. I imagined Father hearing news of the tea the following morning. I knew his temper well—he would brandish his anger upon any whom he saw fit. I, having abandoned my family for this cause, would surely be at the top of his list.

If I meant that much to him—if I was even a thought to him any longer.

Why did I long to be? What, truly, did it matter? I had the love of Noah, an honorable, good man. I had a sure friend in Sarah and now a purpose beyond myself in joining the cause of liberty. I no longer needed my family. I needn't depend on them for strength, for all they did was make me feel inferior, weak.

Yet as I tried to convince myself of that fact, a niggling sensation wormed its way deep within my being. I wondered if I would ever be truly content again, if in separating myself from those whose love I yearned for, I had cut off a piece of my heart forever.

✠

I opened my eyes to a slight tickle along my nose, my frightful dream still vivid in my mind as it vied for a place beside Mohawks and wharves and tea. I shook my head, moved my face from Mary's braid, where she slept soundly on the bed we shared. I rolled onto my back, tried to convince myself the dream had no merit in life.

Yet the memory of it clung to my consciousness, rendering me powerless to separate vision from reality. I closed my eyes, succumbed to its beckoning terror—Father, forcing himself into the Fulton house accompanied by customs soldiers. Tearing apart beds and drawers, searching every corner for evidence of Mohawk treachery.

A dream. Only a dream.

Even so, it loomed large in my mind, causing my heart to beat a frantic pace beneath my chemise.

I thought of the previous night's events with a mixture of anticipation, anxiety, and elation whirling in my head as I sought to replace my terrifying dream with reality.

I forced my thoughts on all that the night before had brought me. Noah's declaration of love and now an impending future with him. 'Twas that which was real. 'Twas that which I should dwell upon.

When Noah and John had come home late last night, complete with Mohawk feathers stuffed in their pockets, exhausted from their endeavors, the lampblack running into their eyes from sweat, Sarah and I had dipped cloths in warm water to help dispose of any last trace of disguise. After Sarah and John had gone to bed, Noah and I sat by the keeping room fire, him detailing every aspect of the night.

After he had told me of the quiet work, of the complete disposal of the tea, we spoke of our future together. Of a simple spring wedding, perhaps forgoing the more traditional reading of the banns. We entertained the notion of following John and Sarah to Medford, where Noah would open his own printing business. I told him more of my childhood, how I had conflicting feelings over leaving my family forever, and yet how, when it came right down to it, I didn't regret it, couldn't imagine another choice before me.

When he left for the night, he drew me into his arms. I swiped at a smudge of lampblack beneath his ear, horrified that I had missed such a telling sign when helping him wash. He pulled me closer, his arms making me forget the lampblack, the disguises, the tea, my family, the seriousness of the situation altogether.

"You have made me the happiest man in Boston this very night, Emma. I can hardly wait to make you my wife."

His words hinted at an intimacy that thrilled and filled my being with a sense of longing that made me dizzy. My heart thrummed beneath their sweetness, Noah's closeness intoxicating, the scent of hyson tea mixed with lye soap and ink. I longed to stare at the nuances of his face, to map each dip and valley and commit it forever to memory.

He ran a finger beneath my chin. "Do you wish me to seek your father's permission? I would do this in an honorable manner. I don't wish you to regret any of this."

I think I might have fallen in love with him all over again in that moment. I laid my hand on his arm, conscious of how close we were, giddy that I might plan the rest of my life beside him. "In an ideal world, that would be wonderful . . . but I'm afraid these times are less than ideal. Father has threatened you before. I can't imagine what would come of your going to him. Nay, Noah. He has certainly disowned me. I will answer for myself from now on, and my answer is you."

"You are brave and beautiful and strong, Emma."

He thought me brave. Strong. Perhaps, in seeking out my own path in life, my own love, I was becoming the very thing I longed for. That the man I loved recognized as much, and thought me beautiful for it, was enough to affirm my decisions of the last few days.

I smiled, mesmerized by the hazel flecks of his eyes, reflecting the firelight.

He pressed his lips together and I was drawn to them, to every movement he made.

He ran his thumb along my jaw, gentle, prodding. "I might kiss you."

I swallowed down my apprehension, thick in my throat. Brave, indeed. I opened my mouth to speak, my words filled with tremors. "I . . . would like that, I think."

He smiled, causing my nerves to rest. Dipping his head, he captured my mouth with his own, drew me closer.

I sank into the solidness of his arms, the movement of his lips over mine so intimate and tender, I fought to remember where I was, who I was. He tasted of mint and adventure, of sunshine and new beginnings. And as he deepened the kiss, I felt a shared force between us—something so powerful and foreign, it frightened me with its intensity as much as it excited me. In that moment, I knew my heart had been lost to him forever, but a better place to lose it I could not fathom.

When we finally parted, I breathed deep, my chest heaving, my head swirling.

"I should look forward to more of that," he murmured in my ear, his breath warm.

I laughed. I would also, though I would not be so bold to say.

"I had best be going. 'Tis not overly wise we are without a chaperone, and the mischief this night has set upon us bids me home."

He kissed me again then, long and just as sweet. It was enough to keep me warm the entire night through.

"Until tomorrow then, my sweet Emma. I will visit you in my dreams."

And while I'd fallen asleep thinking on his kiss, my actual dreams had been of a much less pleasant quality, forecasting disaster instead of fond new love.

Now, lying in the dark beside Mary, I wondered why such dreams should invade my mind when I'd never been happier. Could they be a prophecy of sorts? I raked my thoughts for anything Father could find should he decide to search the house. Absurd, truly, but I could not release the premonition that I was not safe—that I had put Sarah and John and the children, and even Noah, at risk by being here.

We had washed off the lampblack, stored away the shawls and blankets.

Nothing else here would implicate the men. . . .

I sat up at the sudden remembrance of the feathers John and Noah had brought home. I remembered them on the seat of a chair, taken from their cloak pockets. Could we have been so careless as to leave them?

I slid out of the bed, careful to replace the covers around Mary's warm little body. Outside, the barest hint of dawn lightened the eastern sky, shining faint light onto Mary, curled up in the bed, her braid a long, wavy tangle on the bolster pillow. I donned my clothes, careful not to wake the sleeping girls.

I made my way downstairs, hesitated on the creaking steps for only a moment.

The bright feathers lay where I'd seen them last, and I mentally berated all four of us for our carelessness. I scooped them up and faced the hearth, where the coals from last night's fire glowed. I laid kindling upon them, then moved to the stove and did the same.

Would the feathers burn? I had no assurance they would, could only imagine a horrible stench clogging up the house, the bones of feathers still visible in the hearth. Better to remove their damning evidence from the house altogether.

Images from my dream manifested themselves anew. But this time it was Father barging into the Fulton home, demanding an alibi for John last night, smelling the stink of burnt feathers, seeing their skeletons in the stove.

The feathers must be disposed of . . . I looked about the keeping room, caught a glimpse of paper beneath the chair Noah had sat in the night before. Vaguely, I remembered it fluttering to the ground as he doffed one of the blankets he'd wrapped around himself. I'd meant to mention it but had gotten caught up in John's telling of their adventure, and then, later, in the conversation Noah and I shared.

I went over, scooped it up. My blood flowed cold as I realized what I held.

Noah's round-robin. The oath the Mohawks had taken. He'd been careless. Yet the night had been filled with such excitement, I couldn't blame him. He had likely tucked it deep within a pocket—perhaps the strenuous work had caused it to come loose, or perhaps it had come out when he removed his cloak. At least it had fallen here and not in the streets.

And I'd been worried about feathers.

I briefly considered casting the paper in the stove. The flames would devour it easily. But I stayed my hand, thinking Noah would want to keep this pact. The remembrance of my dream returned to me, and having no time to find a secure hiding place for it, I carefully folded Noah's paper and slid it beneath my corset.

Donning my cloak, I unbolted the door and left the house, making my way east. I would see Noah later this day and return the oath to him. He would be happy I'd taken care of it—that I had already proved a worthy helpmate.

The morning chill bit my skin, but I hastened toward

the ocean to dispose of the Mohawk feathers. No one would associate them with John and Noah if they were found in the waters of the harbor—where tea surely floated in abundance this morning.

With quick steps, I braced myself against the cold and worked my way down Auchmuty Street, then South, then Summer until I reached the wharves alongside Flounder Lane, where a small stretch of beach met the water. A gull poked at a reed near the shore, where the tide—blanketed in tea leaves—pulled away. If I flung the feathers in the harbor, nature would certainly do its work in taking them out to sea, far away from Noah and the Fulton home.

The tide had swelled that night. I stepped down to the beach, the tea leaves bobbing heavy in the water and along the shore. Griffin's Wharf lay not far from here, but this day it seemed the entire ocean was adrift in tea leaves. Their exotic aroma mixed with the scent of the harbor.

In what I hoped to be a nonchalant manner, I looked behind me. All seemed quiet, the distillery John worked at looming large in the distance, the smattering of houses alongside it quiet and barely visible from such a distance, their inhabitants still sleeping or tucked within their keeping rooms, lighting their stoves. Afar off came the sound of a horse and carriage.

But nothing else to cause alarm.

I lifted my skirts slightly so as not to pick up wet tea leaves in my petticoats, and squatted at the water's edge. I pulled the feathers from the pocket of my cloak and pressed them beneath the next tide swell, allowing cold water to sweep over my hand.

I swished my fingers around in the sea to rid them of tea leaves and sand, then stood.

There. 'Twas accomplished. Nothing to fuss over, truly.

I almost turned to go but thought of the oath beneath my corset. Had it not already served its purpose? How easy to rip it to shreds and fling it in the cold waters of the harbor, never to be seen again.

I craned my neck in the direction of the distillery. Still no one. I slid my fingers beneath the top of my corset, grasped the list with two fingers, and pulled it out. I held it beneath my cloak, praying for the right course of action.

Mayhap the Lord had sent me the dream for a reason. Mayhap I was meant to dispose of the oath here and now.

I felt its thickness and wondered at the wisdom of standing here, shredding such quality paper with my hands. Surely a fire would be better to destroy it.

Mind made up, I slid the paper back where it belonged, safe against my bare skin. Noah's shop was just yonder. Mayhap he would be starting the fires in the shop, and I would not be intruding if I knocked upon the door. I could give him the round-robin and be done with it.

I turned, running headlong into a tall, solid body.

I gasped, could not fathom how I hadn't heard another's presence.

Large hands steadied me, the scent of pipe smoke familiar. I remembered my dream yet still could not reconcile the fact that Father could be here now.

"Now where are you off to so fast, dearest?" Not Father, then. Oh, so much worse. I tried not to cringe beneath

Samuel's hold, but his fingers tightened. "More importantly, what do you have in your stays?"

I looked up into my captor's face, set in an ugly sneer.

And I very much regretted ever leaving the safety of the Fulton house that morning.

CHAPTER ELEVEN

Emma

This destruction of the tea is so bold, so daring, so firm, intrepid and inflexible, and it must have so important consequences, and so lasting, that I can't but consider it as an epocha in history.

JOHN ADAMS

"I'VE MISSED YOU, dear Emma." Samuel's fingers dug into my arms, talons digging into tender flesh. "Your father insisted you ran off, never to return. He said he wouldn't waste his energy looking for you. But I knew he was wrong. You wouldn't run from me, now, would you?"

Noah said I was brave. Now I must prove it. This man didn't have a hold over me any longer. I had broken away from him—even from my family—to have my freedom.

I wrenched myself from his firm grasp. "I am no longer beneath my father's dominion. Nor yours. I am a free woman."

He threw back his head and released a cackle that scared away the gull I'd seen earlier. "Are you, now? Well, that puts me in a precarious position, does it not? Because you were promised to me. And your dowry was promised to me as well. I intend to have you both."

No doubt it was the connection to Father's royal position he coveted more than my dowry. Either way, I had denied him. "I'm promised to another, Samuel. I'm sorry . . . perhaps I should have sent you a missive."

He stared at me, his gaze like the ice that dripped from the eaves of the distillery. "Flitting from one man to another, Emma? Quite the trollop, aren't we? I hadn't realized you were so . . . free with yourself."

I could scarce comprehend his words. No one had ever accused me of such indecency.

"Who's the lucky chap, then? Not that slovenly Yank who ogled you through my very own house window the night I fought off that unruly mob, I hope."

Inwardly I scolded myself for mentioning my relationship with Noah. 'Twould have been better to let Samuel believe I was truly on my own, with no intended in my future. "No— not him. Another." All I could think to do was protect Noah. If Samuel knew of my beloved's identity . . . there was no telling what travesty might come upon us.

He looked down at me, his eyes slits within his face. "You lie." His gaze continued downward to where my chest grew heavy beneath my cloak. "And what is it you hide in your underpinnings?"

My heart lurched taut under my corset, where Noah's oath lay, suddenly unsafe. "Nothing. Now if you'll excuse me, I must tend to breakfast." My words did not shake, and as I moved to go around him, I thought he might not cause me further distress after all.

How very wrong I was.

He stepped sideways to block my way. "I saw you hide something. If you will not reveal it to me, I shall have to go searching myself."

I crossed my arms before me, shook my head with vigor. From where I stood on the sand, I sprang forward, thinking to outrun him. But he caught me in his arms, his force sending us both falling upon the sand. He clamped a hand over my mouth, his palm locking my jaw together so tight I could not attempt to bite him.

"If you continue to make a fuss, be certain I will find your beau. 'Twouldn't be difficult. He runs with rebels—and Mohawks, it would seem. After the treasonous unrest last night, I should think the king would like to learn of him."

I shook my head against his hand, my eyes drawn to the tea leaves swirling in the water, a tea chest in the flats beyond. Samuel knew nothing except for what he'd seen the night Noah dispelled the mob at the Clarke home. Noah had helped his family. No, Samuel's words were only to elicit a reaction, poking at me like the tithingman poked a sleeping child during service. I squirmed beneath his grip.

"Whatever you are concealing, you can either withdraw it yourself, or I will be forced to retrieve it for you."

I imagined his hands slithering beneath my cloak, his fingers searching for the oath beneath my corset. Spots danced before my eyes. I had no doubt he would do as he threatened.

I nodded as best I could with his hands pinioning me.

He loosened his arms just a bit to allow me room to move. Taking the chance, I propelled myself forward with all my strength, but to no avail. The muscles of his arms locked me in place.

I bade my tears stay put.

"No more nonsense, Emma. This is your last chance. I am being kind."

I had no choice.

Beneath the privacy of my cloak, I slid Noah's oath from my corset. Samuel grabbed it up, releasing me.

I pushed my boots against the sand, then made one last desperate lunge for the paper.

He held it easily away from me, pushed me firmly back onto the sand. "My, now, you are a feisty one, aren't you? Perhaps you'll be better marital sport than I anticipated." With deliberate show, he unfolded Noah's list. "What have we here?" His eyes scanned the paper, near lighting up as they comprehended the information. "My, oh, my, is this what I think it is?"

My bottom lip trembled as I watched, helpless. I'd been trying to help Noah. How could I have been so careless?

"Emma, dear, I'm not certain I could have imagined anything better beneath that dress of yours—" he chuckled—"though I suppose we shall see upon our wedding night, shan't we?"

Sour bile rose in the back of my throat. My world came crashing down upon me, obliterated by the events of the last ten minutes. "What do you intend?" I whispered, my voice hoarse.

Samuel refolded the paper in neat quarters, slid it with care into a pocket of his cloak, patted it twice before focusing his attention on me. "Now *that* is entirely up to you."

I closed my eyes against the morning sun. "What do you want?"

"I've already told you. I want nothing other than what was promised to me. Your hand in marriage."

There must be another way. Though I could not see it in this moment, surely I had not ruined everything by my actions this morning.

"Why do you want to wed me? I've made it clear I don't desire you. My father has disowned me. What do you stand to gain?"

"My dignity, for one. Your dowry, another. And if you must know, I've been looking to seal a more . . . permanent relationship with your father for some time. He will help the Clarke family in ways you cannot imagine."

"Not if the Sons have anything to say about it—which they clearly do."

Samuel brushed sand from his trousers. "They will be squashed soon enough, and all will return as it once was. I've no doubt if you return to your father and beg his good graces, he will accept you back into the fold. Tell him you regret leaving your true family, that you saw firsthand the baseness of those men who mock the name of liberty, that you only wish to have things as they were—to have me as a husband."

I fought to keep from spitting upon his shoes. "Never."

"Very well, then. I will do what I must. You have been warned." He turned to go, and while I couldn't wait to rid myself of him, his words cast fear upon every shredded, shivering strand of my being.

I stood on wobbly legs. "Please. Don't . . ." My voice came out tight, threatening to fly away.

He turned, feigning surprise that I had called out to him. "Don't what? Do my duty to the crown, as any good and law-abiding citizen should?"

"Pray, Samuel. Pray . . . I beg of you, may I have that paper back?"

"Of course. Of course." He stepped closer to me but did not move to take the oath from his cloak. "I promise to return it to you. 'Twill be yours . . . after we are wed."

I pressed a hand to my stomach to fight the ill feeling swirling in the pit of my being. "I cannot marry you."

"Then I cannot keep the contents of this list between us." His expression turned serious, no longer the joking rogue. "'Tis quite simple, in fact. The only way you will receive your list back is if you go straight to your father—immediately. No explanations to your Yank or your employers. You will express your remorse and insist to marry me as soon as the banns can be read. If I find that you are not beneath your father's roof within the hour, if I find that you have not obeyed my demands, I will release the list to General Gage and Governor Hutchinson. If I find that you have ever made contact with any of those associated with this—" he patted his pocket—"consider it a break in our agreement. Surely the Body will not voice opposition to the hanging of men who not only disguised themselves as Mohawks, but who skulk about at night destroying property."

My insides cramped, and I curled myself around my stomach.

"Make no mistake, dear one. Every man on this list has committed treason. Not only that, but he has condemned himself in signing his own name. And you, I suppose, are partly to blame if they should meet their doom. But, Emma, you can be their heroine also. 'Tis quite simple. Return to your father's home and I will forget the list until I return it to you on our wedding night. Their fate is entirely in your hands. You longed for freedom—here it is. You are free to make your own choice in this matter. Choose well, dearest."

And then he was gone, his words and their implications hanging over me thicker than the tea soaking the tides of Boston.

I crumpled to the sand, my mind replaying what had just happened, convincing myself it was a product of my imagination and not the cold, terrible truth of reality. Tears froze upon my cheeks as I fell into a trancelike state until the call of seabirds finally beckoned me. I slid my hands beneath my corset, my despair growing tenfold at the confirmation that recent events had been all too real.

Sarah.

More than anything I wished to seek her advice, tell her of my foolish decision to leave the house, tell her of Samuel's indecency, his attempt to bribe me.

But going to her, or to Noah, would break Samuel's terms. He was likely watching me even now, making sure I was doing as he instructed. And what would Sarah be able to solve? John's name was upon that list—the father of her children. What power did she hold—what power did any of them hold against Samuel and the crown?

I thought of Noah, of our sweet and precious time the night before. Could I go to him? Could we run away together, escape the charges of treason?

Nay. Of course not. For if we were to escape, we would

leave behind a mess of others who couldn't. Men who had trusted Noah with their life when signing his oath. Men who believed it right to stand against the forces of tyranny.

I remembered the warm safety of the Fulton keeping room the night before. Of Noah's arms, strong and secure and gentle against me—the very opposite of Samuel's possessive ones. I recalled his lips against mine, the sweet taste of him as we sealed our future together.

Was that all that was to be ours? A few moments stolen in the middle of the night? We'd been planning a lifetime. Now, it seemed, our plans were slayed.

My gaze fell on the tea chest not far from me. The waves lapped at its solid sides, upon which a pink Chinese tea flower was painted. I wondered if the entire cause of liberty would have been better had I not joined it. Had I stayed beneath Father's dominion, mayhap the Sons would have chosen another disguise. Mayhap there would have been no Mohawk feathers in the Fulton house that morning. Certainly there never would have been an oath beneath my chemise.

It would not be in Samuel's hands this very moment.

I dragged in a shaking breath, felt my heart being wrenched out of my body as I recalled Noah's name clear and bold upon that paper.

He'd called me brave. He'd called me strong.

And I would prove myself so, though it break my heart—and his—in the process.

CHAPTER TWELVE

Emma

The cause of Boston, the despotic Measures in respect to it, I mean now is and ever will be considered as the cause of America (not that we approve their conduct in destroying the Tea).

GENERAL GEORGE WASHINGTON

FATHER'S HOUSE HAD never looked so forlorn, yet so very intimidating. The shutters were latched tight, chasing away the scant winter sun. As I walked toward it, I prayed Father might be out for the day—or better yet, traveling on business.

Mayhap my family had finally retreated to Castle William, like so many other royal officials and their kin. I didn't entertain this thought for long, for Father was far too stubborn to admit defeat, to tuck tail and run because of a few rowdy Mohawks.

The house loomed bigger, and I tightened my arms around the chest recovered from the beach that morning, now covered in a threadbare blanket I'd found in a deserted alley on the way home. I couldn't fully comprehend why I'd taken the chest from the sea. All I knew was as soon as

I made my decision to admit defeat—to return to Father's home and agree to wed Samuel—another, rebellious part of me longed to hold dear the past few days. All of it. My part in the dumping of the tea. In helping Noah turn himself into a Mohawk, lampblack upon his whiskered face. Noah's confession of love. Our precious hours planning a life that would never be.

His sweet words, his sweeter kiss.

I feared I would believe it all a dream if I didn't grasp at something solid and real. Something that symbolized the genuine truth we fought for, the courage I would need going forth, the worthiness of my sacrifice. Something that symbolized that, although I would succumb to a loveless marriage, I *had* known the firm, unyielding form of true love once in my life, if only for a few hours.

'Twould have to suffice a lifetime.

I swallowed down the last of my doubts, the ones that tempted me to run back to Noah's arms. He would think I abandoned him. Betrayed him. Mayhap he would realize I had his oath. He would think I ran to my father. In the coming days, the thought that he would presume me a traitor would surely break my heart.

And yet to protect him, 'twas necessary.

I thought of Mary's little arms, the way they clung to my neck when she gave me a hug. I thought of the book Noah had given me, the cup Sarah had insisted I have.

How it all remained at the Fultons', how the fact that I had gone would only be sharpened by the objects left behind.

I tried not to dwell on Sarah, who would wonder at my

sudden disappearance. In a peculiar way, her disappointment would sting the most. In a time when I'd felt unsure and uncertain, she'd declared me a daughter. She had convinced John of my worthiness and trust, and now I had disproved her confidence. No doubt she would believe me wishy-washy in my resolve to leave my family, believe me frightened by the events the night before. She might believe I set out to betray them all. Somehow, I felt if she understood the extent of my decision, she would approve. Be proud of me, even.

Yet she could never know.

I dragged my weary limbs up the stairs and beneath the covered entryway. I knocked upon the door, uncertain I had the right to enter of my own accord any longer. I tightened my grip on the tea chest, felt defiant at its presence in my father's home and at the same time comforted by what it stood for—the last vestiges of my true self.

For after I crossed this threshold, there would be no turning back.

The door opened a crack, Chloe's dark skin shadowed within. She pushed the door farther when she saw me. "Miss Emma . . ."

"Chloe. May I come in?"

She wavered. "Your father said . . . he said I should not allow you into the house."

Why should I be surprised? "Is he here? Mayhap I could speak with him."

"No, miss. Your mother is resting after a visit from your sister. Shall I inform her of your presence?"

"Please."

The servant girl shut the door to find my mother within, leaving me on the cold steps.

This road would be a hard one. My life appeared before me, leaving a bad taste in the back of my mouth at the suffering I was sure to endure on this path. The only way to survive would be to remind myself—and remind myself often—of the worthy cause for which I fought. One that would no doubt be different from the plight of Noah and Sarah and John and the Sons, yet at the same time one that was very much the same in honor.

When the door opened this time, Mother stood poised beyond it, but unable to hide the tremble of her bottom lip. "You've come home."

"Aye." I looked down at the thin blanket over the tea chest. "Pray, Mother, may I enter?"

She expelled a dainty breath. "Your father . . ."

Looking at her now, ready to turn away her youngest child, I despised her weakness. Was this what I would become upon marrying Samuel? A frail woman who would turn against the child she'd once carried in her womb only to appease a demanding husband?

"Mother, I've come home. To stay, if Father will have me. To beg his forgiveness and admit the waywardness of my actions." I hefted the onerous words, pushed out the last of them, the ones which would ensure my entrance into Father's fold at the same time they ensured that Noah and the Fulton family and all who'd signed that blasted oath be kept safe. "To cast myself upon Samuel Clarke's mercy as well, to hasten our wedding day if at all possible."

A strange light entered Mother's eyes, and she opened

the door wider. "I'm pleased you've come to your senses, then. Come in. You may wait in the parlor until your father returns."

I entered the dark house, wished to put my things upstairs in my bedroom, but dared not ask. I carried the chest into the parlor, and without doffing my cloak, I sat. Mother stood above me, seeming to vacillate between staying and leaving. Finally she placed a hand on my arm, the slight pain at her touch a remembrance of Samuel's hard grip that morning.

Her tone grew intimate. "I am glad you are home, Emma."

My heart softened at the gesture, and I reached for her hand, unable to say the same but willing to squeeze out a "Thank you."

She left me alone then. Chloe did not offer me tea or chocolate or cider. She did not offer to take my cloak or stoke the fire in the hearth. The scent of Father lay heavy in this room—pipe smoke and snuff and leather. The grandfather clock ticked away the seconds, then chimed the hours as I waited for Father's return. I placed the chest to the side of the straight-backed cherry chair and opened the shutter to allow the winter sun to reflect light off the white wainscoting. I prepared my words with care, arranging them in my head so as to feign authenticity. And still, a faint part of me imagined Father opening his arms to his prodigal daughter. Wrapping me in his embrace, telling me he missed me, perhaps realizing the fault in his own hard ways.

When the front door came open and Chloe's soft steps rushed to take Father's cloak, I stood, awaiting him.

He did not show surprise at my presence, and I wondered if Chloe had whispered of my whereabouts.

He strode to the fire and stoked it, laid firewood upon it, then poured himself some brandy. The glint of the flames shone off the shiny brass buttons of his wool coat. I looked at the back of his perfectly powdered wig, not a hair out of place. If only I felt some warmth—some *humanity*—from the man I called "Father." Surely he couldn't be all hard edges and rough stone. Did an ounce of compassion live within him?

"So you come crawling back, do you now, Emma?"

My pride threatened to burst forth, but I did not allow it access to my mouth. This path which I had chosen would be one of long-suffering. One of dying to my own will each and every day.

The remembrance of Noah's face, handsome by the glow of the Fulton fire, bade me stay firm. He would eventually heal from this heartbreak and disappointment. He would go on to live a full life, find another worthy woman with whom to share it. He'd have children to carry on both his name and his ideals. 'Twould be a life without me, but 'twould be life just the same, a better alternative than a hangman's noose.

"I've come to beg your mercy, Father. I fear I made a horrendous decision in leaving. I know—I'm aware I do not deserve your forgiveness, and yet I beg you to grant it. If you will have me back into the family, I am prepared to do whatever you deem fit to redeem my name, including marrying Samuel Clarke."

He raised an eyebrow in my direction. "You can imagine my doubt. My distrust of you. 'Twill take time to earn that trust again. You have sullied my good name, made a mockery of our family. I've half a mind to send you away, to let you lie in the dirtied gutters of this town."

His words hung in the air, and I forced out what was expected. "I know, Father. Though it be audacious for me to ask your forgiveness, I do so nonetheless. I am truly sorry."

Would God curse me for such deceitfulness, even if my intent was to save others? It seemed I could not draw peace from my circumstances no matter which direction I turned.

"Why the change of heart? And where have you been these past days?"

"I thought to escape, to live of my own means if I could acquire a job at a tavern or such. I was frightened to marry Samuel, Father. I pray you understand. I was desperate." With resolve, I prepared to push forth lies based upon a foundation of truth. "Mrs. Fulton works at her mother's tavern. I sought a job there. Forgive me—I know it was an uncomely thing to do, foolish. But I am a foolish girl. 'Tis not the life I want. I see now how well you have treated me. How wonderful my life is. And after witnessing the chaos of last night—those fearful Mohawks romping about through the streets—I wanted nothing more than to come home, to seek solace beneath your roof again." I pressed my lips together, wet them with my tongue. "I truly look forward to making my own home with Samuel Clarke, if he will still have me."

I wondered if the Lord would strike me dead at my lies. And yet they were to protect lives. How could I not do what I must?

Father studied me, his gaze seeming to sear my skin and scorch my insides. He looked away, his eyes dropping to the blanket covering the chest beside me, then slowly moving back to me. "I knew you'd come to your senses sooner or later, but you also must realize the severity of your decisions."

The tight feeling returned to my chest. I struggled to gather breath around it. "I—I do, sir."

"If you want back into this family, you will not be leaving this house without my permission. Is that clear?"

"Aye, sir."

"You will put your full efforts into preparing for your wedding . . . if Samuel will still have you, that is. You will accompany your mother on social outings and speak nothing of politics or of your time away. You will be the perfect match for Samuel, before and after the wedding, in any way he deems fit. Is that understood?"

I remembered Samuel's large hands upon me, what would be expected of me once we wed. The backs of my eyes burned. Was this truly my only choice? In any way he deemed fit . . . Was I no more than a pawn to Father, after all? Did he care nothing for me?

Yet, quite simply, there were no other options. I commanded my tears to stay put. If Father saw them, my entire ruse would be at stake.

"I understand."

"So help me, Emma Grace, if you break this agreement, I will throw you out on your ear for good, mark my words. Better yet, I'll ship you back to London, sell you to one of the bawdy houses myself."

I had no doubt that he would. So much for welcoming his prodigal daughter home.

"I understand, sir."

He jerked his head toward the stairs. "Go, then. Clean

yourself. I won't have any daughter of mine looking like a filthy Yank." He sat at his desk, took out a sheet of correspondence.

I stood, gathered the chest in my arms, but hesitated before leaving. Slowly I went to him, placed a hand on his arm. "Thank you, for your forgiveness."

Was that a softening in his countenance? Nay, I must have imagined it, for he quickly shrugged from my touch.

"Forgiveness is to be earned. Returning here, groveling at my feet, is only a first step. Prove yourself worthy, and earn your way back into my good graces."

"Aye, sir," I whispered, then left the room.

I climbed the stairs as if they would lead me to the Court Street gaol. Once in my chilly room, I set the chest beside my bed, sat on the hearth rug, and slid my hands beneath the sullied rag blanket to the splintered wood beneath.

I should have never left this house. I had only caused hurt for those I loved. Venturing out, believing I had a right to freedom . . . mayhap 'twas all a lie.

Suddenly angry, I pushed the chest beneath my bed, cursing the crown and the Sons and all the trouble that involved taxes and tea. I imagined Noah, hearing news that I'd gone home.

And finally I let the tears come.

CHAPTER THIRTEEN

Emma

There is a certain enthusiasm in liberty that makes human nature rise
above itself in acts of bravery and heroism.

ALEXANDER HAMILTON

I'D NEVER THOUGHT myself a skilled thespian, but after the effort the evening meal required that night, I discovered a hidden talent, born of necessity. At the table with Father, Mother, Mr. and Mrs. Clarke, and a smug-looking Samuel beside me, I plunged into my role, if for no other reason than to not grant Samuel the satisfaction of knowing how deep the wounds of my heart ran.

Amid glittering glassware and sparkling silver, beneath fine Madeira and veal roasted to perfection followed by maize pudding, I performed a show I'm certain even Father approved. And hours later, when he, Mr. Clarke, and Samuel emerged from the parlor, strained smiles upon their faces as they no doubt came to terms over their great loss in the dumping of the tea, I knew I was at the heart of the deal they struck.

As my parents and the Clarkes bade their farewells, Samuel led me to the dark foyer. "You are a wise woman, Emma. And I hope you understand why I had to be somewhat . . . persuasive this morning. I think you'll see in time that all this is for the best. And you will never lack for comforts, so long as you look to my comforts as well." He ran his finger alongside my face and I tried not to cringe at his touch.

I raised my chin, moving from his hand. "Make no mistake, Samuel. I am not fond of you and I desire no marriage. Yet I do what I must. You've given me no choice."

His gaze turned cold and he patted my cheek once, then twice, hard and firm. "With or without your heart . . . I get what I want." The Clarkes rounded the corner and Samuel adjusted his waistcoat, bowed slightly to me. "Farewell, my dear. Tomorrow is not soon enough."

I could hardly bear the two-faced rogue. But was I not also duplicitous? I saw our entire life stretched before us, a dance of hate and scorn, each trying to best the other. Either that, or he would break me altogether.

I turned in a fitful sleep upon my soft feather bed. I missed the straw of the bed at Sarah and John's house, missed Mary's little legs pushing against mine, the tickle of her braid in my face. Here, all was cold and empty. The wind howled under the eaves, calling out a lonely wail that swept over the harbor in eerie waves.

A tapping sounded at my window, as if a tree branch hit it. Or . . .

I sat in bed, clutched my coverlet to my chest. I could just make out a shadow at my window, perched upon the roof over the front door. My first thought was that Samuel had shinnied up the portico to humiliate me further in some manner. But as my eyes adjusted to the dim light of the moon, I made out the familiar form of Noah, his tricorne hat atop his head.

An intense yearning grew in my core, a force so strong I was not sure I could fight it. Everything I longed for was right outside that window. How I wished to go to him.

Yet no good could come of it. Samuel had insisted on no contact, and I could not risk the safety of the man I loved. Instead, I buried myself beneath my covers and pressed them to my ears, willed Noah to take his leave. But the tapping only grew louder, more insistent. Then I heard his voice, calling my name, and I feared he might wake Father.

Pushing the covers aside, I donned my robe and swept my long curls back, uttering a prayer for strength and wisdom as I faced my heart.

I unlatched the window and one side swung open, allowing a cold chill to envelop the room. Noah clutched the ledge, staring at me while staying outside, as if attempting to decipher something.

I could not hold up beneath his gaze, so I walked to the hearth, where I attempted to stoke the fire. I laid kindling upon the glowing embers until one caught, a bright flame flickering within the room. When I turned, he was inside, shutting the window, the pillow slip filled with my belongings in his hand.

We stood like two strangers, spaces apart.

"You forgot your things." He placed them on the floor. I saw the sharp outline of the book he'd given me upon the wide wood boards, the bump of Sarah's cup beside it. I could scarce believe she still wanted me to have it.

I should say something. If I failed to put a wall between us now, I would betray my feelings with words that we would both come to regret.

"You should not have come."

"I should not have come?" He stepped toward me, raised his hand as if to touch me, then drew away, took off his hat instead. "I should not have come?" he said again, disbelief drenching his words. "What would you have me do, Emma, after last night? After the planning of our future together?"

I dragged in a great breath, summoned every last bit of fortitude I could muster.

"I never meant to hurt you, Noah."

He snorted, and the derisive sound of it cut a hole in my soul. He must leave. What if Samuel had guards watching the house? What if someone had seen Noah climb our portico? What if Father heard a man's voice within my chambers?

"Did you plan it all, Emma? Did your father put you up to it? Did you gain any useful information?"

I shook my head, placed a hand over my eyes. "Nay, Noah. Please—you must go. He may be watching."

By the light of the fire, his clenched jaw softened. "Who? Who is watching?"

A sob broke loose from my chest, erupting in a loud sound that I tried to cover with my hand.

Noah grasped my arms, and yet how differently my body responded to his touch than to Samuel's. I could feel his fingers upon my skin, the thin covering of my robe the only barrier between us, intense longing welling within me.

"So help me, Emma. Tell me!"

"Samuel," I whispered. "I'm so sorry. I found your oath this morning—you must have dropped it last night. I went down to the beach to dispose of the feathers. Samuel saw me with your list—you must believe that I tried to keep it from him."

Noah's hands fell to his sides as he stared at the floor, seeming to try to make sense of my words.

"He made me promise to return to my father, to agree to marry him. That's the only way I could stop him from going to the governor with your list. I'm sorry, Noah. I am so very sorry."

Relief swept over his face. "You love me."

I nodded through my tears, and he clutched me, held me close before pushing me back once more, staring at me.

Something foreign stole over his features then, something unrecognizable and hard beneath the shadows of the fire, growing and mounting within him. "I will kill him."

I laid a hand on his arm. "No—no, you mustn't."

"He hasn't a right to extort you in this manner, to ruin both our lives. All those men who signed that oath—what have I done? I do not see another solution. I must have that list back."

I closed my eyes, could understand Noah's urge even as I knew it would be the wrong path. "My love, listen to me, please." My words belied the turmoil in my heart. I lifted a hand to his cheek, stroked it lightly until the murderous look on his face cleared. "Let us not be accused of using violence to obtain that which is honorable and right."

Something terribly forlorn came over his features as he realized I used his own words to argue against what his flesh longed for. His gaze turned glassy as I watched the battle between what he believed as moral and what he longed to take and declare as his own, his right.

I understood.

"I will get your list back and see it returns into your hands." I was proud of the steadiness of my voice, the strength I nearly felt. "We could not begin a marriage with blood upon our hands. We must believe there is another way for us."

"I don't see it," he whispered.

"Nor do I, but we will pray for a miracle. And if none is given, then this must be the sacrifice we are to make, though it breaks my heart to do so."

He sniffed, swallowed. "If it were my life alone at stake, I would take you away now." He pulled me close, burying me in his strong arms. "But it is not. Every man who signed that oath is in danger, and I cannot be so very selfish as to pretend that is not true, that it is not my fault they are in danger."

He tilted his head to mine and brushed his mouth against my own. A sadness lingered in the kiss, and at the same time the realization that this might be all we had. This moment. I sank into it, allowing him to draw me close, savoring the solidness of him along every inch of my body, his surety and steadfastness.

When we finally broke away, he rested his forehead against mine. "I don't know if I can live with the thought of you marrying him. We must find a plan. Surely there is a way to get the list back. I know men who may be able to help. Perhaps search his home whilst he is away."

"For all we know he will keep it in his pocket until our vows are said. It is dangerous, Noah. I can't fathom anyone risking more than they already have."

He turned from me to face the window, raked a hand through his hair, frustration in the hard gesture. "I must do something! I refuse to accept this fate."

I stepped toward him, my bare feet cold on the wood planks. I touched his shoulder and he looked toward me. What I was about to say did not give me pleasure, but we must face the reality of our situation.

"I think what was begun last night—the dumping of the tea—was about more than standing up for our rights or finding our voices. I think it was about risk and sacrifice for the greater good." I continued even as his eyes grew glassy in the firelight, even as he shook his head. "I would not regret saving the lives of the men on that list, Noah. I would not regret saving Sarah's husband and the father of her children. I would not regret saving you. Mayhap the sooner we make peace with that, the better."

He gathered me to him again, hunger and desperation in his embrace, in his kiss. I gave myself over to it fully. When I felt we reached the edge of a passion we could not return from, I pressed my hands to his chest. "I'm sorry," I whispered. "You should go. You've been here too long already. Samuel has forbidden any contact with you or the Fultons. I fear he watches."

"This is not the end for us, Emma." He crushed me to him, then pulled back to grasp my arms and look in my face. "You hear me? This is not the end. I will find a way, I swear it."

I did not see how it could be, yet that precious thing called hope perched within my heart, ready to take flight. I tried to clip its wings, to stuff it down. I had chosen where to give my loyalty and to fight for liberty whilst doing so.

"Please go," I whispered. "Go to Medford with John and Sarah. Begin anew. I will not fault you for it. In fact, I beg you to heed my words."

He kissed me once more before vowing his love forever. And then he was gone, the chill of the night air sweeping in to replace the warmth of his presence. I went to the window, watched him walk up the street with hunched shoulders.

And though I couldn't regret our time together so much as to wish we'd never met, I thought that, for his sake, it would have been better had I never laid eyes on Noah Winslow at all.

CHAPTER FOURTEEN

Emma

Rally, Mohawks! Bring out your axes,
And tell King George we'll pay no taxes!
BOSTON STREET BALLAD

JANUARY 1774

While the dumping of the tea made the accursed beverage scarce in the town of Boston, it also made it all the more talked about. Father purchased both the *Chronicle* and the *Gazette*, and I often snuck into his parlor after breakfast when he was away to glimpse the headlines.

I suppose it should not come as a surprise that my heart cheered the news of the Liberty Boys' victories—of approval from New York and Philadelphia stating Boston had "fully retrieved" the honor we lost, of Charleston refusing to receive East India tea as well, of the new harmony among the colonies beneath the agreement that tea was dangerous to our rights—a plague of sorts to our freedoms.

Some in Boston did not care a whit for the politics behind

tea but did away with it as soon as they read mysterious reports of East India tea being packed into tea chests by Chinese peasants with bare and dirtied, disease-infected feet.

Drinking tea became a disgrace, an idol. No longer was it the fashionable social occasion it had once been. Now, it was looked on as a pastime for the idle, the tea table a place of slander and gossip. It was blamed for scurvy, bad teeth, and weak nerves. Even Mother had ceased to serve it at her table after the image of peasant feet upon her leaves planted itself within her mind.

And then there were bonfires to destroy the tea—one in Lexington, which occurred days earlier, and another in Charlestown on the last day of the year; another in the center of town as news of a Mr. Withington, who discovered a half chest of tea washed up near Dorchester, attempted to sell the leaves to his neighbors. It did not take long for the Sons to get ahold of it and set it burning on the Common.

The *Chronicle*, however, backed by the funds of the customshouse, heralded a different story, declaring the dumping of the tea not a heroic means of defending liberty but a scandalous act of cowardice and vandalism, the dishonorable and unholy disrespect evident in the destruction of private property. Those of the distinguished South, particularly Virginians, turned their noses at the call to give up their tea.

Meanwhile, the Clarkes seemed frantic to regain their loss. Samuel did not come to the house often, for which I was relieved. Instead, I bore much time with Mother and Mrs. Clarke, planning the spring nuptials, the linens and clothing I would need after the wedding, and our trip to London, from which I would likely not return.

Through the hushed tones of Mother and Mrs. Clarke, I learned that Samuel had attempted to save a load of tea from one of his ships at Castle Island. He waited for an opportune time to smuggle the load into Boston—perhaps hide it under containers of coal or in casks of wine, to swear a false oath when declaring his goods at the customshouse.

Father continued to avoid me. I suppose that meant I wasn't yet forgiven. In truth, I found myself quite content with the arrangement. If I were to live the next months beneath his roof, I would rather not bear the direct criticisms and diatribes of guilt. 'Twas clear I would never hold a place in my father's heart—that was not like to change in the few months that remained between us.

And though Mother and I had never spent so much time together, I felt she did not forgive me either. There seemed a hollowness between us as we prepared for the wedding, an emptiness that she attempted to fill with social calls and pleasantries and shallow plans based on financial prosperity.

I heard nothing more from Noah. Or Sarah, for that matter. I hoped they had left Boston, had gone on with their plans to move to Medford. I tried not to imagine a future that could no longer be. I tried not to lie in my bed at night and imagine Noah's strong arms around me, even as I whispered prayers for a miracle I didn't believe would happen. And when I dreamed of the man I loved, I tried not to dwell on the feeling of him by my side, to call my own.

I tried.

But loneliness, defeat, and abandonment crept in. Deep down, I hoped Noah would, as he had vowed, find a way for us.

Meanwhile, the entire town seemed to hold its collective breath. 'Twould be months before news of the tea dumping would reach the king, months longer before the colonies would hear his response.

I'd heard Father and Mother speaking in the parlor one night. Mother pleaded with Father for all of us to leave, or at least join the other agents upon Castle Island.

But Father's pride seemed ever before him. I thought his insistence to stay was born of stubborn protest against the recent handbills appearing throughout the town—threats of punishment for any tea consignees who attempted to leave Castle Island, exhortations to the people of Boston to give the consignees "a reception as such vile ingrates deserve."

The handbill had been signed by the chairman of the Committee for Tarring and Feathering.

Father's tone had been harsh when he responded to Mother. "Do not dare question my decisions for my family, Clara. I've a job to do and I won't leave this town unless it be in a casket."

✝

The two feet of snow that blanketed the city would have been beautiful in another time. Instead, it further served to imprison me. I spent most of my days in my chambers. When I realized that forgetting Noah was useless, I took to writing about him, not much more than musings at first, then longer stories. Beneath my pen, I wrote out our story, however small and tragic, but embellished it with a happy ending—the story I would never live but on the pages of paper.

'Twas highly irregular for a lady to take to scribbling stories, though I cared little. Here, in my musings and imaginings, I could escape. I could live a life other than the one I resigned myself to.

Then, lest Chloe or Mother should find them, I hid them away in the tea chest beneath my bed, trusting this object of rebellion to store my secrets.

I'd been whiling away one frigid morning with my story, clinging to the precious little time I had left with it. 'Twould be painful to burn the papers before I married Samuel, yet by now I was accustomed to the pain of denying my heart. 'Twas for the good of Noah, the good of the Fultons, the good of the cause. And so 'twas worthy.

A loud shout came from outside. I ignored it, assumed it was one of the many boys on wooden sleds taking advantage of the snowy trails of the streets, free of horses and oxcarts. They led a fabulous sledding run from the top of Copp's Hill.

Another shout, but this time the definite voice of a man. I left my story for the window, cracked it open to glimpse a man and a boy at the end of our street a short distance away. The cold cut through my lungs, and I was about to fetch a quilt from my bed when I recognized Father's tall, sturdy form over the boy, perhaps eleven years old. Father's cane was raised above his head. "Do you talk to me in that style, you rascal!"

Another man, one who looked vaguely familiar and who had been passing by our street, held his hand out to Father. "Leave the child alone. He be coasting, is all. He didn't mean to run into ya."

A look of relief passed over the boy's face at the sight of his defender.

I held my breath and waited for Father's response when it came to me who the man was—Mr. Hewes, a shoemaker in the North End. I remembered my lack of surprise when I read his name upon Noah's oath. And though Father wouldn't know Mr. Hewes had secretly played a Mohawk little more than a month ago, he likely realized the artisan's political leanings did not match his own.

Never one to back down from a fight, Father's cackle split the cold morning air, and I cringed, embarrassed for myself and for him. 'Twas one thing to disagree over crown and tea, but must he be so vile toward every man in town? I could only imagine how this situation might deteriorate.

"You—a vagabond, dare you speak to a gentleman such as myself in this manner?"

Mr. Hewes smiled slowly, lazily, it seemed. Apparently he was not one to avoid a fight either. "Be that as it may, at least I never was tarred and feathered anyhow."

As far as I was aware, no one had been bold enough to speak of the incident in Falmouth to Father's face. I could scarce believe my eyes when Father turned his cane upon Mr. Hewes, smashing him with much force in the head. I cried out, gripped the sill of the window.

Mr. Hewes collapsed in the snow, and I watched in terror, willing him to get up, move, make a gesture—something that might indicate life.

The boy looked on, his hands seemingly frozen to the wooden sled which had started the entire fray. But nay, 'twas not the fault of the boy nor the sled. If one were to truly get at the root of the problem, one would find—I was quite certain—the dregs of tea.

I recognized one of our neighbors, Captain Godfrey, walking with brisk steps past our house. He'd seen Father's actions, no doubt.

The captain called out to Father. "Man, what have you done?" He knelt at Mr. Hewes's side, turned to the boy. "Fetch Dr. Warren, lad. Be quick about it."

"I will not be maligned on my very own street, Captain. I've enough of the impudent remarks."

"He's not armed, Mr. Malcolm!"

Father turned on his heel and hastened home. I shrank from view, careful to close the window after he had already entered downstairs.

Moments later, I watched as Captain Godfrey helped an unsteady Mr. Hewes to his feet. I breathed in gratitude that the man was alive. He would see the doctor. Dr. Warren, the Patriot. A friend of John and Sarah's.

What would the repercussions be for such a blow to the head? Surely Mr. Hewes or Dr. Warren would entreat a town official for Father's arrest, at the very least. But nay, they would know that a man of Father's station—a man supported by the crown—would surely evade prison with Governor Hutchinson's help.

Where, then, did that leave Father?

As the afternoon hours wore on, I felt a tight silence outside our house—a warning of an impending storm.

CHAPTER FIFTEEN

Emma

The harder the conflict, the more glorious the triumph.
THOMAS PAINE

THE CROWD ARRIVED after dark.

Their torches lit the street, creating a semblance of daylight, bright against the snow on Cross Street.

At first they were but a handful. Father ordered Mother and me upstairs, and we watched from the window of my chambers as they pressed in close to our home, demanding Father come out from the house.

To our dismay, Father opened the window of the dining room. We could just see the top of his powdered wig as he shouted to the rabble, waving them away as if they were no more than a pesky fly. "Be gone with you! Be assured Governor Hutchinson has promised a bounty of twenty pounds sterling for every Yankee I kill! Be gone, I tell you!"

The mob yelled and cursed at him. From Middle Street, more came to swell its size.

Mother's hands fluttered to her mouth. "Why must he goad them?"

I looked at her, ashen by the light of the pine knot torches, and saw her anew. Had she once resigned herself to the same wretched fate I now faced? Did she wish she had charted a different course for her life or her children?

For the first time, I thought of my future children—children sired by Samuel, a man who matched, even exceeded, Father in his own baleful temperament. I'd only wanted to protect Noah and John and all the Mohawks when I'd agreed to marry him. But what of my own children? Though they be unborn, did they not deserve my protection?

Quite of a sudden, the crowd outside seemed a threat not only to Father, but to me directly, to my future off-spring. 'Twas simpleminded of me to think I could dissuade evil in the marrying of Samuel. Yes, protecting those who'd signed their names to the round-robin was worth my sacri-fice, but would union with Samuel truly bring about good for all my days? Would my children bear the brunt of his ire, as I had with Father? Worse, would Samuel's tempera-ment be passed on to my own sons, a never-ending legacy of my own doing?

My thoughts were interrupted as Mother unlatched my window and leaned out into the cold air, the smoky scent of the mob's torches rising to us. "Pray, leave us be!" Her sobs filled the air. "Be gracious, I beg of you, on behalf of the tender sensitivities of me and my daughter."

I wish I could have called out to the men, told them of

my Patriot activities on the night of the tea party. Would they leave us then? Yet if they did, I would have Father to contend with. He would be apt to murder me himself.

Some of the men wore neckerchiefs tied about their noses and mouths to ward off the cold of the winter night, but a few faces were visible and seemed to soften at Mother's plea. I saw a couple confer with one another, jerk their heads up to the window where we stood watching in terror. Not all, but some. 'Twas enough to give me hope.

Yet while some were distracted by our plight, I watched in terror and disbelief as Father stuck his unsheathed sword through the window. The glimmer of the metal flashed quick before he thrust it within the breastbone of the nearest man.

At this violent turn, the crowd lost any thought of Mother's pleas and feminine sensitivities. They let out a mighty cry, almost animallike, and came upon the house like a swarm of angry bees. The sound of shattered glass and the scent of pitch from their torches filled the air, and I wondered if they intended to burn the house to ash.

I wished for Noah, then. He had saved us all from the mob at the Clarke house with his eloquent words and collected mind. Now, though, in part due to my actions, he was far away—mayhap no longer in the city.

I grasped Mother's hand and pulled her from the window, where men with ladders and axes prepared to invade our home through my chambers. I sought a weapon—something that could be used to defend us—but found nothing more than a paperweight.

Father barged through my door, the bloodied sword in

his hand. He glanced toward the window, the top of a man's head already appearing. "Come," he said, leading us to his chambers.

More breaking glass. Steps upon the stairs. My insides quivered with terror. We should not be here, any of us. Father's pride kept us here. We should have taken leave to Castle Island. Should have known 'twas only a matter of time before a volatile town turned a mob upon an arrogant man who ran amok with his mouth.

Behind the locked door of my parents' chambers, we huddled in a corner, Father muttering something about his musket in the parlor.

I closed my eyes and whispered a prayer for protection for us and the servants downstairs. My hands and arms shook where they wrapped around my middle. More cries of rowdy men, some slurred with drink from the Royal Exchange tavern, no doubt. The thud of more ladders, the terrifying shatter of glass in the very room in which we cowered, the wind sweeping in to chill us as the men entered.

A man took the neckerchief from his face, and a familiar face appeared before us. He caught me off guard with his kind smile, belying the violent evidence of the glass crushed at his feet.

"Greetings," he pronounced, tipping his tricorne hat.

"Mr. Russell, you make sport with this crowd?" Father said.

"We come as friends. We seek to speak with you, is all, Mr. Malcolm." He held out his hand to Father, and after only a moment's hesitation, Father shook it.

I couldn't understand the strange turn of events.

"I ask only that you hand over your sword," Mr. Russell said.

Father wavered slightly, yet what else could we do? The sound of splitting wood, of a hatchet at the locked door sounded to our left. Father and one pitiful sword were no match for the mob.

With a show of reluctance, Father pushed his sword into Mr. Russell's hand.

"You've made a wise choice, Malcolm." Mr. Russell turned and called toward the window, "He's unarmed, men!"

More men and boys rushed in through the window. A final hatchet blow dislodged the door, and bodies rushed in from that way also.

Many hands seized Father. I sank into the farthest corner with Mother, both of us clutching each other in terror and trying to muffle our cries as we watched the men beat Father with sticks and tie a rope round him. They lowered him out the window, his words of "Fie!" only seeming to fuel their task.

They left Mother and me alone, their sole quarry now taken. On trembling legs, we made our way past splintered wood and broken glass to the window of my chambers, whence we watched as the men placed Father on a waiting sled. Four men pulled him toward Middle Street, the rest of the crowd following, and the bob of their torches soon faded, leaving the street dark.

Mother and I stared at one another. Chloe entered, tears streaking her face. "I'm so sorry, ma'am. They were ruthless."

I grasped the dark hands of our servant. "Did they hurt you?"

She shook her head. "They didn't touch me. They only asked for Mr. Malcolm."

"Light some candles; get a fire going in the parlor. Stay there for the night." I donned my cloak, my hat, my warmest boots, and my muff.

"Where will you go?" Mother asked. Her hair came out of her mobcap. I wasn't sure I'd ever seen her so disheveled.

"To get help."

I didn't know what they planned to do to Father, but I could not stand by while the drunken mob doled out whatever madness they called justice.

✠

The night had never been colder, the harbor now frozen for two days. With quick steps, I headed toward the South End, slipping on the icy streets but continuing onward, knowing my only hope for help was the people I loved who had once lived on Auchmuty Street. Samuel would surely understand my need to help Father in this desperate moment. John and Noah had swayed an angry mob before—they could perhaps do so again. Mayhap the Fultons hadn't left Boston after all.

I would soon find out.

My petticoats dragged in the snow, weighing me down. I approached the center of town, lit with the torches of the crowd that had just left our home. The sickeningly pungent smell of tar reached my nostrils. I knew somewhere in the middle of the mob was Father, and I knew what the men planned to do to him. And though some would argue he deserved it, I did not think any living being could possibly deserve such treatment.

I rushed past where Father's clothes were tossed into the crowd. As I hastened toward Old South, I heard Father's cries and I knew the boiling tar was being smeared along his bare skin, that it cooked his flesh. Tears froze upon my cheeks as I changed my gait to a run, my boots slipping in the snow as I passed the Liberty Tree, its frozen branches a skeleton in the night.

When I finally reached Auchmuty Street, my breath wheezed in the cold. John and Sarah's house stood cozy as ever, candles lighting the windows. I approached the door, gasping, knocking frantically and calling out for John to answer.

The door opened, but an unfamiliar man stood before me. My heart dipped to the depths of my stomach.

"Can I help you, lass?"

"John Fulton . . . Sarah . . . are they not here?"

"The Fultons moved to Medford. We took over their rental at the beginning of the year. Is there something I can assist you with?"

I shook my head, backing away from the home where so many of my fond memories lay. No longer. While I had suspected John and Sarah had moved, I'd found meager comfort in not knowing for certain, imagining them on the other side of town should I want to see them again. And as much as I had hoped, for their safety, that they had gone to Medford, I couldn't help the feeling of abandonment that came over me.

They had truly left. Had Noah told them of Samuel and

the list? Did they realize that I had not betrayed them? Or had they left knowing I was to marry Samuel?

Sarah had claimed me a daughter. And yet she had left me alone.

I sniffed back tears, suddenly uncertain of everything.

I continued down Auchmuty toward the frozen harbor, past the distillery where John used to work, past the small beach where Samuel had accosted me with both hands and wits. The printing shop where Noah apprenticed stood on a nearby street corner, the shutters tight. I rapped on the door. No answer.

I turned away, dejected, knowing in my heart that Noah must have left with the Fultons to open his own printing shop in Medford. Hadn't I myself urged him to do so?

Foolish really, to cling to his words of finding a way for us. This was better.

Yet where had I to turn?

As I made my way back toward the Liberty Tree, I saw the mob approach, Father in a cart before them, shivering, a coat of feathers upon his skin. They stopped the cart before the tree, ordered Father to stand and curse the governor.

Now, more than ever, I could see that they did not aim simply to exact justice for the violence done Mr. Hewes that morning. While I knew the crowd held a political agenda in parading Father's tarred and feathered form around the streets, I saw also that Mr. Hewes had little to do with the justice meted out. For before the Liberty Tree, with Father shivering naked within his coat of feathers, Mr. Hewes pushed his own coat upon Father, no doubt taking pity on the man who had smashed him on the head with his cane just hours earlier.

Though I thought to put myself in the midst of the hissing mob, to beg them to stop the madness, I could not bear to face Father in his humiliation. And when he refused to curse the governor, instead letting out a hearty "God save the king!" I was reminded that his very stubbornness and crude spirit had put him in this predicament.

Still . . . not an ounce of honor rested in how they treated him.

My mind turned to Samuel then. Would they listen to him? Could, by some miracle, he help them see reason? While he was not liked by the mob, perhaps all they needed was a bit of persuasion. Samuel was respected in London. Would a voice of the crown be just enough to stop the crowd?

I tried not to think of the broadsides still posted upon the doors of Province House and the Town House, the Royal Exchange tavern, and other prominent places about town. A voice of the crown would likely not dissuade the mob, but rather anger them.

Even so, I must try.

I took off trudging through the snow again, heedless of being seen, of proper etiquette, back toward the center of town until I was before the Clarke house on School Street. I pounded my fist against the door, my limbs spent and aching. I saw a shadow at the window before it opened, a small fire within.

A man I recognized as a servant of the Clarkes' opened the door. I fell across the threshold. "Please, is Samuel here?"

Before the man could answer, I heard footsteps on the stairs and Samuel came into view.

"Emma? What in heaven's name are you doing here?"

"Please, Samuel, I need your help." I hated my groveling, yet if I could not run to my intended when my father's life was in danger, where else could I go?

"You are soaked to the bone. Come by the fire."

I welcomed the heat, tried not to flinch when Samuel drew the cloak from my shoulders and placed it upon a chair near the fire as the servant left the room.

"Wh-where are your parents?"

"Father and Mother left for Castle Island yesterday." Bitterness laced his words. Quite suddenly his demeanor and tone lacked the cocky luster I'd come to expect from him, but he covered it up quickly. "I was just about to settle in for a cozy night with a glass of port. Perhaps you'd like to join me?"

I shook my head. "Have you not heard the news? Father—they've taken him. Tarred and feathered him. I fear for his life."

Samuel's gaze traveled lazily over my body, then back to the window. "I'm sorry. There's naught to be done."

"Please—I've nowhere else to turn. Will you come with me . . . try to talk some sense into them?"

He laughed. The derisive sound seemed to shake the vacant house. "There is no sense when it comes to the rebels." Something in his features softened. "You could come with me, Emma. With the turn of events within the town, I fear I must leave. We could pack tonight. I could hide you away until the situation with your father is sorted out."

"I don't think—"

Samuel grasped my hands. "I know I've been harsh with you, but I do care for you. Come with me and we will see what comes of our circumstances." He ran a finger along my cold cheek and I tried not to cringe at his touch. Without warning, he ducked his head to mine, forced a hard kiss upon my mouth.

I pressed my hands to his chest, fear gripping my insides. His mouth left mine to roam lower, along my neck.

"No, Samuel . . . I must help Father."

"There is nothing we can do." His whiskers raked against the tender skin near my dress collar, his hands lingering at my waist.

With all the force I could muster, I pushed him from me. "No!"

All softness evaporated, a hard anger overtaking him as he stared at me.

But then, with the sudden quiet, the familiar sound of the mob came to us. "Please. They are nearby. Help Father, Samuel."

He strode to the window, pushed back the drapes. The raucous noise grew louder. He turned to face me. "They come this way. You sent them."

"What? No, no, I only wish for them to stop—to bring Father home."

The yells grew close, closer still. Unfamiliar terror came over the man before me. He lunged for his cloak, donned it. "Bartholomew!" He called for his servant, and when the man appeared, Samuel gave orders to ready for departure at once. He turned to me. "Come with me, Emma. You're no longer safe here. We must leave straightaway."

I shook my head. "No. I came for Father. I will not abandon him."

He shoved a hat upon his head. "Suit yourself. You would only make my travel slower, I suppose. I will return for you." He opened the door to the sound of conch shells and whistles, loud "Huzzahs!" at the sight of him and his servant. I went to the door, watched them run from the mob.

The mob did not pursue.

I stepped out into the cold, stopped two stairs above the crowd, held my hands up. "Please! Please, stop!"

They did not listen, and as I rushed to the front of the mob, averting my eyes from the cart that held my father, I near tripped on their many feet, near fell at the press of their bodies.

I yelled for them to stop, was pushed and shoved. I fell to the icy ground, felt the sharp edge of boots stomping upon my limbs and hair, loose from my mobcap.

Then arms lifted me off the street, and I was looking into the kind face of Mr. Hewes.

"Miss Malcolm, where is your cloak, lass? You must go home. It is no use, I've tried to stop them. Leave at once. You will only be injured. Your father has dug this grave for himself. I daresay there is naught to be done."

My bottom lip trembled, and I nodded as the men prepared to march.

Mr. Hewes was right. I had done all I could. I must retrieve my cloak and go home, fetch Dr. Warren if possible. Perhaps the mob would return Father to us. Perhaps he would still be alive.

I hurried back up the stairs, breath tight in my chest.

I shut the door against their madness, crept to the Clarkes' front window, and watched them pass, Father's stiff form in the cart paraded before them.

I closed my eyes, accepting that I could do no more, the ache of my frozen body testifying to this fact.

The sound of the jeering crowd fell away, and as the warmth welcomed me, I realized the circumstance I found myself in.

The Clarke home. Alone.

Noah had mentioned entering the home of his own accord to find the list. Never had we anticipated this opportunity would come to us. Fleetingly, I wondered if God had given us the miracle I'd prayed for—the one I scarce believed could be possible.

Fearful Samuel would return with the parting of the mob, I grabbed a candle, held it to the hearth. It came alive, bright in its polished holder, casting shadows on the papered walls of the Clarke parlor. I scurried up the stairs, searching out Samuel's chambers, praying he hadn't had the oath on his person when he fled.

There was nothing more I could do to help Father. But there might be something I could do to help Noah and the Fultons. There might be something I could do to change the course of my future.

CHAPTER SIXTEEN

Emma

In every human Breast, God has implanted a Principle, which we call love of Freedom; it is impatient of Oppression, and pants for Deliverance.

PHILLIS WHEATLEY

SAMUEL'S FAMILIAR SCENT of leather and bourbon hung heavy in the air as I ransacked his bureau. Whereas I'd felt only shock at the mob's treatment of Father, anger now settled in to replace it. Many men who'd smeared Father's skin with boiling tar had no doubt signed Noah's oath. I thought I recalled the name of Mr. William Russell—the very one who had been first to climb into our home on Cross Street.

I had little desire to protect them now. I acted only for Noah and the Fultons, for my own sake.

I searched beneath a shaving kit, a snuffbox, a few waist-coats and stockings. Knee buckles. A drawing of a woman in a rather provocative pose. With the amount of—or rather lack of—clothes she possessed, I assumed her to belong in a brothel of some sort.

Once again, a married life with Samuel flashed before my eyes. I hoped this was God's way of saving me from it.

Now, though, as I rummaged through his private things, I wondered if the oath was in the home at all. It could be in the warehouse. It could be on Samuel's person. It could be so well hidden I might never find it. My hopes sank as I continued searching to no avail.

After I'd looked through his chest of drawers, I opened a nightstand, then a small cupboard, then the drawers of his desk. Nothing.

I released a small cry of exasperation. I placed the candle upon the desk, ran a hand over my face. I closed my eyes beneath the cold of my palm, suddenly cognizant of the frozen, sodden petticoats clinging to my legs.

Was this out of my hands? Would nothing be gained? Samuel would return to Boston to fulfill his pledge to marry me. True, the Fultons and Noah were safe, but I couldn't ignore the hurt that they'd so easily abandoned me for Medford.

I dropped my hand to my side, opened my eyes before the flame of the candle. Light flickered to a crooked painting above the desk, an oil portrait of an older man, presumably a Clarke ancestor.

Perhaps, after this night of chaos and destruction, I sought only to set something to rights. No, it was certainly more than that. Some otherworldly tug on my heart, some holy whisper, prodded me to stretch out my hand and straighten the portrait. And as I did so, the corner of a paper slid from the bottom.

I gripped its edges and tugged, freeing it from the back of the frame.

I blinked twice, sure that the cold and exertion and terror of the last two hours had finally taken their effect.

The paper's folds spoke of the familiar, and my fingers trembled. I fumbled as I opened it, breathing an exhalation of gratitude at the names radiating out from the center, the words *Oath of Secrecy* in the middle.

I held it to my chest, each breath a prayer of thanksgiving, not bothering to stop the warm tear weaving its way down my frozen cheek.

Noah's oath. In many ways, the key to my freedom.

As I refolded the paper and placed it beneath my corset—the only warm, dry place on my body—I pondered the deep possibilities of a very real grace.

I thought of Father smashing Mr. Hewes upon the head, of striking a man outside our house with a sword, of belittling Noah the night he had escorted me home. I thought of the mob that had visited our home. Of Mr. Hewes, who no doubt wanted Father to face justice for what had been done to him, but who had taken pity on him and given up his own coat at the sight of Father naked and shivering. I thought of how good had been borne of this terrible night. Unplanned, perhaps undeserved, yet nevertheless real.

I took my leave of Samuel's chambers, donned my cloak and muff, and left the Clarke house, wondering what Father's fate—and mine—would be.

⨪

I had been home for well over an hour, attired in dry clothes and coaxing Mother from her worry with a cup of chocolate, when the mob returned. I rushed to the door and opened it against her warnings.

They did not stay this time. Rather, they pushed the cart by our house, rolling a lump of frozen tar and bloodied feathers off like a log upon a hill. I gasped at what I could only assume was Father, patches of skin exposed on his naked body, neck raw and bloodied, flesh mixed with tar.

From behind me, Mother cried out, then fainted straightaway onto the floor. Chloe went to her while I went to Father, unsure how to approach him in his humiliation. Scared to touch him, I knelt by his side, knowing not if he was alive.

"Father—Father, answer me!"

Mr. Hewes came beside me. He laid his cloak upon Father's lower half. "He is alive, though barely. I will help you get him inside."

I grabbed Father's legs, thankful he appeared unconscious. By the time we'd brought him into the parlor, Mother had roused and Chloe had laid several sheets upon our couch, then fetched more to cover Father.

Mr. Hewes left, promising to come back with Dr. Warren or Dr. Young, both Patriots but the only men of medicine left in town.

Mother, Chloe, and I flitted about Father, trying not to stare at the evidence of savagery before us. How could anyone—no matter their grievances—think it right to perform such travesty upon a person?

Mother sobbed as Father's frozen body began to thaw by the fire and he woke, his pain renewed as his tarred flesh began detaching from the rest of his body in strips, all of its own volition. She ended up running from the room, and I heard the sounds of her retching from down the hall.

I felt I would not be far behind.

When a grim-faced Dr. Warren returned with Mr. Hewes, he asked us to light as many candles as the room would hold, then urged us to retire for the night, assured us he would stay with Father and care for him until morning.

But when we made to leave the room to find a set of chambers which still had their windows, he called out, "Mrs. Malcolm."

We stopped at his summons, turned to face him. I could not help my gaze from landing on Father's scalded, peeling flesh, his bloodied neck from where they must have roped him mixed with bits of brown, thawing tar within the wounds.

Dr. Warren, too, glanced at Father, his handsome face a mask of worry. I knew him to run with the Sons. Friend of Mr. Adams and Mr. Hancock, he was a splendid orator, leader of the commemoration at Old South for those who had died in the massacre on King Street almost four years earlier. His wife had died two years earlier, leaving him one of the most eligible bachelors in town. And although he did not participate firsthand in the dumping of the tea, it was common knowledge that Dr. Warren was behind many of the activities of the Sons. Perhaps 'twas he who dubbed himself the chairman of the Committee for Tarring and Feathering.

But nay, the look of pity he now gave us, similar to Mr. Hewes's, did not match a man responsible for the ill-treatment of my father.

"I think we all know I do not share the same politics as

your husband—" he turned to me—"and your father, Miss Malcolm."

I nodded, felt the bold and intelligent eyes of the doctor on us, not a strand of the horizontal rolls of his hair out of place.

"That does not mean I condone what has been done Mr. Malcolm this night. Any grievance against him should have been settled in a court of law. This—" he gestured to where Father groaned in pain upon the sofa—"is inexcusable. And I am certain I am not alone in my thinking."

Mother nodded. She turned on her heel and rushed up the stairs. I stayed back, stirred by Dr. Warren's heartfelt words, relieved by them. For my heart still very much understood the cause of the Liberty Boys. The violence—the means by which they sometimes sought to achieve it—I did not.

So what was right? Which side did I choose? Was it all or nothing? Part of me wished to sit with Dr. Warren, explain to him my part in the dumping of the tea, the way my soul felt torn between both sides of this blasted conflict. I felt he might understand. That, no matter his political leanings, he was like Noah in his intelligent mind, willing and able to at least see the other side in conflict.

Instead, I simply granted him a curtsy. "Thank you, Dr. Warren. And thank you for caring for Father. I realize . . . I realize he is oft a difficult man, but he is still . . . ours."

Dr. Warren gave me a small smile, a dimple upon his clean chin.

"I will wake early. Mayhap you will break your fast with us and instruct me how to care for his wounds?"

Dr. Warren shook his head. "I will share breakfast with

you, but the tending of his wounds will be . . . unpleasant. 'Tis not suitable for a young lady. But rest assured, I will see to your father's recovery myself."

"Will he . . . will he live?"

"He's been to the gates of eternity and back. That he is still alive should give you hope. If infection does not set in . . . he may stand a fair chance."

"Thank you, Doctor."

I left him to go to my chambers. Shards of the window-pane lay scattered across the floor and I swept it up as best I could. Tomorrow, Mother or I would have to go into town to enlist help in either repairing the windows or having them boarded up.

I took Noah's oath from where it lay hidden beneath my bodice. In many ways, I felt like an African slave holding my papers of manumission.

I was free.

I slid the tea chest from beneath my bed, took the rag blanket from it. Before me lay the dark pine wood, and I ran my hand over its cold and sturdy surface, wondered what Noah did in that moment, wondered if he'd truly left thoughts of me for Medford so easily.

I placed the list at the bottom of the chest, beneath my story, and covered it with Sarah's blanket.

I was free. Free to leave and seek out Noah and the Fultons. Free to lead my own life once again, as I'd done for three glorious days in December. And now, with Father incapacitated, I could leave without fear of recompense or him chasing after me.

My words from two months earlier echoed in my head.

Oh, how it felt so much longer since that night Noah walked me home.

"Noah, tell me which is more honorable—loyalty or liberty?"

Still, after all I'd been through, I did not have an answer. While my heart longed to go to Medford, I knew I could not leave Father and Mother in this, their time of deepest need. Margaret had left for the country with her husband, anticipating the birth of their child. Could I live the remainder of my life knowing I'd deserted my parents? True, we did not see eye to eye on most things. But they were my family.

Yet if I stayed, was I in essence putting the shackles upon my own wrists? Would I regret the decision? On the other hand, how would I travel? I had no money to my name, nothing to call my own other than what lay in the tea chest.

My gaze landed on the fresh sheets of paper at the bottom of the chest, my heart chasing a rapid beat at the thought of sending a letter to Noah, of telling him the turn of events that left me with his oath.

Surely he would return for me. Yet what if Samuel returned first, found the oath gone before I could arrange to leave?

'Twould be easy to visit the *Gazette* tomorrow and request they post my letter while I was out looking for help to repair the windows. Neither Mother nor Father need know. I only hoped Noah would receive my letter before Samuel's return.

CHAPTER SEVENTEEN

Emma

The people should never rise, without doing something to be remembered—
something notable and striking.

JOHN ADAMS

THE NEXT AFTERNOON, upon returning from the *Gazette* to post my letter, I entered the parlor to tend the fire. Dr. Warren had taken his leave some hours ago, promising to return before nightfall. On the sofa lay Father's bandaged body.

The fire crackled from behind, and Father stirred. I wondered if I should fetch Mother. She had not come down from her chambers since last night.

I took a tankard from the Carolina tea table and poured some water in it from the pitcher nearby. I approached Father, his form restless, his breathing slight.

I leaned close, saw the pink of blood that soaked through the bandages along his arms and chest. The smell of rotting flesh and tar assaulted my nostrils. How could the Sons have done such a thing? And in the name of such a blessed thing as liberty?

"Father? Dr. Warren says you should have plenty of water. May I give you some?"

His eyes came open, his gaze set upon me.

I tried again. "Some water, Father?"

In a single motion that surprised me with its agility, he hit the water from my hand. The metal clattered to the floor, the water spilled upon the Oriental carpet. "I want nothing from you, disloyal whore."

I backed away. Was he having a dream, a delusion? "Father, 'tis me. Emma."

He laughed, mocking me, then clenched his teeth in what must have been pain from the exertion. I could not stop the tears that fell from my eyes.

"I know who you are and I demand you stay away from me. I don't need your help. Where were you to help when the Mohawks began this mess? You are disloyal—disloyal to your family and disloyal to your king. A whore. I wish I'd never laid eyes on you."

Rapid breaths fell upon me, and with what little strength my legs possessed, I ran from the room.

It had been a mistake to pity him. The man's heart was pure ice. Nothing could thaw it. He blamed me, his own daughter, for the wrong done him—not the Sons, not his own vile actions in hitting Mr. Hewes, in striking a man with his sword, in goading those who already held so much against him.

How could I live beneath his roof any longer? I wouldn't. I couldn't.

I'd been on my own once before. And though I'd had the help of Sarah and John and Noah, surely anything would be better than living beneath the roof of a man who despised me.

A few more days I would manage. By that time I would certainly hear from Noah. And if I did not, I would make my way on my own.

✠

Two days later I came downstairs to hear Dr. Warren and Father talking quietly in the parlor, the good doctor no doubt attending his wounds. Though Dr. Warren estimated it would be months before Father was well enough to be out of bed, he was to make a deposition to a town official the next day.

I had not yet heard from Noah. Surely he'd received the letter by now.

But I could wait no longer. The possibility of Samuel's return was too risky. Upstairs, my things were packed. I would leave that night, seek refuge at Sarah's mother's tavern. Mayhap she could arrange for my travel to Medford.

I paused at the door of the parlor, heard Father's familiar groans, then voices from within.

Dr. Warren's low, soothing voice, then Father's filled with pain and anger.

"Be sure to save a hunk of my flesh—feathers and all—as a trophy for me to bring back to the king."

"You can't be serious, Mr. Malcolm?"

"I'm very serious, Doctor. As soon as I am well enough, I will be paying a visit to him. Mayhap I will request a knighthood. A single Knight of the Tar, in fact . . . for I quite like the smell of it."

I leaned against the wainscoting outside the parlor, disbelieving my ears. I truly had been a fool to think Father's ordeal would soften his prideful heart. If the events of three nights earlier did not humble him, then nothing would.

And now I knew for certain: my family would be returning to London, quite likely to stay. I would not be going with them. I cared not if I had to take work at a tavern, I would not cross the vast breadth of the ocean only to put myself in chains on the other side of the sea.

My hope for reconciliation with Noah had been renewed, but as my letter seemed to have been met with silence, my hope dimmed darker and darker. I wondered how long before 'twould be snuffed out altogether.

✠

For the second time, I stole out of my own home as if I were a thief. My loot? The tea chest, the oath, the book Noah had gifted me and the cup Sarah had, a sparse amount of my belongings, and my stories I hadn't the heart to feed to the flame.

'Twas not as late this time. With Father immobile in the parlor and Mother making little appearance from her chambers, I slid easily from the house after all settled for the night.

I shut the door quietly and turned, the chest clutched to my middle. I gasped at the form of a man upon our steps.

He stood. "Emma."

I near dropped the chest of belongings at the sight of Noah, handsome as ever. The beat of my heart would not slow, seemed to take flight with itself. My arms grew weak. A lock of hair curled at his brow, sending my limbs quivering.

"Noah . . . you've come."

"Of course I've come. I told you I would not leave without a fight. I was in Medford, helping John and Sarah move when I heard news of your father. I just returned and came as soon as I could. I know it is a risk, but . . . I had to see you."

My heart near burst at his words. I placed the tea chest on the ground and fell into his arms. "You did not receive my letter, then?"

His brow wrinkled. "No. What news did you write?"

He hadn't abandoned me after all. Even when I'd asked him to. Even when there was no hope. "I will tell you, but we must leave. Now." I found his hand. "I have the oath, Noah."

His gaze widened beneath the light of the moon, and I took the opportunity of his silence to pick up the chest and thrust it into his arms. "'Tis here. It is our freedom."

He didn't ask for an explanation, rather tucked the chest beneath one arm and me beneath the other, led us toward the South End.

The snow had begun to melt, finding its way of escape through the cracks of cobbles along the crisscrossed streets of the town. We walked fast, clinging to one another. When we reached the printing shop where he apprenticed, I followed him in. He laid the chest down, worked to stoke the fire.

"Mr. Alves is in the next room," he explained quietly. "But tell me what has transpired—tell me everything."

I told him of the mob, how they had taken Father to be tarred and feathered, how I'd come for help and had sought Samuel in the end. How he had fled, leaving me alone, how

I had pleaded with the mob, and how, miraculously, I had found Noah's oath behind the portrait.

He grasped my arms as I finished the story, wet his lips, excitement emanating from every part of him. "This is it for us then, Emma. Our chance. The Lord has delivered us, and we mustn't hesitate."

I nodded, catching his enthusiasm.

"And your parents? Are you certain you are ready to part with them?"

"Aye. I was ready to part before I knew you were on my doorstep." I thought of Mother and Father, of the harshness of Father's words, calling me unspeakable names. "I have loved them the best I know how. But I do not feel I could ever stay in the chains they demand of me. When I saw that list, when I realized I could be set free, I felt something bigger—Someone bigger—was calling me to it. I am fully ready to begin anew, with you."

He pulled me closer, inch by inch, then swept a stray hair from my face. He leaned down and kissed my temple, trailing his mouth to the corner of mine, where he spoke. "Will you marry me as soon as we are able to find a preacher, then? Now that we are together, I don't want to chance anyone tearing us apart."

"Yes," I breathed. He dipped his head to mine then, moved his lips over my own, drawing me in with a restrained hunger that I felt just beyond his gentleness.

This was what love was. My heart sang with gratitude for the gift.

Finally we parted, both of us unsatisfied with the too-brief moment. "If I thought it safe, I would wake the reverend from his sleep this minute. But we should leave early tomorrow for Medford, at first light. Sarah and John will keep you until we can be married. I will find us a home and open my shop, and while it may be meager, I will work my fingers to the bones if it means supporting you. If it means having you as my wife."

I felt as if I would float on air the rest of my days. This was all I imagined and more. He kissed me again, and though it took all of our strength to part, I felt I could live on the anticipation of the rest of our lives together for the small hours until I would become his wife.

Noah made up a bed of straw for me between the hearth and the press, told me he would wake me early, then gave me one last sweet kiss. "I am overcome with gratitude this night." His eyes shone and I felt mine smarting as well.

As I settled against the straw, I realized that had Father not been tarred and feathered, this moment would not be. Quite likely I would yet be planning a wedding to Samuel.

I remembered a Scripture verse I'd heard from the pulpit at one time, how it had struck me as odd and almost nonsensical, but how in this moment it seemed to make perfect sense.

"Ye thought evil against me; but God meant it unto good."

As Noah left to go to his bed, I breathed in the toasty air of the fire, my chest light.

God meant it for good.

I closed my eyes, sank into the knowing that a Creator cared for me enough to arrange the events of the past month. Overwhelming certainty and love flowed through my being, and I clutched it, begged for this holy presence to never leave my side.

Sounds of men cheering came from the direction of the Liberty Tree, and I pulled the quilt tighter around me, grasped on to the promise of peace I'd just felt, trying—very hard—to ignore the growing tumult right outside Noah's door.

CHAPTER EIGHTEEN

Hayley

THE HOLLOWNESS of the phone's ring sounded in my ear. He wouldn't answer. Certainly he had better things to do. And yet the thought of sharing my find with Ethan—of sharing what appeared to be a legitimate historical document that had been right under our noses—caused me to hold the phone tighter to my ear.

"Hello?" The sound of tinkling glassware echoed in my ear alongside a woman's soft laughter. Words froze on my tongue.

"Hayley? What's up?"

"Nothing," I mumbled. "I should have texted you. I'm sorry to interrupt."

Then I hung up.

I paced the kitchen. Stupid. I was stupid. He'd said some

nice things, wanted to clear up the past, but that didn't mean he wasn't already well past it. He'd been *married*, after all. His wife had died years earlier, and he dated.

I'd interrupted his date.

Stupid, stupid, stupid.

I shook my head, looked at the paper I'd pulled from the bottom of the chest. It had lost its luster in my mind, its sparkling possibilities.

I didn't need Ethan, or any man, to come alongside me in this endeavor—this search for the remarkable. I could, and would, do this on my own. Hadn't I always prided myself on just that?

I brought the paper, slivers of wood still attached, to the dining room table and flipped on the light. I googled one of the signatures on the right side of the list. Henry Bass.

Nothing but a couple of personal pages. I added the word *historical* at the end of his name and tried again. An ancestry page and some historical town pages appeared. I scanned the list again, the first result causing my heart to pick up speed.

Henry Bass—Boston Tea Party Ships and Museum.

I clicked on the result, found a two-sentence page stating Henry had been a merchant from Boston who had participated in the Boston Tea Party. He died in 1813.

I stared at the two sentences. Could this oath actually have something to do with this history? I thought of the chest, my contemplations jumping ahead to what it could have been used for. No way.

I began typing in the next name, but a harried knock came at my door.

I left my phone on the table, peered through the peephole before opening it.

An apology flew from my lips, this time sincere. "I'm so sorry, Ethan. I didn't mean to interrupt—I shouldn't have called."

His chest heaved. "What's wrong? The way you hung up—I thought . . ."

I would not blush. "I felt bad about taking you away from . . . whatever you were doing."

"I was having dinner. No biggie. Why'd you call?"

I looked back at the chest lying on its side on the kitchen island. "We can talk about it when you have more time. Maybe I can stop by your shop tomorrow? Really, go back to whatever you were doing. We'll talk tomorrow, okay?" I started to close the door, but he stopped it with his hand.

"Hay, I wasn't doing anything. And I'm done with dinner, so why don't you tell me what's going on?"

I wondered if his date was waiting for him outside. I looked back at the chest again. "You sure?"

"Yeah. Let me in already, will you?"

I allowed him entrance. His gaze landed on the chest, the splintered pieces of wood on the laminate counter.

"I dropped it. It was dark and I don't know the apartment well . . ."

"You dropped it . . . then ripped it to pieces?"

"I saw something in the bottom after it fell. A paper wedged in there. I took it apart." I brought the brittle piece of parchment from the dining room and handed it to him. "Look."

He scanned it, flipped it over. Scanned it again. "This was in the bottom?"

I nodded. "It's legitimate, right? I mean, the thing is *old*."

He shook his head. "This is amazing. It looks authentic. But what is it? And why was it at the bottom of the chest?"

I stepped closer, caught up in his excitement. "It says it's an oath, but it's hard to read the rest of the writing in the middle. I looked up one of the names. Some information about the Boston Tea Party came up, but I was going to see if the same came up for the others."

He sat at the table, nodded toward my phone. "Let's check it out."

I googled the name below Henry Bass's. George Hewes. A Wikipedia entry stated that George Robert Twelves Hewes (August 25, 1742–November 5, 1840) was a participant in the political protests in Boston, including both the Boston Massacre and the Boston Tea Party.

I typed in the next name, tried to rein in my excitement. John Fulton. There were more entries this time, but still, at the bottom of the page was one relating to the Tea Party. "This is amazing. This paper must have to do with the Tea Party, then, right?"

Ethan took out his phone, began googling more names.

We spent the next hour searching each, reporting our findings to one another. More often than not, we'd find a record tying the name to the Tea Party.

"Hey, look." Ethan showed me the screen of his phone. "I knew it looked familiar, but I can't believe I didn't realize why."

I took his phone, scanned the page on the Boston Tea

Party Ships and Museum website titled "A Box Worth Keeping." There, at the top, was a close-up picture of a tea chest found the morning after the Tea Party. A chest that looked nearly identical to the one on my counter.

"No. Way." I breathed the words, a lucid sort of magic heavy in the air. "You think this was actually a chest that was dumped that night?"

Ethan scrolled through his phone. "There are two still in existence. One on display at the Boston Tea Party museum. The other at the Daughters of the American Revolution Museum in DC."

"And maybe this one."

His mouth pressed into a thin line.

"You don't think it is?" I asked.

One corner of his mouth inched up in half a smile. "I guess I've learned the hard way. When something seems too good to be true, it usually is."

I tore my gaze from his, suddenly uncomfortable. "Let's keep looking," I said, my voice soft.

We worked together until we'd gone through as many of the names as we could make out among the nearly 120 of them. Not all of them yielded an entry pertinent to the Tea Party, but at least three-quarters of them did.

Ethan and I sat back, the paper between us.

"This is an oath they took, then? Maybe something having to do with dumping the tea? It has to be."

Ethan let out a short breath. "It seems it is, but we have to check it out. The smaller text in the middle is hard to read. You okay with me bringing this to my appraiser tomorrow? He'll be able to tell us if there's a chance any of it is authentic."

"Of course. Maybe he can tell us what the words in the middle say." I dug through the kitchen drawers until I found a gallon-size freezer bag. I held it open while Ethan slipped the paper inside.

"We might have to hand it over to the museum, Hayley. Finding out if this is authentic could cost thousands of dollars. I don't know how much the Navy pays you, but my antique shop isn't going to be able to foot that bill."

I nodded. "Let's see what your guy says. Call me tomorrow?"

He smiled and I realized how natural it seemed for him to be here. Comfortable. As if we hadn't been apart for six years.

He hefted the chest into his arms. "Hate to take your present back, but you can pick something else in the shop if you want."

"No way, Gagnon. That chest—and the list—is mine. I'm letting you borrow it, is all—got it?"

He laughed. "Got it. But I'll have you know I have a moral obligation to hand it over to the museum if my appraiser thinks it's the real thing."

"It doesn't mean we can't do some investigating first, right?"

"You really want me in on this with you?"

I thought to throw out a witty, sarcastic comment. Something about only wanting him for his connections and historical insight, but looking at him, the chest beneath the crook of his arm, his head tilted endearingly to the side, I couldn't thrust the joke from my mouth.

"You're the one who obtained it in the first place. You're a part of this too."

He smiled. "You bet I am. Makes me wonder about the previous owners, though. They didn't realize what they had."

I stared at the chest, nodded. "What's the story behind it all, right?"

"If it's authentic, you mean."

"Why would someone go through the trouble of forging an oath like that, then hide it in the bottom of a chest never to be seen again? It has to be real."

He didn't look convinced, but I could tell he didn't want to squash my hopes.

I recognized something in him, then. Something I hadn't seen in him in high school. Something that made me sad.

Defeat.

The world had worn on Ethan, I saw that now. He had a weathered look about him as if afraid to hope for too much. I wondered at the disappointments life had dealt him. The death of his wife, perhaps the death of a career. He'd claimed to be making the best of it, but were those just words of bravado? What lay beneath them? And why did I feel guilty that maybe, just maybe, years ago, I'd contributed to that hopeless look, that shadow of defeat?

CHAPTER NINETEEN

Hayley

THE VOICE ON THE OTHER end of the phone caused unexpected tears to poke my eyelids.

I pushed them back. Tough and tears didn't mix. I think Uncle Joe had told me that once.

"Hey, kid. I got your text and I had a minute."

He was probably on some top secret mission. Soon I would be alongside him, soon we would share a camaraderie of serving our country in the most elite division of the United States military.

"Thanks for calling, Uncle Joe," I said.

He swore softly. "Kid, I think it's great you're back home. And you know Lena—you never can tell, she just might surprise you."

"You think it's crazy I feel I have to see her before BUD/S?"

"No. I think you're doing everything you can to prepare, and that's smart."

His words soothed my soul, even as I wanted to push back at them, reach for deeper assurance.

"You know, kid, if any woman can make the team, it's you. I'm sure of that. But remember, this life . . . yeah, I wouldn't trade it for the world, but it takes everything. Most of the guys who were married are on their way to divorce, either that or their wives are warming the beds of other men. And their kids? Forget it. They're almost strangers. Some of them can hold it together, I guess, but for most of us, it's a dead-end road. And if we have to choose, we choose the team. Always the team."

I thought of Uncle Joe's own brief, failed marriage. I had never prioritized such things in my life. A spouse. Marriage. Family.

For a fleeting second, I thought of Ethan, of how my life might have played out if I'd stayed in Massachusetts all those years ago, if I hadn't enlisted in the Navy. Would Ethan and I have gotten married? Had children? The thought was so preposterous, so out of sync with anything I'd dreamed before, that I cast it aside.

Who would I have become if not for the Navy? Military life was hard, but it had made me strong. It had given me the gifts of independence, knowing I was capable, and a dependable family. It had stripped down the distraction of outside forces and in many ways, simplified my priorities to what I knew I could count on—myself and my team.

I recalled Ethan leaving the night before, the tea chest beneath his arm. I still hadn't heard from him, and though I hated to admit it, I looked forward to his voice on the other end of the phone as much as I looked forward to any information he'd found.

Yet a relationship? It could never work. Ethan would never understand the part of me that would always long to be free. Independent. If I were to ever marry, it would no doubt be to a military man, not a civilian, someone who respected my need to fly free, someone who understood my near-obsessive commitment to my Navy family.

"When you gonna go and see her?" Uncle Joe asked.

"I tried to yesterday. She's in *Barbados*." Bitterness dripped over my words, and I hated myself for it.

Uncle Joe didn't take the bait. "Tell her I said hi."

"Sure."

A sigh from him. "You're ready, kid. You don't have to be afraid to face your past if you're certain of what you're about now."

He was right. In a way, it was why I'd come back home in the first place. To prove I'd conquered my troubled childhood. To prove I was beyond it all—to myself, yes, but maybe also to Lena.

"Thanks, Uncle Joe."

"Text anytime, kid. I'm praying for you."

We hung up and I stared at the phone screen until it went black.

I'd always chosen to believe that pain made you stronger. That growing up with Lena had made me more resilient, more mentally capable. Had I twisted my circumstances around to force something positive from them?

Uncle Joe's words came back to me.

"You don't have to be afraid to face your past if you're certain of what you're about now."

I knew what I was about. I was about serving my country and my team. I was about strength and determination and not letting anything hold me back.

Why then did Ethan's image, tea chest beneath his arm, pop back into my mind? Why did it make me doubt, maybe for the first time, if all of that was enough?

CHAPTER TWENTY

Hayley

THE BELL ABOVE the door of Revere Antiques called a greeting when I opened it. A smattering of customers perused the downstairs clutter.

Ethan had called not ten minutes ago, asking me to come down, said he thought he had some answers about the oath. And while I convinced myself it wasn't desperate to show up so soon—I'd already completed a ten-mile run that morning—there was a small part of me that couldn't reconcile the contradiction: training to save my country from its most dangerous threats, yet practically jumping out of my skin over a phone call.

I would sort it all out soon enough. I had twenty more days before I reported for BUD/S—plenty of time to tame my mind. I had this under control.

"Hello." An older woman in a flowered blouse—Braden's

grandmother, I assumed—called out from behind the front counter.

"Hi. I was looking for Ethan?"

"I think he's upstairs."

I smiled my thanks and went around the corner, lightly jogging up the stairs, the burn in my muscles familiar and satisfying.

When he heard me, Ethan turned from a crouching position in front of a Radio Flyer wagon. "Hey, Hay."

I rolled my eyes. "You always were a bit of a dweeb—you know that, right?"

He smiled, his jovial mood infectious. "Is that why you first went out with me? Sympathy date?"

I tried to suppress a smile. "Something like that."

I'd first met him in a co-ed gym class. Four-hundred-meter run. I'd finished before all the boys.

All except one.

That was the draw for me—not his intellectual mind or National Honor Society grades. It was because he was the one guy I couldn't beat in a race.

He'd teased me often after that, mostly in the halls in passing. I could still remember his tousled hair, just a bit too long. The way he would pass my locker and lean down. "Let me know when you want a rematch, Ashworth."

I'd push him away in a flirty kind of way, something foreign for me until that moment. I remember him winking at me. That wink sent heat deep into the pit of my belly and then all the way down to my toes.

He'd smiled, leaned closer again. "I don't push girls, but it's nice to know I can outrun you if I need to."

I scowled at him, actually enjoying the attention. Most boys looked past me. Except on the track, I was good at blending in. But Ethan . . . for whatever reason, I had earned my way onto his radar.

"Seriously, Ashworth. You want to run together sometime? I'm thinking about joining the cross-country team at Framingham this fall, and I need a training partner. You interested?"

I hadn't said yes right away. He'd asked several more times before I finally gave in.

He stopped calling me "Ashworth" after our second run. He'd asked me to the movies on our fourth. By that summer, we were seeing each other every night after our respective workdays—me as a lifeguard, him running the go-karts at the rec center.

I sighed, blinked. We were a long way from cross-country and go-karts, high school and first loves. We were adulting it now, forced to live in the world even if we didn't feel quite ready or "grown-up" enough for what the world brought us.

"So what did your guy say?" I held my breath. If Ethan's appraiser deemed the chest a fake or simply an old relic without a significant past, where did that leave us? And why did the answer to that question bother me?

"He said he can't be 100 percent sure without taking chemical samples, but based on the artwork, the script of the letter, the deterioration of the wood and the type, which seems true to the time of colonial Boston, he said it all seems authentic, including the paper."

"No way."

"Way." That contagious smile again. He truly was the king of corniness.

"So what now? You want to bring it to the museum, is that it?"

"I think it's the only right way to go about this, don't you? If they think it's real, they'll put the money behind it to find out. And as far as the oath, they have the top historians in the country at their disposal to figure it all out. What do we have?"

"Us," I said, the word sounding ten times more intimate than I'd meant it to.

He caught my gaze. "We have to hand it over, Hay. For the sake of historical preservation."

"Seems it's been preserved pretty well all these years without the bigwigs behind it." I closed my eyes, shook my head. "Yes, you're right—of course you're right. I was just excited about figuring out the story, you know? Maybe we can hold off bringing it for a little bit?"

This was crazy. *I* was crazy. How did I think I had time to solve a mystery in the middle of training to be a SEAL?

He shifted from one foot to the other. "I don't know. . . . It feels like a big responsibility to hold on to something with so much potential value."

"Two weeks, Ethan. I have to be in California in twenty days. Let's give ourselves fourteen days to find what we can find. Besides, I could use the distraction." Was I really inviting him into this with me? Did I really want to spend more time with this man who seemed to draw me into the past, who created feelings as rocky as a trawler in the teeth of a storm?

"Let me get this straight. You want me to risk one of the

greatest finds of this year—probably of this century, definitely of *my* life—so you can have a *distraction*? What about your training? Hayley, what about Lena?"

"There'll be time for all that. If anything, it will help my discipline. I need to use both my mind and my muscles, and this will be a great project for that."

He raked a hand through his hair, his short-sleeved shirt pulling upward to show tanned biceps. "Ten days."

I stuck out my hand. "Deal."

He broke into a grin, gripped my hand. "You're not the only one excited. I've been waiting for a find like this since I took over the store. Crazy that it was right under my nose. I want to find out what's behind that chest too."

My breaths came fast. For the first time since I'd gotten accepted into BUD/S, I felt . . . alive. Was it the history surrounding the tea chest, the fact that finding it with Ethan seemed like so much more than coincidence, or was it only as I claimed—simply a matter of distraction? Maybe all I was doing was procrastinating about seeing my mother.

And yet something deep within niggled. As if it were so much more than distraction or procrastination. As if it were the feel of his hand in mine, the personal history winding around us and between us, beckoning us back to another time and place. I'd told myself once that it had all been a lie. That for me, real love would never exist. But now, with my hand warm within his own, I faced the possibility that for Ethan, our love, though young, had never been a lie.

I took my hand from his, ready to grasp at something else. Anything else. I ignored my skin, warm from his touch. "So what's the next step? Did your appraiser say anything else?"

He pointed to the stairs. "I'll show you."

The shop had emptied. The woman behind the counter took cash from a couple holding an old decorative sign shaped like a cow that read, "Be Healthy. Drink Milk."

The couple finished their transaction and left. Ethan gestured to the woman. "Hayley, this is Ida, my one and only loyal employee."

I shook hands with Ida. Her palm was cool. Her glasses slipped down her nose and she pushed them up to her graying brows. "You're the young woman who helped my Braden, aren't you?"

"That's her," Ethan said.

Ida threw fleshy arms around me, pinning me in a tight embrace. I stood frozen, patient while she finished the hug. "I've been thanking the Lord you were there when you were." She pulled away. "Thank you, dear. Thank you."

I shifted from one foot to the other, uncomfortable. "No problem, really. That undertow was brutal, though. It really wasn't Ethan's fault."

"I'm sure it wasn't. I'm just thankful all is well." She turned to Ethan. "I'm going to head out now, boss. We did good today. Sold your last walnut round table, with a request for five more from a restaurant owner in Boston. Looks like you got your work cut out for you."

I perused the shelves of military paraphernalia near the counter to allow them to talk business.

"Thanks, Ida. I have a proposition for you."

"I'm listening."

"You were going away at the beginning of August to see your family, weren't you?"

"That's right."

I walked farther away from them, felt like an intruder, but still listened to Ethan's voice. I studied a clock made out of wood planks, the numbers roman numerals.

"Any chance you could take over the daily running of the shop for the next week? Open and close, keep up with the orders as best you can?"

My stomach fluttered. Was Ethan taking the time off for me? For the chest, rather?

"I suppose so—"

"I was thinking a fair trade would be an extra paid two weeks off in August. What do you think?"

"That sounds mighty fine to me, but August is busy, Ethan. Can you do without me?"

"If you can manage without me for the next week . . ."

"Okay, let's give it a shot."

I could hear the smile in Ethan's voice. "Great. I'll come in early tomorrow and go over a few things. I'm not going far, so I'll only be a phone call away."

"Okeydokey. I'll talk to you then."

I smiled and waved good-bye to Ida as she bustled out the door. Ethan locked it behind her, flipped the sign so it read Closed.

"Nice lady," I said.

"She's the best. After Allison died, her parents tried to stay on with the shop, but it was too much for them. I'd met Ida at church. She'd just lost her husband to a long battle with cancer and was looking for a way to fill her time. We just fit together well."

I swallowed. "What happened to Allison's parents?"

"They moved down to Florida. Wanted to get away from the memories."

"And you kept the shop running."

"It was a healing thing at first, felt like a way to keep her alive." He sighed, looked around the crammed shop. "She loved this place, grew up here."

I wanted to ask if he ran the shop for his wife's memory alone, if any part of him truly felt passionate about it, but it all seemed too invasive.

"Is it hard for you to be here still? You know . . . because of her?" I wondered if it was odd for him that I should be here now, his old girlfriend.

"It was at first. I guess it still is in some ways. But I've also changed the shop a lot too. Added original pieces, made it my own. Somewhere along the way it stopped being Allison's parents' shop, or even Allison's shop—it became mine." The tender way he spoke left no doubt in my mind that he didn't run the shop only for his dead wife. Listening to him, trying to understand him better, I felt happy for all he'd accomplished, for all that was ahead of him.

"So what did you want to show me?"

"Right." He knelt behind the desk and picked up the chest, placed it with care on the front counter. He scooped up a photocopy on the inside of the chest, showed it to me. "My appraiser was able to scan the list, play around with some of the color and contrast settings with his editing software. Look."

I took the paper. The list was blown up and darkened to magnify the center of the paper. The words that were illegible last night beneath the heading *Oath of Secrecy* were now clear.

Bound together in secrecy, we pledge our silence for the cause of the colonies. If any man should break this silence or bear witness against his brother, he forfeits the right to honor and will subject himself to publik ridicule, claiming himself an enemy to his country. Each signer agrees to vandalize no property save tea, to commit no mayhem, and to guard this secret until his dying breath.

"Wow," I breathed. "Serious stuff."

Ethan nodded. "I knew the destroyers of the tea took an oath of secrecy, but I never thought they went so far as to sign their names to paper. Seems that would be incriminating."

I placed the paper back inside the chest. "And yet it would be something to hold them accountable. A solid proof of honor in a time when a man's honor was everything."

"I did more research online last night. There's a list of participants, numbering around 115. Most did indeed remain anonymous for years after the dumping of the tea, not only scared of punishment but fearful of ridicule long after our country was founded. Destroying private property wasn't looked at as something honorable by all. George Washington himself condemned the dumping of the tea. So yes, it was a matter of honor—an honor to keep their secret, but also a possibility of ruining their good names if found out."

I shook my head. "I don't get it—didn't Sam Adams and all them put these guys up to this? Wasn't this the Patriots' doing?"

"It was. But the Patriot leaders—Sam Adams, John Hancock, Josiah Quincy, and the like—were very careful to disassociate themselves from the men who dumped the tea. From what I read, they went as far as to have an alibi, staying at Old South meetinghouse well past the hour when the tea would have been dumped."

"So they got these men to do their dirty work."

Ethan laughed. "I think they were eager to do the work, but let's try to find out ourselves."

I leaned my arms on the counter, pressed the toe of my flip-flop backward on the wood floor, causing the separation between my toes to press into my skin. "Where do we start?"

"I think we should visit the museum. Get a better feel for what we're dealing with. Then I'd like to take a trip to Medford, where I bought the chest in the estate sale. Maybe we could find someone who could tell us the history of the family. I mean, why didn't they know this was hidden in the chest? And who on this list was a part of their family, if anyone?"

Though my heart quaked at the mention of my hometown, I knew he was right.

I looked at the chest, worn and not incredibly pretty, but precious all the same. What had it been through? Out of all those names on that list, would we ever find which one belonged to the chest? And if we did, would we find the story behind it all?

"I'm in, of course," I said.

"Great. Tours start at ten. Eight thirty too early for me to pick you up?"

I raised my eyebrows. "You clearly have never been on a ship. Eight thirty is practically midday for me."

He laughed, looked at me with those piercing green eyes

again as if he were trying to see beyond me, as if he searched for clues not just to the historical mystery before us, but to the life I had lived without him.

Maybe I only flattered myself to think so. Maybe I thought such things because I was wondering about him, too. Wondering how he'd met Allison, wondering how her death still affected him. He'd said things were complicated when she died—what did that mean?

I had the next ten days to find out.

CHAPTER TWENTY-ONE

Hayley

I LOOKED DOWN at the card the woman in colonial costume handed me. Ethan and I sat in a pew, the room with wide windows crammed with other tour guests, a single pulpit raised before us and off to the side. We'd been given a feather upon entering the Boston Tea Party museum—this room being a simple replica of Old South meetinghouse.

The name on my card dubbed me Joseph Shed, a forty-one-year-old carpenter who had helped with the reconstruction of Faneuil Hall. The card stated some men disguised themselves at Joseph's residence before dumping the tea.

I looked at Ethan's card: Joseph Lovering, a fifteen-year-old who snuck out past his curfew to join those at Griffin's Wharf.

"Do you remember either of their names from the list?"

Ethan shook his head. "There were so many."

Neither rang a bell for me either.

The tour started and the woman who gave us the cards introduced herself as Frances Gore Crafts, wife of Thomas Crafts, one of the Loyal Nine who had participated in the Stamp Act riots. She stated how her husband was recently accused of being a Tory over his hesitation to aid in violent protests. She told us of her own father being loyal to the king, and though the political tension in their home was great, she had chosen to stand on the side of liberty, believing something must be done to make their voices heard.

Samuel Adams came to the pulpit amid a chorus of "Huzzahs!" He explained the dilemma of the tea that must not be unloaded, how one of the owners of the ships had gone to see Governor Hutchinson to ask that the tea be returned to England.

The costumed Sam Adams effectively riled up the crowd with reminders of the colony's own losses in the French and Indian War, the Boston Massacre, being taxed without the same rights as Englishmen.

The meeting ended with information that the merchant had returned with the governor's refusal of the colonists' requests. More groans and shouts of "Fie!" before we saw our only option before us: dump the tea.

We made our way onto the ship, the cool breeze from Boston Harbor serving to sweep away the stickiness of the hot air. Some of the kids dumped "chests" of tea tied to the ship. We toured the replica of the *Dartmouth*, full of hogsheads and tea chests marked with the East India logo. A guide explained to us how the Tea Party members would haul the chests up to the deck of the ship, hack open the chests, which were protected by a lead lining, scoop firmly packed tea leaves into the harbor, then destroy the chests as best they could and throw them in the water alongside the tea. With such destruction, I didn't see how a tea chest from the night of December 16, 1773, could possibly still be intact today.

My hopes that our chest—the one Ethan and I discovered—had actually been involved in the dumping of the tea faded. What were the chances?

We climbed the stairs of the ship, following the crowd into the back of the museum.

Before I could ask Ethan his thoughts, we rounded a dark corner and came face-to-face with a beautiful cylindrical display case. Inside sat a chest similar to the one we'd found. Lights shone down upon the circling artifact, so obviously old and worn, whispering a hundred historical secrets.

I grabbed Ethan's arm in my excitement. We'd known it was here, had seen pictures of it online, but being in the same room as such a relic of history assured me that if this one survived the dumping, no doubt there could be another.

He rested his hand over mine and squeezed, the gesture natural.

Our guide explained how the chest on display had been discovered by a young John Robinson on a beach near Dorchester Heights on the morning of December 17, 1773. It had stayed in the family for seventy years until it was passed to a distant family member as a thank-you gift. The chest was passed down within the family—even used as a bed for kittens at one time—until finally, it landed in the hands of a Helen Ford Waring, who would begin a ten-year quest to weave together the provenance of the relic.

The group filed out of the room, but Ethan and I lingered, watching the chest—identical to ours save for a marking on the bottom—as it revolved inside the case.

"Ten years it took her to piece together the history of her chest. Guess we're a little arrogant to think we're going to figure it all out in ten days, huh?" I said.

Ethan smiled. "Ahh, but we're millennials. Helen didn't have the technology of the twenty-first century." He led the way out of the room and into another. Our group stood to watch a documentary depicting the beginnings of the American Revolution in colonial Boston.

These were ordinary men—and women, too, no doubt. Their portraits scrolled by; their voices were brought to life in reenactments. They risked their reputations, their property, their families, their lives. Here I was, trained by the military, prepared for war, yet the thought left me shaken. It was so much more than tea.

Ethan and I grabbed a couple of hot dogs at Quincy Market, then walked back to the parking garage. As we drove north to Medford, I felt myself detaching from the quest of the tea chest, instead focusing on all the personal history that lay in Medford for me.

The Mystic River flowed sparkling to our right, and we passed the Mexican restaurant I'd worked at for one cold high school winter. My skin seemed to crawl along me, and I wondered if this town made me crazy, if it was something in my blood—in Lena's blood—that associated Medford with poison.

"Your folks end up going to Arizona?" I asked, grasping for diversion.

"Yep. After I graduated. Dad got a job with a good company in Phoenix."

"And you stayed here, went to Framingham." That had been his plan when I'd left at least.

"I did."

I forced my thoughts outside myself. "Is that where you met Allison?"

"Yeah, I bumped into her running down a Frisbee near Linsley Hall."

I didn't know how to respond to this piece of information. I wanted to know more, though I wasn't sure why. Commenting on how romantic running into his future wife with a Frisbee was didn't seem to make the cut of possibilities.

"You must have hit it off to get married so quick." As soon as the words were out, I wanted to snatch them back.

Ethan gave me a sideways glance as we turned right on Powder House Road. I breathed easier as we headed up the hill, to a more affluent part of town than I grew up in.

"Maybe too quick."

I returned his glance.

He shrugged. "I don't know if I really believe that, actually. Lots of couples get married fast and hold lasting marriages."

I kept quiet, any question I could think to form seeming too intrusive. Instead, I let his comment hang between us.

He pulled his Ford to the side of the road and put it in park before a For Sale sign. He reached over to the glove box and pulled out the freezer bag with the paper I'd found in the chest. His arm brushed my knee. "We're here."

I didn't move to get out of the car, waited an extra second to see if he would comment more on our conversation, but he opened the door of the Ford.

Guess not.

We walked up a cobblestone path to a Victorian cape with scalloped eaves. A full-length screen door was the only thing between us and the inside of the house. From within, a baby's happy babbling echoed in a room filled with boxes.

Ethan rang the bell. A woman in her thirties came from within, red hair in a kerchief, a purple T-shirt and workout pants on. "Hello."

"Hi, ma'am. We're sorry to bother you, but I was here for your estate sale and I had a question."

"All sales are final, I'm afraid." Her mouth pulled downward, revealing faint lines in the corners.

"No—no, I don't want to return anything. You see, I purchased an old tea chest about this big—" Ethan gestured with his hands—"for my antique store. Long story short, we found an old paper in the bottom that seems to be authentic. We're trying to solve a little mystery and thought to start here."

The baby started crying and the woman looked at us, vacillating. "Why don't you have a seat on the porch and I'll join you in a minute with my little guy." She disappeared back inside.

Ethan and I lowered ourselves onto a rather rickety-looking porch swing. It creaked when we tested our weight on it. When it didn't break, we slowly sat, relaxing into the worn wood.

Ethan pushed slightly with his Vans, the freezer bag in his

lap. The baby stopped crying and the sound of a wind chime came to us from the corner of the porch—a deep, melodic call. Poppies hung heavy beyond the porch, the burden of their tufted petals drooping yet beautiful, their sweet scent wafting to us. I allowed myself to relax within the swing, moved my feet in rhythm with Ethan's, the sound of the chimes calling to mind things of the sea.

This was . . . nice. Too nice, maybe. Without warning, visions filled my mind—of growing old together, of porch swings and babies. Possibilities I'd not thought on in a long time, if ever. Possibilities I couldn't afford to entertain now.

Thankfully the woman stepped outside before the images could go further. In her arms, she shifted a chubby infant with hair identical to her own from one hip to the other. She sat on a white rocker angled in our direction.

"You gave me a reason to stop working." She smiled. From where he sat on her lap, the infant grabbed his bare toes, examined them. I'd never been around babies much, but if they were all like this little guy, I just might understand the draw.

The woman must have noticed me staring. "This is Wyatt. I'm Melissa."

Ethan held out his hand. "Ethan and Hayley."

She shook each of our hands in turn. "I've been cleaning and packing up this place for the last week, getting ready for prospective buyers. I'm afraid Wyatt's had enough of it." She laughed. "Me too, if I'm honest. It's all filled with memories of Gram, sometimes too much for me. I'm anxious to sell it."

"Well, it's beautiful. I'm sure you'll have buyers before long."

She looked toward the front yard, seemed lost in memories before turning back to us. "Now, you're asking about an old chest, is that right?"

"Yes, ma'am," I said.

She waved her hand through the air, caught the attention of Wyatt, who followed it with his eyes, near swallowed up by his chubby cheeks. "Please, call me Melissa."

I nodded. "Melissa."

"I do remember the chest, actually."

Ethan scooted forward on the swing. "You do?"

"Very well, in fact. We found it in the attic when we were cleaning it out. My sister and I were over to Gram and Gramps's a lot as kids. We used to flip it over and use it as a seat when we put on plays upstairs." She stared off past the porch. "It was hard to part with a lot of the things in the estate sale, but we simply couldn't keep them all, you know?"

Ethan's mouth pressed into a line. "I'm sorry about your grandmother."

"Thank you. It's not fun, but it is the course of life, I suppose. Now what did you say you found in the chest?"

Ethan opened the freezer bag and held out the paper. "Kind of amazing, really. Hayley dropped the chest and the bottom splintered. She saw this paper. I had an appraiser check it out yesterday, and he seems to think it's the real deal."

Melissa took the paper. I tried not to cringe when Wyatt reached for it with wet fingers that had been in his mouth. Melissa pulled it off to the side, squinted at the list, handed it back to Ethan. "I'm afraid I don't understand."

"We didn't at first, either," I said. "Until we started googling some of the names. Almost all of them are attached to the Boston Tea Party. This appears to be a secret oath they took before the dumping of the tea in December 1773."

She crinkled her nose. "And this was in the chest the entire time?"

"It would seem so," Ethan said. "We were hoping you could enlighten us, maybe tell us some of your family's history. Do you know if your ancestors have roots in colonial America?"

Melissa reclined in the rocking chair and Wyatt fell back against her chest. "I know one fought at Bunker Hill, but I'm afraid I don't know much more than that. And I never thought of the chest going back that far. Are you sure it's legitimate?"

"Ninety percent sure, maybe?" He looked at me for confirmation.

I would have said ninety-eight. I wondered about my need to believe in this thing when so often it was the solid, concrete things I put my hope in—my work ethic, my drive, the strength of a team, of the military. When it came to hazy hopes such as relationships, love, and faith, more often than not I checked out. What was it with this chest?

"My uncle did a genealogy project some years ago tracing our ancestors. I remember it being a pretty big deal finding out we had a Revolutionary War veteran in our family line. I was in elementary school at the time. But I don't remember anything being said about the Tea Party. I could ask my mother about the research my uncle did. Other than that, I'm just as surprised as you."

Ethan looked at the document. "So your grandmother . . . she never said anything to you about the tea chest or its importance?"

Melissa shook her head. "She said it was handed down to her from her mother, but she had several things that were. I kept some of them."

I thought of Lena then. She hadn't much—anything of value had been sold long ago to get her next fix—but did that mean I wouldn't want anything of hers after she was gone? I remembered a Christmas ornament I'd always been drawn to, a tiny ceramic mouse with a nightcap cuddled in a sleeping bag. Lena would let me hang it on our scraggly tree every year. She'd always made an effort on Christmas Day, even making hot chocolate and letting me put as many tiny marshmallows in the cup as I cared to. No boyfriends, no drama, no drugs. Just me and her.

And while the ceramic mouse didn't have any history more fascinating than a flea market, I thought maybe that bit of *my* history—mine and Lena's—might make it valuable enough for my own tree one day.

"I'm sorry I can't be of more help . . . unless . . ." She stood. "Hold on, I seem to remember an old photo I just packed up yesterday. Let me see if I can dig it out." She left us, returning momentarily with a large photo album propped against her hip. Wyatt reached for it, but she handed it to me. "Would you mind? I think it's at the beginning. I need to fix his bottle."

I took it from her, placed it on my lap, and opened it while Melissa disappeared back inside the house. Several black-and-white pictures dominated the front before giving way to colored photos, worn with age. I moved closer to Ethan, sharing the album with him as we started at the beginning. Photos of a small group on a lawn, dressed in their best for a wedding. A bride in a lacy white dress with a handsome groom. Then snapshots of toddlers in sailor outfits.

Melissa came out with Wyatt, the infant holding the bottle with his own hands. She looked over our shoulders, pointed to the toddler on the right in a sailor dress. "My mother." She flipped the page back a few times, then showed us a black-and-white picture on the right bottom of the page. "There."

I lifted it closer. A couple stood in the picture, dressed for a formal event. At first, I couldn't make out why Melissa had pointed out this particular picture. Then I saw it in the bottom corner in the background. The tea chest. Our tea chest. What looked like a Sears catalog poked out from the top of it.

Melissa sat back in the chair. "That's a picture of Gram and Gramps before they were married. It was taken in this house, only it belonged to my great-grandmother at the time. I'm afraid it's all I have."

I kept the album open on my lap. "No, that's okay. It's neat to think all that chest has been through. I wonder, though, if it really is from the Tea Party . . . why was the story of it not passed along?"

Melissa shifted Wyatt in her arms, her bare feet pushing against the stained boards of the porch as she shook her head. "If I'd known some great secret surrounding it, I probably wouldn't have sold it. But like I said, except for some fond memories I shared with my sister, it didn't mean all that much to me."

I thought of the chest, how quickly I'd become attached to this inanimate object. Good thing Melissa didn't mention wanting it back . . . yet.

Ethan tapped his fingers on his thigh. "I'm curious about that genealogy research your uncle did. He was the one who discovered you had an ancestor at Bunker Hill?"

"That's right." Wyatt's bottle fell out of his mouth, leaving droplets of milk on his cheek. He looked at me and let out a small giggle. Melissa wiped his cheek with a burp cloth and replaced the bottle in his mouth. He pulled it out with a slurping sound, milk splattering his face once again. This time, he gave a bubbly laugh. A smile pulled at my lips.

"I guess you're done with this, mister." Melissa placed the bottle on the deck boards, sitting her son up for a burp. "My mother has a copy of the genealogy book. I'll be here again tomorrow, trying to finish up if you want to stop by. I could show it to you."

Ethan stood and I closed the album. "That would be great," he said.

A large bubble of air released itself from Wyatt's mouth. "Wonderful. I hope it helps. I have to admit, I'm curious to see what you find."

I took out my phone. "Could I take your number? We'll definitely keep you up to date."

In the car, Ethan replaced the freezer bag carefully inside the glove compartment. "That's a start."

We drove down the hill toward the center of Medford, and I fought the urge to close my eyes against memories, even the good ones, like meeting up with my friends for ice cream at the corner store.

"I can't help but wonder if whoever put the list inside the chest never intended to share the history of it with his family."

"We might never find out, but I'm feeling lucky that Melissa's uncle did some legwork for us." We neared the rotary and my stomach clenched at being so close to Vine Street. Ethan must have picked up on my nerves—he'd always been good at that. "You want to swing by your mom's? She's back, isn't she? Barbados, you said?"

I opened my mouth to tell him no, I didn't want to see Lena now, especially not with Ethan in tow. Then a sudden impulse came over me to get this thing done. It was what I'd come for, after all. Why put it off any longer?

"You know what? Yeah. It's been hanging over my head, but maybe—you know, having you around for moral support would help."

He turned onto Vine Street and pulled alongside the house, where a Ford Taurus was parked in the drive. He took the key from the ignition. "Man, this place didn't change, huh? Weird to be back."

I'd forgotten how many memories the two of us shared here. How many nights we sat on the decrepit front porch, delaying our good-night with both words and kisses. How many times I'd watched out the window for him to come pick me up, how he'd take the stairs two at a time before seeing me in the window, his smile brightening my dreary home.

I sighed. "Yeah, it is." I opened the car door, then looked back. "I'll just be a minute. Thinking this could be a sort of icebreaker. I can make plans to chat another time."

"I have nowhere to be. Take your time."

"Yeah . . ." I scooped my phone from the console and tucked it in my back pocket, trotted up to the ripped screen, just as I'd done three days before. I knocked once, then twice. Then again.

I ground my teeth. There was a car in the drive. Why wasn't anyone answering?

I pictured my mom passed out, dead to the world on the couch. I banged harder. "Lena! Come on, open up!"

This wasn't supposed to be so hard. I'd done the difficult part twice in bringing myself to this place, in dragging my open and bleeding heart to the epicenter of my painful past.

Unbidden, the memories came. The yelling, the slamming of broken bottles, my mother half-dressed on the couch as I left for the school bus, too afraid to wake her up or touch her for fear I'd find her dead, wondering if she'd be in that same spot when I came home, if I'd have to call an ambulance to take her body out of the house. I remembered the boyfriends sneaking into my room, seeking to steal what wasn't theirs, what Lena didn't seem to value in the least—her daughter.

I banged again, my throat tight. Adrenaline rushed to my limbs. I opened the storm door and wiggled the handle, banged some more. The old helpless feeling returned, like an attack from the enemy.

I was *not* this powerless little girl anymore. I'd gone away, matured, made something of myself. I was strong, and I'd come back here to prove it.

No matter if it took everything within me, one way or another, I would win this battle.

I took a step back, readied myself to kick the door open, to face it all then and there. I was done with wondering, done with trying to do the right thing by coming here. I wanted it over.

Without warning, solid fingers circled my arm. "Hayley."

My breath caught, and I froze beneath Ethan's touch. Reality exploded within me, then embarrassment. What was I thinking? How could I have gotten so involved with my memories, so oblivious to Ethan's presence? "I—I'm sorry. I got caught up in—"

"Hey, it's okay. We'll try again tomorrow."

I hated the way he spoke to me, as if I were weak, like a child. But wasn't I? How did I expect to get through BUD/S—mentally and physically—if I couldn't keep it together on my mother's front porch?

He tugged me down the steps, put an arm around me to open the passenger door of the car. Though I hated to admit it, I needed his strength in that moment. In a way, it felt like he'd never left me. And how had I treated him? By skulking off without a good-bye, by leaving without warning, by proving myself disloyal when he'd been—still was—the exact opposite.

I hadn't deserved him then, and I didn't deserve him now.

What was worse, with his tender touch, I felt us barreling back to where we started, felt the draw to be something more than I'd been, to prove my honor and loyalty to this kind man. And at the same time, I felt like running before things could get any deeper. Before I could hurt him like Lena had hurt me.

Quite obviously, I sucked at this relationship stuff. I'd

brushed it all off these past six years, convincing myself that I could find my purpose in my military family. Things were simple there. Do your job, be loyal to your team, whether you felt like it or not. Why then was everything so much harder back home? And while excelling in relational intimacy wasn't something I needed to pass to become a SEAL, I was beginning to wonder if it was the one thing that—no matter how hard I worked—I wouldn't be able to wrangle for myself.

CHAPTER TWENTY-TWO

Emma

*May we ever be a people favoured of God. May our land be a
land of liberty, the seat of virtue, the asylum of the oppressed,
a name and a praise in the whole earth.*

GENERAL JOSEPH WARREN

MEDFORD, MASSACHUSETTS

APRIL 1775

The hard lump that spoke of new life growing within my
womb seemed to contradict the preparations for battle
around me. The preparations for the taking of life, rather
than the birthing of it—endlessly grinding sulfur, saltpeter,
and charcoal to be made into gunpowder; wrapping it in
paper packets crudely called "cartridges"; even melting lead
and pressing it into molds to make musket balls.

Life with Noah, living out our love in the back of his
simple printing shop, had proved everything I dreamed. Yet
while the work of being his wife was satisfying, I couldn't
ignore the doubt that rose within me at the melting of the
snows that seemed to propel us toward an inevitable future,
one that included battle.

Noah would be a part of it—that much was never a question. Among the first to join the Medford militia, he spent most of his time hunched over his press, printing news for those hungry for it in Boston's outlying towns, mostly Patriots who had fled Boston more than a year ago after word of the port closure—our punishment for the dumping of the tea.

It did not seem to matter a whit that the Sons tried to separate themselves from the unruly Mohawks and mobs that ran amok in Boston's streets—King George peered right past it all. But the rest of the colonies did not. Like siblings who sympathized over the harsh discipline of a brother, all rallied around Boston, even as loyalists sought refuge there, among some four thousand members of the King's Army.

Supplies coming out of Boston had dwindled with the increasing presence of the king's troops. The distillery where John worked ran short on molasses. The thriving marketplace, where so many country traders from New Hampshire and Vermont visited to peddle their brassware and broadcloths, silks and spring locks, grew pitiable. And Mr. Hall's—now Captain Hall's—lightering business, which made it possible to send Medford's goods down the river and into Boston, had become nonexistent.

The call to arms came in the dark of night before dawn on the nineteenth of April. A rider came barreling through our streets, shouting. I woke to it, stretched my fingers to the warmth of Noah's body beneath our coverlet, terror seizing my chest.

I knew the time would come, and yet I had denied it.

Noah pulled me close for a moment, where I huddled in the crook of his arm for much too short a time; then he pressed a kiss to my forehead and caressed the expanding mound where our child grew before throwing the covers back and pulling on clothes.

I emerged from the bedroom in my dressing gown, poked to life the embers of the stove to heat water for something warm to fill my husband's belly. Noah went outside to confer with Captain Hall, the commander of our militia. A moment later, he returned. He scooped some bullets he'd cast last night into his pocket, grabbed up his powder horn, and faced me. "It is as we anticipated. They are on their way to raid our stores in Concord."

'Twas happening. Unlike the time last autumn when the Redcoats came up the Mystic River to retrieve the casks of gunpowder they'd left in an old silo south of town, this time the stores did not belong to them. This time, so much more was at stake—both in firepower and in the lives of our men.

I grasped for a reason for him to stay. "The water has not heated yet. You cannot leave until I get something to sustain you." I tried to keep the tremor from my voice but failed miserably.

He drew me close, cupped my face in his hands, and kissed me deeply—now, fifteen months into marriage, a bit more familiar. "I must go," he said.

I clutched at his shirt, willed myself to be brave and strong even as I wished to cling to his legs like a toddler and demand he not leave me. I could make excuses for him. He was needed here, at his press, ten times more than he was in battle. While I helped him as I could, setting the letters on occasion, working beside him to get the news out to Medford and her outlying towns, I could not do it on my own. I thought of the apron he'd purchased for me, hanging alongside his own. To have but one more day with him in his tiny shop, the smell of paper and ink around us, the smudge of it upon my hands, the markings something like a proud brand I wore that I belonged with this man.

I opened my mouth to try to convince him one more time, then snapped it shut.

I knew he would go. Just as he'd felt compelled to dress as a Mohawk and dump the tea, just as he'd felt compelled to drill with the militia, he would go. We'd been round these tables before, and I did not wish to make our parting harder on him now. I did not wish to dishonor the cause both he and I considered worthy enough to fight for.

He kept his hands on my face. "'Twill be well. And I have hopes to be back before nightfall. We will have some cocoa and dinner." He stooped to plant a kiss on my womb.

Cocoa and dinner, mayhap some seedcakes . . . aye, that sounded lovely. A few hours he would be gone. Then he would return.

He scooped up his hat and supplies, looked at me as if he wished to say something, then decided against it before nodding and closing the door, its echo shattering the night.

I pulled my robe tighter and made myself a cup of cocoa in the well-used cup Sarah had gifted me all those months ago. I could still remember her pressing it into my hands, near prophesying over the events to come.

I had followed my heart. I had found my voice. I had proved myself strong in leaving my parents.

Why, then, did I feel so weak?

I sat by the fire, my hands going to the small babe within

my belly. My gaze landed on the tea chest—what had become a symbol for our beginning and in which Noah had secreted away his oath, hiding it under a false bottom with strips of additional wood.

I could still hear his words to me as he did so.

"We swore an oath of secrecy, all of the men on this round-robin. Yet I have an inkling that one day, we may want to share with our children, or perhaps our grandchildren, what we took part in this night. Could we have a greater source of proof than this paper?"

I could still recall his enthusiasm. Though it seemed none of the men regretted what they'd done that night, it still felt less than honorable. The way 'twas kept quiet, the way the names were hidden. I understood it—after all I would not wish Noah to ever suffer the recompense of being found out—but would he ever be proud enough to share the story with our children? Could the dumping of the tea ever be a source of pride?

I closed my eyes, grasped for memories of all the Lord had done for us in the weeks following the tea party—how he'd delivered Noah's oath into my hands, how he'd made a way for us here in Medford, given me a new family with Noah and the Fultons and, now, with what would soon be my own child. Surely—surely—he would once again deliver Noah from the hands of our enemies.

Heavenly Father, may it be so.

✝

When Sarah opened her door to me in the predawn hours, the slaves from the surrounding orchards of the Royall plantation were just beginning their morning work. She surprised me by grabbing me up in an embrace—a rather emotional display for her, yet becoming more frequent, as we had grown closer these past months.

In a world where my letters to Mother and Margaret had gone unanswered, I gleaned comfort from this place, this home, a family I gave my complete loyalty to. And I tried not to think of Father and Mother off to England, carrying with them the lump of flesh Father deemed a sort of trophy for his time of persecution in Boston. I tried not to think of the words they exchanged over my betrayal. I tried not to ponder whether they missed me or not.

I tried.

"Noah's gone with the militia."

"Aye. John as well, despite his recent illness. He's asked me to take the children to the Phips home."

"Will they come through Medford?"

"Medford is out of the way, but we do not know what the day will bring. I trust our men can stop them. Still, 'tis safer we all leave the main road. While I'm not afraid of a few Regulars, I don't want the children in harm's way." Sarah draped a shawl over Lydia and handed baby Francis to me. Mary clung at my skirts, her blue gaze wide. "I need to run upstairs for a few things. Would you stay with them?"

I looked to the spot where Sarah's two oldest children prepared a basket of food and supplies. "Of course."

She left and Mary tugged at my skirts. I knelt with care, as I had baby Francis in my arms and my own burgeoning belly to contend with. "What is it, Mary?"

"Are you afraid, Miss Emmy?"

I thought to lie to the child. We did not need the children worrying—'twould only make it worse for them. And yet I thought of Sarah's strength in the face of her vulnerabilities, of my own strength the Lord had provided when I was at my weakest. Could the same be true in fear?

I brushed a strand of hair from her face. "I am a wee bit frightened," I admitted, feeling the eyes of the oldest children upon me. "But I think it's not a bad thing to be afraid. When we admit our fears to one another, they lose their tight grip on us. Do you want to try that?"

Mary nodded solemnly.

"Very well, I'll go first," I said despite my sudden hesitance to be so dreadfully honest with the children. "I am afraid for Noah, even though I trust he will be a big help in stopping those Redcoats." I exhaled a deep breath. "You know what, though? I feel better just telling you all what I was afraid of. And truthfully, I am trusting God that Noah and your papa will be fine. Do you want to go next?"

Mary bit her lip before speaking. "I am afraid the Redcoats will come be mean to us."

"Oh, darling." I drew her into my arms. "They don't have an interest in us, only in Concord. And your papa and Noah and a lot of other brave men will make sure they don't even get that."

She nodded where I held her alongside the baby near my chest.

"Do we have everything?" Sarah asked her older children as she descended. They nodded and she opened the door and led us to the Phips home, where we would battle our fears as we awaited news.

'Twas evening before word arrived. The militia had not only stopped the Regulars from obtaining the stores in Concord, they had chased them back to Boston.

Word also came that the victory had come at a heavy cost.

My worry seemed to stir to life the first flutterings within my womb. Mr. Phips took us back to town in his wagon, the older children following behind. When we reached the bridge, we near ran to the Fulton house, elated to see candles in the windows.

We found John and Noah sitting in the keeping room, tankards of flip before them. Noah stood at my arrival and I ran to him, nearly knocking him back in his chair. I drew away, searched his face and body for sign of injury. "You are well?"

He smiled, dirt creasing the folds of his skin. "I am well."

Little John came bounding into the room. "Tell us! Tell us!"

Sarah ordered the wee ones upstairs.

Young John continued his begging. "Did you fight, Father? Tell us everything."

A slow smile came to John's face. "What would you like to know, Son? Mayhap how your old father made a stand in Menotomy alongside Doctor—or should I say, General—Warren? That man is to be lauded—the most active man in the field, I tell you. Got so close to those Redcoats, a musket ball struck out one of the pins holding up his curled hair."

"Dr. Warren?" The very same who had tended my father's wounds?

Noah nodded. "He may be a military novice, but his ability to inspire was just what our men needed."

It seemed preposterous that a group of provincials had

the King's Army locked up in Boston. Preposterous and wonderful at the same time.

"And what is to happen now?"

"We must leave first thing tomorrow, join those gathered in Cambridge and Roxbury. More will come. Many more. We must stay strong against them, refuse them exit from Boston."

I felt as if a lead ball weighted my stomach instead of a wee babe. I had thought of this battle—this day—as the one thing to conquer, but now I realized that this was just the beginning of a very long road we'd begun on those ships that December night.

Young John tugged at his father's torn and dirtied shirt. "Father, may I go with you next time? May I?"

John tousled his son's unruly hair. "Nay, Son. Battle is . . . not for young ones. I am telling you the glorious parts so you will be proud of your father, but there are other parts I should never wish you to hear."

✠

Noah was quiet on the way home. Our life seemed to stretch before us in an uncertain tangle. He would leave. For how long? To what end?

Once we'd lit candles and started the fire in the hearth, I fixed us each a cup of cocoa and got to work warming some seedcakes. "You can tell me."

"Tell you what?"

"How 'twas. All of it. Noah, I am not only your wife but your friend. If you need to release your thoughts, then pray, release them to me. I promise I will not question it or that for which you fight. You risked your life today. I could have lost you. Your child could have never known his father. I don't say this to guilt you but to convince you." I stepped closer to him, his gaze directed to the flames licking wood within the hearth. "I stand with you, my husband. You deem this cause worthy, and I deem you worthy. I will fight alongside you how I can. You have my word."

In the shadows of the room, it seemed his bottom lip trembled. I went to him, wrapped him in an embrace, pressed my lips to his dirtied, sweatied hair. He clutched at my waist, ran his fingers up and down my sides, stroked the spot where our child rested with loving, sure fingers.

Finally he spoke. "I've never killed a man before this day, Emma. Now I've done so at least twice over. That fact . . . it shakes my soul. How can it not?"

My heart near broke in two for him. I stroked his hair as I stood beside him, thinking he might speak his mind more freely if he did not have to look into my eyes. 'Twas one thing to drill with the militia and practice shots, to talk of shooting down the coats of red. 'Twas quite another to actually take a man's life.

"I remember the swishing sound of the grass as they came from behind, not on the road as we thought. We'd been hiding in the orchard and ran for a house. John and I survived only by using the cellar as our fortification. When they finally retreated, we came forth. Those they shot, they stabbed numerous times . . . a viciousness we hadn't expected. Yet it seems it all began in Concord, for they were breathing murderous threats about how the rebels were barbarians, scalping the Regulars that very morning. I think war . . . it unleashes something of an animal within a man. One vicious act leads to another and then another, until we have enough anger and ambition and desire for revenge that it threatens to stifle that for which we truly fight."

My stomach swayed and sour bile filled my throat. I swallowed it down. "Noah . . ."

He pulled away, looked at me this time, his gaze searching. "I admit—when I killed the Redcoats, in that moment, I was not fighting for our liberty. I was fighting to save myself, to avenge the deaths of those I saw around me. Is that wrong?"

I had never felt so inadequate to answer a question. Was it wrong that war took away our compassion? Aye. Was it necessary if we were to achieve freedom? I did not know, nor could I pretend to have an answer. I only knew, looking into the gaze of the man I loved, that I wanted nothing more than to comfort him.

"I think 'tis normal, Noah. Yet I think 'tis important to remember why you fight. To not allow the battle to steal your heart."

He smiled. "'Tis why I must make visits to you often, though this bloody conflict takes me away. You. Our children. That is why I fight."

I pressed my lips to his, his mouth hungry on my own, and I knew he longed to forget the events of the day by burying himself within my arms.

I drew back, suddenly decided of how I could help. "I will run the shop in your absence."

"Emma . . ."

"I know how to set the type, and your messenger will continue to come. I am not so terrible at writing a story, am

I? I will keep them short and simple, keep our business running whilst you are gone."

His gaze seemed to dance beneath the flickering firelight. "*Our* business, is it?"

I crossed my arms before me, challenging him to continue his thought.

He sought my hands instead. "If any wife can run a home and a printing shop, it is you, my dear. But you must promise me you won't work yourself too hard. You have my child to take care of, after all."

"*Our* child," I corrected again, not resisting when he pulled me close and kissed my head.

"Yes." He squeezed my hand. "*Our* child."

CHAPTER TWENTY-THREE

Emma

Boston has been like the vision of Moses:
a bush burning but not consumed.

REVEREND SAMUEL COOPER

JUNE 1775

I straightened from where I'd been hunched over the printing press and kneaded my fingers along my back. The babe within was now a noticeable, active mound, and I was not certain how long I would be able to keep my hours at the press.

I looked at the letters I'd just finished setting.

GAGE PLANS ATTACK

Noah had come home as often as he could for a wash and food and to aid with the shop, but for the most part he stayed in Charlestown with the provincial army, awaiting General Gage's next move, anticipating that the commander would not be content to stay trapped in Boston forever.

Meanwhile, our lives—and our town—seemed to turn

upon themselves. John stayed home. The warehouses and the distillery alongside the river had taken on the role of supply depots, in which John served as bookkeeper. Meat and rum were shipped down the Mystic to where Noah and the army waited at Charlestown.

Shortly after the battle for Concord, Colonel John Stark and his fellow commander, a very tall and handsome Major Andrew McClary of the New Hampshire militia, arrived in our town, determined to set up a field office. A weathered veteran of the French and Indian War, Colonel Stark took dinner with the Fultons his first night, regaled us with stories of his Indian captivity. I sat, transfixed, remembering Mary Rowlandson's story, admiring the man before us who possessed such grit and fortitude. Colonel Stark set up his headquarters at the Admiral Vernon Tavern, not far from the Fulton home, and began recruiting at once. Within days, more than a thousand New Hampshire militiamen arrived, and our town became a whirlwind of activity and noise. Not long after, the colonel moved into the Royall mansion, as Isaac Royall had fled to England with a handful of his slaves a few days before the Concord battle, leaving his estate unattended.

Soldiers came and went through Sarah's home as John took to helping Major McClary gather what supplies he could for the troops. Talk of war and lack of gunpowder became the fiber of our lives. When word leaked out that General Warren had granted Captain Benedict Arnold two hundred pounds of powder to capture cannons at Fort Ticonderoga, we held our collective breath, waiting for our salvation.

Now, I looked down at the letters, glistening with ink, set in the press that would soon turn upon paper. Mr. Adams and Mr. Hancock were in Philadelphia at the second meeting of the Continental Congress. But Noah and the army needed their help now. They needed the cannons at Fort Ticonderoga now. Yet General Gage surely knew this. He would not wait in his plans to break out of Boston.

✝

I woke to the sound of cannon fire.

Its solid, powerful booms called from the east, causing a cramp of worry to form within my chest and work its way to my gut. I eased my hands over the solid mound of my belly, feeling my wee one move within even as my heart seized in fear for his father. Remembering my own advice to Mary the day of Lexington and Concord, desperate prayers poured from my mouth as I voiced my fears and consciously released them to the Almighty.

I rose and dressed, set out to Sarah's house as soon as I was able. Despite the early hour, both soldiers and civilians crowded the main thoroughfare. I pushed across the bridge and finally entered Sarah's home, where Major McClary pleaded with John.

"Is there no more to be found anywhere?"

John shook his head, a frown on his face as he broke into an unhealthy cough. "I'm afraid not, Major."

The man cursed and Sarah looked on, her mouth pressed tight.

"I'm sending my men into battle with naught but a cupful of powder, fifteen balls, and a flint per man. Inexcusable."

He left the house and Sarah placed a hand on John's arm.

"There is nothing you can do. We've given all we have and now there is simply none left to give."

After Colonel Stark's troops marched away, we gathered upon Pasture Hill. The rumble of cannons shook the sky. From the direction of Charlestown, billowing smoke rose to the heavens. I tried not to cry, truly I did, but thinking of Noah alongside all the men on the receiving end of the cannons of the king with not enough ammunition to defend themselves caused a large lump to form in my throat.

I'd felt that God had bestowed such grace upon me in allowing me a life of my own—a life with Noah. Would He continue to allow me to live beneath this grace? And what of those whose husbands and brothers and sons lay dying amid that smoke?

I breathed a prayer into the air, releasing it toward the gray swirls curling against the blue of the sky. What terrors were happening upon the hills of Charlestown, on both sides, we could only imagine.

Lord, be with Noah.

Be with us all.

☩

When we could stand to watch the smoke and listen to the cannons no longer, we turned for home.

"There will be wounded. We must gather supplies. We'll set up a hospital on the field near the bridge," Sarah said.

John nodded. "Little John and I will ride to every house and gather what lint and linen we can."

Sarah turned to her oldest. "Take the children back home.

Keep a kettle of hot water on the stove all day, you hear? As much as you are able." Young Sarah nodded, solemn.

We all went to our intended tasks when we reached the Fulton house.

"Where is Dr. Brooks?" I asked.

"Major Brooks," Sarah corrected. "He is with the men."

"Dr. Tufts is to care for them all? Who will work alongside him?"

Sarah looked at me. "We will." Something passed between us then. A solidification of the bond we shared. While she was as much mother and sister to me, in that moment she was also friend and fellow freedom fighter.

We could not go to battle alongside the men, even if we wanted to. But we could do this. Help the hurting. Heal the sick. Together. I vowed not to leave her side.

We gathered what instruments we could from the kitchen and from John's small shed, and though I couldn't imagine using them on injured men, I reminded myself that I would do what I had to—for Noah. For all the men who risked their lives for our cause. And while I might not be convinced of the rightness of war, I was convinced in the rightness of helping the injured.

I would be strong.

We set up tables and lined them with old sheets, gathered what honey and camphor we could to make a tincture for wounds. The townsfolk responded to our call, donating as they could—a chair, a table, tools and axes. Butcher knives and torches. Lint and bandages and sheets. In early afternoon, a dirtied Major McClary came down the road. Far from the organized officer I'd seen just this morning, his shirt was torn and his hair a clump of dust and sweat.

"We need more dressings."

We collected what we could, taking some from a group of women stripping sheets for just such a purpose, all the while keeping an ear for Major McClary's report.

". . . not enough gunpowder . . . reinforcements . . . holding them off . . . should have been on Bunker Hill . . ."

I wanted to ask him news of Noah but knew it was foolish to expect him to know how my husband fared among so many. We watched his retreat atop his horse.

I did not expect that the next time I glimpsed Major McClary's handsome face, it would be with vacant, hooded eyes, eclipsed in death.

☩

As night fell, our hospital grew busy. Both the dead and the wounded were brought to Medford. Little John lit torches alongside the beds of the men, and his father assisted Dr. Tufts in holding the men down during amputations. Reverend Osgood helped transport the men from wagons to the tables and workbenches that served as the makeshift beds of the hospital, praying with as many as possible.

I was sure the screams of the soldiers would haunt me until the end of my days. If the screams did not, the visions of open wounds and dangling limbs and tendons and, in one instance, a man's bowels would certainly do so.

I wiped my cheek against my shoulder as I fought a rising nausea within me, but continued at my task, trying to ignore the obvious pain of the man beneath me as I dug a bullet from his upper thigh.

At first, at the sight of any serious injury, I had waited for Dr. Tufts. After the fourth time calling the doctor away from his immediate duties, Sarah had turned to me, exasperated. "Do what you can. He can only help one man at a time." She'd handed me iron tongs. "If it is a musket ball, dig it out with this. If it is a laceration, apply lint and a bandage. If amputations are needed . . . tie off the flow of blood as well as you are able. They will have to wait for the doctor."

Now, digging within this man's flesh, the smell of blood and sweat and dirtied leather shoes rose up to meet me; the ground swirled around me. I would be sick. The flame of a nearby torch created a devilish vision before me, ghostlike in its fiery embrace. The mortifying scream of a man broke through it all. Then Sarah's voice and Dr. Tufts's. I turned in time to empty the little contents of my stomach onto the muddied ground beside me.

Almost at once, my vision cleared and the nausea left. I took my tool and continued the work of probing within the man's leg for the bullet that plagued him.

"Almost there, soldier," I said, trying to mimic the calm tone Sarah had mastered. I felt the solid mass of the musket ball—the size now familiar from treating so many similar wounds—and grasped it, pulled it up through the man's loud groan.

I placed the bloodied ball and my tool on top of his stomach and began applying the tincture of honey and camphor, then packing lint into the wound, taking my tool back up, and turning to see who else needed aid. The man mumbled his gratitude behind me.

With each survey of a man's body, I would drag my reluctant gaze to his face and search for my husband's features, both longing to see him and holding out hope that he would appear beside me—upright and healthy—at any moment.

I lowered myself to the ground beside a body—a colored boy of no more than thirteen—who shook uncontrollably. I ran a hand over his face, grabbed some lint from my basket and applied it to the quivering stump of his leg. Someone on the field had tied a rope around it to stop the bleeding, but there was nothing more I could do for him.

I sought his hand with my own bloodied one and squeezed. "Shhh . . . the doctor will be over soon." A woman with a tray of flip passed by and I scooped one up, lifted the boy's head to sip. He swallowed the tiniest of sips, but mostly his lips just bathed at the rim. After a moment, I lowered his head back to the ground.

"Do you know where my m-mother is? I r-ran away to the b-battle without her knowing."

I made more hushing noises. "You will see her soon enough, now. Just rest."

"Will you get her for m-me? She's in the keeping room making b-biscuits."

I blinked away tears. 'Twas the first time in hours that I had stopped to gaze upon the soul of the wounded. The boy's eyes grew vacant.

"I w-want to tell her . . ."

As I watched the young man prepare to give up his life, I felt at the brink of insanity. I wanted to cover my ears and close my eyes to it all. Block my nose from the smells of reality around me. Would *this* truly give us freedom? This boy— was he a slave? Did he fight with freedom in mind? "She's coming, dear. You can tell her. . . . Lord, be with him. . . ."

And then he was gone.

I blew my nose in my apron. If I dwelled on the boy's death, if I pondered the heartbreak of the mother he'd spoken of, if I continued to sit holding his stiffening hand, I would weaken. I would not be able to rise and help others. In order to survive, I must somehow separate myself from it. I must continue on for the sake of us all. For Sarah, who labored alongside the broken, wounded men. For Noah, who gave his all for this fight. For my own child, growing within my womb, a legacy of liberty the inheritance we longed to give him. For every man who had given his loyalty to this cause of freedom, putting action behind ideals.

I gently pulled my fingers from the boy's, laid one last lingering hand alongside his face, and rose, my basket of lint and bandages clutched in my arm.

"Emma."

I turned at Sarah's voice, prepared to give her aid, my dressings, whatever she had need. I held out the tool she'd given me, blood drying upon it.

She shook her head, her gaze flicking to me, then back to the tool. "'Tis Noah. He's with the doctor. You must come quickly."

CHAPTER TWENTY-FOUR

Emma

In the midst of death's relentless power,
I yet among the living stand.

MERCY OTIS WARREN

I FOLLOWED SARAH through the maze of wounded, bloodied men. My stomach threatened to rebel against me again, but I continued forward, the pale pink of dawn just now showing itself on the horizon.

Part of me wished Sarah to stop walking, to simply tell me what had happened to Noah or make him appear before my eyes. Another part wished she would walk forever. That I would never have to see what waited for me at the end of this march.

Whatever it was, I vowed to be strong for my husband. We would make it past this. I would help him. Unless . ... what if it wasn't something to be past? What if he already lay like so many others, like the boy I'd just left who cried for his mother? What if he was already dead?

The ground swayed before me and I stopped, my hand grasping for something solid.

And then Sarah was there, supporting me, strong as ever. Yet she could be strong, couldn't she? 'Twasn't her husband we went to see.

For a moment, I regretted that Noah was so young and healthy, that he didn't suffer an infirmity like John. He could have stayed. He had the work of the press, after all, itself a worthy cause for liberty. Why had he left us? Me and our unborn child? What would I do without him?

Sarah guided me toward the edge of the field. "A cannon hit his leg. Took it clean off. Dr. Tufts says it's better that way, without an amputation. They were able to stop the bleeding on the field and dress it, but he's lost a lot of blood. When I saw him . . . I had to tell you. The doctor gave him some opium to help with the pain."

Her words lay like a jumbled mess in my head, as slow moving as custard. I couldn't comprehend them, and at the same time, I could.

Noah, hurt. No leg. A lot of blood.

I curled over, Sarah's arms around me.

Help . . .

'Twas the weakest of prayers, but it came straight from my soul.

"I . . . I need a moment." My breathing was shallow and rapid as I whispered to Sarah, who held me, crouched in the mud.

I was selfish. Men needed her right now. Men worse off than I. Or were they? Was the pain of the heart sometimes capable of a greater suffering than that of the body?

Sarah rubbed my back, and I remembered Mother doing the same for me once when I was sick as a young girl.

Mother. She'd never written. Did she think of me? Did she care? Surely, when I had run off, she did not wish such travesty to be a part of my life. If she knew, what would she say?

"Emma." Sarah's voice broke through my thoughts. Strong, sure, where Mother's was nothing but a figment of my imagination. "All will be well."

Was it a lie meant to soothe, as I'd told the dying boy that his mother was on her way? I didn't care. In that moment, I would believe it.

And yet as I felt my entire world crashing down, a greater call impressed itself upon me.

This moment could not be forever. I would have to rise, to walk and see my husband, to be strong for him in this, his moment of need. I would not disappoint him. 'Twas my turn to take up arms in our little family. To fight for goodness and peace amid chaos and destruction.

And I would do so by facing my husband with a brave face.

I dragged in air through my nostrils, decided and steady. Once. Twice. Three times. I felt my brain begin to clear, the call of duty to my husband stronger than my desire to curl in the mud and deny and sob and plead with the unfair reality of this turn of events.

"I am ready." My voice didn't waver and with Sarah's assistance, I got to my feet.

"Good girl," she said, directing me to the table, my husband's still body upon it.

The first thing I noticed was not the stump of his lower leg, 'twas the steadiness of his breathing. His chest rose and fell in a rhythmic manner, so unlike the boy's erratic and shaking breath. Such a small matter, a husband's breath, yet it fulfilled in me no small hope.

Sarah left me, and I approached the table. When I came to him, I laid a hand on his shoulder and he startled awake, his eyes wide. I glimpsed the terror he'd been through that day in his wild and unfamiliar stare, the light from the lanterns reflecting a gaze that saw me and, at the same time, didn't.

"'Tis me, Noah."

He seemed to return to his senses at the sound of my voice. He grasped at me, mumbled my name, his words slurred with the effects of the opium.

I held him close, pressed his dirtied head to my bosom, and made gentle hushing noises as I'd done with the boy not minutes ago. Only, I vowed, Noah's ending would be different. I would do everything within my power to see it be so.

☩

Dawn came early the next morning, shedding light on the writhing mass of wounded and bloodied men lying in our field hospital. I did not go far from Noah's side, tending those at the edges of the field as best I could.

Something otherworldly pushed me forward. My stomach cramped around my nausea, but I considered it a small sacrifice compared to those around me. I stopped by Noah often, but the opium kept him sleeping, which I deemed best. When I passed him in his sleep, I dared glance at the abnormal stump of his bandaged left leg, propped up with a crude wooden crate. He still had his knee, but my husband's foot and calf were gone.

I grieved that part of him, tried not to think on its implications, tried not to think on the dangers of infection setting in.

I prayed.

I prayed over him and over the patients I worked on. I prayed that something would give in this war, that the madness of wounding and killing one another would stop, that King George would see our side and that, perhaps, the Sons might see his.

As I moved from patient to patient, the lint and dressing within my basket beginning to dwindle, I sensed that we were not alone through the suffering, that a presence greater than us understood it.

It did not make a whit of sense. For the very life of my husband was in danger, my future in question. Despite my tiredness, I felt a purpose in serving, in being Noah's wife and helping him through his darkest hour.

When he woke, the drugs seemed to have worn off, for he grimaced in pain, and I ran my hands over his arms, looked around for a tankard of brandy, which would have to do, for Dr. Tufts had run out of opium long ago.

When Mrs. Phips came with a tray, I took a cup and put it to my husband's lips. He drank heavily before resting his head.

"I'm sorry, Emma . . ."

I sniffed back tears, tried to ignore a sudden harsh cramp climbing my belly.

"Whatever do you have to apologize for, you silly man?"

I forced my tone light, not yet ready to face the heaviness of our situation.

"I made a . . . poor decision on the battlefield. I should have stayed behind the fortification . . . tried to help . . ."

I smoothed his hair back upon his head. "Noah Winslow, you are the most intelligent man I know. If you made a poor decision, 'tis not a matter to dwell on."

He dragged in a shaky breath, and I tried to keep myself upright, showing no signs of pain as another cramp—stronger this time—tore through my middle.

"You should rest. Go home, please."

"I will. Shortly. Though I can't imagine leaving your side. Mayhap I can get some able-bodied men to bring you home?"

"Aye. That would be good." His watery gaze flicked to a flock of geese flying across the sky, their calls echoing in the silent morning. "Is it . . . bad?"

"Noah, as long as you are well—"

"Please, answer me. I need to face it sooner or later."

"'Twill take getting accustomed to, is all."

With much effort, he propped himself up on his elbows, stared at the bloodied stump of his bandaged leg, closed his eyes in defeat before lowering himself back to the table. When he opened them to look up toward the sky, foreign bitterness showed upon his features. "I am but half a man."

I positioned myself over him so he could see my face. The cramp that had gripped me dulled and I grasped the moment to encourage my husband. I placed my hand over his heart. "Noah, 'tis not your legs that make you a man. 'Tis your heart. I did not run away with you because you could dance a jig better than the others, but because you are a good and honorable man. One who believes in liberty. One who loves me and one whom I love. Last I checked, you needn't two legs to do any of that."

His face crumpled at my words, and he breathed deep, trying to control his emotion.

"Emma, can you come?" Sarah's voice from behind.

I squeezed Noah's hand, kissed his whiskered face, and turned before he could see my own tears.

Sarah met me several yards from my husband. "You're bleeding."

I looked down at my dress, streaked with blood and mud. Searched my arms, my sleeves pushed up to my elbows. "'Tis the men's blood. It—"

Just then a massive pain tore through my womb. A gush of liquid burst between my legs.

And I knew.

Once again, Sarah supported me. "'Tis too early," I whimpered.

She waited for the pain to pass. "Let's get you home." She guided me toward the edge of the field, and when she saw a wheelbarrow loaded with dressings, she dumped it out on the dew of the lawn and eased me into it.

We must have been a sight, her pushing my rounded body over Cradock Bridge and up the main thoroughfare in the wheelbarrow, but no one questioned us or bothered to assist, so busy were they with the wounded soldiers.

I placed my hand over my full womb, praying the child within would hold tight. Mayhap once I rested . . .

Sarah stopped at the entrance to my home and helped

me out just as another pain ravaged my body. This time I cried out.

I must keep this baby. I must.

For Noah, who considered himself a broken man. One who had fought for the liberty, for the betterment of his children.

I must keep this baby. I must keep it for my husband.

CHAPTER TWENTY-FIVE

Hayley

MELISSA APPEARED BEHIND the screen door, this time with Wyatt in her arms. "Good, you came back!"

She opened the door, allowing us into the house.

"Thanks for letting us." Ethan's words echoed off the bare walls and empty room, nothing but scuffed wooden floor. I tried to imagine it filled with both furniture and people, some that I'd glimpsed in the album the day before. For some reason, it saddened me to think of its end with this family.

"I'm afraid the chairs in the back are all that's left." She scooped up a rather unwieldy brown book with a picture of a tree on the front and led us to the back patio. A near-empty hummingbird feeder hung beside the table, and flowers of all colors grew abundant along the paths, lending a cheery quality to the place.

We sat, and she slid the book toward us. The front read, *Our Family Tree. Kinsleys.*

Ethan opened it, flipping through with care. Not only was it filled with branches of the Kinsley family tree, it included pictures and notable newspaper articles.

"Wow, this is really . . . extensive." I didn't know what I had thought—that we'd be able to flip through and find something of meaning, maybe? Something that might connect us to the chest and the oath within? But looking at the all-encompassing project, I realized this clearly could not be done in an hour or so.

Melissa laughed. "Yes, it is. Full of interesting history, too. Of course, it's my family—probably more interesting to me than you two."

Ethan turned another page. A newspaper article stating a local election win. If I could peel back the past of my own family, would I find some long-lost relative who had run for selectman? Someone who had fought in a war, fallen in love with a high school sweetheart, or chased dreams of owning their own business? Seeing the book through Melissa's eyes made me think of how precious family could be, and suddenly I felt hollow.

"No, it is interesting," Ethan said. "And who knows? Maybe something having to do with the chest is in here."

"I don't remember seeing anything, but if you guys want to borrow it for a few days to look into it, that'd be fine with me."

I looked up. "Really? I mean, we'd take good care of it, but . . . I don't know if I feel okay with that."

Ethan shook his head. "Yeah, me neither."

"It is valuable, and it means a lot to me, but my uncle had extras printed for future generations, and it's all digital now, too. My mom had one copy, but there are more if something happened to this one. Besides, whatever that chest meant to Gram, I can tell you're just as invested. Go ahead, take it. Give me a call when you're done with it and we'll meet up somewhere."

"Are you sure?" Ethan asked.

"Absolutely." She smiled in a sheepish manner. "I have to admit, you have me curious, only I don't have time to look into any of it myself right now. Maybe we'll both find some interesting history by the time you're through." She stood, signaling the end of the conversation. I closed the book and cradled it in my arms, knowing its worth to Melissa, wanting to live up to the trust she placed in me and Ethan. Wyatt bounced himself on his mother's hip, then reached a hand to me.

I held out a finger, let him grasp it. Wow, kids could be really cute.

"Thank you so much, Melissa. We promise to take good care of it."

"I know you will." She led us back through the house and opened the screen door for us. "Have fun, now, and don't forget to call me when you find what you're looking for."

If we found what we were looking for.

⊹

Ethan didn't ask if I wanted him to turn down Vine Street this time. I'd probably scared him with my little episode the other day. Truth be told, I scared myself, spent most of the night convincing myself that one weak moment did not mean I *was* weak. I would learn from the experience, be more careful not to let my guard down in the future.

SEALs didn't let their guard down.

SEALs didn't fail.

Now we sat in the cool of the slight shade of the deck off my apartment. The ocean stretched before us, the beach packed on the warm day.

I leaned back in my chair. "I don't know, Ethan. This is all interesting, but do you really think it's going to lead anywhere?" I looked at a drawing of Tufts College, circa 1854. Below told the story of William Davis, an ancestor of the Kinsleys who taught at the college.

Ethan took a swig of his iced tea. I'd asked him if he wanted a beer, but he'd declined with an explanation that he didn't drink anymore.

Definitely not the Ethan I remembered.

Not that I was a lush or anything, but especially since joining the military, I associated downtime with a drink or two. I sat back, eyed the man before me. He'd seen an unpleasant side of me yesterday, a side most of my comrades hadn't seen, a side I barely saw. Maybe it was his turn to open up. "How come you don't drink anymore?"

"That's a change of subject." He pushed the book onto the table, raked a hand through his hair. I could tell before he opened his mouth that he would once again bare a part of himself to me. His honesty and sincerity wore at one of those soft spots in my heart, and I braced myself.

"The boat accident that killed Allison? We were drinking.

Us and another couple. Allison and I had been arguing. I went below deck to get away from her, and Allison took over the ship's wheel. The next thing I remember is waking up in a hospital with two broken legs, being told my wife was dead."

"I'm so sorry."

He sniffed, hard. "Me too. Allison and I . . . we'd been arguing a lot. Trying to figure out if our new marriage was even worth working for. We drank a lot too, especially when we couldn't find the answers we needed. Seemed a better alternative to arguing. The alcohol made us forget why we were so angry in the first place. Sometimes. Other times, it brought that anger to the surface. That night was one of those nights. What was said . . . it's not important now, but I haven't taken a drink since." He shrugged. "It's a personal thing, you know? Like I don't trust that I could handle it."

My insides grew tight. "I had no idea."

He gave me a small smile. "Of course you didn't."

Why did I feel like that was my fault?

I noted storm clouds in the distance, billowing high on the horizon.

I pulled the book toward me, wishing I hadn't brought up the drinking thing at all. I turned another page, chronicling the members of a branch of the Kinsley family tree and their role in the Civil War. Two men of the family had given their lives for the cause of the North. A Jack Kinsley and a Michael Ashworth.

I hesitated at the last name of the latter but brushed it off quick. Surely my surname was common enough.

"I wish there was more information on the women in

the family," I mused, hoping Ethan would let the previous subject drop.

He seemed to take the hint, for he turned another page, then another and another.

"Wait, what are you doing?"

"Getting right to the Revolution. Maybe we'll actually find something about the chest there."

I leaned closer to him, saw a sketch labeled *The Battle of Bunker Hill*. It looked familiar—a wounded man central to the painting in the arms of another, who attempted to ward off advancing Redcoats. Smoke and raised flags appeared in the background, wounded or dying men in the foreground.

Below it the caption read: *Noah Winslow fought alongside General Warren at Bunker Hill.*

"Noah Winslow," Ethan said, the previous tension between us disappearing beneath the possibility of discovery.

I put my hand on Ethan's arm. "Wait." I went inside the apartment and grabbed the photocopy Ethan had made of the oath, scanned the page for the familiar name. "Yes!" There it was.

Noah Winslow.

Ethan squeezed my shoulder. "All right. We got something."

My face warmed at his touch. I curled my leg beneath me, pointed at Noah's name in the genealogy book. "This must be him then, right? The guy who put the oath in the chest?"

Ethan's brow furrowed. "Maybe . . . but why, if it was handed down all those years as something of import, did Melissa not know about it?"

"The chain was broken. Someone didn't pass on the information."

"Or Noah didn't reveal the information, or the history of the chest, but it got passed down anyway."

"And then there's the question of how he got the chest in the first place. If he was a participant in the Tea Party, from what we learned at the museum yesterday, there is no way he should have walked away with anything, much less a chest of tea. Didn't they nearly tar and feather someone who pocketed the tea?"

Ethan nodded. "Yeah, I don't understand it. Seems if he was keeper of such an important oath, he would have been trusted, a man of integrity. Not one to sneak a chest of tea off the ship."

I laughed as I remembered carrying home the empty chest. "Besides the fact that there was no sneaking around with something that unwieldy."

"Right." Ethan pointed to a small paragraph below the Bunker Hill caption on Noah Winslow.

Noah Winslow was the husband of Emma Malcolm and the father of Jacob Winslow. It appears he was a close friend of John Fulton, a bookkeeper at the Medford distillery, who wrote of Noah's participation in the Battle of Bunker Hill.

A picture of a handwritten list—this one in columns—sat below the caption. It was filled with the names of those who had fought at Bunker Hill. Noah's name was circled in red.

Ethan flipped the page, but it contained nothing more

than a brief note to the reader from Melissa's uncle, Jed Kinsley. "Not much more to go on."

"Maybe we should take a trip to the library or search Bunker Hill online. Or John Fulton. Wait . . ." I scanned the list we'd found in the chest, pointed to John Fulton's name.

Ethan took out his phone, navigated to the Boston Tea Party website. "John's listed as a participant. Noah isn't."

"Maybe he wasn't there."

"Maybe . . ." He typed on his phone again. Within minutes, he'd pulled up a page of the National Park Service, Boston division. It was a roster of those at Bunker Hill. I looked over Ethan's shoulder as he scrolled to the *W*s.

I pointed. "There."

Again, our guy's name.

Noah Winslow* (W)
    Town: Medford
    Rank: Lieutenant
    Regiment: Prescott's

"What does all that mean?"

Ethan scrolled back to the top of the page. "The asterisk means he received money for his service in the battle. The *W* means he was wounded."

"The book didn't mention all that."

"The book was written a while ago. Researchers may have found more details since then. I say we visit the historical society, ask for help with more information finding Noah." He opened a new tab on his phone, typed the society's name into Google. He groaned. "They're only open on Sunday afternoons. Looks like we have a couple days to wait."

"Let's try the library, then."

Ethan agreed and we gathered our things just as large drops of rain splattered on the composite deck boards. A crack of thunder sounded, and we slipped inside as a colorful swarm of beachgoers across the street packed up and headed to their cars.

A chill washed over me upon entering the air-conditioned apartment and I rubbed my bare arms. "I can fix us some sandwiches before we head out."

He was staring at me again, and I felt the tension crackle in the air. A bolt of lightning flashed over the sky. "Why do you do that?" I asked.

"What?"

"You know . . . get all intense on me."

"I was thinking that it wasn't weird . . . talking about Allison with you. And that I'm enjoying this." He patted the genealogy book on the island of the kitchen, left his hand there.

I gulped in a breath. "I'm glad you can talk about her with me. No matter how things were when she died, she was a part of you. An important part from the sound of it." I stared at his hand, still on the genealogy book. "I've felt guilty leaving the way I did before, but knowing all you had to go through—her death, the broken legs, and that I didn't know, that I wasn't there to help you through it . . . I think I feel most guilty about that." I stepped closer, placed my hand on his, even as I wondered if it were the wisest decision, this initiation. But I wanted him to see my heart. To understand.

Not to hate me for what I'd done. "I am sorry, Ethan. If I could do it all over again, I would do it differently."

"How so?"

This was foreign territory—this wearing your heart on your sleeve type of stuff. Ethan had changed. But of course he had. Going through whatever he had with Allison, it seemed to have made him more vulnerable. I wasn't sure I was a fan.

But I'd changed too. If anything I'd grown harder, more relentless in pursuing what I thought would make me happy, what I thought would give me purpose and identity beyond my broken family, my broken mother. And yet, in the six years since I'd left Massachusetts, I couldn't really claim I was happier. More self-satisfied, more confident, maybe. But happy?

What was happy anyway? Happy was working alongside my crew. Falling into bed exhausted from a grueling day at sea. Here, discovering bits and pieces of the tea chest history, discovering bits and pieces of Ethan again. But those things were all dependent on circumstances, on succeeding even, or on another person.

I gathered a breath, forced myself to answer honestly. Standing here, before Ethan, I felt like a failure once again. I prided myself on being loyal to my crew—to near strangers who came together for a common goal. But what about this man whom I'd first given my heart to? How could I have ever been faithful to him while pursuing a military career? How would I do things differently if I could do them again?

"I think I still would have left."

He turned his hand upward, our palms now touching, the gesture a thousand times more intimate than it had just been. "I would have understood, you know. I would have gotten it. I had dreams too. We could have chased them together. I only wish you had trusted me with them."

His calloused fingertips grazed the inside of my wrist, causing my heart to thud with steady beats. My senses heightened, every cell of my hand aware of his nearness, seeming to transport that wakefulness to the rest of my body.

He stared at my lips, and I forced myself to concentrate on my words.

"How would that have looked for us, Ethan? Us seeing each other once, maybe two times a year? I left without telling you because I thought that's what would be easier—for both of us."

No matter my loyalty. In the end, making a clean break had seemed the best choice, the least painful.

The thought shattered me. For didn't I put myself through pain every day in order to strengthen my muscles? Wouldn't BUD/S training put me through the worst physical and mental pain I'd ever known? Yet I sought it out. Trusted it to hone me.

Why then, when it came to people I cared about—Ethan and even my mother—did I shy away from the hard? Was it possible that going through the fire in these places could make our bond stronger, could heal it even?

While I didn't make a habit of keeping and coddling memories from childhood, there was one I couldn't shake. I was eight, sitting on the toilet of our apartment, trying to muster enough courage to rip a Band-Aid off a scraped knee from a bicycle fall. I stared at the grout in between the tiles, grimy from wear and lack of cleaning. I'd wanted to keep the Band-Aid on; Lena insisted I take it off. She came into the bathroom, a silky light Victoria's Secret robe around her skinny waist, the polished toes of her tanned, bare feet on that dirty grout. She knelt beside me, looked at me for the first time in a long time. "Sometimes you just have to take the pain, Hayley. Rip it off and then it's over."

Now I wondered if that's how she felt when jabbing needles into her arms. Feel the pain, then it's over. Why had I ever thought to listen to this woman's advice?

That day on the toilet, Lena had ripped my Band-Aid off, and it hurt. But she was right about one thing: I didn't have to agonize over it anymore. The pain was gone.

That's kind of what I thought I'd been doing when I enlisted in the Navy without a good-bye to either Ethan or Lena. Ripping the Band-Aid off. Yes, it would hurt, for all of us. But once it was done, I wouldn't have to wonder about making the right decisions anymore. I wouldn't have to wonder about saying good-byes.

Now, staring both Ethan and my past in the face, I wondered if my reasoning had been all wrong.

"Was it easier for you, then?" Ethan asked.

I swallowed. His fingers pressed against my skin now, finding the delicate pulse that throbbed heavy at not only the topic of conversation, but at his nearness. "I missed you," I whispered. "Is that what you want to hear?"

"Yes," he said, bringing my hands up against his warm chest. I felt small beside him, safe—things that once reminded me of weakness, but I didn't mind in this moment. He mapped my face with his eyes, seemed to explore every part of me. "Was that too much to ask after all we shared that summer?"

Some sort of mysterious force held us together. Desire churned within me, sending pulses of deep want to every inch of my limbs. Another crack of thunder rolled outside. Finally Ethan lowered his mouth to mine, slight stubble on his face brushing against my skin. I deepened the kiss, and passion erupted inside me.

With the remembrance of his touch, of his lips, I felt a teenager again. A blanket of sand beneath us, waves sounding around us, Ethan had shown me that physical love didn't have to be a forced and dirty thing. It could be tender, beautiful.

We'd found stones that night, smooth, with white swirls.

"Let's bury them here, Hay. To remember this night. To remember us."

Were they still there? Did Ethan ever think of them?

I ran my hands beneath his shirt, found warm skin and muscle, longed to draw him closer.

But he took my hands in his own and ended the kiss on a groan. "We can't."

I looked at him, rejection setting something on fire within me. "Why not?"

"Because it's not how we ought to do this."

I'd been good enough for him in high school, but now that we were adults and didn't have to skulk away and hide on a beach, I wasn't?

"Fine." I turned away, searched in the cupboard for the can of tuna I'd bought earlier in the week, trying not to show my hurt.

"Don't do this, Hay." His tone had an edge, a warning.

I flipped my ponytail over my shoulder. "What?"

"You know what." He came around the island. "You're the

one who left us. There's still this bond between us, but no way for me to even know where you'll be tomorrow. Maybe you can sleep around with your Navy guys and not give it a second thought, but I'm not one of them. And I don't play that way." His voice softened. "You know what it took me to get over you? I'm not ready to go through that again."

Why did I feel like the bad guy here? And why did I want to abandon ship, demand he leave this very moment? Maybe take his stupid tea chest with him.

And at the same time I wanted to fall into a pile of girlish tears and beg that he forgive me, ask how he could be so very honorable and good while I didn't seem to have a chance at finding anchor.

Some things, it seemed, would never change.

CHAPTER TWENTY-SIX

Hayley

ETHAN HAD STAYED for lunch. Stilted conversation, awkward embarrassment over tuna sandwiches with too much mayo. After we'd finished our meal, he took our plates, rinsed them before placing them in the dishwasher. When he was done, he turned to me, dish towel over his shoulder, arms crossed. "Ready to go?"

"I should really get in a run, actually. Probably try Lena again. Why don't you go on without me? Maybe I'll catch up later." It wasn't a total lie. Another run would do me good. BUD/S was coming fast and maybe letting myself get distracted hadn't been the smartest move.

"It's raining."

"A little rain doesn't stop a SEAL," I said.

He looked at me, mouth tight. "Right. A SEAL." He put the dish towel on the counter, grabbed his keys off the island. "Okay, no problem. Call me when you're ready."

I pointed to the genealogy book. "Don't you want to take all that?"

"No, we'll catch up when we catch up." He opened the door, then he was gone.

I rubbed my eyes with my palms, stared out the slider window to where streaks of rain ran like tears on the glass.

He was so relaxed about everything. Why couldn't he *not* be in control for once?

I blew my hair away from my face and went into the bedroom to change. A run would clear my head. Then I would go to Medford, see Lena. This time I'd camp on her porch until someone came home or opened the door.

I laced up my sneakers. It wasn't too late. I'd come here for a purpose, and I would carry it out. I wouldn't let my mother define this Ashworth legacy.

My last name echoed around in my head, making me think of the genealogy book and Ethan, the Michael Ashworth we skimmed over.

I got off the chair, ignoring the sudden urge to call Ethan and apologize. I took the Kinsley genealogy, flipped to the Civil War page, stared at the short information on Michael Ashworth and Jack Kinsley. I paged to an outline of Noah Winslow and Emma Malcolm's family tree, saw that Michael and Jack were both great-grandsons of the couple, but while the branch of Jack's family tree seemed to continue, it appeared Melissa's uncle hadn't researched Michael's further than the three children he'd had prior to the war.

Looking at the tree, I understood why. Noah and Emma Winslow had two granddaughters—one had married a Kinsley;

the other had married an Ashworth. To research every branch of the family tree would have proved overwhelming, certainly.

The chances were slim, and yet I couldn't help but wonder . . . I grabbed up my phone, tapped out a text to Uncle Joe.

Kind of an offhand question . . . you don't know if we have a Michael Ashworth who died in the Civil War in our line of ancestry, do you? If not, how far back can you trace our lineage? You know, anything before Grandpa Dan?

My thumb hovered over the Send button as I pondered how absurd it was that I suddenly cared about my family heritage. Honestly, except for being related to Uncle Joe, I'd never particularly cared about where I'd come from, hadn't known my grandfather except through Lena's scathing remarks.

I sighed, hit Send, and put the phone down. Uncle Joe never responded right away—sometimes, with his missions, I didn't hear from him for weeks.

I stared at the screen. When no response came, I chastised myself for thinking I could be related to this chest—and its originator. Besides, we were trying to figure out the story behind the chest, not my family ancestry.

Still . . .

I went to my phone again, found Melissa's name this time.

Hi Melissa, it's Hayley. I was wondering if you might be willing to connect me with your uncle Jed? I have a few questions.

Her reply came quick.

Sure. He loves talking about all that stuff and will probably be very interested in your find.

She listed an e-mail and a phone number. I opened up the mail app on my phone, composed a quick note explaining how we'd been in touch with Melissa, what Ethan and I had discovered, and finally asked if he'd done any additional research after he'd published his genealogy. I didn't say why I asked but did sign the note Hayley Ashworth, hoping he'd notice the connection. I sent it, put my phone aside, rubbed my temples, and wished I hadn't been so childish about what had happened between me and Ethan.

Our time together, our time to figure all this out, was limited. Of course I had trouble seeing that in the midst of my anger, in the humiliation of rejection.

Yet calling Ethan to apologize didn't sit well with my pride.

I didn't particularly care for this part of my personality—the part that worked hard to shield me from emotional pain, from rejection. But I had no idea how to open it up, pry it loose from where it had been firmly locked since childhood.

Outside, the sun broke through dark-gray clouds, shining light upon the drenched boards of the deck. Droplets gathered on the boards beneath the brightness, splendid like a million diamonds. They hadn't looked beautiful until the sun had touched them with its brilliance.

Too bad my soul couldn't change just as easily. A little touch of sun to make it more beautiful, more loving, more forgiving, more soft.

Yet I knew, from experience, that allowing for such things would only increase my chances for hurt. It was simply safer this way.

All those things that made me vulnerable and weak brought nothing but pain.

CHAPTER TWENTY-SEVEN

Hayley

ETHAN MET ME outside the Medford Public Library. I allowed him to take the chest from me.

It had taken me an entire day to call him. An entire day of sending e-mails to Melissa's uncle, an entire day of willing my uncle Joe to text me back, an entire day of pouring myself into my training, nursing my wounded pride, and again knocking on Lena's door and not receiving an answer.

Ethan let me enter the library ahead of him. "Did he say where he'd meet us?"

I shook my head, my attention drawn to an older man in a dress shirt with a prominent stomach, who raised his hand at us and shuffled over, arm extended long before he reached us. "Hayley?"

I held my hand out. "So nice to meet you, Mr. Kinsley."

"Please, just Jed. And you must be Ethan?"

Ethan shifted the artifact under his arm and held out his hand, gave Jed a firm shake. "Nice to meet you, sir."

"I asked the librarian if we could use the learning center to talk for a few minutes." He led us to a room, where Ethan placed the chest on the table before us.

Jed held his hands out to it but didn't quite touch the sides. His glasses slid down his nose. "Would you look at this . . . ? Amazing. I haven't seen it in years and now . . . well, it's taken on a whole new meaning, hasn't it?"

I opened the freezer bag with the original oath. We had only shown Melissa, but I felt Jed should see it too. I took it out, unfolded it with care. He didn't touch it, just looked it over with such respect and admiration that both the oath and the tea chest seemed to grow in value before my eyes.

Ethan cleared his throat. "We plan to hand it over to the Tea Party museum. We were just giving ourselves a few days to find out more, if possible. We hoped to figure out why the list was in the bottom of the chest in the first place. And why your family didn't know about it."

Jed nodded slowly, his eyes never leaving the round-robin. "And you've narrowed it down to Noah Winslow."

"He was the only one from that time in your family, and his name is on the oath." I pointed to Noah's name, upside down and angled toward the bottom of the paper.

"Unfortunately, colonial writings are rare, though they did increase with the war. I took it upon myself to research a bit last night and this morning—I hope that's okay?"

I nodded, released a nervous laugh. "It is your family."

He smiled—a kind smile. I noticed a worn ring on his

finger and wondered if he and his wife were happy. If they had been married for a long time, if their children—Ian and Elizabeth, I knew from his research—would pass on the genealogy book, if their family line would continue to record their history.

Again, that foreign sensation of loss over not knowing my own family's history—over maybe not even really caring—came to me. A sense of loss over what would likely never be. To be proud of my family line, committed, loyal—as I was to my military family. But that happened over time. It was born of sacrifice for one another, going through tough times and sticking by one another. The only thing that linked me to Lena was a chain of tarnished memories: abandonment, neglect, manipulation.

Why then couldn't I release the idea of seeing her before going to BUD/S?

Ethan shoved his hands in his pockets, looked at Jed. "Did you find anything worth noting?"

He placed a stack of photocopies on the table. "I found some journal writings from a Reverend David Osgood, who served in Medford. He mentions Noah and his wife, Emma, a couple of times."

He handed us the papers, some margins marked here and there. Ethan and I pulled out chairs and sat, the papers between us. I skimmed the first page, my gaze stopping at the star in the right margin. I looked at the text beside it.

There are many in my flock who endure the consequences of battle. Samuel Reed suffered a minor wound to the shoulder, yet infection set in

quite of a sudden. We lost him last night. He left a
wife and three wee ones. Noah Winslow lost a leg
and seems to rely heavily on the rum to deliver him
from pain. With so much recent loss, I see a sadness
gripping the family. I pray for my flock. I pray the
Lord works out good in the midst of darkness. I pray
we comprehend what it is we fight for and are able
to stand firm alongside that which we have decided
is worth so much suffering.

Ethan flipped to the next notation.

I buried little Mary Fulton today. Such a sad state
of affairs, 'twas. Though Mrs. Winslow tells me that
some of her last words were of trusting the Lord.

Another flip of a page, another notation in the margins.

I pray in earnest tonight for Mr. and Mrs.
Winslow. Word has it that Mrs. Winslow found
herself captured in Boston. I fear it is due her
own foolishness, and that of Mrs. Fulton. Rumor
spreads that General Washington plans to attack
the city imminently. Mr. Winslow is beside
himself, insisting he go to his wife. I tried to
persuade him of the uselessness of such an attempt.
A man with two good legs could not enter safely
into Boston.

   Mrs. Winslow is in the Lord's hands, may He
save her.

Ethan turned the page, but no more existed.

"That's it?" I looked up at Jed.

"I'm afraid so."

"Well, what happened to them?" I'd cared about Noah Winslow before I'd read Reverend Osgood's entries, but though it was only a few sentences, Noah and his wife had suddenly become more than just names—they'd become people, those who'd fought for their country, who'd struggled and had known tremendous loss.

They were real.

What had their ending held?

"We may never know." Jed took off his glasses, rubbed his eyes. "But I think while we're here, we should look in the library's database, see what we can find."

We agreed, letting Jed guide us in our search on one of the library's computers. He started with Noah and Emma Winslow's names but came up with nothing we didn't already know. Slumped over the computer, Jed stared at Reverend Osgood's missives, his eyes landing on the last passage, the one that told of Emma Winslow being caught in Boston due to her own foolishness and that of a Mrs. Fulton.

"Sarah Fulton," he said. "There's been more written on her than most. I ran into her often when studying this area's Revolutionary history. When I researched our genealogy, I found her husband, John Fulton, was a friend of Noah Winslow. It appears Emma Winslow and Sarah Fulton knew one another as well. Maybe if we search the Fultons, we'll find something more to go on." With renewed energy, he searched both John and Sarah Fulton. Pages of information came up. What we learned fascinated me—Sarah's role in disguising the Mohawks the night of the Tea Party, her later foray into spying and being honored by General Washington himself.

But we didn't find the Winslows' names anywhere.

Ethan tapped a pointer finger on the table beside the keyboard. "Do you think Mrs. Fulton's spying had anything to do with Emma Winslow being captured in Boston?"

Jed's brow crinkled, a thinning piece of silver hair crossing the wrinkled skin, falling over his forehead. "I would think if Emma were a part of such a venture, she would have been given credit for it by General Washington. Unless . . ."

"Unless . . . ," I prompted.

"Unless her involvement was kept secret. Much of the Fulton history we're reading is based on what was passed down from the family. I'm not saying it isn't based in truth, but perhaps there was more to it that didn't get passed down."

Like the chest. Where did it all fit?

I groaned. "We may never find the story behind it all."

Jed bestowed a kind smile upon me. "Sometimes the past is not meant to be known. And sometimes, it just takes a bit more persistence in finding. Your next stop should be the historical society. They often have records the library doesn't. It's worth a shot. And what of you, Miss Ashworth? Did you research any more of your history?"

It was Ethan's turn to sport the crinkled brow.

"No," I mumbled, avoiding both of their gazes.

"I did my own quick search into your surname, and it is indeed one of the least common names. I'd say your chances of being related—however distantly—to Michael Ashworth are decent, especially with you being from the Medford area.

Do you have a grandfather who could shed some light on his grandparents, their history? That's a great place to start. I'd be happy to help how I can after that. And who knows? Maybe we'll discover we're actually related, eh?"

That would be . . . weird. But cool. I'd never thought of my family consisting of more than Lena and Uncle Joe. That I could be distant kin to Melissa and Wyatt, to Noah and Emma Winslow, it all stirred up a foreign hope within me.

Jed gathered his things and shook our hands, wished us luck with our continued search, and urged us to let him know how we made out. Then he stepped out, leaving us alone with the tea chest.

Ethan held up his hands. "So what did I miss? What's this about you and him being related?"

"I'm sure it's just me being ridiculous. I don't see a resemblance at all." I forced a laugh.

"He thought it was probable."

"Remember Michael Ashworth, the Civil War veteran we read about in the genealogy?"

Ethan's eyes lit up. "Right." He whistled low, swiped a hand above his head. "Didn't connect the last names."

"I figured the name was common, but I googled it, and turns out it's pretty rare. Got me thinking . . . that's what made me e-mail Jed in the first place."

"We can't go to the historical society until Sunday, so you want to switch gears and look into it?"

I cleared my throat. "I don't expect you to jump on board with this." We had effectively ignored how we'd left things at my apartment the other day, but now the tension suddenly returned. A teenage boy with earbuds walked by the room we were in. The bass of his music reached us where we sat in silence.

"Do you not want me to? I took the week off from work. I'd hate to waste Ida's time."

A prickle of guilt over our squandered day yesterday—mainly due to my pride—nipped my conscience. I tried not to dwell on it.

"I'm waiting for my uncle Joe to call me back." I shrugged. "I don't know any further back than Lena's dad—and he was no picnic. Makes me wonder if I really want to find out more about my family."

"You could be waiting weeks to hear from Joe."

I remembered then how Ethan had actually met Joe once, the summer after graduation. I'd been nervous to introduce Ethan to my uncle, the closest thing I had to a father. I shouldn't have been. The two hit it off. I remembered Uncle Joe saying good-bye to me once again, putting a hand on my shoulder, squeezing slightly with those strong fingers. "He's a keeper, Miss Hayley. Good kid."

I'd smiled. "I like him."

He'd stared at me, his tanned features firm. I couldn't hold his gaze, studied his tattooed arm below his T-shirt, the dark-blue ink depicting an eagle, anchor, and pistol. The SEAL Trident. "You like him, but . . ."

Had I placed an unspoken *but* at the end of my short sentence? I inhaled a deep breath, said the words I knew my uncle Joe expected, said the words I expected of myself. "But I like the idea of enlisting a lot more."

I remember Uncle Joe's small smile of acceptance and something else . . . pride, maybe? "Well, try not to break the poor kid's heart, then. He's head over heels for you, case you're blind."

I'd laughed, felt uncomfortable with the thought of anyone being in love with me, never mind the boy who occupied so much of my time and thoughts. I hadn't meant to get attached. I would need to ease out of the relationship soon, before he got hurt. Before I got hurt. Before I believed that such a thing as real love existed.

That'd been easier said than done, though. Every time I told Ethan I couldn't hang out, he'd find me—either at Lena's or my lifeguard job or on the beach—and give me that irresistible smile that wheedled its way inside my heart . . . so naive of the fact that I was trying to ditch him, so positively endearing, that my heart would trip over itself and I would doubt my plans to join the Navy.

That's why I'd had to leave like I did. Because I wouldn't be able to hold up against a proper good-bye.

"Hay?"

I blinked, brought my attention to Ethan's smile—a bit more worn around the edges than it had been six years earlier but still doing the same amazing things to my heart.

"Sorry," I mumbled. "What did you say?"

"Are you going to just wait around on the chance Joe will call you?"

I breathed deep through my nose, gave Ethan credit for *not* mentioning my only other viable option.

Lena.

I *was* a warrior. It was time to go through with my vow to camp out on Lena's porch until she either came home or opened the door.

It was time to put on my armor and fight, face the past, face the possibility—rather, likelihood—of being hurt.

I thought of Reverend Osgood's words.

"I pray the Lord works out good in the midst of darkness."

I thought of first glimpsing the tea chest in Ethan's shop. Of how it had dropped off my counter. Our visit to Melissa in my hometown. The genealogy book.

Was Someone bigger than me working something out for good in my own life? And why, though I dared hope it, was it so hard to believe?

I *would* face my past. I *would* enter this old battleground, a place where nothing of promise ever grew, where only ashes and blackness remained.

Yet one question persisted: When I had completed this mission, this revisiting my past, would it bring any type of closure or healing to my battered soul? Would it help me move on, prepare me in every way to be among America's most elite warriors?

Or would I find myself more bruised and scarred than I was to begin with?

CHAPTER TWENTY-EIGHT

Hayley

THE RIPPED SCREEN of Lena's storm door stood before me again, representing the torn and broken pieces of my past. All waiting for me behind that door.

But it would not break me. No matter what this visit brought, I vowed I was stronger. I would conquer.

I will not fail.

I knocked again, loud and firm. No answer.

I dragged in a breath, huffed it out, then sat down on the top steps of the front porch. I'd vowed to wait, and wait I would.

Behind me, a door squeaked open. I turned, saw a shadow beyond the screen, squinted to make it out.

"Hayley?"

I stood, saw my mother in jeans and a T-shirt, more weight on her bones than I remembered.

"Yeah, it's me."

Lena opened the screen, her hands shaking. My first thought was withdrawal, but she seemed too aware of my presence, too undistracted. If she needed a fix, she'd never be able to keep a focused gaze.

"Hayley." She almost fell through the door, pawed her way around the screen. I tried not to pull away from her tight embrace but instead closed my eyes, inhaled the familiar scent of cigarettes and Suave coconut shampoo even as I longed to pull away.

When she finally released me, she held me at arm's length. "Look at you! You're all grown up, Hayley girl. I'm so glad you're here. Come on inside."

I looked at the still-open door behind Lena, a neatly painted wooden bench in the small entryway, two pairs of shoes beneath. One a man's. I glanced at Lena's left ring finger, saw a glittering diamond upon it.

For the hundredth time, I wondered if this was a new one. Or was it a man I knew, one who'd slipped into my room at night, who slid his hands beneath my sheets, searching, groping, pressing the comforter to my mouth when I whimpered too loudly?

I looked toward the two pairs of shoes again, a tight lump forming in my throat. *I would not fail.* "Um . . . okay, I guess."

She practically leaped over the threshold. The way she acted, the way she looked—it was so far from what I expected. It made me feel uncomfortable, out of place. If she had answered the door with a half-drugged stare or in obvious withdrawal, I could have walked in with confidence, heaped condemnation upon her. I'd even practiced the words in my head.

"Wow, Lena, looks like not too much around here has changed . . . same old story, huh?"

She would be nice because she'd be glad I was back, but she would also be ashamed. Ashamed I'd caught her exactly how I'd left her.

I walked into the house, still clinging to the line I'd prepared. Lena could put on a good show for a short amount of time, but her true colors would show through soon enough. Then I'd finally get the satisfaction of delivering it.

But as I walked into my childhood home, I couldn't deny that things *had* changed. The house was the same, and yet it was completely different. Fresh paint, new windows and curtains. Brighter. More airy. A sofa rejuvenated by a well-fitting slipcover. Furniture that looked familiar . . . yet seemed to be refinished in a way that reminded me of the furniture at Ethan's shop.

I choked on the words I'd been clutching tightly, almost ashamed that something akin to disappointment stirred in my chest over my inability to say them.

I was a horrible person. I'd rather see my mother fail, I'd rather put my pride on a pedestal, than sacrifice it and be happy for these small changes in Lena. Ugh.

I looked at my mother in her short-sleeved shirt with clean, bare arms. She looked back at me and gave me a clear smile.

No, it couldn't be. Had Lena . . . changed?

But she'd been in jail just a couple years ago—Uncle Joe had told me. He'd never spoken of her getting clean. Then again, whenever Joe tried to bring up Lena, I'd either ignored him or told him I didn't want to hear about her.

Lena pulled out a chair for me. I sat in it, my knees wobbly. "Want some coffee?"

Coffee.

I shook my head.

"You look good, baby. Navy treating you well?"

I nodded, slow, forcing myself to open up against the invisible vise threatening to clamp my lips shut.

"Did you reenlist? Or are you home for good?"

I found my voice. "I have another year and a half before I reenlist. I'm about to head out to California. To train as a SEAL."

"A SEAL? Like Joe?"

"Yes," I whispered. This was what I'd come to do. Tell Lena my plans, get the satisfaction of telling her I'd turned out okay, despite her nonexistent efforts. But here, now, waiting for the satisfaction . . . it didn't come.

"That is mighty impressive, baby. Imagine, my daughter . . ."

"Don't," I ground out.

"Don't what?"

"Pretend like you can take credit for anything good I've done with *my* life."

"I—I wasn't . . . I didn't mean—"

I swiped a hand through the air, exasperated with both her and myself.

Reconciliation. Yeah, right.

"Forget it," I said. "It doesn't matter." I rubbed my eyes. "How are you?"

A small smile forced its way to the corners of her mouth. She looked . . . worn, but good. Not at all like she'd been using recently. "I'm . . . good. I'm glad you came, Hayley."

"I—I actually had a question."

She twisted her hands together, seemed to wring them out upon the tabletop. "Okay."

"I was wondering if you could tell me about Grandpa, if he ever spoke of his parents or grandparents."

She stared at me, blinked. I guess I could have started with some small talk first, could have broken the ice a bit better. You know, *"Lena, the place looks nice. You seem like you have your act together a little. Do you really, or did I just catch you on a good day?"*

Yeah, small talk.

She looked nervous at my inquiry, and that's when I noticed it. Her hands started shaking. Slightly, almost imperceptibly, but so, so familiar.

I closed my eyes, didn't realize that as soon as I'd admitted to myself that Lena had improved, I'd started hoping. Hoping for what, I wasn't certain. Maybe a normal relationship with my mother? Some sort of connection? A bond I could depend on?

But as I stared at her quivering hands, it seemed the evidence shouted up at me.

Nothing had changed. I needed to get what I'd come here for and leave, forget things such as hope and all that.

"I'm doing some research into our family tree, and I thought the best place to start was here, with what you already knew."

She seemed to notice her shaking hands and stuffed them

beneath the table, leaned forward, pressed her upper arms into the edge of the table a little too hard. "Your grandfather mentioned his father—Bradford—often. He did speak of his own grandparents, too . . . I can't remember their names right now, but if you give me some time to dig around, I'm sure it'll come up."

The promise to dig around didn't seem that promising, but I nodded anyway, couldn't stop myself from wondering how the drugs she'd used for so many years clouded her brain.

I stood. "Thanks, Lena. If you find anything else out about your great-grandparents, will you let me know?"

She stood, a panicked look in her eyes. "I'll call you, okay, baby? Can I call you?"

I heard her unspoken request in the question. *Will you answer?* It found and poked at the tender places of my heart. Wow. I guess against all odds, there was still some part of that left when it came to Lena.

I nodded. "Yes." I started for the door.

"Wait." Desperation soaked the one word. Made it ooze and drip with vulnerability. Not only were Lena's hands shaking again, so was her bottom lip. "I ain't been using, Hayley. I been trying to clean myself up. Lord knows I ain't been doing perfect, but I been trying." She turned to the cabinet, to several orange prescription bottles, grasped the closest one, and shook a pill from the near-empty bottle. She downed it with a glass of water. She closed her eyes, inhaled deep.

The pill seemed to calm her. It didn't seem possible that something taken orally could work so quickly. I wondered if it were a psychological thing more than a physiological. And how ironic that she would claim to be clean, yet need to dig out a pill just to carry on the rest of our conversation.

But this was prescription. Not that that mattered—people abused prescription drugs all the time. But I supposed, considering the other option, it was the lesser of two evils.

"Joe sent me to rehab. Long-term inpatient. After I got out of prison eighteen months ago. Hayley, I don't know if I'll ever be free of all this junk, but I am better. Met someone there, too. His name's Will. We been living together for six months now, helping each other in our weak moments. He has a job parking cars at the children's hospital. It's a good job, and he's done well. Even won us a trip to Barbados on some raffle from his work. We're getting married—you know, something small—in the fall. I . . . I'd love it if you could come."

I tried to take in the information, not to simply write it off as another failed attempt, another excuse. Uncle Joe had paid for Mom's rehab. She'd found a guy—what a surprise. Another recovering addict. Super. And yet while I couldn't see how healthy that was, looking around the home, it seemed they truly were trying to make the best of it.

"I work at Walmart now. In the ladies' department. I like it, Hayley. Better than cleaning houses."

I nodded, unwilling to dash her optimism, unwilling to be the one to pop her balloon with reality.

And you know, maybe this was it. The one time Lena was going to change and it was going to stick.

"I'm glad for you, Lena. The house . . . it looks good."

It cost me something to say those words. I might be a horrible person for wanting to cling to my self-righteousness, but I felt justified in being angry over all Lena had put me through. I felt it near killed a part of my soul to push out those words, to not ridicule my mother for her attempts at a better life.

I needed to get out of here. Now. "Call me, okay? If you find anything?"

"Maybe we could grab some ice cream sometime? I'd love you to meet Will."

I didn't give a flying flapjack about Will. Her shiny new object she hoped would prove something. He was just another boyfriend to me. A distraction of hers, a crutch. And if he were anything like the others, I most certainly did not want to meet him.

I hiked in a breath. "I came here to let you know about my training. Just to . . . check in. I'm not sure about ice cream . . . I'm just not sure."

It wasn't much to offer, but it was all I could seem to give in that moment. Had I accomplished what I'd come for? Could I leave for BUD/S and feel like I'd closed this chapter of my life?

No.

The answer came swift and sure, and I grasped for words that would turn that mental *no* into a *yes*.

"You've done good, Lena. Maybe I'll visit on my next leave. Maybe I could meet Will then."

I felt suddenly claustrophobic, more so than in the cramped corridors of any ship. For a woman who spent so much time below water, I felt as if, in that moment, I must escape from the tight confines of the house I grew up in—from the tight confines of these bright and cheery walls that masked the true colors of my childhood. They stripped me of my confidence, diminished me to the scared little girl I once was, uncertain of my future, uncertain if I would sleep in my bed undisturbed. Part of me wished to pour out my thoughts to Lena, to demand an apology or some kind of remorse, and part of me couldn't stand the thought of shaking her up so badly that she might turn to something more dangerous than whatever was in those prescription bottles.

Instead, I turned at the sight of her quiet tears—tears my words had no doubt produced—and then was out the door into the glorious open air.

I was halfway to my car when Lena called out to me. "Thank you for coming. Baby."

I turned, looked at Lena's outstretched hand, her bare feet on the stoop, one hand against the screen of the storm door, probably ripping it further. She looked so pitiful there, and for a moment I tried to picture how she felt. Not hearing from her daughter for six years, then having her show up without an apology, running off again within minutes. She probably wondered if it would be another six years before she heard from me.

I smiled enough to let her know it wouldn't be. As far as that apology . . . well, hopefully she wouldn't hold her breath for that.

CHAPTER TWENTY-NINE

Hayley

"AND HOW WAS SHE?"

I shrugged, didn't make a move to leave the passenger seat of Ethan's car though we'd just parked on Governors Avenue near the Medford Historical Society. "She was . . . good."

"Yeah?"

"I mean, not totally together of course, but her house was nothing like I remember it being. It was . . . clean. And she said that she was too. I kind of believe her."

"Wow. That's great." I felt that intense gaze again. "That's great, isn't it?"

I nodded. "Yes. Of course. I guess I'm just a little gun-shy."

"It's good that you went there, you know? I'm proud of you."

Why did I not feel proud of myself? I'd done what I'd come to do, and yet I ended up feeling emptier for it.

Ethan tapped his thumb against the steering wheel. "Did she know anything about your family?"

"She knew the name of my great-grandfather. Jed called me last night, asking if I found out anything. He offered to look into it for me. I took him up on it."

"The guy's into this stuff. And who knows? Maybe he'll find you are actually related to Michael Ashworth. And to Noah Winslow. And I guess, very distantly, to him and Melissa and little Wyatt."

I didn't want to get my hopes up. It was no secret I wasn't proud of what little family legacy Lena left to me. To find out I had a rich family heritage—one dating to the founding of our country, one that included a man who had risked not only his life, but his reputation for the sake of freedom—stirred to life something small and hopeful within me. Thinking I could be related to someone like Melissa and the adorable Wyatt . . . well, it was simply more than Lena had ever been able to give.

"Maybe," I said.

We sat in silence for a moment before he took the keys out of the ignition. "Ready?"

I nodded, slid from the seat while Ethan grabbed the photocopies Jed had given us along with the photocopy of Noah's oath.

We walked down the hill to the historical society, pulled open one of the big wooden doors. A set of carpeted stairs lay in front of us, and we climbed them to the foyer.

"Hello!" an older man called from where he dusted an antique chair to the left, up the short flight of stairs. "How can I help you folks today?"

Ethan strode up the stairs, held out his hand, and once again introduced us to a stranger we hoped would be able to help us. I joined him at the top of the stairs, peered into a spacious room with plentiful windows and various displays to the left. A large painting of a woman took up a spot to the right, along with some antique swords.

Ethan explained our entire journey, beginning with the oath in the chest, all while the man listened intently. When Ethan finished, the man, whose name was Gerald, touched the photocopy with a sort of reverence, studied it carefully.

"I can hardly believe it."

"We couldn't either, at first, but we brought it to an appraiser. It appears to be authentic. We only wish we knew the story behind it."

"I may be able to help with that." He turned and walked quickly to the back of the spacious room, obviously excited.

We followed the man's wobbly steps. Wobbly, but filled with enthusiasm. I squeezed Ethan's arm, couldn't deny my own excitement.

Gerald led us across the wood floor to a display of various writings and pictures in a glass display case. He pointed to a picture of a broken stairwell on the left side of the case, just above an old teacup without handles, its blue pattern smudged with age. "This house dated back to the Revolution. It was just north of Cradock Bridge. They did a major renovation last year, completely tore out the original stairs, and found these." He gestured to the documents behind the glass. "Revolutionary writings of Emma Winslow, Noah Winslow's wife. I've studied them many times, wondered at the missing pieces . . . and now it seems some of them have been found."

I stepped closer, put my hand to the glass where the first paper lay. That the answers to our questions could be so close seemed incomprehensible. Beside Emma's journal entry was a familiar-looking cartoon. The caption read, *An artist's depiction of the tarring and feathering of loyalist John Malcolm in Boston. (The Granger Collection, NYC).*

It pictured five angry-looking colonial men surrounding a gray-haired, feathered man. They yanked his head back with a rope tied about his neck, shoved a kettle labeled *tea* down his throat. Two streams of liquid squirted from his mouth, mirroring those in the background, tea chests being dumped from a boat. Also in the background stood the Liberty Tree, a hangman's noose upon it.

I read the first line of the journal with some trouble, the script in cursive and a bit faded.

Gerald opened the case for me, and I leaned closer.

I've nowhere else to turn, and so I turn to a blank page, where lies the only hope for a promising future. One day soon, I will have to lay these musings aside. One day soon, when I become his wife.

I stepped back, my mind already full of questions. Was she nervous because of what Reverend Osgood had hinted at in his entries? Was Noah a no-good, lousy drunk?

It saddened me to think a man despised by his own wife might be behind the tea chest, behind my own family perhaps. And yet that was life, was it not? Allowing hope, bracing for disappointment. Rinse and repeat.

Ethan stepped beside me. "This is amazing." He turned toward Gerald. "Is it okay if we stay here a bit, try to read through this?"

His smile seemed to take on the look of a teacher who had answers he couldn't wait for his students to discover. "We're open until four. But this is just part of the entries. The rest are upstairs."

"Thank you so much. We'll start with these," I said. "I'm also wondering about Sarah Fulton. I read she was a spy. Do you have any record of that?"

His smile broadened. "We do. Though I suggest you begin with Emma Winslow's journals first." He returned to his desk.

Ethan placed the photocopies on a nearby glass display of an old quilt. "We're finally about to get some answers."

I rolled my eyes. "Finally? Seems this fell into our laps pretty quickly if you ask me."

"That's just because you always expect things to be difficult."

"Things *are* always difficult."

"I think you like them that way."

I didn't want to argue, or rather delve into some sort of psychology debate, so I simply shrugged. "Maybe."

Maybe I did like them that way. Less expectation, more work. But when the good things happened, I knew I'd earned them. And when they didn't happen, well, maybe I just hadn't worked hard enough.

But at least they were within my control.

I thought of the training that would await me in California in just over a week.

I'd worked hard. I'd come back to Massachusetts to see Lena, find some sort of closure. Surely that would equate to success.

Yet finding the story behind the tea chest was something thoroughly out of my control, and it seemed the answers had fallen in place. Maybe Ethan was right. Maybe things didn't always have to be difficult.

"I pray the Lord works out good in the midst of darkness."

I wondered if this—the getting without the deserving, the good in the midst of darkness—was the sort of thing I longed after, maybe even the answer to some of my emotional hang-ups. What would it be like to let go? To trust in something besides my own ability?

Ethan and I stood side by side, working out the words together, forming them into sentences beneath squinting eyes, slowly coming up with a picture of Emma's life. Emma Malcolm, if we were to be accurate. Boston resident. Daughter of a hated customs official. Soon-to-be wife of a man she did not love.

We read with rapt attention of her friendship with Sarah Fulton, of her role in the Tea Party. Straining to rush forward, to connect the pieces, we were forced to put up with the slow pace the antique reading demanded.

Still, we formed a picture. A picture of a marriage proposal on the eve of the Tea Party. Excited young love. Rebellion, and the pressing question of what to give one's devotion to—liberty or loyalty. The all-too-familiar oath.

When we'd reached the end, we stepped away, rubbed our eyes. We'd been at it an hour, each word a struggle but with a reward waiting. And now this—a beautiful discovery.

I felt something around my heart crumble. A guard of sorts. Looking here at this old document that Emma Winslow had left behind, knowing how we would find the chest she spoke of years later . . . I felt I was suspended in some sort of in-between place. Here, with Ethan, trying to solve an ancient mystery. And yet very much hundreds of years away with Emma, in despair over her future.

Liberty or loyalty.

I'd chosen liberty.

I longed for Emma to choose it also. To flee from the family that smothered her, stunted her growth, as I had. To leave behind the unpleasant and think what was best for herself. To serve her country how she could. In this desire, I felt bound to her.

"But she married Noah. This isn't the end." I felt lightheaded from the squinting, from the emotional exertion of the journey. I dug in my bag for the two water bottles I'd packed, handed one to Ethan, and twisted the cap off the other.

"You sure you want to keep going?"

"I can go upstairs and work on it for a while if you want to look around some, take a break." I knew my tone held a challenge, and I remembered the runs Ethan and I used to go on together, thought how it might be fun to do so again.

"You're crazy, Ashworth." He put the cap back on his water bottle. "I only asked for your sake."

I hit him lightly on the arm, knew we were flirting. Here, in this building of secrets—secrets that were fast becoming personal at the same time that they were becoming so much bigger than us—it seemed that anything was possible. Anything . . . maybe even me and Ethan.

My chest warmed at the thought. This wasn't in my plans. There was no room for a man, especially a civilian man, in my life. Especially *this* civilian man. I would go on to California, I would become a SEAL. I would bask in the comfort of strictly regimented days, in the purpose and calling of a military life, a military family—my real family—and there, I would be far away from Lena and Ethan and tea chests and everything that caused me to do the one thing I hated to do.

Feel.

Foreign tears pricked the backs of my eyes. They taunted me, calling out my weakness, and I hated them. I stepped toward the glass, chose to focus on Emma instead of my petty problems.

Gerald came back into the room. "How's it coming?" he asked.

"I think we're finished over here. Would it be okay if we had a look upstairs?"

He waved his arm toward the stairs. "It's already set out on the table for you. If you wouldn't mind washing your hands first in the bathroom over there, you can get started. The oils on our fingers are known to damage old documents."

We both washed thoroughly, then followed him up a winding staircase to a single dark room, two tiny windows letting in scant sunlight. A lamp sat on the table, along with a small manila file folder, open with a stack of creased, brittle papers like the ones we'd read in the display case downstairs.

"You're free to look at them all. Just treat them with care, of course. We want them around for a good long while." He winked at us.

We thanked Gerald and sat at the table, our arms pressed against one another in the small space.

We turned our attention to the pages, the top one seeming to pick up where the last one in the display case left off.

We read.

Emma wrote of the morning after the Tea Party, waking in the Fulton house but hoping to destroy the evidence of treason. She wrote of going down to the beach, seeing a tea chest in the waters . . .

The tea chest?

And now I will depart from the truth of my history. Now I will tell the story I wish were my ending instead of the one that must be. Had Samuel not found me that morning, had he not found Noah's oath, all would be different. And here I will allow it to play out in my mind—mayhap only a foolish girl's fantasies, but dear to me all the same.

If Samuel had not found me that morning, I would never have returned to Father's house. I would not be here now, writing these pages, desperate for a second chance. I would have gone to the Fultons' that morning, helped Sarah make breakfast, greeted Noah at the end of the day . . .

The entries went on. A story. A wedding, children, a genteel correspondence with somewhat-estranged parents. It was sweet, but it lacked authenticity, and even if she hadn't said as much, I would have been able to tell that this was not

Emma's real story. It seemed to fizzle out until it changed drastically with one sentence.

> All this time I have sought to comfort myself with this story, resigning myself to the fate of my future. Yet Providence has smiled upon me, even at the ill-fated mistreatment of my father. The town is mad, it seems, and still Father provoked without mercy. Still, I fear the image of his tarred, naked body will be forever branded upon my mind. 'Twas too cruel. Too inhuman an act. But 'twas just such an act that sent Samuel away. 'Twas just such an act that caused him to leave in haste. 'Twas the Lord who led me to the spot where he'd hidden Noah's oath. I have sent a letter to Noah. Meanwhile, I hold out hope . . .

I fended off a sudden chill by rubbing my arms with my hands. I had never quite thought of all the drama surrounding the birth of our country. To me, it had always sounded glorious and worthy, but here, reading of Emma's father, seeing the picture of men who claimed to stand for liberty mistreating a man, I wondered. There was so much left untold, it seemed.

"Wait." I left the table to go back downstairs, Ethan following. We went to the display case, to the painting of the feathered man. "She's the daughter of this man." I pointed to the picture. "John Malcolm."

Ethan's mouth pressed into a thin line. "She was definitely caught in the middle." We studied the painting another minute before going back up the stairs. The society lay quiet, and I wondered briefly where Gerald had gone before we sat down and continued our deciphering.

> As Father lies suffering in the parlor, calling out curses upon me, seeming to blame me for his troubles, a small part of me can't help but wonder if my disloyalty has indeed brought about these circumstances. What those men did was not right, and yet neither were Father's actions. Both proceed in the name of liberty, though I do not see that either one promotes freedom. I cannot help but think of Noah. His honor and goodness. I miss him.

"She really did love him, then. And it appears his alcohol problem came later, maybe after he was wounded at Bunker Hill."

Footsteps came up the stairs, and I slipped my phone from my pocket—4:32. We'd already overstayed our welcome.

"How is your reading coming along?" Gerald asked.

Ethan nodded. "Fascinating, but I'm afraid we could be here for hours more before we finish. Forgive us. We lost track of time."

"I can be here tomorrow if you'd like."

"Thank you so much, Gerald. We appreciate that." I looked at the papers again, Emma's now-familiar writing within reach. "Could we take some pictures?"

"As long as they are not posted publicly, you certainly may."

I snapped a series of pictures of the next several pages of Emma's journal, hoping we could see the words well enough to continue deciphering them. We thanked Gerald, gathered our things, and headed to the car. The sun began its descent, blocked by the large hill to the west, but hours of summer light would still be ours. I thought of Melissa and Wyatt, of the tea chest stored in one of the houses at the top of that hill for all these years.

"You up for more?" Ethan asked.

I looked at him, my heart aching in an unfamiliar way.

I would leave soon.

We would continue our adventure, hopefully find the rest of Emma's story . . . and then? I would go to California. To my dreams. To the schedule and structure and routine and hard work I loved. I supposed Ethan and I could keep in touch. But it wouldn't be the same. I felt the press and crunch of time closing upon us. This mystery, this discovery of the past, together.

Perhaps there was more to life than personal ambition and proving one's strength and capability. I'd thought those were the things that made me alive, but looking into Ethan's now-familiar gaze, the sun highlighting specks of blond in his hair as he held the car door open for me, I wondered if there wasn't more—much, much more to be had from life.

I smiled. "I'm definitely ready for more."

And that thought alone scared me more than anything else.

CHAPTER THIRTY

Hayley

WE HADN'T TAKEN enough pictures. I looked across the table of my apartment to where Ethan sat. Outside, night had long ago enveloped the patio, and when a chill had swept in off the beach, we'd come inside to finish working on the pictures we'd taken at the historical society.

Work on our phones was tedious, and Ethan had gone to get his laptop to put the pictures on some time ago. Still, they'd been so much clearer in person.

And now, we'd read of Noah leaving for Bunker Hill, of Emma serving bravely alongside Sarah Fulton to help the wounded men, of Noah's injury, his struggle with drink.

But we'd reached the end. We'd have to wait until we went back to the historical society tomorrow.

"This was real," I said.

Ethan nodded, his mouth in a grim line.

"I mean, I know history is real, but reading this, thinking of what they all went through . . . it makes it more to me."

"You ever think how we're not so very different than those who've come before us?" he asked. "Yeah, we have social media and more technology, but humanity . . . it really doesn't change. It's scary, but Noah, the drinking . . . I can relate. It's how I used to block out pain."

I nodded, knew exactly what he meant. I felt a bond with Emma. We'd both broken away from family circumstances to serve our country. We both often felt caught in the middle, perhaps sure on the surface but filled with doubt underneath it all. And though I didn't like to admit it, we both searched for ourselves in the security of our country.

I wondered how Noah and Emma would handle their hard times ahead.

"Hay, you ever think about leaving?"

"Leaving?"

"Your ship. Or the training you're preparing so hard for."

I felt my defenses rise. "Leave the Navy?"

He shook his head, laughed. "I know you wouldn't think of that. I mean, get a desk job or something in Boston. For the Navy."

I raised my eyebrows. "A desk job? Really, Ethan? Do you know me at all?"

He shrugged. "Wouldn't have to be behind a desk. Just something that would keep you in Boston."

I forced down the emotion bubbling in my throat.

No.

This was why I should have never come back home.

Home.

That was my problem. This place wasn't my home. My home was on the *Bainbridge* or at a training base in California, or a desert in the Middle East. Home was where the military told me to serve.

If only I didn't feel the pull of this place. I hadn't expected to feel this force, this sense of the unfinished—not just between me and Ethan, but between me and the chest, me and Medford, me and Lena.

I'd come to seal this part of my life shut, and instead, it had burst open.

I dragged in a breath, closed my eyes. "Ethan . . ."

He tapped a finger on the table. "What?" *Tap, tap, tap.* "I mean, you wouldn't miss me, even a little?" *Tap, tap.* "I think I would miss you a lot."

He raised his gaze to mine, his vulnerable words dancing over the table that separated us.

Was it reading of Noah and Emma's journey that had made him sentimental? Was it memories of high school? Or was it this . . . us . . . now?

He cleared his throat. "You ever think of us, Hay? Of starting over again, seeing where it might all lead?"

His words threatened to undo me. And I needed to view them as just that—a threat. One to be taken out and destroyed. Eliminated, so that my position could be secure.

I could never be loyal to Ethan. I'd decided on my future already, and it didn't include him. It certainly didn't include Massachusetts. I was free to make my own decisions. And this was what I'd chosen.

I will not fail.

"We're different people than we were six years ago," I whispered. "But I still have a dream, just like I did back then. And just like then, I plan to see it through. Please don't ask me to do differently—you know what my answer will be."

He slumped over, looked at the ground, gave a small, humorless laugh. "A smarter man would have given up on you long ago."

Couldn't argue with that.

Without warning, he left his seat. My heart felt like a bull pummeling my chest, looking for escape. He crouched down, grabbed my hands, looked at me with those beautiful, intense eyes. "What do you feel, Hay? Right now. What do you feel—how do you feel—about me?"

I felt my defenses rising at the pressure to admit things I wasn't sure of, at the pressure to take my focus off all that was important to me. I rolled my eyes. "Civilian guys."

"What? Because I'm being honest? Because I'm not hiding behind some tough-guy act or behind a six-pack of beer to tell you what's on my heart? Does that mean I'm weak? You think I'm weak because I can own up to my feelings, face possible rejection?"

No. No, of course not. If anything, he was the strongest man I knew. I saw that now. Appreciated that. Longed for it. But rearranging my life goals? For a guy? I'd promised myself I would always and forever look out for me first, and while that might sound selfish, it was also self-preservation. No one else was going to do it for me.

"It's not weak to let someone see your heart, Hay. I . . . I've been hurt, too. It scares me to make myself vulnerable again, you know? It's a risk—I know that better than anyone.

It can all be gone in a second. But I'm willing to take that risk. With you."

My breath came fast, and though I told myself to, I could not break his gaze. "I don't know if I can get past my fear," I whispered.

"What's here?" He put my hand to his chest, where his own heart beat strong and steady. "What do you feel when I tell you that I think I'm still in love with you?"

I closed my eyes, let his words sink in. I felt . . . hope. And fear. And heights of elation I'd never known. No matter how I tried to keep him at arm's length, he'd pushed through my walls—not with muscle or brawn but with gentleness and tenacity and patience and honesty.

Who would have thought?

"I feel . . ." Would I regret my next words come morning? "I feel like I want you to kiss me."

His gaze dropped to my mouth. He stood, pulled me up alongside him, and ran his thumb along my cheekbone. He lowered his lips to mine, and as I tasted him, my world seemed to fall away.

He loved me.

I felt it in his kiss, gentle yet ardent and hungry. His mouth moved over mine and it grew deeper, more intimate. My head swirled. This was different from our previous kiss, when I'd thought of him as a nice distraction, a pleasant fling. This was a kiss from a man who loved me.

Had he ever told me that, even in high school?

Had anyone ever told me that? Certainly Lena had never outright said it, though I assumed she must in an obligated, mother sort of way. Uncle Joe loved me, of course, but he never made himself vulnerable enough to say it. But this . . . this was different. In the midst of the kiss, anything seemed possible.

And at the same time, everything was threatened.

Silly, really, to fall in a mushy puddle at the feet of the first person to tell me such things. Yet that's exactly what I was doing. I felt it happening fast and sure, felt myself valued and worthy.

Was I also in love with Ethan, or was it the idea of having such immense worth in someone's eyes?

The thought of it all washed over me in a dizzying wave and I ended the kiss, though I wasn't sure why. Because now I would have to look into his eyes, speak words I wasn't eloquent enough to say.

He put my hands against his chest, his heart thrumming. I'd read a *Newsweek* piece explaining that one reason members of Special Forces units seemed to succeed under intense pressure was their "metronomic heartbeat"—a heartbeat with almost no variability between beats, which wasn't something most people could claim as normal. I'd often wondered if I possessed such a quality. But here, now, with my hand over Ethan's heart, I knew neither of us had a metronomic heartbeat. Rather our hearts, in this moment, were alive and feeling and filled with emotion. Vulnerable.

I could not be vulnerable.

"Hayley?"

"I—I can't do what you're asking me to do." I pressed my lips together. "I'm sorry."

A sad smile tilted the corners of his mouth. I knew he wanted me to tell him I loved him, that we would find a way to make us work, find a way to start over. But I wasn't a rush-into-it type of girl. I wasn't a feeling girl. I was a think-and-plan kind of girl. A be-cautious-with-my-heart kind of girl. And being a SEAL was my dream. Ethan would either get in the way or get hurt. I'd been disloyal to him once. I would not make the same mistake again.

He lifted my knuckles to his mouth, touched them with a kiss, causing my skin to tingle. "I get it. I guess I knew your answer, but I had to ask." He released my hands, looked at the floor for a moment before gathering his laptop. "I'll pick you up tomorrow to meet Gerald. About nine okay?"

I nodded, still dwelling on all he'd said.

My gaze fell on the tea chest, at the farthest end of the table. "You know, in all the excitement of discovering Emma's writings, we almost forgot that we discovered what we've been looking for all along."

He tilted his head to the side.

"The story behind Noah's oath. We have it now. No matter what the Tea Party museum authenticates after we hand all this over, we know the truth. And we have an entire handful of men who no one knew participated in the Tea Party, including Noah."

He nodded, that sad smile again. "You're absolutely right."

Why did he look so incredibly forlorn, then?

I looked at the chest, the freezer bag tucked inside. "Maybe we should hand it over tomorrow. We're done with it, right? We don't need the chest or the oath to finish knowing what the story is."

"Whatever you think."

"Okay."

"Okay."

He walked toward my door, then turned. "Hayley?"

A strand of hair fell over his forehead and I resisted the urge to place it back where it belonged.

"Don't leave without saying good-bye this time, okay?"

My heart crumbled in my chest.

And then he was gone, the soft click of the door echoing behind him, the faint scent of someone's burnt supper lingering from the hall.

I put my hands over my face, the realization that he knew me better than I knew myself undoing me.

I went to the bedroom, dug out my duffel bag, the one I used as a carry-on. I didn't know how to deal with what Ethan offered. I didn't know how to do vulnerable and real and feeling. And while I could blame Lena until the cows came home, when it came right down to it, it was my own shortcoming, my own deficiency.

Quite simply, I didn't know how to love.

Ethan deserved better. He didn't deserve me holding him back from finding real love. It had happened once before, with Allison. If I left, it would happen again.

And I *needed* to leave. I would not—could not—sacrifice so much for a romantic fling. I'd done what I'd come to do in seeing Lena. Mission accomplished. I would not compromise being a SEAL for a few feel-good emotions. That's not who I was. I must follow through with my plans.

I will not fail.

I took out my phone, booked a flight for early the next morning to San Diego, and packed the remainder of my things.

I looked at the tea chest, lonely on my table. Ethan knew the code to the apartment. He would come in tomorrow after I didn't answer the door. He would find the chest and make sure it got to the museum.

I wondered about the rest of Emma's story. For just a moment, I tried to talk myself out of leaving or at least putting it off for another day. But it would only prolong the inevitable.

I searched for a piece of paper and found some computer sheets in the utility closet. I sat down, pen in hand.

This time, I would not leave Ethan without a good-bye.

CHAPTER THIRTY-ONE

Hayley

Ethan,

I hate that you know me so well.

Please realize I don't take what you told me tonight lightly. Though I know I must leave—for both our sakes—I must tell you that I don't think of you as weak.

Ethan, in many ways, you are the strongest man I know.

You will find someone worth your love. I know you will.

I hope you find the rest of Noah and Emma's story. I trust you will get the chest and the oath where they belong, and I look forward to seeing you on the news when you do.

Thank you, Ethan. No regrets, okay?

Hayley

✛

When I turned on my phone after landing in San Diego, a voice message notification popped up. As the plane taxied, I listened to the excited voice on the other end.

"Hi, Hayley, it's Jed. I have some news. Give me a call when you can. Bye."

I tried not to let the call affect me. I'd left all this behind, again. But I couldn't ditch the niggling idea that Jed had found what I'd been hoping to find—that which I tried to cast off as unimportant but could not release.

I'd spent the plane ride planning my last few days of training before BUD/S, reciting the SEAL code, trying to block out images of Ethan knocking on the door of my Revere apartment, of him finally entering, perhaps knowing what he'd find, of him seeing the empty apartment save for the tea chest, of him reading my note.

No regrets, okay?

It sounded so good at the time. So light and airy and *Here's looking at you, kid*dish.

Now, thinking about Ethan reading it, it fell flat—false and inauthentic.

I'd left him again, managed to convince myself it was what was better for him. But really, I wondered if it wasn't just better for me.

And maybe not even better. Maybe only safer. That would explain why what I considered a strong decision had made me feel so awful and so very weak.

As soon as I gathered my duffel bag and made my way down the Jetway, I found an out-of-the-way spot near a large window. Outside, the nose of a plane pointed at me. I had absolutely nowhere I needed to be. I still had three days before I needed to report to Coronado. I would use those days to continue my training, to mentally prepare myself for all that was ahead.

I bit my lip a little too hard as I scrolled to Jed's profile and hit the Call button. He picked up on the second ring.

"Hayley, I've been waiting for your call. I have some exciting news."

I looked at my phone. Twelve o'clock. Three o'clock Eastern time. Had Ethan kept his appointment with Gerald?

"I'm sorry. I ended up taking a flight out of Boston this morning."

"Oh? Are you coming back soon?"

"I don't think so. I have to report for duty in a few days."

"I was hoping to show you all the work I did on your family tree." The disappointment in his voice was apparent, and once again I questioned my impulsive decision.

"I'm so sorry, Jed." He'd obviously worked hard. I'd been so eager to get away from Ethan and his words that I hadn't thought how my actions might affect anyone else, including Jed.

Briefly, I thought of Lena and her offer to go for ice cream. She'd been the one to abandon me, to not be the mother I needed. When I was eighteen, I used that as an excuse to believe it was okay to leave her. Now, realizing how disappointed she'd likely be to find me gone so quickly, I couldn't help but feel low. Real low.

"Well, I could tell you now, send you the information via e-mail. Does that work?"

"Yes—yes, thank you. And tell me how much I owe you, too. I appreciate all the time you've taken on this."

"You don't owe me anything. It's my pleasure. Besides, after what I discovered, I can say we're family."

His words sank in. All they meant, all they implied.

Family.

The word had certainly never given me warm fuzzies before, but when Jed said it, my mind raced to the tea chest, to Ethan, to a woman I barely knew and her small son, to the kind man on the other end of the phone who went through so much trouble to help me. To Uncle Joe bringing me out of Massachusetts for the first time to glimpse a beautiful bell that symbolized liberty. To Noah and Emma, their struggle and tussle with their own relationship, with their fight for the colonies' freedom.

"You mean . . ."

"Yes. I was able to trace your great-grandfather, Bradford Ashworth, four generations back to Michael Ashworth, the Civil War veteran in the genealogy. To Michael Ashworth, Noah Winslow's great-grandson."

"I can't believe it."

"Believe it. I have the proof now. We're so distantly related I suppose I can barely call us family, but we both *can* trace our heritage to Noah and Emma Winslow."

"That is so . . . amazing. I don't know what to say."

That I had found the chest, that it had led us to the story of Noah and Emma, that I could claim them as part of my legacy . . . it was all too much to take in. I couldn't wait to tell Uncle Joe.

And Ethan.

"I'll e-mail you my findings and the official family tree. It's all on ancestry.com now."

"Jed, I really don't know how to thank you."

"Are you kidding me? This is the most fun I've had in months. Any luck finding anything more about Noah?"

I filled him in on our discovery at the historical society. "Unfortunately, you'll have to contact Ethan if you want to know the rest of the story. I can give you his number if you want."

"Okay, yeah. I think I would like to give him a call."

"I'll text his number to you."

"Great. Thank you."

"Thank you, Jed. What you've done . . . I really can't thank you enough."

And I'd run away with barely a thought to him and all the work he poured into Noah and Emma's story—in a way, my story.

We said good-bye and I lowered the phone.

A little girl skipped to the window before me, pressed her palms flat to the glass, turned to look at a tall woman with long brown hair, and pointed at the plane.

I thought of Emma, distancing herself from Noah to protect him after Samuel's blackmail. Then being set free, running away with Noah to Medford, away from her parents.

Yet had she been running away? Or had she simply chosen a better life for herself? What qualified as running away? Was it the leaving without the good-bye? The sneaking away when no one expected? When someone made a decision to leave and shared their choice with the ones who cared for them, that wasn't running away. The *running away* happened when one refused to face one's problems, one's feelings.

Holding the phone in my hand, contemplating my choices, I felt like a coward. I'd always striven to be strong, to prove myself everything Lena wasn't.

And while I thought I was a fight-over-flight girl, my actions said otherwise.

I texted Ethan's contact information to Jed. Then I put my phone away, looked out at a Delta plane inching higher and higher into the clear sky.

I dragged in a breath, pushed aside my self-doubt. *That* was what made me weak. Anything that got in the way of my focus, of putting my country and my training first, of knowing what I was about, was what made me weak.

I'd left. Doubting this tactical move would not help me gain ground or secure my mission goal.

I grabbed my duffel bag and walked past the many gates of people waiting for flights. Anticipating their vacations or business meetings or time with family.

I continued walking.

Away from the plane that had taken me from Boston, away from the chest and Ethan and Lena and Emma and Noah.

I wasn't running away. I was making a choice. A choice that was necessary in order to be that special breed of warrior, in order to have that uncommon desire to succeed.

☩

Hayley,

I thought you'd like to know what I found at the society today, so I'm e-mailing you the rest of Emma's story.

Jed called.

These people . . . Noah and Emma . . . they're your people, Hay. I know you want to search for meaning somewhere far away and off by yourself, but maybe your answers are closer than you think.

Go chase your dreams, but remember, you are not alone.

I am waiting.

Love, Ethan

CHAPTER THIRTY-TWO

Emma

Which is the side that I must go withal?
I am with both; each army hath a hand,
And in their rage—I having hold of both—
They whirl asunder, and dismember me.

MARGARET GAGE, QUOTING
SHAKESPEARE'S *King John*

I SHOULD HAVE never held him.

The bloodied bundle lay in Sarah's arms, the cord tied round his neck. "I am so sorry, Emma. . . . Do you want to . . . ?"

I nodded, my body spent from working through the night over the wounded men followed by hours of wasted labor. I knew it had been too soon, and yet I hoped. I held my arms out for my son.

She cleaned him off the best she could, removed the cord, placed the tiny mound in my arms. He was beautiful. Aye, some might consider a babe so small and underdeveloped an ugly thing, but I saw past it all to the child Noah and I had created together.

"Your father would have loved you," I whispered against

slick skin still wet from birth. A sudden sob shook my body, and I wondered if I would be haunted by the weight of this tiny babe in my arms for all my days. 'Twould have been better not to know the still-warm feel of him.

So much death these last two days. So much darkness in a season that surrounded us in light. Was my babe's death a curse upon me for leaving my parents? Was it simply a result of staying up all night, of witnessing the sights and sounds of so much death? Had it been catching to my babe somehow?

Noah would wonder why I had been so long away from him. And yet when I saw him, I would have to tell him of our sweet son, borne away with the angels.

I asked Sarah to fetch me the soft-yellow blanket within the tea chest that I had made for my child, and I wrapped my babe within its warm folds—so unlike how I'd once imagined.

Sarah took the child away, and I fell into an exhausted sleep, longing for the peace I'd felt in the field hospital, longing for that presence to come alongside me in my suffering. But like my womb, I felt only emptiness.

✠

My babe was buried two days later, alongside a handful of Medford militia. Because we did not allow our dead to cross bodies of water, the majority of the burials were performed in the South burying ground, on the side of Cradock Bridge which held the hospital.

Our little one was buried in the North burying ground beside our church. I stood alone at our wee one's final resting place when Mary came up to me, a carefully arranged nosegay of wildflowers in her little hands. I knelt down to her height and welcomed the child in my arms, holding her tightly, wishing never to let go.

Noah hadn't attended the burial. Though Benjamin Hall had fashioned crude walking sticks for him, Dr. Tufts had ordered Noah abed for at least a fortnight, saying if the wound began to bleed again, the risk of infection would be all the greater. When I returned from our son's burial, I fixed Noah a meal of creamed vegetables and told him I would see what needed to be done in the shop.

He shook his head. "I think we will close the shop for a time, Emma. Just for a time."

I nodded. "Very well. Whatever you deem best." I propped a bolster pillow behind him, noticed the new lines on his face. "We *will* have more children, Noah. I am sure of it."

I said it for my benefit as much as his. He held his arms out to me and I leaned over, careful not to touch his injured leg as I nestled against his solid chest, so grateful that he showed no sign of fever or infection, yet so cognizant of the impending emptiness that hovered between us, so aware of the awkwardness of not sitting upon his lap as I once had.

"How are you, Emma? You have been through so much . . . You are a strong woman, my wife. Stronger than I realized. I appreciate that, especially now . . ."

I sniffed. "Does it hurt much?"

"Less with a mug of ale or some flip." He forced a laugh, but I knew he spoke truth, for he was never far from his cup these past two days. I didn't fault him for it. 'Twould take time, but we would heal. Noah's leg would soon not hurt quite so much, and someday, though I could not imagine, the ache in my arms would lessen as well.

The night before I'd asked him if he wanted to talk about what happened upon Breed's Hill, just as we'd spoken of the Concord battle.

And though he'd never raised his voice to me before, I would not soon forget his visible frustration as he tried to settle himself upon our small sofa. His face red, droplets peppering his brow as he held himself up to readjust his lower half, the bandage soaking with blood from the activity. His low growl. "No, I do not wish to talk of it. I do not wish to talk of anything unless it is of the rest of the colonies coming to aid us."

I heard news of Dr. Warren's death upon Breed's Hill from Sarah. I heard of the defeat of our troops, of the massive injury done to the Redcoats. With Mr. Adams and Mr. Hancock in Philadelphia, and with the defeat of Bunker Hill still very much a part of our memories, a gloom seemed to hang over us all.

And I tiptoed around my husband and filled his request when his mug became empty of strong drink.

Liberty. 'Twas a strange notion. Noah would be bound to crutches or mayhap a wooden leg for the remainder of his days. Dr. Warren's children were left orphans. Many a woman was left without a husband, without a son. I hadn't pondered the full extent of the sacrifices we would be called to make in the name of freedom.

If I tallied them up, I wondered, would it be worth the cost?

CHAPTER THIRTY-THREE

Emma

While we are contending for our own liberty, we should be very cautious
of violating the rights of conscience in others; ever considering that
God alone is the judge of the hearts of men.
GENERAL GEORGE WASHINGTON

JULY 1775

The provincial army officially became the Continental Army
with the arrival in Cambridge of a new leader, sent by the
Continental Congress. General George Washington seemed
to invigorate the raw and ragged troops around Boston, even
as the conditions in Medford grew bleak.

Refugees from Boston and burned-down Charlestown
poured into our town. Rumors flew that General Gage was
evicting those crippled with smallpox into provincial territory. A smokehouse just south of Sarah's home was set for
anyone seeking shelter in our town.

And still they crowded in. Noah could not yet climb the
stairs without aggravating his wound, so he gave our room to
three soldiers. Another three stayed in the shop. They came

and went, and I tried to keep them fed, but the market was slim, the town dirty, the scent of human waste pervasive. Many died of dysentery.

I went about my household tasks with arms that physically ached for our son. Milk long dried up, I could almost understand what Noah spoke of in feeling the pain of a leg he no longer possessed.

☩

The house lay quiet. The soldiers had been out all afternoon, as had Noah. I tried not to think of where my husband spent his time, but I knew. The tavern seemed to call his name every afternoon this week. He'd only just started venturing out of the home, and I could scarce comprehend that he would rather spend his time among men deep in their cups than at home with me.

I sighed and put the now-cold ham and biscuits on the warm stove. The door opened, and I startled as Noah hobbled through, shoving it closed with one of his crutches. A curse passed his lips and I cringed, unable to recognize the man before me—not because of his missing leg but because of what losing that leg was causing him to become.

I thought of two nights before, when we had come together as husband and wife for the first time since before he'd been wounded. What had once been an act that bonded felt graceless and uncomfortable. I felt Noah did battle in our lovemaking. As if he fought something unseen that he didn't want to remember, the stench of ale heavy on his breath. In the end, he had become frustrated, and I wasn't quite sure that I wasn't the one he was frustrated with.

I'd turned on my side and cried myself to sleep, praying for the lost man I loved to come back to me.

Now, as he stumbled toward his print shop, his drunken gaze wavering, I could not help feeling a rise of disgust within me, and I felt ashamed.

He did not speak a word, but I heard him sit on the chair near his press and leave the door open. I turned to the cupboard, tears stinging my eyes. I swallowed them back. I had not left my parents and all I knew to give in to defeat the first time it presented itself. I must fight for my husband. If he was not strong enough to do so at this time, then I must do it for him.

I reached into the cupboard on the uppermost shelf, taking down the cup Sarah had given me all those months ago. I let my thumb travel over the Oriental pattern and then down to the chip at its base. I hadn't taken much into this new life—the tea chest, Noah's book, my writings, and this cup were all the vestiges of my old life, and the only reason I held them dear was because each, in its own way, was also a part of Noah.

I set the cup down and went about heating some water to steep some dried mint leaves. When it was finished, I carried the offering to the shop, sure that Noah would see the significance of me bringing out this special relic. Perhaps we could talk. Truly talk. I could assure him of my love, and maybe he would take me in his arms as he used to. Maybe I would welcome his embrace and feel safety within it instead of fear.

He didn't look up when I entered the room.

"I brought you something," I said, forcing cheer into my voice.

His gaze flickered toward the cup, but he kept his elbow resting on the end of the press, his face pointing toward the open window. "I don't much feel like drinking tea, Emma."

I held it out to him anyway. He hadn't seen the cup. If he would only look . . . "Are you certain? It'll do you good."

He ran a hand over his face. "You drink it."

I pushed it toward his chest. "I made it for—"

But with one quick motion, he slapped it from my hand. "I said I don't want it!" I gasped as hot tea sloshed upon my skirts and the cup shattered on the floor, its simple pattern broken in many pieces. I went to it, in disbelief that he had done such a thing—reminiscent of what Father had done when I'd once offered him a cup of water after his tarring.

It couldn't be fixed. Looking at the cup now, tea seeping into the wood of the floor, I could hardly remember how I'd once felt about my husband. What was more, I hardly cared to remember. I should have never run away with him. If I had left Boston with Mother and Father, if I had gone back to England, mayhap I would have met a gentleman whom I could have come to love. I could have lived in a fine house with servants. I could have bathed often and not endured the putrid stench of human waste baking in the hot sun the moment I stepped out of doors. Mayhap I would have borne healthy children.

How did God expect me to keep such an impossible vow to this man who had become a stranger to me? I'd joined him with liberty in mind. Was this—suffering the behavior of a husband—freedom?

✠

I closed the door and allowed a breath of relief to pass my lips.

'Twas not right for a wife to sneak out of her own home with pale excuses of needing a measure of precious flour. But I did it more and more often of late, particularly at this late-afternoon hour, when Noah had been in his cups the near livelong day.

His wound had closed up. And yet while the pain should have dulled, he continued his drink.

Despite my attempts to urge him to think what he might write in his paper to stir the colonies to recruit more men, his old passion could not be spurred. I never knew which moods might strike the day. Sometimes he would lash out in frustration and humiliation; other times he would beg my forgiveness and tell me how he loved me. Both times, it felt as if there was a part of him I could not reach, even with my love. That a part of him had indeed died that day on Breed's Hill. Or perhaps he had sealed it off himself, deep enough for me to never find.

I walked to Sarah's, crossing Cradock Bridge, hoping to arrive before John came home. I knocked on the familiar door, and when my friend answered it with a raised brow, saying, "Out of flour again?" I could not stop the tears that came.

A look of pity came upon her face and she closed the door behind her, put an arm around my shoulder, and led me down toward the river away from the ever-present crowd of soldiers.

We didn't speak at first, and though I hadn't outright spoken of Noah's struggle, I also knew that Sarah understood. I suddenly felt selfish. People died every day from dysentery;

soldiers were in need of supplies. And here I wept over a surly husband.

We stared at the river for a moment, its muddy banks growing dry from the summer heat and the little rain we'd had of late.

Finally Sarah spoke. "This river is like a roaring lion in the spring, when the snows melt and the rains come. It's peculiar how circumstances can reduce it to a pitiful stream." She dragged in a breath. "Noah is fighting right now, and at the same time, he's given up his fight. He's realizing how weak and dry he is. It's your turn to be the roaring lion, Emma. You must fight for him. I don't mean for you to stand by and allow him to overtake your spirit. I don't abide with drunken men who don't know when to shut their mouths or keep their fists at their sides, but this drought is new for Noah. I trust God will help him to see in time, to restore him to the roaring lion he once was. And I'm trusting He will use you to do it." She put her arm around me and I tried not to sob into the shoulder of her dress. "Be patient, dear. And come and get as much flour as you need."

I laughed through my sniffles, grateful to have her on my side.

"Emmy!" Mary came barreling down the hill, her blonde braid flying.

Sarah squeezed my arm. "Take all the time you need. I'll have your flour for you when you're ready." She left, tugging Mary's braid as she passed.

The five-year-old launched herself at me, and I clung back, inhaling the scent of lavender her mother used in her hair to keep the nits away. Though I loved all of Sarah's children,

I couldn't deny the bond I felt with Mary. She had always adored me more than the rest, and after we buried my sweet babe, we'd only found a closer tie, the precious child often bringing me wildflowers for my wee one's grave.

Now, I sat down beside her, arranging my skirts to cover my legs.

"Why are you crying, Emmy?"

I swiped at my wet cheeks. "'Tis nothing, dear. Grown women get sad sometimes too."

"Remember when you told me that if we tell each other what we're afraid of, our fears lose their grip?"

"I do."

"Maybe that's true for what makes us sad, too."

My bottom lip trembled at her thoughtfulness, her desire to help. "I—I am having trouble helping Mr. Winslow."

"Because of his leg?"

"Yes . . . though I think it may be his heart that needs the most help."

"I will pray for him. Reverend Osgood says Jesus knows about everyone, so He must know about Mr. Winslow's leg, and his hurting heart. I will pray he gets better."

I put an arm around her and pressed her close. "You are a sweet child. Do you want to know a secret?"

She leaned closer until our foreheads were touching. "What?" she whispered, her face all conspiratorial.

"Someday I hope to have a daughter just like you."

She smiled, her entire face wrinkling with the idea of holding such a secret.

We stood, and I hugged her one more time. "Mr. Winslow's going to get better, Emmy. I just know it. You'll see."

CHAPTER THIRTY-FOUR

Emma

As the season is now fast approaching, when every man must expect to be drawn into the field of action, it is highly necessary that he should prepare his mind, as well as everything necessary for it.

GENERAL GEORGE WASHINGTON

OCTOBER 1775

I pressed the edges of a pie crust together with a fork, the utensil creating lines on the dough. While many household staples were in short supply, I had managed to grab a few apples from the orchards beyond our home to make this special treat.

A knock came at our door, and I brushed my hands over my apron and opened it to the sight of a teary-eyed little John.

I thrust a hand out to him. I had not seen the Fultons since last Sunday meeting. "John. Whatever is the matter?" I'd never seen this boy cry.

He surprised me by throwing his arms around me, tucking

his wet eyes into my floured apron. "'Tis Mary. Mama says you must come and bid farewell."

Mary . . . nay. Not Mary. My chest grew tight at the thought of the child. She'd been fine the last time I'd seen her. I couldn't imagine her anything but a ball of energy. Yet the devil had surely gained a foothold in our town, the dirtiness of it causing the deaths of dozens—at least half of them children.

I held the boy close, felt the burn and prick of my own tears behind my eyelids. I lowered my voice. "We will come. Allow me to get Mr. Winslow." I watched my feet as I made my way to the shop. It had been months since the battle of Breed's Hill. Months with no change to either his heart or our marriage. I could not fathom what to expect from him any longer. Would he be angry? Deny that our friends needed us now? Would he refuse to come?

As usual, Noah sat on a chair, his crutches leaned against his abandoned press. He stared out the window to the dusty roads, the wooded hills beyond dotted with vivid color.

I came behind him and placed a hand on his shoulder. He jumped, and I realized he'd been deep in thought or, as so often was the case, a drunken haze.

"Little John is here. Mary is sick. Very much so. I'm going there. . . . Will you come?"

He looked at me, his eyes clear. "Mary?"

"Aye."

He looked out the window, and I noticed the full growth of whiskers he hadn't bothered to shave for some weeks. I thought he might tell me to go alone. He did not go out much, except to meeting and sometimes the tavern. I know he did not like to be seen, to be stared at and whispered of.

But he rose, grabbed up his crutches. "Aye, we will go."

The three of us started the walk down the dusty road. When we crossed Cradock Bridge, we nodded to Colonel Stark, who spoke with some officers outside the tavern, before following young John into the Fulton house.

He led us upstairs to where Mary lay, her breathing ragged, her face leached of color. Sarah turned, eyes glazed, from where she sat at her daughter's bedside, holding her hand. With the aid of his crutches, Noah went to where the girl's father stood against the wall and put his hand on the arm of his friend.

'Twas one of the first gestures of compassion I'd seen in him in a long time.

Sarah opened her mouth to speak, but no words came forth. John spoke for her. "Dr. Tufts did all he could. We also called an old friend, Dr. Brooks from Reading. But both say there is nothing more to be done. Only that we keep her comfortable."

Mary's siblings gathered around. Sarah and Ann lovingly stroked her blonde locks, splayed on the pillow. Lydia sat at her feet, her hand upon her ankle. My heart bent in two.

'Twas not right. It should be another. It should be me. Not this child, a light in so much darkness.

Sarah stood, offered me her chair. I slipped my hand into Mary's and her eyelids fluttered. A small smile etched upon her face.

"Miss Emmy . . ."

I pressed my lips together at her nickname for me. How would this family survive without this ray of sunshine?

"Darling . . . I love you, dear." I did not care that the entire family heard me. For in that moment, I cared only for this little girl, always so bright and alive.

She licked her lips, tried to speak. I leaned close so I could hear her faint voice. "Mama says I may get to visit the angels soon. Do you think they'll like me?"

I blinked away my tears. "Dear, they will absolutely adore you. And when you get there, you must say hello to my little one. Will you do that?"

She smiled, seemed pleased with her mission. "If I can't find him, I will ask Jesus. He knows about everyone."

I stood, trying to disguise my tears. "That's right, little one. He will love to meet you." I pressed a kiss to her head, then left the room with Sarah. I embraced my friend, her arms shaking, her normal strength wilted.

"It happened so quickly. Her sickness. If only there were more . . ."

"What can I do, Sarah? Would you like me to take any of the children home with us for a bit?"

She shook her head. "We must be together in this. They may regret they are not here when . . . the time comes. And I can scarce bear to let any of them out of my sight, anyhow." Her teeth chattered and I ran my hands along both her arms.

"Do you wish us to stay?"

"Nay. Only to say farewell. Thank you for coming."

We embraced again and reentered the room. Noah sat in the chair this time. He held out a beautiful hawk feather, wispy lines of tan and dark brown perfectly formed. He placed it in Mary's palm. "I think this was left for you. Mayhap 'twill help you fly with those angels."

Another weak, small smile. "Is your heart better, Mr. Winslow? I asked God to help it."

Noah cleared his throat of emotion even as my own threatened to burst forth. "I believe He has, little one. Thank you."

I placed my hand on Noah's shoulder, and he rose, took his crutches from John. "Tell us if you need anything. Anything at all. We will be praying for a miracle."

John nodded, his eyes red.

We left them to face what they must.

This time we walked home, just the two of us, our hearts heavy in silence along the road. When we arrived at our house, it seemed unusually quiet, the soldiers who stayed at our home having gone to meet up with General Washington in Cambridge. Rumors of a planned attack against Boston had begun to circulate, the general waiting for the harbor to freeze over to aid in the attack and catch the wintering troops off guard.

And still we awaited the hoped-for arrival of the cannons from Fort Ticonderoga.

The crust of my pie had dried. I brushed water over it, put it upon the hearth to bake. Noah stood beside the table, watching me.

When I could think of nothing else to do, I sat and allowed my tears to come—soft at first, then guttural, heart-wrenching half prayers of anguish. I felt I was losing my babe all over again, and my arms ached afresh at the thought of little Mary giving up her life.

I heard the hobble of Noah's uneven step behind me, then the weight of his hand upon my shoulder. I leaned into him, uncaring that my tears made me look weak and emotional, uncaring if I ever moved from this spot again.

He slid his hand along my shoulder until his arms were around me, and I let him hold me for a long time, the tears exhausting me as much as they washed me of some hidden need to acknowledge the pain of my heart.

When they finally settled to hiccuping sobs, I straightened, knowing I should check on my pie but having trouble finding the strength to lift my body from the chair.

"I know things need to change, Emma."

I looked at my husband, standing with the aid of but one crutch. He had filled out some the last few months, his upper arms and chest gaining new muscle. It suited him.

"I need to change."

My heart tripped upon the words, hope sprouting somewhere deep beneath the pool of sadness that gripped my heart. I drew back on its reins, tried to suppress it. "How so?" I asked.

"You've been patient beyond belief with me. And I don't mean only with my physical limitations. I mean with the sourness that's been eating me alive. The heavy drink. I've known for some time that it all needed to change, but here, now, I am telling you for the sake of accountability. Looking at Mary . . . at Sarah and John's beautiful family . . . The Lord has allowed my leg be taken, but He has still granted me life. I saw that on my walk this morning. I saw it just now in the sadness of that house." He paused, leaned a hand on the back of a chair. "I've behaved inexcusably. And I don't expect you to forgive me. But I wish to prove myself to you."

My bottom lip quivered, my breath came fast. I swiped at my eyes, then wiped the wetness on my apron. "I—I should like that."

He held his arms out to me and I came into them. He gripped me, the perfect contradiction of gentleness and fierceness in his embrace. I thought of Sarah's words, comparing my husband to the Mystic.

"'Twill not be easy," he whispered into my hair. "But I refuse to hurt you any longer. I am so very sorry that I have." His chest shook with silent tears and I thought his emotion was not only over our circumstances and over little Mary's sickness, but over the fact that for the first time in a long while, he was very, very sober. He could feel.

"I think you should open your shop again. We should open it again." We could print writings to aid the troops' morale, to put new life into the cause. We could do it for Mary, who had prayed for Noah.

He pulled back from me, gripped my arms, and kissed my forehead. "Aye, I think that is a good idea."

Something like a wall came down that night between us. And though we were drenched in sadness for the Fultons and for the loss we felt over Mary's battle, I felt that at least this time, we were in it together.

Before we settled in for bed, he came to me, the precious cup he'd shattered sealed back together, and though the cracks covered it entirely, it was sturdy as ever. I hoped 'twould last. I hoped 'twould be enough for a lifetime.

✣

JANUARY 1776

The miracle had not come for Mary, but it did come for Noah.

After that day in October, he never took a sip of strong drink again. He attributed it to Mary, being with the angels and Jesus, somehow helping him along on his journey. He told me often that whenever he thought of taking a drink, he needed only think of Mary and the promise he made to himself and to me the day she died.

By now, loss was so familiar, I came to expect it. When news of a young one's death came, it did not surprise. Rather I sought to wrestle out the pleasantness in life, to be grateful for each drop of goodness, to trust the Lord, as Mary had, to take care of the eternal.

The winter set in dreadfully cold. We printed a manual titled *Common Sense* by a man named Thomas Paine, sold them along with news of the needs of the troops at Cambridge. The manual seemed to strengthen our resolve, for which I was grateful.

A group of Medford women gathered to make coats. Sarah seemed more avid about her wartime role than ever before. Mary's death created an almost-reckless need in her to get behind the Patriots. Though she did not state it, I wondered if she blamed her daughter's death on the presence of the soldiers in town, on the fetid conditions we fought daily. I did not think she could bear to consider the war being lost—her little girl dying with no reason behind it.

I visited her one cold winter day to deliver a coat I'd

made. The keeping room fire glowed warm and Sarah sat by it, sewing on a button for a soldier's coat with fluid, vigorous strokes. Deep crow's-feet lined her eyes, along with the corners of her mouth and brow.

"John went to meet the delivery of wood intended for the Cambridge army."

"That is good."

She poked her finger and let out a small curse. I took the coat from her and finished where she left off.

"I hope you rest once every seven days or so."

She stoked the hearth, jabbing it with the poker. "No time to rest. Our men don't rest, nor should we."

I stood, placed a hand on her arm. "Sarah. You must take time to grieve."

She near slapped my hand away.

The door opened and John came in, hat folded in his hands.

Sarah looked up. "Well?"

Sarah had never been a particularly feeling woman, but she'd always held compassion for her family. Now though, with Mary's death, she seemed on edge, anxious to complete this thing that had been started. It seemed to drive her every action, her every word.

"I purchased the wood from the trader, but on my way home I ran into a gang of Redcoats. They seized the wood, held me away with their muskets. There was naught to be done."

Sarah's face grew hard; she breathed deep. "They stole our wood."

"Aye. Some men are planning to see what we can gather in the hills tomorrow afternoon. 'Tis a shame."

"Aye," she said.

John said he must find Colonel Stark and tell him the bad news. A few moments after he left, Sarah had her shawl on.

I stood, wondering what she had in mind. "Sarah . . ."

"I am going."

"Going? Where?"

"To get our wood."

And then she was gone.

I threw on my cloak, raced after her to their crude stable, calling to her. "Sarah!" She ignored me, saddling their mare. "Sarah, these are not the same men you served at your mother's tavern. They've been hardened by war. They are defensive, in enemy territory. How can you expect to stop them?"

"I don't know, but I will not stand by and do nothing. You may either come and help or go home and pretend you know nothing."

I hadn't thought to help her until she suggested it. Still, I wavered, thought of Noah at home on his press. He'd found purpose again. Mayhap I could enlist his help. But nay, he was still not confident upon a horse. Yet could I let my friend go alone? What if something happened? She had an entire family depending on her.

"Allow me to go in your stead." I would certainly be more pleasant than Sarah. Mayhap the soldiers would see the error of their ways and relent.

Sarah laughed. "Emma, I would be glad for your help, but you are too sweet to accomplish this task alone. Now, I'm going. Do not stand in my way."

Whoever thought being sweet could sound like a cause for ridicule? I was not too sweet. I loved this cause—and the men behind it—just as Sarah did. She was not the only one who had suffered loss.

"Very well." I turned to saddle their other horse. Sarah did not wait for me but started ahead. I flung myself atop the mare, wishing I'd spent more time letting Noah teach me to ride when we first moved here. But no matter. The horse was eager to go after Sarah, and I clung tight to the reins, allowing the mare to run free. We raced north past our home, where Noah, if he glimpsed anything out his shop window, would see a blur of horse and cloak and hair.

We rode past the marketplace, veered right onto the road to Malden, the wintry dust kicking up with the horses' steps, the thrum of their hooves echoing to the center of my being. Another two miles or so and we spotted the coats of red, muskets at their sides, leading a team of oxen pulling a massive cart of lumber.

Sarah gained upon them and they stopped, no doubt wondering what this petite lady intended. She dismounted and marched up to the lead oxen, taking them and attempting to turn them around.

I could not fathom her boldness.

The soldiers looked at one another. One readied his musket. I dismounted, prepared to be the voice of reason to save my friend.

"What are you about?" one of the Redcoats asked, visibly shaken by Sarah's audacity or mayhap, as I did, wondering at her sanity.

"I've come to claim the wood my husband paid for."

The oxen began to turn back to Medford. The other soldiers followed their officer, readied their muskets.

"Ma'am, if you don't move, we will have to shoot you."

"Shoot away, then."

'Twas her grief that made her careless. Either that, or she waged bets that they wouldn't dare harm her. Legs as sturdy as custard, I came alongside her, my hand finding the smooth horn of an ox. I straightened my shoulders. They'd taken what was not theirs. Our men depended on this wood. And they would have it.

Something akin to fire sizzled in my belly at taking a stand against them. At directly fighting for the cause I had so many uncertain feelings for. Like Sarah, though, I knew Noah's leg and the loss of my babe and Mary's death could not be for naught. I had wanted to fight where Noah couldn't. All this time, I had wanted to find a purpose, find my voice. Here lay my chance.

The men vacillated. The officer in charge was the first to put down his musket. "We must let them have it, men. 'Tis theirs."

They turned and were gone.

My heart had never beat so fast in all my life. We watched the backs of the Redcoats, waiting for them to turn and change their minds. When they didn't, we grasped one another's arms. Sarah smiled for the first time in months.

We led the team home, and though we acquired some strange looks at the sight, no one questioned Sarah. No one usually did. She insisted we stay silent so as to spare her husband any unneeded embarrassment.

The next day, John brought the load to Cambridge, much to the appreciation of the troops.

Though Noah was appalled when I told him the story, I did not breathe a word of it to anyone else. I did, however, add the account to my journals and tuck them within the tea chest. If I were to ever have a daughter, I wanted to tell her how her mother had once stood up to a band of armed Redcoats.

CHAPTER THIRTY-FIVE

Emma

It is a noble cause we are engaged in; it is the cause of virtue and mankind.
GENERAL GEORGE WASHINGTON

AT THE END OF JANUARY, word came that our very own Boston bookseller, Henry Knox, had successfully returned from Fort Ticonderoga with not only cannons, but howitzers, mortars, and sixty tons of artillery.

We waited with bated breath for General Washington to make his move. Though we did not know when or where, we knew it must come.

I thought of Mother and Father often. While we had parted on unpleasant terms, I did hope they had left the city as planned. I imagined Father clutching the box that held his tarred-and-feathered flesh as he boarded a ship that would take him to England. I imagined him showing it to the king, having the audacity to request being made a knight for his immense suffering and humiliation at the hands of the Bostonians.

Father was a bold and stubborn man. A strong man, however misguided. I had always seen that as a strike against him. Yet after I helped Sarah obtain the wood, I wondered if mayhap I had inherited some of his bold strength. Was it those who came before us who gave us the individual characteristics that made up our personalities, or was it those who came alongside us—Noah and Sarah and Mary—who shaped us to become who we were?

We visited the Fultons often in the weeks after Mary's death. Noah grew stronger and, with the help of Dr. Tufts, fashioned a wooden leg for himself. While he still used a cane and progress seemed slow, we enjoyed the excuse to walk, even in the cold. Food staples being slim, I often shared what we had with the Fulton family so the children would not go without.

One afternoon in early March, Noah and I made our way south, a basket of biscuits hung on the crook of my arm. I'd donned my warmest cloak and muff, for though thawing temperatures gave reminders of spring, the night air still bit one's skin.

When Sarah opened the door, the heat from the hearth enveloped us. I offered the basket and she took it with much thanks.

"John is upstairs. He started a fever last night."

Noah and I exchanged worried glances. Sarah caught our look. "'Tis not what Mary had. He will be fine." Her tone was sure, hard, as if she could force something to be simply by saying so. But I caught her tense shoulders and thin form as she turned to tend the hearth.

Noah cleared his throat. "I will see to the horses." I tried not to admonish him with my gaze, to warn him to take care.

I knew it niggled him when I did. He needed to go about everyday chores, forge new ways to do old tasks.

I grabbed up the kindling. "Here, Sarah. Allow me. Why don't you go for a walk? 'Tis beautiful out today. Or perhaps rest a bit?"

She jutted out her chin. "Are you telling me what to do, Emma Winslow?"

I matched her chin with my own. "Aye. I've learned a thing or two about being stubborn, Sarah, and your kind of stubbornness will put you to an early grave. Would it harm you to take a bit of aid when 'tis offered?"

She pressed her lips together. "I suppose 'twouldn't hurt to catch a breath of fresh air while the little ones nap."

I raised my eyebrows and nodded, trying not to gloat in my victory over her will—no small feat. A knock came at the door and she smoothed her hair beneath her mobcap before opening it.

"Major Brooks. Come in, of course." She allowed the tall doctor to step inside, the long tails of his blue coat brushing against Sarah's table. The red waist sash and gold epaulets that symbolized his high rank seemed to dwarf the two of us. While I knew that General Washington worked to restore order within the Continental Army, I also knew that before he arrived in Massachusetts, soldiers were awarded ranks by how many they could recruit. I wondered if the fact that Major Brooks was a doctor and a respected and learned man had also contributed to his rank.

I thought of my husband in the barn, who had given his all for his homeland, how he would never ascend to such honor attributed in coat adornments. Did it bother him?

While he'd been granted a pension due to his injury, the outcome of the war would no doubt determine how long, or if, such a pension would last. I couldn't ignore how he no longer earned the same respect he once had when walking into a room—the same respect Major Brooks now commanded. Noah had won out over strong drink, but I knew he was haunted by things he did not yet share with me. Now, looking at Major Brooks, strong and immensely capable, I wondered how Noah felt when he was beside such a figure, knowing that his injury would never again permit him to contribute to the fight for liberty. How did that sit with a man? How did it sit with my husband?

Sarah closed the door behind the major. So much for her rest. "A cup of sassafras tea, Major? Tell us to what we owe this pleasure."

"No tea, thank you. I just came from the distillery, but they reported that John was home. Is he here, ma'am?"

"I'm afraid he is ailing with fever. I was just going to look in on him. Can I be of assistance to you?"

His gaze flicked to me and I chastised my face for reddening.

I gathered my cloak. "I will go see to Noah—"

"Nay, Emma." Sarah squared her shoulders at the major, much as she had done the day we'd retrieved the wood from the Regulars. "Whatever you need say, you may say it to Emma, Major. She is my dearest friend and I don't keep secrets from her."

His mouth drew into a straight line. "Are you certain John is not well enough for conversation? Mayhap I could examine him whilst I am here."

Sarah obliged and went with the major to see John as I waited by the fire. When their steps sounded on the stairs as they returned to the keeping room, I caught the major's words. "He needs plenty of fluids. Try to keep his fever down with cold compresses. And aye, you were correct, Mrs. Fulton. He is not fit for conversation, nor for what I had in mind."

Sarah gestured to a chair. "Tell me what you need, sir."

"I am not sure 'tis wise work for a woman . . . Then again, this may be the hand of Providence."

"Major?"

Again, his eyes came to me. I drew myself up, too curious to take my leave now but feeling I must assert myself. "Major, I aided the Mohawks in the dumping of the tea. I still hold a paper of oath with all their names upon it, secreted away so one day I might tell my children of their father's hand in our freedom. My husband gave up a leg upon Breed's Hill and nearly his life. He was not one of the cowards who ran . . . and neither am I."

I had never felt so certain of my place, so proud of the cause for which we fought.

The major nodded at my words, and I saw something akin to respect in his eyes. "Very well, then." He took a small bundle of papers from the bag he carried. "I came to see if John might be willing to deliver some important dispatches inside Boston this night. 'Tis urgent they are received. I'm aware of his familiarity with Boston, particularly the South End, and I thought of him." He dragged in a deep breath. "Time is of the essence. They are from General Washington himself."

The room grew silent at the name of our respected leader. But to go into loyalist-occupied Boston beneath the cover of night?

In a strange way, my heart ached at the thought of my old home. I remembered the fire in my chest that had burned to life as I stood alongside Sarah to retrieve the cart of wood. It kindled within me now at the prospect of helping Major Brooks and General Washington, at helping the cause for which I was now so deeply entrenched I could not tell where it began and I ended.

"I will go." My voice echoed in the room and I realized that Sarah had spoken the words in unison with me.

The major looked between us. "You both will go?"

Sarah shook her head. "Nay, Emma, you must stay. I will go. 'Twill be quicker with one."

"'Twill be safer with two," I countered. "And if something were to happen to one of us, there might still be another to see the dispatches delivered."

The door opened and Noah stopped short at the sight of the major. He recovered quickly, hobbled inside, and offered his hand to the officer to introduce himself. The major stood, taking Noah's hand. Then the two men sat as the major quickly explained the predicament we found ourselves in.

I watched Noah do battle within himself, hating the inadequacy of his leg. "I could go upon a horse."

"'Twill require going through Charlestown, rowing across the river to Boston, then much more walking to get to the destination. I'm sorry, Mr. Winslow. I greatly value all you've given in the name of liberty, but I fear one of these ladies is the better choice."

"Ladies?" Noah nearly sputtered, looking at me.

"'Twould be safer for us to go, Noah. No one would suspect a woman of carrying such dispatches."

"They may if they catch you rowing across the Charles in the dark of night! Nay, Emma. I may not have say in Sarah's decisions, but I cannot in good conscience allow you to risk it."

I tried to see past his determination to what truly lay at the heart of the issue—fear. I knelt at his side, put my hands upon his lap.

"Noah . . . were you not fearful when you built the fortifications atop Breed's Hill, when you faced the Regulars that day?"

He kept his mouth closed, breathed deep.

"You moved past it, my love, because you knew liberty was worth the fight. Now you are being asked to put it aside again. 'Tis not foolish to allow me to take up the struggle in a fashion I am able. 'Tis not wrong. It is for that same fight that I am willing to do it. I've knowledge of Boston. I am young and strong enough to see it through." I licked my lips. "You once stated it was my strength of mind that drew you to me. Would you snuff it out now, in the Patriots' time of need?"

Sarah stood. "And she will not be alone."

I turned to her, glad to have her on my side, and smiled. "Aye, we will go together."

The major looked at Noah. "Seems if any are capable, 'twould be these two women."

Sarah nodded. "If we are stopped, I have dozens of stories in my head that any dunderheaded Redcoat will believe. No one would dare harm us."

Noah shifted in his seat, looked down at his wooden leg with a sadness that squeezed my heart. "What is so important that my wife is bent on risking her life, Major?"

The officer's Adam's apple bobbed. "Dispatches from General Washington. As you may have heard, and as I implore you not to repeat and only impart to you now because I trust you, there will be an attack from Dorchester Heights in a few days' time. The general feels he must warn a certain friend of his—a Patriot—behind enemy lines. This man will relay the news to the other Patriots within the city. Surely you see he cannot attack in good conscience with innocent men in harm's way."

Noah lifted doleful eyes to me. "Aye." He looked at Sarah and Major Brooks. "May we . . . ?"

The major nodded. "I will explain the details to Mrs. Fulton in the parlor."

They left.

Noah inched his fingers to the back of my head, slid them beneath the hair piled below my mobcap. "Emma, if anything should happen to you . . . I do not think I could live with myself."

"All will be well. And if it be not, you would go on and be strong with the Lord at your side, as I would have been forced to do if you gave your life at Breed's Hill." I knew my words spoke simply—too simply, perhaps—of immense suffering. Yet here was not the time for such ponderings. "I will have Sarah with me. They will not harm two women."

"This is so important to you?"

"It is."

He sighed. "Then I suppose you must go."

I kissed him long, my gratitude evident.

"Be sure to use that beautiful mind of yours, though. No unnecessary risks."

I nodded. "We will be back and well before morning. You will see."

"I will be praying 'tis so all the long night."

CHAPTER THIRTY-SIX

Emma

Every temporal advantage and comfort to us, and our posterity,
depends upon the vigor of our exertions; in short, freedom or
slavery must be the result of our conduct.

GENERAL GEORGE WASHINGTON

THE STONE POSTS of the carriage entrance to the Royall mansion stood like sentinels in the dark of night. Everything, in fact, seemed to take on a different quality beneath the dark of a secret mission. The trees seemed to possess eyes, ones that might betray the whereabouts of my companion and me.

The grounds of the Royall property were no longer the rolling wonder of peaceful orchards. Beneath the scant moonlight, I saw how they'd been stomped and drilled and marched on by many soldiers, battle-worn just like the people who refused to give up their fight.

In her warmest cloak and muff, Sarah moved soundlessly in the night. She had sewn General Washington's dispatches into the hem of her skirt, and as we walked, I remembered the last time I had possessed knowledge of such an important document.

I thought of the oath, concealed within the tea chest. How long ago it seemed that Noah had first shown it to me. I remembered him then, sure and full of youth. He was different now. And yet so was I. Was that not what journeying through life together meant? Not that we stayed unchanging but that we lived and learned and clung and wept and laughed and danced and grew and changed, all alongside one another.

As Sarah and I continued our walk toward Charlestown, we did not speak. We'd chosen not to go by horse, for fear we might give ourselves away. A wispy cloud darkened the moon, the cold silence seeming to echo our steps along Medford Road. We passed Winter Hill without incident, and before long, we saw the gleam of the Mystic to our left once again.

We approached enemy territory—Charlestown Neck. Bunker Hill rose in the distance, its fortification eerie lumps of shadowy earth. I knew that the colonial militia had been given orders by the Committee of Safety to base their fortifications upon Bunker Hill. I also knew that the command was ignored as the officers directed the soldiers to build their battlements on the smaller Breed's Hill, closer to Boston and to the Regulars, evoking a potent response from the King's Army. A forceful one that could not be engaged with so little gunpowder.

Colonel Stark had told us how he'd ordered his men not to fire until they "could see the enemy's half gaiters," hoping to save their gunpowder until it was bound to hit.

I tried not to wonder how any small change that day might have changed the course of Noah's fate—either for the good or the bad.

"Do you see anyone?" My breath hit the cold air in a visible puff, my heart sounding so loud within my ears I feared any soldier within a mile might hear it. Certainly the Regulars would post a sentry at the neck. Certainly they would protect what they had fought so hard for last June.

Sarah had a story at the ready—something about needing to get to her uncle to tell him of his dear cousin's impending death. But with much surprise, we crossed the narrow strip of empty land without resistance.

Bunker Hill stood to our left and I glimpsed the second hill—Breed's—the one where my husband lost his leg. For an insane moment, I walked alongside Sarah in silence, mourning my husband's leg, morbidly preoccupied with what had happened to it. Had the cannon that had blown it away simply blasted the limb to pieces? Or had it been torn from Noah's body to land somewhere on that hill, where it now rested?

I dragged in a shaky breath to ward off the image. We approached the empty remnants of Charlestown on our right, its charred shadows rising black and ghostlike beneath the moon. Hollowed-out homes and a tower of stones that once denoted a chimney poked through crumbled bricks and timber. The Regulars had torched the town during the battle, and as far as I could see, no life endured.

We continued down to the beach, where several rowboats were tied at the wharves. I breathed a prayer of thanksgiving that our journey had been undetected so far, that it seemed the Lord paved a way for our success. If only it would continue without delay.

Sarah untied the boat and I stood watch, noting the bob

and flow of the Charles River. Many had died while swimming in its waters. Sarah told me of the death of her own grandfather, found drowned while on a canoe outing. While the North End of Boston seemed deceitfully close, I knew it was not so. Stories had come to us of the rider Revere lighting lanterns at Old North Church, its white spire a glint in the moonlight now, and then of having two men row him across to Charlestown to warn of the impending invasion upon Concord.

Mr. Revere had taken this same path. At night. Only he'd had two men to row him. Would Sarah and I be able to handle the boat? What if the tide carried us away from our destination or flipped us upside down, General Washington's papers and our bodies nowhere to be found save for the bottom of the sea?

Though it did not make sense, I longed to hear the bells of Old North again. To let their chimes cast out the demons they were believed to defeat, one more time, on this night, for me and Sarah.

Noah had a right to be frightened. Perhaps I had been callous and disrespectful of the dangers of this mission. And yet some part of me grew determined to conquer these perils, to do this thing not only for myself and for my husband, but for the innocent in Boston, for General Washington, for the legacy of the Sons and Daughters of Liberty, for my own unborn children even.

I tamped down my fear as I slipped into the boat behind Sarah, the frigid wind biting my cheeks. I drew my hands from my muff, inched the edges of my cloak around my face, and took up an oar. Sarah adjusted the hem of her skirt, placing it protectively in her lap so it would not become wet and ruined by the slosh of the oars.

We rowed without speaking, our breaths counting out a rhythm, our oars in unison as the boat sliced through the water. In the distance, a man-of-war stood guard over the Charles. When we spotted a sentry patrolling its decks, we stilled our oars, waited for him to disappear below deck before continuing.

Chunks of ice surrounded us, the harbor only now beginning to thaw from a long winter. I thought of General Washington's plans to use the ice to attack Boston. Though I couldn't be certain, it appeared his plan had been denied, or mayhap he had thought better of it. A second plan was now in place. One that would occur within a few days' time, mayhap on the anniversary of the bloody massacre on King Street.

My fingers turned numb with the cold, the icy water slashing at them with frozen fingertips. Once I nearly dropped my oar. Sarah and I took two short breaks to catch our breath and warm our fingers as best we could, but still my toes grew numb beneath the flimsy covering of my boots.

The river kept pulling us away from our destination, and my muscles strained as we aimed for Copp's Hill. We could not afford to miss our mark.

The shore inched closer, almost tantalizing for the respite it offered. My arms burned, my fingers throbbed numb and painful all at once.

When the keel of our boat hit a small beach, I breathed out long and slow, tried not to succumb to tears. We had made it, and at the same time I could not imagine how we would have enough strength to return this night. 'Twas a good thing we had both decided to come, for I did not see how one alone could have made the journey across the river.

Sarah pulled the boat in, and careful to avoid the ebbing waves, I gingerly stepped out, both of us seeking the warmth of our muffs for our hands.

The town stood quiet, as it was well past midnight. British detachments might be out, patrolling the streets, but if we listened for them, we should be able to stay clear.

We passed Uncle Daniel's burial spot and wound our way south, where I could not resist a look at my old home on Cross Street.

Like much of the town, it stood lonely and abandoned, Mother's flower boxes long ago cut off for firewood. I glimpsed my window, remembered Noah climbing the portico to see me. How very long ago it all seemed.

An intense longing for my husband overcame me. A longing for the man he was when we'd met—the one with the dancing eyes; a longing for the man he was now—the one with the patient smile and tender touch. I could not wait to be home the next day, to bury myself in his arms and never leave his side again.

Sarah and I crossed Mill Creek, and I dared hope that our destination would lead us to a cup of chocolate and a bit of warmth by an open hearth before we made our journey back. In the distance, marching feet sounded off cobbles. We ducked in an alley, held our breath as a group of dragoons passed us, red coats worn and faded beneath the moonlight.

Lights of the Royal Exchange tavern glowed and we

skirted around them, keeping toward Long Wharf to avoid the center of town.

Everything about the city spoke of weariness. Dirt and ice had pressed between tired cobbles, making them uneven and lopsided. The roofs sagged; once-booming businesses were boarded up, their ragged fronts chipped of paint. The Clarkes' warehouse lay on the left but it too looked abandoned.

I did not hear the steps upon us until 'twas too late. I pushed at Sarah, told her to run. Hands grabbed at my cloak. I stifled a scream just as I saw my friend making her way around the next corner.

As hard fingers turned me around, I could only think on my relief that Sarah—and General Washington's dispatch— had gotten away safely.

Then I looked into the face of my captor.

CHAPTER THIRTY-SEVEN

Emma

It [is] impossible to beat the notion of liberty out of the people,
as it [is] rooted in 'em from their childhood.

GENERAL THOMAS GAGE

SAMUEL.

I had supposed he had gone back to England. But clearly he'd been hiding with the loyalists in the town, cowering beneath the protection of the King's Army.

"It *is* you," he said, a slight slur to his words. "I thought my eyes fooled me." He dug his fingers into my arms.

"Pray, Samuel. Let me be. I—I must see my kin to tell them of an impending death in the family."

The words, which had sounded so reasonable when Sarah had relayed them, sounded lifeless and false to my own ears now.

His hands continued to knead my arms. "I've missed you, Emma. I thought you were gone, off with your parents to England."

"I—I did not go with them."

His fingers loosened but did not release.

I wondered if Sarah kept to an alley, waiting to help me, or if she had gone on with our mission. I could not fault her if she had. 'Twas part of the plan. Still, I felt suddenly alone and trapped, abandoned. I had escaped this town and this man long ago only to walk back into their clutches.

He stood, unsteady before me, and I thought to run from him. He was drunk. I could surely escape him in the dark alleys. But I must wait for the right opportunity.

"How do you fare?" I asked, knowing nothing would distract him better than talk of himself.

"I would be better if I weren't stuck in this insufferable town." He looked at me more closely. "You are frozen. Come home with me and warm yourself."

I near succumbed to the invitation, as I now shivered beyond control. I had never been so frigid in all my life. "N-no thank you. I must see to my kinsman."

He narrowed his eyes at me. "You did not go with your parents. Did you marry him, then? That Yank of yours? Why is he sending his lady to do such dirty work?"

I didn't answer, for to lie felt to dishonor Noah, yet to tell the truth would prick Samuel's pride.

He nodded, knowing. "I see. If I were your husband, Emma, I would never let you wander the streets of town alone and cold. I would keep you home, nice and warm." His fingers went to my icy cheek and I turned from them. "A real man would not allow you into such danger."

I slapped his hand away. "None of this is your concern."

His grip grew stronger. "Perhaps it should be. He is obviously not taking care of what belongs to him."

My bottom lip trembled. "You know nothing. Now excuse me, I must take my leave."

"I will escort you. Tell me your destination."

I searched my mind. He needed to get as far away from Sarah as possible. The North End. I knew it well and might be able to escape him there.

"Ship Street," I said.

"Very well." With a viselike grip upon my arm, we began our journey north.

I wondered what I might do when we arrived at Ship Street, if I could simply pick out an abandoned home and feign disappointment if no one answered. Hoping no one answered.

We crossed back over into the North End. I waited for Samuel to loosen his grip. I would run and hide near Copp's Hill Burying Ground. I would wait for Sarah in sight of the boat. We would return this night, across that frozen expanse of water and on toward home. By dawn's light, I'd be in the cozy home Noah and I had made together. I'd have naught to fret over but a loaf of bread to be made, mayhap a press to be set. I could near taste the contentment, the freedom, remembering all Samuel had symbolized to me—the tight chains that once bound me.

When he laughed at one of his own jokes and stumbled on a cobble in his drunken haste, he lost his hold of me.

I ran.

Though my toes were numb and unwilling to propel me forward, I forced my feet fast up Middle Street, my breath heavy in my ears, my muff in one hand, the burying ground my goal. I took a sharp left on Beer Lane but ran into a solid mass.

A pleasant chuckle reached my ears. "Well, what do we have here?"

I looked up from my wincing to see a red coat, brass buttons shiny in the moonlight, epaulets upon his shoulders. I sensed more Regulars behind him.

"Now, lass, where are you off to in such a hurry?"

More footsteps behind me, then Samuel's voice. "There she is! Sir, don't let her get away. She is not loyal to the crown. She is likely here to betray us all."

My heart sank at Samuel's words, at the solid brick of a man before me, backed by his patrol. It seemed all my efforts were for naught. I should have heeded Noah and not come at all. What help was I to Sarah and Major Brooks and General Washington if I only drew attention to myself and our secret endeavor?

The man in the bearskin hat spoke. "Those are serious allegations, sir. What cause have you to make them?"

Samuel seemed to sober under the intense gaze of the officer, and I inwardly begged him not to implicate me. We were not friends, that much was true, but our families had been, at one time. Could he not spare me?

"I was to wed this woman. She is daughter of John Malcolm, honored servant of the king, who was humiliated by the rebels. This woman ran away with the rebels, from me and from her own loyal father. I see no reason for her to be in the city now and suspect her intentions are less than honorable."

The man cleared his throat. "This is hardly discourse to have in the middle of the street. You both will be escorted to Province House, where we will continue this conversation with General Gage."

The long, cold walk back to the center of town and then on toward the South End caused my brain to numb. By the time we'd reached the grand entrance of Province House, the copper weather vane at the top depicting an Indian archer, I could only anticipate the warmth within, not the intense questioning—and the answers I didn't have—that would surely ensue.

Somewhere in my frigid mind lay the thought that Sarah must have certainly accomplished her mission by now. She would take the boat back to Charlestown, for what else could be done for me? 'Twas one thing when it was only Samuel, but now I was in the hands of General Gage himself.

As I followed the red-coated officer inside, the warmth enveloped me like a thick afghan. I went to the fire of the sitting room, put my hands to it without invitation so they might begin to thaw.

"General Gage will not be pleased to wake at such an hour, but your allegations are cause for urgency." The officer sent a man in the direction of the stairs.

A short time later, my limbs still frozen through, the general came into the room in full uniform, red sash and waistband, epaulets and brass buckles gleaming. I began to shake at the sight of him, certain my reaction was not entirely from the cold.

I'd heard rumors the general's wife sympathized with the Patriots. Might he be a reasonable man? Certainly not as hard as Father. What was my best course of action?

He sat in a large wingback chair, crossed his legs, and raised his eyebrows at Samuel. "State your case, Mr. Clarke."

He was familiar with Samuel, then. Was that to go against me in this inquisition?

Samuel stepped forward. A stray hair fell before his face, the only sign of his drunkenness. The fresh air and circumstances had apparently sobered him nicely.

"I've reason to believe this woman should be investigated."

"Go on."

"Her name is Emma Malcolm. We were to wed two years ago. Our families had been close, until her father was tarred and feathered by the rebels, until this woman ran away with those who committed such a crime, until she ran away from our nuptials and into the arms of the rebels. I have not seen her since, which leads me to believe she has no due cause in being here tonight." He left out the oath, surely knowing it would implicate not just me, but both of us. I realized then that his bringing me here was likely a result of his anger. He'd thought I had gone to England with my parents—that, he could accept. Now, knowing I had stayed, realizing that I had wed a Patriot instead of him, he was determined to make me pay.

General Gage listened to Samuel's words. He stared at the worn Persian rug at his feet, and when Samuel was done, he released a tired sigh. He seemed so very human in that moment, weary, and I saw how this conflict weighed on him.

"And what have you to say for yourself, young lady?"

This was so far removed from anything I could have imagined when setting forth from Medford with Sarah. Then, I had assumed we might be stopped at Charlestown Neck, that

I would allow Sarah to explain our unlikely whereabouts in her confident manner. I had even pondered being stopped in Boston, but not alone. And not required to give an explanation to the commander of the King's Army himself.

I could argue with Samuel, state that he had been the one to flee Boston, yet what did the general care about such a paltry matter?

I swallowed down what felt like a hot stone lodged within my throat. Still, my body shivered. I would need to lie.

What made a lie worthy? Was the cause of liberty worth it? Was my life?

"I c-came to seek out a kinsman for my husband. 'Tis his uncle. My husband's father is ill and his brother needed to be told."

I felt the sear of General Gage's gaze slicing hot through my chilled body. "Why did your husband not come himself? Why send you?"

Samuel's words came back to me, accusing, and I felt the need to defend Noah.

"My husband is not able to travel, as he is unwell also."

More untruths, or rather, part untruths. 'Twas a dirty business, war. In that moment, I wondered why I had involved myself. I'd considered it honorable, this fight for liberty. And though it might be, war perhaps was not. It caused men—and women—to do dishonorable things. To deceive and kill. I'd been a fool to think I could make a difference, to think I could earn the respect of Sarah and Major Brooks and General Washington—and aye, Noah—by accomplishing such a secret mission.

What did it matter now?

"And what might be the name of the kinsman you came to inquire of?"

I scurried to think of the name of a Patriot within the town, but I knew none. I thought of a common name, one that I hoped wouldn't draw suspicion. "Charles Smith."

"On Ship Street," Samuel added, and I tried not to glare at him.

"Is that right, Miss Malcolm?"

I didn't bother to correct my last name. "Yes, sir," I said, wondering if my words would condemn me.

General Gage's eyes didn't leave my quaking form. "Very well, then. Captain Wells, be sure to check for a Charles Smith on Ship Street first thing in the morning. Meanwhile, Miss Malcolm, you will stay in one of the rooms upstairs tonight, under guard of course. Until we verify your story, I'm afraid I will not be able to release you."

I did a slight curtsy, grateful he didn't send me to the gaol this night. I had time. Yet time for what?

Samuel left Province House smirking, and I was led upstairs to a spare bedroom, a fire already burning. I thanked the guard before closing the door. I heard the creak of the wood boards as he patrolled the hallway.

I knelt by the fire, removed my cloak, and hung it on the back of a Queen Anne chair to dry near the heat. Slowly my fingers thawed. I turned sleepy beside the warmth of the heat, forcing myself to come up with a plan that would save my life.

General Gage's officer would not find a Mr. Smith on Ship Street. At least no Mr. Smith who recognized my name. What would they do then? What untruth could I tell to allow my escape? I went to the window and looked down. Two red-coated soldiers guarded the entrance of Province House.

I was trapped.

The room that held me was finer than any I'd seen in years. Yet it held no friendliness. I had disappointed Noah. Sarah would return to Medford and tell my husband how I had landed myself in enemy hands. He would be mad with worry, in an anxious fit that there was nothing he could do. Or perhaps Sarah would spare him the guilt of being able to do nothing and tell him I had drowned in the Charles. Aye, I could picture her telling such a lie if it meant keeping him safe in Medford. In fact, I prayed she did tell him the untruth.

Staring into the fire, allowing it to lull me into sleep, I thought of little Mary, her last words to me.

"Jesus knows about everyone."

Did He see the predicament I'd gotten myself into, then? Did He see my heart? My desire to act with honor, to help those who loved me and the cause for which we fought? What did *He* think of this war, these battles?

With not a little guilt, I realized this was the first I pondered the question. I'd been so eager to have a part, to assist those I loved, I'd never stopped to wonder which side Christ loved. A verse of Scripture came to me, one that Reverend Osgood read often.

"Love your enemies, bless them that curse you, do good to them that hate you."

Who were my enemies? Was General Gage my true enemy? We believed in different causes, but did that make him my enemy? I thought of Samuel, who truly did show his hatred for me this night. Either way, I was to bless them both.

Whether 'twas the warmth of the fire or the late hour, a peace came over me, even in my weakness. I prayed for Sarah's safe return home. I prayed for Noah. I prayed for the Redcoats I'd encountered that night.

I prayed for Samuel.

The light of morning would bring more troubles, but here, now, I rested in the arms of One who was stronger.

CHAPTER THIRTY-EIGHT

Emma

The waves have rolled in upon me—the billows have repeatedly
broken over me: yet I am not sunk down.

MERCY OTIS WARREN

THE LIGHT OF DAWN stretched and yawned lazy in the early March hours. I woke in the feather bed, my toes and fingers warm.

General Washington would attack Boston soon, and it seemed that I would be trapped within the city when he did.

I splashed water upon my face from the pitcher beside the bed. I donned my dry boots and smoothed my dress and cloak as best I could.

And waited.

Not long after, a knock came at my door. 'Twas the same officer I had run into the night before.

"Miss, General Gage wishes to see you in the parlor."

I nodded, started down the hall. My boots echoed against the pine planks. He would have found out by now, of course. There was no Mr. Charles Smith on Ship Street. Quite likely there was no Mr. Charles Smith in all of Boston. And if there were, he certainly did not know an Emma Malcolm. Quite likely he did not have a brother outside of Boston.

I entered the parlor, my knees trembling. Outside, bright sunshine shone down on tired streets. Sarah would be home by now. Had Noah slept at all last night? I imagined him at the Fultons', peering past the entrance to the Royall estate. I imagined him seeing only one form coming up the road. I imagined him seeing Sarah, tired, haggard from her trip. He would hobble to her as best he could, demand answers, deny her words.

What would she tell him?

It truly didn't matter. There was no help for me now. I was in the hands of the crown, all but convicted. Boston would be attacked with the cannons Henry Knox had obtained from Fort Ticonderoga and I would be held within its gates.

General Gage stood as he had the night before in front of the hearth, his hands behind his back. On a table lay a large map, and I imagined him with his officers, planning an attack or perhaps anticipating General Washington's.

"Miss Malcolm," he said as I stood before him, two soldiers and an officer flanking my sides.

"Sir."

"My officers have searched and scoured for this Charles Smith of Ship Street, and they have come up empty-handed. Mr. Clarke is trusted by the crown, and so I have no choice but to believe his words. Still, I entreat you to supply me with another explanation, or else tell me honestly what you are about, young lady."

I scrambled for another untruth, but it seemed vile,

useless. Would this man—this man who possessed a wife who sympathized with the Patriots—find it in his heart to understand?

But what could I say that would not implicate Sarah and General Washington? That would not give away the imminent plans the Continental Army had to attack Boston?

Nothing. I could say nothing.

"Miss Malcolm, I implore you. Tell us why you were in the city, and I will have my men transport you to the town gates at once."

To be out of Boston . . . yet I could not waver. I must decide, now, that I would be strong. That I would serve the cause I loved. I would serve General Washington and all of the Patriots, Mr. Hancock and Mr. Adams, Dr. Warren's memory, all in Medford, Sarah's precious little ones, Mary's memory, and my beloved Noah.

I would serve them with silence.

What was my life, after all, compared to those who depended upon me in this moment?

"I am sorry, sir." I dragged in a breath, thought again of Father's stubbornness. I would need to adopt every last shred of Malcolm tenacity to survive this moment.

"You refuse to tell me? You refuse to speak?"

"I cannot, sir. I am sorry." Beneath my skirt, my knees wobbled.

"Miss Malcolm, I truly, truly wish you would not be difficult. The task ahead is most unpleasant, for I fear the safety of my men and the King's Army is at stake with the information you hold." I tried to fix his words in my mind, couldn't fully piece them together until he turned to the officer in the room. He sighed, swiped a hand over his face. "Captain, take her down. Be as gentle as you can."

My breath hitched within my chest as the captain led me back into the hall and then opened a door that led to the basement. My boots skidded on the rug as I glimpsed the dark hold below, the general's words echoing in my thoughts.

"Be as gentle as you can."

I thought of Father's immense suffering at being tarred. Of Noah lying wounded on the battlefield, his leg severed. Of Sarah crying at Mary's graveside, of all the men whom I had dug a bullet from in the Medford field hospital.

I was not made of the same strength as them. How would I hold up to whatever lay before me in that darkness, alone with this red-coated captain? What did General Gage intend? And would I be able to keep my silence through suffering?

✠

When the captain led me below, I expected him to leave me there in the cold. Perhaps allow me to go hungry in an attempt to pry information from me.

Those alternatives would have seemed like heaven compared to what was done me.

After the first blow, my mind and body seemed to go into a state of shock, which aided in my silence through the pain. I had seen the results of the horrors of war on the Medford field after Charlestown. Father had struck me on more than one occasion. I had seen the tortures of his brutal tarring and feathering.

But my brain could not comprehend that such things

were being done to a woman. To me. And all for the information I held.

I sensed their desperation, felt they would not have resorted to such measures if they were not so very frantic to know General Washington's plans, if they were not so very certain that I knew something, if they were not so certain that time was of the essence.

Their blows pummeled me. They were deliberate, methodical—one would not expect anything less from the King's Army—beginning with the knuckles of my hand and then moving to my middle, where once I had carried a small babe and where I would likely never do so again.

They left me for some time and I huddled around myself in the cold dark, sobbing aloud, begging the Lord to spare me or kill me quickly, begging Him to give me strength not to betray my comrades.

A small window cast light in the very top of the wall and I saw the boots of soldiers walking back and forth. I moved an inch, and my entire body screamed with protest as though a million knives were being plunged along my skin. The blood dried quick upon my knuckles, the air cold and clotting.

I prayed.

I did not feel the peace of earlier, but I did feel a knowing, a certainty. I would see this through to the end. No matter my pain, no matter my fate, I would bear it for my fellow Patriots.

Adrenaline pulsed through my veins when a soldier's boots returned upon the stairs. I drew my knees to my chest to protect myself.

He knelt by my side. 'Twas the man who had escorted

me to Province House the night before, the one who began this torture. He spoke soft. "Please, Miss Malcolm. Enough shilly-shallying. Tell us what we seek. 'Tis not my pleasure to harm you, and I fear it will only get worse from here if you do not comply."

I looked at him with chattering teeth, wound my arms tighter around my legs, my conversation with Noah long ago playing in my head.

"Which is more honorable—loyalty or liberty?"

Here, now, they lay tangled together, both the honorable choice.

"Miss Malcolm, once I leave this room, you are no longer in my hands, but in the charge of ones whose job it is to force information from you. And they do their jobs well. You *will* give in. Why not relent now and spare us both the heartache and pain?"

My flesh begged me to. I had never feared so much in all my life. I imagined Sarah in my place. She would spit in the face of this soldier. We were different, Sarah and I.

Could I be so strong?

I remembered the tea chest and the oath it held. The part Noah and I played in this story.

"Very well, then." The captain rose and left, his boots sounding up the steps slowly, as if he expected me to call out to him. He opened and closed the door and then was gone.

The basement grew silent again. I released a shaky breath into my knees.

I prayed for strength.

Mary's little voice again.

"Jesus knows about everyone."

He saw me now, in this moment. A swift certainty fell over me, and I suddenly felt not quite so alone. In a blur of time, I recalled the many stories Reverend Osgood spoke on, particularly those of the Gospels.

Jesus, flogged and on a cross. Beaten for the sake of others. Dead.

"He is not here: for he is risen, as he said."

As He said.

He did know all.

As I heard the door open and two sets of boots descend the stairs, I pondered instead the strength the Lord must possess to burst forth not only from a sealed grave, but from death itself.

I leaned into it, felt a burgeoning within my soul that He would give me strength in this moment—not because He cared so much about my keeping General Washington's secrets and not because He cared so very much about the Patriot cause perhaps, but because He cared about *me*.

"Love your enemies, bless them that curse you."

The red-coated soldier approached, and as he held up a knife that gleamed in the scant sunlight coming from the window, as he grabbed for my hand, splaying my finger upon a hard rock, choosing the smallest of them to begin the torture, when the other soldier held me still until I could no longer wriggle from his grip, I buried my head in the crook of my other arm and did the unthinkable: I prayed for them.

As blinding pain tore up my arm and into my body until I could no longer tell the source of it, I muffled my screams in my elbow. I did not feel strong.

But I depended on One who was.

I was not alone.

CHAPTER THIRTY-NINE

Emma

The passion for liberty cannot be equally strong in the breasts of those who have been accustomed to deprive their fellow creatures of theirs. Of this I am certain that it is not founded upon that generous and Christian principle of doing to others as we would that others should do unto us.

ABIGAIL ADAMS

I'M NOT CERTAIN when I swooned, but the sound of cannons woke me.

General Washington had begun his attack.

General Gage and the Regulars seemed to forget about me in their haste to muster a defense. Two of my fingers had been bandaged—the soldiers likely did not want me to bleed to death yet. I saw the bluish, blood-drained nubs of them not far from me, and I kicked them away, near fainted at the sight of my familiar fingernails upon them.

I heard footsteps above, felt so cold I wished to swoon again and be done with the pain of bone and flesh being taken from me, be done with the pain of being so very cold it felt my body would freeze like the frozen banks of the Charles in January.

More sporadic cannon fire, bringing me reminders of the battle at Charlestown. I drifted in and out of consciousness. Night descended again, and all grew quiet. I wondered if the Regulars had abandoned the city, if they had left me here to die, if I could summon the strength to move, if I could manage an escape.

The sound of breaking glass startled me, and I assumed a cannonball had blown open the basement window. Shards of glass landed at my feet and in my delusion, I felt as though I were back at my home on Cross Street, huddled with Mother and Father as the rebel Bostonians searched out Father to drag him away.

A form scurried through the opening, but I could not make sense of it, thought I was hallucinating. For only one man could walk with such a limp, only one man could be big enough to take up the corners of my mind with his presence, only one man could seem perfect even as I knew his faults.

I was dreaming, was all.

But the hallucination knelt before me, said my name so tenderly, I had trouble convincing my mind 'twas not true.

"Emma."

I convinced myself I should swat at the hallucination, even as I tried to reach for it, to test its solidity, at the same time bracing for disappointment.

A calloused finger stroked my cheek. Firm. Real.

"My love, what have they done to you?"

I let out a soft gasp, part cry, still disbelieving that my husband was before me. "Are you truly here?" My words slurred. I could not form them.

Almost at once I was in his arms, felt myself being lifted

from the frozen dirt, being thrust through the window into another set of arms—these smaller, more feminine.

I wondered where the soldiers were. The burst of cannon fire sounded louder. And then I was back in Noah's strong grip, and I did not care if it were dream or real, I did not care how he managed to carry me with but one leg. I only cared that my husband's arms were there to hold me.

CHAPTER FORTY

Hayley

I RUBBED MY EYES, burning from reading on my phone. I looked at the words of Emma's story that I'd just read, of her trapped in the cellar of Province House. Facing torture was one of those things I'd thought I was mentally prepared for, had even expected a taste of it at the end of Hell Week. I couldn't imagine being an eighteenth-century woman, unprepared for such horrors. I wondered, if I were in Emma's place, would I have held up under such pressure?

I thought of her reliance on a different sort of strength, a strength that came from God.

"Jesus knows about everyone."

In this lonely hotel room, reading Emma's story, I felt the truth of those faint whispers. What was more, for the first time, I longed for them. Almost like an invisible force called to my heart.

I thought to shake it off, to cast it aside as emotional weakness while reading a story, anticipating the challenge before me, but the thought of leaving it alone produced such an intense sadness within me, I immediately discarded the idea.

What was it—or who—that Emma trusted in that called to me now?

Though Ethan had sent the e-mail with the attachment of the rest of Emma's story late the night before, it had taken me most of the day to read it. I hadn't even gone for my usual morning run, telling myself I would run double as soon as I finished the story.

I couldn't deny how my blood ran hot at the sight of Ethan's name in my in-box. I'd hoped he would reach out, and at the same time I didn't. His words about waiting for me niggled in a wonderful, annoying way. I thought he just might mean them.

This thing—being pursued—was new for me. I never thought I'd wanted it. I wanted independence, to be left alone.

At least that's what I'd told myself.

I was not alone.

"Jesus knows about everyone."

I continued scrolling but hit the end of the document.

No.

There simply had to be more.

Was that the end of her story? Emma must have made it out in order to go on and have children, to pass the chest down to the family, to write this very account . . .

But was that the end of what Ethan found? Or had he purposely left me with only this?

I scrolled more, unable to believe he would do this. Or that this was the end of Emma, my eight-times great-grandmother.

I got off the bed, paced beside the large window overlooking a luscious green courtyard.

I'd left Ethan in the midst of our discovery, and now he had, maybe rightly, left me at the pinnacle of Emma's journey.

I huffed, scuffed the bottom of my foot against the carpet until a slight burn started. Then, before I could think on the consequences, I picked up my phone and dialed.

"Hello?" His tone sounded nonchalant, as if my name hadn't shown on his phone, as if he didn't know who called.

"You're really going to leave me with that?"

"Oh, Hayley, it's you. Nice of you to call."

"Please, just answer me. Is there more of her story? You're not going to leave me with that, are you?" I was being unreasonable. I knew it: I knew it, and I didn't care.

"And what did you leave me with?"

"Ethan . . . I—you knew I would leave!" I said in desperation as if that were an excuse for my doing so. "We were . . . It was too much. We were getting too . . ."

"Close? Why does that scare you so much? Why can't you accept that you're not your mother and I'm not one of her boyfriends? Why do you have to be such a—a . . . ?"

"A what?" I knew what he'd been about to say, and I used it to fuel my anger, to jettison me forward instead of dwelling in the past—both the recent and not-so-recent past.

"Forget it."

"No. Say it. We'll both feel better after you do." I kicked harder against the carpet, almost savoring the rug burn at the bottom of my foot—a physical pain to replace the mental anguish his words would bring.

Why do you have to be such a coward?

I braced myself for the impact of the words. Maybe a normal girl wouldn't feel so offended at them. But I'd known I wasn't normal the first time one of Lena's boyfriends snuck into my bedroom.

And the truth of the words would hurt.

I was a coward.

I was nothing like Emma or Uncle Joe or Ethan.

"Hayley, I'm sorry."

Wait . . . what? "What in tarnation do you have to be sorry for?"

"For hurting you."

I sighed, long and deep, the apology breaking something inside me. "I shouldn't have left, Ethan. Not like I did. Again. Just—being with you, it was like I couldn't think, like you threaten my existence or my purpose or something. Like you threaten who I know myself to be."

They were the most honest words I'd spoken aloud in a long time.

"We can go slow, Hayley."

There it was again. The still-existing invitation. "You don't give up, do you?"

"There's something here for us. Even if we have to wade through a whole lot of fear and uncertainty, this—us—we could be worth it."

"There can't be anything. You—a relationship . . . it's not in the stars for us, Ethan. I'm all the way in California.

I'm going to be a SEAL. Do you have any idea what that involves?"

"Enlighten me."

"It means never seeing each other. It means you not knowing where I am or if I'm alive 80 percent of the time. It means you not getting why I will always be more loyal to my team or to my country or to the Navy, more than you."

I swallowed at the truth, naked between us. It had to hurt.

Silence over the line, then a long intake of breath. "Jed called. You're really related to her."

"Emma."

"Yeah." His voice sounded low and husky, so close. "You want to read the rest of her story?"

I snorted. "Silly question."

"Then I guess you're going to have to come home and read it yourself."

"Ethan, that's not funny."

He cleared his throat. "I'm not joking. This is your family, Hay. Your history. And you shouldn't be alone in some California hotel room when you read it. You should be with me. You should have always been with me."

I winced at the crack in his voice, tried not to imagine a different sort of future, a different ending to me and Ethan.

I thought of Emma, of her fight for not only her country, but for the man she loved. Did it have to be one or the other? It hadn't for her. But what about me?

"I'm sorry, Ethan."

"Because you won't come home?"

"Yes. But I'm also sorry for hurting you." I sniffed.

"But in all fairness, you knew I was dysfunctional from the beginning."

"You're not dysfunctional. Think of Emma and Noah. They definitely had some issues. But they worked through them."

"They're different."

"Why?"

Why. Because they leaned on each other. They leaned on Someone greater.

Another sigh from Ethan. "You know . . . I've been trying to get you to see my side for some time . . . to control things. Maybe—maybe it's just not my place. Maybe it's time I depend on God too. Maybe I shouldn't try to hold you so tightly."

I didn't know what to say to that. He was letting me go. I should be happy.

"I'll send you the rest of the story tonight."

CHAPTER FORTY-ONE

Hayley

I DID NOT SLEEP much that night, after I read the rest of Emma's story.

The next morning, I texted Ethan. That's really how it ended?

Yes. You don't think that's a good ending?

I'm glad he rescued her, but I thought we'd learn about their children and why they didn't hand down the story.

Gerald said there could be more information in Sarah Fulton's records.

You didn't look?

No. I did hear from the museum this morning. They sent the chest and letter out for testing.

That's good.

I stared at my phone, but no response. What was there

left to say? We'd discovered almost everything we'd wanted to know—the story behind the chest and the oath, the fact that I was, unbelievably, a descendant of Emma and Noah Winslow.

Perhaps we simply wouldn't ever know where the break in the family's story was.

I should be able to feel peace with that, and yet I felt nothing but anxiety.

⛨

I didn't hear from Ethan until I'd been training at BUD/S for a week.

He texted me an article.

CHEST FROM THE BOSTON TEA PARTY DISCOVERED

A symbol of the American Revolution has been discovered and is now returning home.

When Ethan Gagnon purchased an old tea chest from an estate sale in Medford, Massachusetts, for his antique shop in Revere, he had no idea he was purchasing a symbol of our country's freedom. He gave the chest away as a gift to Lieutenant Hayley Ashworth of the United States Navy, an old childhood friend. It was Ashworth who discovered a historic document hidden in the bottom of the chest. A secret oath in the form of a round-robin, signed by participants in the Boston Tea Party.

Both the chest and the oath have undergone rigorous testing and have been proven authentic. The Boston Tea Party Ships and Museum are now in possession of both artifacts and are currently updating their list of those who participated in the Tea Party.

"It's absolutely exciting," said Steven Preston, museum director. "We assumed when the Robinson chest came home to the museum in 2012 that this would be the last artifact to be discovered, but history continues to surprise us."

Gagnon shared his journey of discovery, relaying how he and Ashworth alerted the Medford seller's family as to the historical value of the chest. The family, who did not realize the chest had been more than an heirloom, is happy to see it on display at the museum. They will come, along with Gagnon, to the unveiling ceremony Thursday, July 20, when the chest will return to the very spot where it was thrown overboard nearly 250 years ago.

When asked if the Navy might allow Ashworth to return for the unveiling, Gagnon simply smiled and said, "She had a big hand in getting the chest this far, but she's doing something very important right now, something any friend would be proud of. I truly hope she can come, but if she can't, I understand. She's a strong woman. I'm glad to know her."

CHAPTER FORTY-TWO

Hayley

HELL WEEK

NAVAL SPECIAL WARFARE CENTER

CORONADO, CALIFORNIA

Strong arms dragged me up from the sand. "You got this, Ashworth. Don't leave us now. You got this."

I blinked, pain returning to my body as I woke from where I'd passed out. It couldn't have been more than a minute or two, yet I already grieved the time. I grieved the remembering of my time in Massachusetts, my time with Ethan, my time learning about Emma. It all seemed so far away, like a fairy tale compared to this hard, cruel place.

I imagined the bell again, remembered Emma staying strong to the end for the good of her country.

Unable to speak, I stumbled toward the O course, more for Carpenter's sake than my own.

Over the first wall I went into a mess of mud and scum-filled seawater goop, my head knocking hard into what I assumed to be someone's boot. My brain numbed. Bitter bile gathered in the back of my mouth, then burst forth from my stomach onto the ground. I crawled beneath the barbed wire through it.

Explosions filled the air. Smoke, whistling, gunfire. I couldn't remember anything—why I was there, which way was forward or backward. How many days we'd been training. I could barely remember my name.

It was there, in the sludge and slop of my own vomit and mud and scum, barbed wire and explosions above me, that I froze. And again, Carpenter was there, dragging me through the sludge. This was a race—he would be punished with extra push-ups for not finishing in the first group. And yet I knew one thing: he would make it. No man left behind. It was who he was, and in that moment I loved him for it.

Something buckled deep inside me then. I couldn't stop thinking of Emma, the sacrifice she made for freedom. While she certainly held fondness for the Patriots, her sacrifice had been more than that. It had been for the man she loved, for the friend she loved, for all those who'd sacrificed so much for the cause she'd come to believe in.

In the haze of that mud pit, in the haze of being dragged by my friend, I wondered why I wanted the Trident so badly. Was it for the good of my country, my family, and my friends? Did I truly think I would be an asset to a SEAL team, or was it as I feared—only a means to prove myself? To prove myself strong, to prove myself worth more than what Lena had given me? To prove myself to not only my mother but to Uncle Joe, to my hometown, to my country, and to Ethan?

I thought of the hazard I was to Carpenter in this moment.

I thought of Emma, alone in that cellar. She hadn't cared about proving her loyalty or her strength, for she garnered those things from Someone bigger. No, Emma had only cared about loving those who may be hurt by her failure.

I looked at Carpenter, knew I held him back. I thought of where my heart was during this entire training—in Massachusetts. I thought of the hope I hadn't realized I was holding close to my heart, even now—a hope that there was indeed Someone stronger than me that I could count upon. That maybe real strength wasn't in proving my endurance or my stamina; maybe real strength was in surrendering.

There, in the mud, I pondered my hollow attempts to find meaning in a career, in the military, when my family had failed me. I'd locked myself into a mad race to be my best in military life, and when the chance for love or a purpose outside of my set plans presented itself, I refused to give it voice. I refused to give it a chance.

I was tired of running. Tired of chasing after meaning and strength with the eyes of the world. I had refused to fail, and yet, what if failing—surrendering—was the beginning of finding my true self, of finding real strength?

I wiped mud from my eyes, felt myself release the very thing I wanted more than anything else. I felt myself release the Trident.

"Leave me," I said to Carpenter. "I'm done."

"You can do this, Ashworth. I know you can."

"No. You can." I didn't recognize my voice, had to focus

every last bit of concentration to form words. "I'm ringing the bell."

"No."

"Yes." I looked at him, resolute, my mind clearing. "Carp, it's okay. It was meant to be this way." Somehow, I felt it in my bones. And while my pride would be wounded, I felt there was something more waiting beyond the wounds.

Carpenter looked up the wall that was next to scale. I knew he wondered if he could carry me on his back. "Are you sure?"

"I am sure. Go get that Trident. You got this."

He looked as if he would leave, then finished pulling me from beneath the barbed wire, up to the next wall. I swore at him. "Go!"

"I'll see you on the other side," he said.

But I wasn't going anywhere, and really, it had nothing to do with those blasted explosions and everything to do with the absurd peace flooding my being.

When the explosions finally stopped, I crawled around the course, made my way to the center of the compound, following a handful of my comrades.

I gripped the rope of the bell and gave it three tugs, signaling my DOR. A note of finality echoed through the compound.

All those times I imagined ringing the bell, I imagined it would be entrance into a prison of sorts—a prison of failure. But something surprised me when its solid chime sounded from the ancient metal. The note didn't quite sound like failure.

Instead, it sounded an awful lot like freedom.

CHAPTER FORTY-THREE

Hayley

I FELT OUT OF PLACE in my maxi skirt and flip-flops. My Navy whites would have been a better choice, but I didn't want to draw attention to myself. I stood outside, searching the crowd in front of the Tea Party museum. I spotted the top of Ethan's head, his unmistakable solid and tall form by an empty bench, his head bent over his phone. My heart did a flip.

As I drew closer, I pondered how right this felt, how coming home felt . . . good.

I could only hope Ethan would think so.

"Hey, stranger."

He looked up from his phone, his mouth dropping open. "You—you're here."

His eyes raked over me. I knew I looked like I'd gone

through torture. No amount of makeup could cover the bruises along my face and arms, and I wondered if he would view me as a broken failure.

He raised a hand to my face, ran a gentle thumb along the curve of my jaw. Beneath his gaze I didn't have to guess if he thought me broken because succumbing to his touch, I felt only valued. Precious.

"Are you okay?" he asked.

A smile pulled at the corners of my mouth. "I am now." I swallowed, knew words had to be said, yet I felt inadequate to say them. "So I realized some things at BUD/S. I rang out. But knowing I was able to come back here, knowing you were waiting for me, it didn't feel like failure. In those trenches, in all that torture, I knew what Emma had felt. That Someone stronger was over her. It made me feel like maybe getting my Trident wasn't the most important thing after all. Maybe . . . surrendering is. Maybe loving is. Something changed for me over there. I can't explain it, but it's like something inside me is new . . . beautiful, even. Crazy, huh?"

He was looking at me, and my heart sped up. I'd shared too much. And yet I wouldn't turn back now. "I guess what I'm saying is . . . I'm not sure what all this means, but I was hoping to explore it . . . maybe with you."

Without hesitation, he drew me to him, dipped his head to mine. I sank beneath his lips, relishing the feeling of giving myself over to this man, of releasing my need for control. His mouth moved over mine in tender restraint, and I surrendered to it.

When we broke our kiss, he held me close, whispered against my hair. "Feels like victory to me."

Me too.

It dawned on me then. I could be loyal to Ethan and not lose my freedom. Because he loved me. Real love gave freedom. Emma and Noah had taught me that.

"I have a lot to sort through, but I promise you something—I will never leave again. Not without intention of returning."

"How long until you have to go back to your ship?"

"Three days."

"Then we better make the most of every moment."

He didn't ask questions, he didn't beg for an apology; he just accepted me.

I'm thinking that's how love—real love—acted.

"Hayley, you came!" I turned at the sound of the familiar voice.

"Lena?" I looked at Ethan, questioning.

"I invited your mom, thought she might want to share in the celebration of her daughter."

"I don't think—"

"I'm proud of you, honey. Ethan told me all you two did. I read about you in the paper, too." She turned to her side where a broad-shouldered man with gray in his hair smiled at me. "I want you to meet William. William, this is my daughter, Hayley."

I shook the man's hand, couldn't get over the glow on Lena's face. She was *proud* of me. And while it wasn't exactly a SEAL Trident, for the first time in a long time, I felt fond emotion toward my mother. Maybe it was only the sentiment of being home, of that kiss from Ethan that still lingered on my lips, but it wasn't bitterness and it wasn't hate, so I'd take it.

I thought of Emma, longing for reconciliation with her parents though they'd treated her horribly. I thought of her in that Boston basement, being tortured, praying for her enemies. I thought of Ethan, accepting me with open arms despite my flaws.

That was how love was supposed to act.

And right then, I released whatever hold Lena had on me that kept me from thriving. I wasn't sure if I'd call it forgiveness exactly, but beside Ethan and his acceptance over my many flaws, I thought I might well be on my way toward it.

He slid his hand into mine. "We need to talk."

"I know." We had a lot to say to one another, a lot to figure out. I'd done some soul-searching these past several days, prayed for wisdom regarding my feelings for Ethan, and yet I still wasn't 100 percent sure of the path before me.

We entered the museum, and I clutched his hand, felt the strength of his grip, and for the first time, I took comfort in it.

✝

We bid good-bye to Lena and William shortly after we'd finished our cones from Ben & Jerry's. I promised Lena I wouldn't leave without saying good-bye, and even though the thought of seeing her again caused no small amount of anxiety, I meant it.

Ethan and I strolled along Long Wharf hand in hand, alone for the first time.

"That was . . . special. The ceremony. Lena and Jed and Melissa's family being there. It was nice."

Introducing them to Lena, knowing we were distant

family, was . . . weird. Weird, but totally amazing. A newspaper reporter took our picture with the chest, jotted down notes on how we'd discovered our distant relations. It was the first family photograph I had ever taken. Ethan had snapped a shot on my phone, and though others might think it sentimental, I knew I would cherish the picture forever.

"You know . . . I don't feel like I want to run away right now."

He smiled. "That's good, because I'm hoping we can talk. And if you're interested, swing by the historical society later. Gerald said he found something for us."

☩

The air conditioner in the window of the upstairs room of the historical society ran on high, blowing cool air to where Ethan and I sat at the table, a written account from Sarah Bradlee Fulton before us.

I dragged in a breath, hadn't realized how tense I was. "Do you think this is it?"

"Let's find out."

We got to work, the papers easier to read and better preserved than those of Emma's journal.

October 29, 1789

I am certain if I live to be one hundred, there will never be a more memorable day for me, nor for my family.

President Washington visited today. I am in awe of his generosity and the honor he bestowed upon me and my family. Oh, the scrubbing our home endured in preparation for his visit! The children wore their best, as did John. I wore my pale-green damask dress.

At the sound of the horses, I doubt my heart beat as fast when I went into Boston under siege, Emma beside me. We all waited outside—the children, our oldest son and his new bride—as His Excellency came closer. I could not imagine a more stately figure if I were to try, and though John had naught to worry over, I feared my blushing made him a bit anxious.

President Washington bowed to me and I led him inside, gave him the Windsor armchair, served him John's best punch. As we all sat still and quiet, His Excellency spoke, expressed his extreme gratitude for my willingness to risk my life for the cause of our noble country. As I absorbed the adoration and the children's proud smiles, there was one face among the wee ones that stood out to me most. I wanted to be certain he remembered this moment, remembered that I was not the only one to be honored. That his mother, brave soul, not to mention his father, deserved every bit of recognition, if not more, than myself.

I called four-year-old Jacob forward, his face reminding me so very much of Noah's, his eyes those of his mother. Once again, my heart ached over the loss of them both in the meetinghouse fire. I remembered Emma's words, on the brink of death, asking me to care for their dear, long-hoped-for child as if he were my own, to teach him the things of faith that Noah and Emma so adamantly clung to.

For the last three years, I had kept my word.

And now, I would teach him something else.

I gripped his little-boy hand, ushered him before His Excellency, told our president of Emma's heroic deeds and of Noah rescuing her while Boston was under siege.

After hearing Emma's story, President Washington bowed to Jacob, the child quite flustered at near royalty bending a knee for him. He then put a hand on Jacob's shoulder, thanked him for his parents' bravery, and urged him to live a life of honor and love, to carry on the legacy of Noah and Emma Winslow.

There was not a dry eye in the home.

After His Excellency left, I hugged Jacob to me, hoped he would remember this day, a testament to the legacy left him. 'Twas good he had the tea chest from his parents, but in some ways, memories mean more.

I wiped my eyes after reading the last sentence, the silence swallowing up the historical society in a sort of reverence.

"They never got to tell him the story of the tea chest, of the oath hidden in the bottom."

Ethan sniffed, hard. "And it seems Sarah hadn't known either, that Emma had written her tale and hid it in the stairs, thinking they had many years left."

"And yet in her last moments, she focused not on the glory she'd obtained from the war, but on things of faith. In the end, that was most important to her."

Pondering this newness of faith I was just beginning to explore, I felt in some mysterious way that Emma's faith was meeting me, her eight-times great-granddaughter, here in this place.

She'd never had the daughter she'd longed for, but here, in a strange and intimate way, I felt I could possibly be that daughter. I thought of little Jacob, how he would have two children, one daughter whose family line would include Jed and Melissa and Wyatt, and another whose line would include Michael Ashworth and Uncle Joe and Lena and me.

Had the legacy Emma wanted to pass on survived? I felt, beyond a doubt, that it had.

We put the folder away and wandered downstairs, stopping in front of Emma's display case. Ethan knelt down and pointed at the teacup I hadn't given much thought to when we'd first seen the exhibit.

"It's her cup. The one Sarah gave her, the one Noah put back together."

I knelt beside him, placed my hand on the glass. "Still in one piece after all these years."

We shared a smile and rose. Ethan squeezed my hand.

After we shared our findings with Gerald, we walked into the center of Medford toward Cradock Bridge, the very one where the Fultons and Emma and Noah had once lived. We looked out over the bridge to the warehouses, to where John's distillery had once been.

The Mystic flowed beneath us, and a breeze caressed my skin, stirring something within me that was becoming less and less foreign. "Maybe I'll come to church with you one of these days," I said to Ethan.

He raised an eyebrow. "When you're on leave?"

"No. When I have a weekend off in between work and my classes in Boston."

He turned to me, hope in his eyes. "Classes?"

"It won't be until January, but it looks promising. I requested a switch in positions. I'm ready for a new career direction, and I've been inspired by Emma and Sarah, all they did to help those men after Bunker Hill. I think I'm going to try my hand at being a medic, go to school for nursing, maybe even become an NP someday."

"In Boston?"

I smiled, nodded.

He swept me up, pressed his mouth to mine, and I had to admit that there, in Ethan's arms, in the very place where the Winslows and Fultons fought and lived and loved and died, I felt very, very much at home.

There was no more running away from it. No more wallowing in failures and a need to prove myself brave or strong. I was already loved, just as I was. I was already strong, not because of my muscles, but because of *who* held me.

That knowledge, more than anything else, called forth a freedom more precious than any I'd ever known.

HISTORICAL NOTE

IN JULY 2017, it was announced that for the first time, a woman would enter the training pipeline to become a Navy SEAL. A couple weeks later, it was reported that she had dropped out. I couldn't help but imagine what this unidentified woman had gone through and what had propelled her to enter such rigorous training. I decided to explore her story in fiction.

While Emma Malcolm is fictitious, her father, the customs official John Malcolm, is not. In actuality John and his wife had five children, two of whom were deaf. Records indicate he was a harsh man, and while I attempted to remain true to what I read of him, I am hopeful the actual John Malcolm was more caring. John was tarred and feathered by a Boston mob and he is said to have taken a hunk of his tarred flesh to King George and requested to be made a "knight of the tar." His brother, Daniel, was revered among the Patriots.

Another true-to-life historical figure I explored was Sarah Bradlee Fulton. Though little is written about her, I based much of my findings on information from the Boston Tea Party Ships and Museum website (Sarah is given credit for the idea of disguising the men as Mohawks) as well as a book written by one of her family members, *A Woman Fearing Nothing* by Brenda Ely Albus. I found this book extremely helpful in aiding this story. And though it seems Sarah helped the "Mohawks" at her brother's Boston home, for the simplicity of the story I have omitted her brother, Nathaniel.

There is not only record that "a paper was handed out in a very confidential manner," encouraging the men to ready themselves to destroy the tea that December night in 1773, but according to apprentice Joshua Wyeth, the men had "pledged our honor, that we would not reveal our secret." Another account tells of a group of the men signing their names to a round-robin—my basis for the oath found in the tea chest. Many Tea Party participants kept their secret until death. Not until the nineteenth century did stories begin to come out surrounding the night of the Tea Party, though descendants took great pains to make the destruction of the tea sound honorable. As the participants became celebrated, stories grew until it seems no one could be certain who truly participated and who did not.

Samuel Clarke was modeled after Jonathan Clarke, who was indeed a consignee for the East India tea and did shoot out the window of his home into the mob in the weeks before the Tea Party. There, the similarities end, and I have fictionalized Samuel for the purposes of the story.

I read no evidence of General Gage himself ordering women spies treated with the cruelty Emma endures, though I have come upon other reports of harsh treatment done to women suspected of spying during the Revolution.

Continuing to research Revolutionary Boston, I thought

of my present-day heroine, Hayley. She, like Emma, longed to serve her country and, at the same time, to show her strength and worth in doing so. I don't think I will ever get over the wonder of exploring both historical and contemporary characters within the same story. Though hundreds of years apart, Hayley and Emma share struggles that many of us can relate to.

In his book *Defiance of the Patriots*, Benjamin L. Carp says that "the Tea Party opens up Pandora's box—out comes chaos, but also hope. In this way it exemplifies an ongoing struggle in America between law and order and democratic protest." Just as today, the characters in this book struggle with the contents of this box. I hope readers will be spurred on to discuss these things upon finishing the book.

I pray we will ponder history as we move forward with our own. I pray that as we explore our own purposes in this precious life, we would not hesitate to look to the One who is not only able to grant us renewal and strength beyond ourselves, but in whom our true—and greatest—identity can be found.

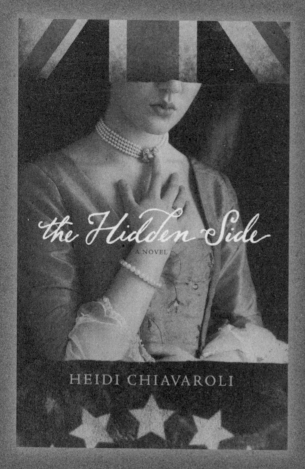

NATALIE

———◇———

When I was fourteen, I hid a pack of Virginia Slims in the top drawer of my dresser. I never smoked them, just kept them there for over a year. I remember glimpsing the package beneath old training bras and lacy underwear I bought at Victoria's Secret with my friends, feeling a sense of accomplishment over their very presence in my room.

Something about seeing them—the thin white package with the brown strip, the gold seal still unbroken—made me feel powerful. As if I had some autonomy outside my parents' overbearing control.

Now, twenty-six years later and about to breach the slender link of trust that remained between me and my sixteen-year-old son, I lifted my hand to where the partially opened drawer of Chris's desk called to me, beckoning. The laminated wood finish peeled around the edges, revealing smooth, pale plywood beneath. It would be so easy in this empty house. Ten seconds was all it would take.

I could pick a song to play for one of my callers at the radio station in ten seconds. I could fold one of the undershirts my husband, Mike, wore beneath his police uniform. I could shed a tear. Order a coffee. Give a hug. Check a Facebook message. Speak words I could never snatch back.

Gathering a breath, I pulled at the knob of the top drawer. It came open several inches before jamming against an object.

Now committed, I wiggled my finger inside the drawer to free it of the problem—a slim book, from the feel of it. I caught a glimpse of my concentrated face in the reflection of Chris's blank computer screen. Shame tunneled through me as I faced my act of invasion, yet continued at my task.

The book slipped down, allowing the drawer to glide open. I stared at the unexpected item, its hard cover muted with soft shades of blue, green, and brown.

The Velveteen Rabbit.

I slid the children's book from the drawer, the tattered paper jacket catching on the sides. In a whisper of time I was back in this very room—the walls a dusky blue with brightly colored truck-and-airplane decals sticking to them. A Furby stuffed animal in Chris's lap, one tiny hand clutching an oversize ear. Beside him on the carpet, his twin, Maelynn,

holding *The Velveteen Rabbit* across her legs. She read loudly
to Chris, who'd taken out his hearing aid in preparation for
bed. He peered over her arm at the picture of a bunny on
top of a pile of books, thick glasses sliding off the bridge of
Chris's small nose.

*There was once a velveteen rabbit, and in the beginning he
was really splendid.*

I sniffed, shoved the book back into the drawer, and closed
it. I hadn't realized the story was in the house anymore. Sweet
that Chris would keep it as a reminder of his childhood. No
doubt I worried over my son for nothing. He was busy with
school and work, maybe tired from adjusting to his junior
year. So he didn't talk to me like he used to. What teenage
boy confided in his mother?

*For a long time he lived in the toy cupboard or on the nursery
floor, and no one thought very much about him.*

*He was naturally shy, and being only made of velveteen, some
of the more expensive toys quite snubbed him.*

I pulled the shade open, allowing bright sunlight to
stream into the room onto the postered walls. A collection of
vintage prints, boasting Winchesters and Remingtons, amid
paintings of wild birds and hunting dogs. I recognized one
at the bottom: a picture of a severed snake, symbolizing the
colonies at the time of the Revolution. Below the snake were
bold letters: *JOIN, or DIE.*

A chill chased my gaze from the walls and back to the window where a flock of geese sounded their calls over the house.
Across Brewster Court, the Nielson preschoolers ran through
a sprinkler, enjoying the unseasonably warm afternoon.

I turned from the squealing children to draw the covers

up over my son's unmade bed, careful to smooth out the wrinkles. The scent of old roasted coffee from his part-time job at Dunkin' Donuts infused the room.

"What is Real?" asked the Rabbit one day.

"When a child loves you for a long, long time, not just to play with, but really loves you, then you become Real."

A pile of books beside Chris's bed caught my eye. He always kept library books there. The top one read *Nathan Hale: The Life and Death of America's First Spy*. I flipped through the remaining titles, similar to the first. Except for one—an older book the same Aegean blue as Chris's eyes, save for a maroon strip across the binding. *The Journal Entries of Mercy Howard*. I turned to the first page, a musty scent rising to meet me.

September 22, 1836

Every year, on this date, when I find the leaves hinting at near death, I remember. It's been sixty years since my Nathan died—strung up from the gallows at the Royal Artillery Park in New York City. All remember his name. And yet I am the one who loved him. His death spun into motion the most tumultuous time in my life, of which I now take up my pen to write.

I can no longer bear to take this secret to my grave. I wish to unburden my conscience and make my story known.

A horn honked outside the window and I jumped, closing the book. A Chevy Impala backed out of the Nielsons' driveway. The driver beeped and waved good-bye to the glistening children on the lawn.

I replaced the books how I'd found them. They must have been for a school report. Chris had always been into stories of espionage, dreaming of working for the CIA. I hadn't heard him talk about that for some time—or any other dreams for that matter. I vowed to ask him about the report later, maybe strike up more than a two-sentence conversation.

I exhaled a shaky breath, looked to the desk I'd just invaded—a desk with nothing more to hide than childhood memories. What had I been looking for anyway? Drugs? Porn? A pack of cigarettes? I should be ashamed of myself.

Talk about spying.

I stared at the berber carpet, where the picture of peace still clung to my mind's eye.

"Does it hurt?" asked the Rabbit.

"Sometimes," said the Skin Horse, for he was always truthful. "When you are Real you don't mind being hurt."

I took one more look around Chris's tidy room, now awash in bright sunlight. All was well. Good, even. Mike was right. I worried over nothing.

I opened the door, my world once again right-side up. My baby—my only son—was fine. My family was fine. Everything was fine.

I left the room, the memory of my daughter's five-year-old voice echoing through its walls.

"Once you are Real you can't become unreal again. It lasts for always."

The Rabbit sighed. He thought it would be a long time before this magic called Real happened to him. He longed to become

Real, to know what it felt like; and yet the idea of growing shabby and losing his eyes and whiskers was rather sad.

He wished that he could become it without these uncomfortable things happening to him.

Mercy

The sound jolted me from sleep, and I straightened in bed, still upon the feather mattress, my senses heightened. The scent of smoke tainted the salty sea air, and a moment later the bells of Trinity Church called out, beckoning any able men to aid in snuffing out flames.

The men.

They were all gone. The redcoats now in their place.

Another crack came at my window, causing my heart to take up a frantic beat that echoed along with the church bells. I kicked the covers from my feet, cursing the king's soldiers in my head. Though fresh to Manhattan, I was accustomed to their revelry from my last month in Long Island. If they weren't deep in their cups at night, they were making mischief in the barn with one of the local village girls. Or trying to woo my sister, Omelia, with Cathay silk or hair adornments or some other inappropriate imported gift. Now, they seemed bent on throwing pebbles at one of the finest homes in the city.

I crept to the sill and peered below to Aunt Beatrice's fading hydrangea bushes. Moonlight illuminated faint wafts of smoke. In the far west, in the lots of land leased by Trinity Church, lay the taverns and dens of ill repute which had been dubbed "Holy Grounds." There, orange flames lit the sky.

If only Uncle Thomas were still alive. Though I had pleaded with Aunt to escape with me when General Washington fled and the Regulars arrived, she refused to leave Uncle Thomas's body, still laid out in the parlor awaiting burial. His funeral had been conducted just the day before, and Aunt Beatrice had taken ill immediately after. I hadn't the heart to broach the subject of leaving the city again.

A shadowy figure below caught my eye. I shrank back within the room, pressed my cheek to the trim, and looked again. Not a redcoat, but . . .

No, it could not be.

Donning my dressing gown and boots, I lifted the latch of my chambers carefully so as not to wake my aunt in the next room. The wood of the floor protested beneath my slight weight as I descended the stairs; scents left from dinner—chicken pie and roasted apples—drifted to my nose.

I wished Frederick had not left. At the first sign of smoke several hours before, the butler asked for a time of leave. Brow sweating, he had looked out the western window anxiously, claiming he had a mother who needed his assistance to escape the flames.

Aunt Beatrice said this was the first she'd heard of his family.

I opened the front door, where the pungent scent of smoke assaulted me in fresh waves.

Not wanting to leave the safety of the door, lest I was mistaken about the identity of the figure, I imitated the sound of a mourning dove, and held my breath to wait.

A call echoed back to me and a lump lodged within my throat. I closed the door behind me. "N-Nathan?"

'Twas impossible. Nathan was a captain in the Continental Army. Manhattan now belonged to the king's Regulars. And yet . . .

Strong arms came around me, a familiar smell blocking out that of smoke. I sank into them, relief and instant desire soaking into my limbs. "Nathan!"

"Mercy, forgive me, I knew no other way to see you."

I turned, stared into the moonlit face of the man I cared for more than any in the world. I cast my arms around his neck and pressed my nose into the black wool of his jacket. He still smelled of leather and books and safety. "It truly is you. But how—"

He placed a finger over my lips, gestured toward the path that led to Aunt Beatrice's gardens. I clutched his arm, allowed him to lead me away from the house and along the deserted trail.

As the house disappeared from view, my excitement over seeing my intended waned and my questions increased. When finally we reached the stone bench in the back of the garden, I turned to Nathan, put a hand on the stubbled cheek of his handsome face. Moonlight accentuated the delicate smattering of scars upon his forehead, the result of a flash of gunpowder in his face as a boy. In this moment it all seemed bittersweet.

"The fire . . . is it being contained?"

Nathan looked to the west. "I fear not, though I have not seen it firsthand."

"You should not be here. The Regulars—they are numerous."

Nathan gritted his teeth. "And yet 'tis safe for you?"

"Uncle Thomas fell ill weeks ago. Aunt Beatrice sent word to Setauket asking for help, and when Abraham offered to escort me, I did not hesitate to come." Aunt Beatrice—so unlike Mother. So capable and strong. Some of my happiest memories as a child involved spending summers in Manhattan with her and Uncle Thomas. But Uncle's illness had shaken her. She had needed me, and I did not regret coming, even now being hemmed in behind enemy lines. "He passed earlier this week."

"I am sorry, Mercy. I know you were fond of him."

"Aye. Aunt Beatrice is beside herself with grief. It made me realize how short life can be . . . It made me think of us." I would not say outright that we had held off our nuptials for far too long, but I could certainly hint it.

A look akin to defeat crossed Nathan's face. 'Twas unfamiliar and it made my stomach curdle. I sought to fix it. "Forgive me. I know you must finish this fight. I love you all the more for it."

As a woman, I could not take up arms and go to war.

But I could wed a man whose beliefs mirrored my own, who might even redeem our traitorous family from the shame which now marked us.

"Word has come that my uncle William was the one to lead General Howe through Jamaica Pass." I allowed the words to settle between us, wondered if Nathan would condemn me for the actions of my family.

"'Tis not your burden, Mercy."

"You were there, at Brooklyn. Had you been killed, it would have been due to my own blood."

He pulled me close and I leaned against his solid chest, wanting nothing more than to forget about war and traitorous family members and red-coated soldiers who seemed to gain the upper hand in our fight for freedom. His heart—strong and certain—beat through his coat to my ear. I leaned into it, remembering the first time we'd met at a picnic in honor of our mutual friend, Benjamin Tallmadge, the son of our pastor. He was one of the few young men who'd made their way out of our hometown of Setauket. He'd met Nathan while studying at Yale, and the town had been proud to celebrate his graduation.

I could still remember the way Nathan had sought my gaze from across the green. How he'd approached me and introduced himself with all the courtly manners of a gentleman, his sun-reddened skin betraying how acclimated he was to the insides of a classroom. We'd taken a short walk, found ourselves at the boulder not far from the common where we spoke long hours of politics and Paine, poetry and Pope, captivity and *Cato*. He spoke of his mother's death when he was twelve, regaled me with stories of his years at Yale—how as freshmen, he and Benjamin had been charged a shilling and five pence for breaking windows following a visit to a local tavern. How the duo had argued successfully at a debating society on a woman's right to education. And when he left at the end of the evening, he'd kissed my hand, asked if he could write me. If only we were back in that time. In safety.

"I am learning that war is not so cut-and-dry as I once imagined."

I lifted my head. This was not the Nathan I knew—the one who stood certain for the Cause, who vowed to put loyalty to the Cause before his very life. "Nathan?"

"I am only saying that we don't know how they pressed your uncle. How they used his family . . ." He shook his head. "But you are right. There is no excuse for betrayal. Still, you need not blame yourself."

I ran my finger over the lapel of his coat, inhaled his scent. I suppose it was easy to think my uncle should have stood up to the officers in His Majesty's service. He would have been shot, no doubt, my aunt and cousins left unprovided for. But I could not stomach his betrayal—an act which led to a British victory at Brooklyn, an act which left hundreds dead and many more captured. I wondered, if I were a man, would I have enough gumption to stand for what I believed with every last ounce of my being—to risk even death—for the Cause?

"Pray, Nathan, tell me why you are here at all. Surely you put yourself in danger."

His Adam's apple bobbed and he placed his hands on my waist. They tightened, and I felt something unfamiliar in their grip. A fierce type of longing, yes, but something more. Something that smelled of fear.

"What is it?" My voice shook.

"I cannot say, but I only know my heart could not rest if I did not see you whilst I was here."

"You frighten me, Nathan." Who was this man? This man who could not trust me with the burdens of his heart? Was this what war did to men—made them hard and untrusting, forcing them to draw within their own hearts and shut others out? I could understand Nathan's distance of late in his letters, but here, where naught could hear but the distant seabirds asleep at the naked masts of ships, why should he hold himself back from me?

"I have always enjoyed your mind, Mercy. And now I have a question for you I would very much appreciate an honest answer to."

I put a small amount of space between us. "Very well."

"Do you believe that whatever is necessary to the public good becomes honorable by being necessary?"

I blinked.

"Pray, my love, tell me your thoughts. Would you agree?"

"Yes, I suppose so, but whatever does this have to do with why you are here? Nathan, you can trust me—I hope you know that. Please, tell me your heart."

He drew me to him, then. His hands ran along my waist until foreign desire ignited my insides. I pressed into him and he kissed me with gentle, prodding lips that loosened my own. He tasted faintly of mint and smoke, and I sank into the kiss, allowing it to deepen and hold.

As I became further acquainted with this affection,

I sensed his desperation. A physical urge, certainly, but also the deep-seated fear I'd intuited before. I broke the kiss, gazed into his eyes. Perhaps I could have confided in my family regarding my engagement. I could hardly wait to tell my mother and sister the news of my young swain. But Nathan had been so hesitant to make plans with this foul war disrupting the colonies.

Perhaps Nathan had foreseen this time—a time when redcoats would occupy our towns and our homes. A time when it would be dangerous for it to be known that he had taken up the insignia of a captain in the rebel army.

"You will not tell me, then?"

"If I could, I most certainly would, Mercy. 'Tis for your own good, as well as that of the Cause. I am safe. I have met someone just today who is of the same regard as me and will help return me to General Washington."

I could not argue with that.

He tightened his grip on my waist again, drew me a breath closer. "I *will* marry you, Mercy Howard. Soon. I will find a way to bring you to Connecticut with me, whether or not this war be over. Watch for me within the month. After . . . after I do what I must."

My innards trembled like wool strained tight on a spinning wheel.

"For now . . . play the part you must whilst among the redcoats."

I allowed his words to soak into my being, but I couldn't recognize them as true to the man before me—a man who would rather die than utter allegiance to the Crown. Yet now he bade me put on a facade of loyalty to the king?

I trailed my finger along the stubble of his jaw, trying to read his thoughts. "You are a mystery to me, Nathan Hale."

"I regret not marrying you sooner, Mercy. Perhaps then you wouldn't be here, in harm's way."

"My stay will not be for long, I suspect. Abraham is a fine escort. He knows the roads well."

Nathan closed his eyes in defeat. "I suppose we both must do what we are called to do, the Lord help us."

I fell into his arms once more, allowed him to press me close.

Yet as close as we were, he was only half-present in the embrace. Another part of him was lost in some great secret— one that troubled him—one that he would not share with me. And though we were close in a physical sense, I felt a great foreign chasm between us.

It frightened me, and though I wanted to be happy for his promises of love and future and marriage, I could not summon the strength to do so.

Instead, his words tumbled around in my mind, causing me to doubt how well I even knew him any longer.

"Whatever is necessary to the public good becomes honorable by being necessary."

Whatever could my Nathan undertake that he feared I might find so repulsive?

And why, if he was so bent on spending the rest of his life with me, did he feel the need to hide from me?

DISCUSSION QUESTIONS

1. Hayley longs to prove herself by achieving what no woman has ever achieved. What is the most ambitious thing you've ever attempted? What motivated you to tackle it?

2. As Emma is torn between her choices, she wonders, "Was not loyalty more honorable than liberty?" Which of these qualities do you find more appealing?

3. How has Ethan's personal tragedy shaped him? What do you think binds him and Hayley together?

4. Whether from shame or fear, many Boston Tea Party participants never disclosed their involvement. But today we laud their actions. How can a person determine when a law is unjust enough to warrant breaking? Have you ever had to stand against an established rule or law? Would you make the same decision now?

5. Did Emma make the right choice in the face of Samuel's blackmail? How would you have responded?

6. At the end of chapter 17, Emma realizes that what she thought was for evil, God intended for good. Have you or someone close to you experienced hardship that God reshaped into blessing?

7. Hayley strives to move beyond her past, but she keeps falling into it—her relationship with her mother, her history with Ethan, and other memories. What are some ways God uses her return home to transform her and help her grow?

8. Compare the challenges Emma faced in Boston before her marriage to the difficulties she encountered after leaving Boston with Noah. Was she ever tempted to regret her decision? How did she respond to the hardships she dealt with once she left home?

9. Hayley and Ethan are reunited by their quest to discover the history behind the tea chest. What about the mystery is so enticing to them? How does it help them rebuild their relationship? Have you ever found common ground with someone through a shared experience or interest?

10. In chapter 33, Emma asks herself, "How did God expect me to keep such an impossible vow to this man who had become a stranger to me? I'd joined him with liberty in mind. Was this—suffering the behavior of a husband—freedom?" How did Noah's change affect Emma? In a situation like this, what is a spouse's responsibility? How can a person know when to fight for their marriage and when it is utterly lost?

11. Hayley learns that she has distantly related family members she never knew about. How does this revelation impact her? Do you have any ancestors who were involved in historically significant events—and if so, what do you know about them?

12. Was Hayley's decision to drop out of training a victory or a failure? How did she define it? Do you agree with her assessment?

ABOUT THE AUTHOR

HEIDI CHIAVAROLI writes women's fiction, exploring places that whisper of historical secrets. Her debut novel, *Freedom's Ring*, was a *Romantic Times* Top Pick and a *Booklist* Top Ten Romance Debut. She makes her home in Massachusetts with her husband and two sons. Visit her online at www.heidichiavaroli.com.

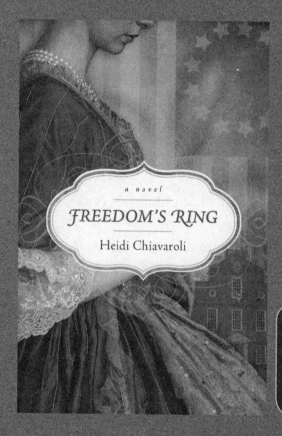